Ordinary Thunderstorms

William Boyd

W F HOWES LTD

This large print edition published in 2009 by
W F Howes Ltd
Unit 4, Rearsby Business Park, Gaddesby Lane,
Rearsby, Leicester LE7 4YH

1 3 5 7 9 10 8 6 4 2

First published in the United Kingdom in 2009
by Bloomsbury Publishing

A CIP catalogue record for this book is available
from the British Library

ISBN 978 1 40744 243 3

Typeset by Palimpsest Book Production Limited,
Grangemouth, Stirlingshire
Printed and bound in Great Britain
by MPG Books Ltd, Bodmin, Cornwall

FSC
Mixed Sources
Product group from well-managed
forests, controlled sources and
recycled wood or fiber
SA-COC-1565
www.fsc.org
© 1996 Forest Stewardship Council

For Susan

Ordinary thunderstorms have the capacity to transform themselves into multi-cell storms of ever growing complexity. Such multi-cell storms display a marked increase in severity and their lifetime can be extended by a factor of ten or more. The grandfather of all thunderstorms, however, is the super-cell thunderstorm. It should be noted that even ordinary thunderstorms are capable of mutating into super-cell storms. These storms subside very slowly.

Storm Dynamics and Hail Cascades
by L.D. Sax and W.S. Dutton

CHAPTER 1

L et us start with the river – all things begin with the river and we shall probably end there, no doubt – but let's wait and see how we go. Soon, in a minute or two, a young man will come and stand by the river's edge, here at Chelsea Bridge, in London.

There he is – look – stepping hesitantly down from a taxi, paying the driver, gazing around him, unthinkingly, glancing over at the bright water (it's a flood tide and the river is unusually high). He's a tall, pale-faced young man, early thirties, even-featured with tired eyes, his short dark hair neatly cut and edged as if fresh from the barber. He is new to the city, a stranger, and his name is Adam Kindred. He has just been interviewed for a job and feels like seeing the river (the interview having been the usual tense encounter, with a lot at stake), answering a vague desire to 'get some air'. The recent interview explains why, beneath his expensive trenchcoat, he is wearing a charcoal-grey suit, a maroon tie with a new white shirt and why he's carrying a glossy solid-looking black briefcase with heavy brass locks and corner trim.

He crosses the road, having no idea how his life is about to change in the next few hours – massively, irrevocably – no idea at all.

Adam walked over to the high stone balustrade that curved the roadway into Chelsea Bridge and, leaning on it, looked down at the Thames. The tide was high and still coming in, he saw, the normal flow of water reversed, flotsam moving surprisingly quickly upstream, heading inland, as if the sea were dumping its rubbish in the river rather than the usual, other way round. Adam strolled up the bridge's wide walkway heading for midstream, his gaze sweeping from the four chimneys of Battersea Power Station (one blurred with a cross-hatching of scaffolding) to the west, past the gold finial of the Peace Pagoda towards the two chimneys of Lots Road Power Station. The plane trees in Battersea Park, on the far bank, were still some way from full leaf – only the horse chestnuts were precociously, densely green. Early May in London . . . He turned and looked back at the Chelsea shore: more trees – he'd forgotten how leafy some parts of London were, how positively bosky. The roofs of the grand, red brick, riverine Victorian mansion blocks rose above the level of the Embankment's avenue of planes. How high? Sixty feet? Eighty? Apart from the susurrus of ceaseless traffic, the occasional klaxon and whooping siren, he didn't feel as if he were in the middle of a huge city at all: the trees, the quiet force of the surging, tidal river beneath his feet, that special luminescence that a body of water throws off, made him grow calmer – he'd been right to come to the river – odd how these instincts mysteriously drive you, he thought.

He walked back, his eye held by a clearly defined, attenuated triangle of waste ground to the west side of Chelsea Bridge, formed by the bridge itself, the water's edge and the four lanes of the Embankment. It was bulked out with vegetation, dense with long grass and thick unpruned bushes and trees. He thought, idly, that such a patch of land must be worth a tidy fortune in this location, even a thin long triangle of waste ground, and he built, in his mind's eye, a three-storey wedge of a dozen bijou, balconied apartments. Then he saw that in order to achieve this he'd have to cut down a huge fig tree, close to the bridge – decades old, he reckoned, drawing nearer to it, its big shiny leaves still growing, stiffly fresh. A venerable fig tree by the Thames, he thought: strange – how had it been planted there and what happened to the fruit? He conjured up a vision of a plate of Parma ham and halved fresh figs. Where had he eaten that? On his honeymoon in Portofino with Alexa? Or earlier? On one of his student holidays, perhaps . . . It was a mistake to think of Alexa, he realised, his new mood of calm replaced at once by one of sadness and anger, so he concentrated instead on the small surges of hunger he was experiencing, and felt, thinking

3

of the figs and Parma ham, a sudden need for Italian food: Italian food of a simple, honest, basic sort – insalata tricolore, pasta alle vongole, scallopine al limone, torta di nonna. That would do nicely.

He wandered into Chelsea and almost immediately in the quiet streets behind the Royal Hospital found, to his considerable astonishment, an Italian restaurant – as if he were in a fairy tale. There it was, tucked under yellow awnings badged with a Venetian lion, in a narrow street of white stucco and beige-brick terraced houses – it seemed an anomaly, a fantasy. No shops, no pub, no other restaurant in sight – how had it managed to establish itself here amongst the residents? Adam looked at his watch – 6.20 – a bit early to eat but he was genuinely hungry now and he could see there were already a few other customers inside. Then a smiling, tanned man came to the door and held it open for him, urging, 'Come in, sir, come in, yes, we are open, come in, come in.' This man took his coat from him, hung it on a peg and ushered him past the small bar through to the light L-shaped room, shouting genial instructions and rebukes at the other waiters, as if Adam were his most cherished regular and was being inconvenienced by their inefficiency in some way.

He sat Adam down at a table for two with his back to the street outside. He offered to look after Adam's briefcase but Adam decided it would stay with him as he took the proffered menu and glanced around. Eight tourists – four men, four women – sat at a large round table, eating silently, all dressed in blue with identical blue tote bags at their feet, and there was another solitary man sitting two tables away along from him, who had taken his spectacles off and was dabbing his face with a tissue. He looked agitated, ill at ease in some way, and he glanced over as he replaced his spectacles. As their eyes met the man gave that inclination of the head, the small smile of acknowledgement – the solidarity of the solitary diner – that says I am not sad or lonely, this is something that I have happily chosen to do, just like you. He had a couple of folders and other papers spread on the table in front of him. Adam smiled back.

Adam ate the house salad – spinach, bacon, shaved parmesan and a creamy dressing – and was halfway through his scallopine al vitello (green beans, roast potatoes on the side) when the other solitary diner leant over and asked him if he knew the exact time. His accent was American, his English flawless. Adam told him – 6.52 – the man carefully adjusted his watch and they inevitably began to talk. The man introduced himself as Dr Philip Wang. Adam reciprocated and supplied the information that this was his first trip to London since he had been a child. Dr Wang confirmed that he too knew very little of the city. He lived and worked in Oxford – paying only short, infrequent visits to London, a day or two at a time, when he had to see patients taking part in a research project he was running. Adam said he'd come to London from America, was applying for a job here, wanting to 'relocate', to come back home, as it were.

'A job?' Dr Wang asked, looking at his smart suit. 'Are you in finance?' His speculation seemed to carry with it a tone of disapproval.

'No, a university job – a research fellowship – at Imperial College,' Adam added, wondering if he might now be vindicated. 'I just came from the interview.'

'Good school,' Wang said, distantly, then, 'Yeah . . .' as if his mind was on something else, then, collecting himself, asked politely, 'How did it go?'

Adam shrugged and said he could never predict these things. The three people who had interviewed him – two men and a woman with a near-shaven head – had given nothing away, being almost absurdly polite and formal, so unlike his former American colleagues, Adam had thought at the time.

'Imperial College. So, you're a scientist,' Wang said. 'So am I. What's your field?'

'Climatology,' Adam said. 'What about you?'

Wang thought for a second as if he wasn't sure of the answer. 'Immunology, I guess, yeah . . . Or you could say I was an allergist,' he said, then glancing at his newly adjusted watch said he'd better go, had work to do, calls to make. He paid his bill, in cash, and clumsily gathered up his papers, spilling sheaves on the floor, stooping to pick them up, muttering to himself – suddenly he seemed more than a little distracted again, as if, now the meal had come to an end, his real life had recommenced with its many pressures and anxieties. Finally he stood and shook Adam's hand, wishing him luck, hoping he had got the job. 'I have a good feeling about it,' Wang added, illogically, 'a real good feeling.'

Adam was halfway through his tiramisu when he noticed that Wang had left something behind: a transparent plastic zippable folder under the seat between their tables, half obscured by the hanging flap of the tablecloth. He reached for it and saw that on the front was a small pocket that contained Wang's business card. Adam extracted it and read: 'DR PHILIP Y. WANG MD, PhD (Yale), FBSI, MAAI', and under that 'Head of Research & Development CALENTURE-DEUTZ plc'. On the reverse there were two addresses with phone numbers, one in the Cherwell Business Park, Oxford (Unit 10) and the other in London – Anne Boleyn House, Sloane Avenue, SW3.

As he paid his bill, pleased to remember his new pin code, tapping it without hesitation into the handset, Adam asked if Dr Wang was a regular customer and was informed that he'd never been seen in the restaurant before. Adam decided he'd drop the file off himself – it seemed a friendly and helpful thing to do, especially as Wang had been so enthusiastic about his career prospects – and asked directions to Sloane Avenue.

Walking along the King's Road, still busy with shoppers (almost exclusively French or Spanish, it seemed), Adam thought suddenly that perhaps Wang had deliberately left his file for him to discover. He wondered if it was a way of seeing him again: two lonely men in the city, wanting some company . . . Was it, even, a gay thing, a ploy? Adam had sometimes wondered if there was something about him that gay men found attractive. He could recall three precise occasions when he had been flirted with and another when a man had waited for him outside the lavatory of a restaurant in Tucson, Arizona and had forced a kiss on him. Adam didn't think Wang was gay – no, that was preposterous – but he decided it would be wise to phone ahead and so eased Wang's card out of its tight plastic niche, sat down on a wooden bench outside a pub, fished out his mobile phone and made the call.

'Philip Wang.'

'Dr Wang, it's Adam Kindred. We just met at the restaurant—'

'Of course – and you have my file. Thank you so much. I just called them and they told me you had it.'

'I thought it'd be quicker if I dropped it off.'

'That's so kind of you. Please come up and have a drink – oh, there's someone at the door. That's not you, is it?'

Adam laughed, said he thought he was five minutes or so away and clicked his phone shut.

8

Come up and have a drink – perfectly friendly, no sexual innuendo there – but perhaps it was the American accent, professionally flat, giving away nothing, that made Adam think that Wang had been insufficiently surprised to hear he was on his way round . . .

Anne Boleyn House was an imposing, almost fortress-like 1930s art deco block of service flats with a small semicircle of box-hedged drive-in and a uniformed porter in the lobby sitting behind a long marble-topped counter. Adam signed his name in a register and was directed to Flat G 14 on the seventh floor. After his phone call he had thought over the necessity of seeing Wang again – he could have safely left the file with the porter, he now realised – but he had nothing else to do and he didn't particularly want to go back to his modest hotel in Pimlico: a drink or two with Wang would kill some time and, besides, Wang seemed an interesting and educated man.

Adam stepped out of the lift into a wholly feature-less long corridor – dark parquet, pistachio walls, identical flush doors differentiated only by their number. Like cells, he thought, or, in a film, it might have been a lazy art director's vision of Kafkaesque conformity. And there was an unpleasant nose-tickling, odorous overlay – of wax polish mingled with potent, bleachy lavatory cleanser. Small glaringly bright lights set into the ceiling lit the way to Flat G 14, where the corridor made a right-angled turn to reveal another length of soulless, service-flat

9

perspective. A glowing green exit light shone at its end.

Adam saw that Wang had left his door slightly ajar – a sign of welcome? – but he rang the bell all the same, thinking that it wouldn't do simply to walk in. He heard Wang come through a door, heard a door close, but no call of 'Adam? Do come in, please.'

He rang the bell again.

'Hello?' Adam pushed the door slightly. 'Dr Wang? Philip?'

He opened the door and stepped into a small, boxy living room. Two armchairs close to a coffee table, a huge flat-screen TV, some dried flowers in straw vases. A small galley kitchen behind two louvred half-doors. Adam set his briefcase down by the coffee table and placed Wang's file beside a fan of golfing magazines, all smiling men in pastel colours brandishing their clubs. Then he heard Wang's voice, low and urgent.

'Adam? I'm in here . . .'

The next room. No, please, not the bedroom, surely? Adam thought to himself, urgently regretting coming up as he stepped over to the door and pushed it open.

'I can only stay five min—'

Philip Wang lay on top of his bed in a widening pool of blood. He was alive, very conscious, and a hand, flipper-like, gestured Adam towards him. The room had been trashed, two small filing cabinets up-ended and emptied, drawers from a bedside table tipped out, a wardrobe cleared with a swipe or two, clothes and hangers scattered.

Wang pointed to his left side. Adam hadn't noticed – the handle of a knife protruded from Wang's sopping sweater.

'Pull it out,' Wang said. His face showed signs of a beating – his spectacles distorted but unbroken, a trickle of blood from a nostril, a split lip, a red impact-circle on a cheekbone.

'Are you sure?' Adam said.

'Please, now . . .'

With fluttering hands he seemed to guide Adam's right hand to the hilt of the knife. Adam gripped it loosely.

'I don't think this is the sort of thing—'

'One quick movement,' Wang said and coughed. A little blood overflowed from his mouth down his chin.

'Are you absolutely sure?' Adam repeated. 'I don't know if it's the correct—'

'*Now!*'

Without further thought Adam gripped the knife and drew it out, as easily as if from a scabbard. It was a breadknife, he noticed, as a surge of released blood followed the withdrawal, travelling up the blade and wetting Adam's knuckles, warmly.

'I'll call the police,' Adam said and placed the knife down, unthinkingly wiping his dripping fingers on the coverlet.

'The file,' Wang said, fingers twitching, moving, as if tapping at an invisible keyboard.

11

'I have it.'

'Whatever you do, don't—'Wang died then, with a short gasp of what seemed like exasperation.

Adam stepped away, appalled, horrified, stumbled against a pile of Wang's jackets and trousers, and went back into the living room, looking for a phone. He saw it sitting on a neat, purpose-built shelf by the door and as he reached for the receiver saw that there was still some blood on his hand, still dripping from an unwiped finger. Some drops fell on the telephone.

'Shit . . .' he said, realising this was his first articulated expression of shock. What in the name of fuck was going on?

Then he heard the window in Wang's bedroom open and somebody step heavily inside. And the terror he was feeling left in an instant. Or at least he thought it was the window – maybe it was from the bathroom – but he had heard the clunking sound of a catch being released, one of those brass handles that secured the mass-produced steel-framed and many-paned glass windows that gave Anne Boleyn House its slightly depressed, institutional air.

Adam grabbed his briefcase and Wang's file and left the flat rapidly, closing the door behind him with a bang. He looked towards the lifts and then decided against them, turning the corner and striding normally, not running, not unduly fast, towards the green exit light and the fire stairs.

He descended seven floors of the dimly lit stone

12

stairs without seeing anyone and emerged on to a side street behind Anne Boleyn House beside four towering grey rubbish bins on sturdy rubber wheels. There was a powerful smell of decomposing food that made Adam gag and he spat, squatting down to open his briefcase and slip Wang's file inside. He looked up to see two young chefs in their white jackets and blue checkerboard trousers lighting up cigarettes in a doorway a few yards off.

'Stinks, dunnit?' one of them called over with a grin on his face.

Adam gave them a thumbs-up and headed off, still at what he imagined was an easy saunter, in the opposite direction.

He wandered Chelsea's streets for a while, aimlessly, trying to sort things out in his mind, trying to make some sense of what he had witnessed and what had taken place. His head was jangled, a shocking, fractured mosaic of recent images – Wang's battered face, the hilt of the breadknife, his twitching, tapping hand gesture – but he was not too jangled to realise what he had just done and the consequences of his importunate, natural reactions. He should *never* have obeyed Wang's instruction, he now realised. He should never have pulled the knife out, never – he should have simply gone to the telephone and dialled 911 – 999, rather. Now he had traces of Wang's blood on his hands and under his fingernails and, even worse, his fingerprints were on the fucking knife itself. But what else could anyone have done in such a situation? another side of his brain yelled at him, in frustrated rage. You had no choice: it was a dying, agonised man's last request. Wang had practically fitted his fingers around the knife's hilt, begging him to pull it out, begging him—

He stopped walking for a second, telling himself to calm down. His face was covered in sweat, his chest was heaving as if he'd just run a mile. He exhaled, noisily, slow down, slow down. Think, think back . . . He set off again. Had he interrupted Wang's actual murder? Or was it just some robbery gone hideously wrong? He thought: the door he had heard close as he came in to the flat must have been the perpetrator leaving the bedroom – and the sound of the person re-entering must have been the perpetrator, again – the murderer, again. He must have come in from a balcony, he realised, as he now remembered noting that some of the Boleyn's higher service flats had narrow balconies. So the man had slipped out when he heard Adam come in and had waited on the balcony and then when he heard Adam leave the bedroom to phone . . . Yes, the police, must call, Adam reminded himself. Perhaps, he thought suddenly, it had been a terrible, foolish mistake to have left, to have run away down the stairs . . . But if that man had caught him, what then? No – completely understandable, had to get out, *had* to, fast, or he might be dead himself, now, Jesus . . . He reached into his jacket for his mobile and saw Wang's blood now dry on his knuckles. Wash that off, first.

He wandered into an open space, a kind of wide square giving on to a sports ground and an art gallery, oddly, where small grouped fountains spouted from holes in the paving stones, couples sat around on low walls and a few kids whizzed to and fro on their expensive metal scooters.

He crouched by a fountain and washed his right hand in the cold water, a wobbling vertical column flowing upward, defying gravity. His right hand was now clean – and now trembling, he saw – he needed a drink, he needed to calm down, give his thoughts some order, then he would call the police: something was nagging at him at the back of his mind, something he had done or not done, and he just needed a little time to think.

Adam asked directions to Pimlico and set off, once sure of where he should be heading. On his way there he found a pub, reassuringly mediocre – indeed, as if 'average' subsumed all its ambitions: an averagely stained patterned carpet, middle-of-the-road muzak playing, three gaming machines pinging and gonging away not too loudly, a shabby-looking blue-collar clientele, a perfectly acceptable number of beers available and unexceptionable pub food on offer – pies, sandwiches and a dish of the day (smearily erased). Adam felt oddly re-assured by this pointed decision to settle for the acceptable norm, to strive for nothing higher than the tolerable median. He would remember this

15

place. He ordered a large whisky with ice and a packet of peanuts, took his drink to a table in the corner and began to reflect.

He felt guilt. Why did he feel guilty – he'd done nothing wrong? Was it because he had run away? . . . But anyone would have run in his situation, he told himself: the shock, the presence of a killer in the next room . . . It was an atavistic fear, a sense of illogical responsibility – something every innocent child knows when confronted by serious trouble. It had been the obvious, natural course of action to run out quickly and safely and take stock. He needed a little time, a little space . . .

He sipped at his whisky, relishing the alcohol burn in his throat. He chomped peanuts, licking the residual salt from his palm, picking the impacted shards from his teeth with a fingernail. What was bothering him? Was it what Wang had said, his last words? 'Whatever you do, don't—' Don't what? Don't *take* the file? Don't *leave* the file? And then he thought of Wang dead and the delayed shock hit him again and he shivered. He went to the bar and ordered more whisky and another bag of peanuts.

Adam drank his whisky and consumed his peanuts with a velocity and hunger that surprised him, emptying the packet into his cupped palm and tipping the nuts carelessly into his mouth in an almost ape-like way (stray peanuts bouncing off the table top in front of him). The packet was

16

emptied in seconds, crumpled and placed on the table where it cracklingly tried to uncrumple itself for a further few seconds, while Adam picked up and ate the individual peanuts that had escaped his immediate furious appetite. He wondered, as he savoured the salty, waxy peanut taste, if there were a more nutritious or satisfying foodstuff on the planet – sometimes salted peanuts were all that man required.

He went to the gents' lavatory, stooping down a narrow, bendy staircase – as though it had aspired to be spiral once but had given up half-way through the transformation – to a pungent basement where beer and urine competed on the olfactory level. As he washed his hands again beneath the unsparing glare of the light above the sinks he saw that his shirt and tie were freckled with tiny dark polka-dots – polka-dots of blood he assumed, Dr Wang's blood . . . Adam felt suddenly faint, remembering the scene in Wang's flat, remembering the withdrawal of the bread-knife and the bloody surge that followed it. The delayed shock at what he had done and witnessed returned to him – he would go back to his hotel, he resolved suddenly, change his shirt (keeping this one for evidence) and then call the police. No one would blame him for leaving the crime scene – what with the man, the murderer on the balcony, re-entering. Impossible to remain calm and lucid under these circumstances – no, no, no – no blame attaching, at all.

He rehearsed his story as he walked back to Pimlico and Grafton Lodge – his modest hotel – pausing a couple of times to check his bearings in these near identical streets of terraced, white-stuccoed houses, and then, once he was sure he was going in the right direction, setting off again with new confidence, happy in the certitude of his decision-making process, pleased that this awful night – the terrible things he had witnessed – would have their proper judicial closure.

Grafton Lodge consisted of two of these terraced houses knocked together to form a small eighteen-bedroom hotel. Despite the overt pretensions of its name, the owners – Seamus and Donal – had a cursive pink neon sign in a ground-floor window that flashed 'VACANCIES' in best B-movie fashion and the front door was badged with logos of international travel agencies, tour groups and hotel guides – a shiny collage of decals, transfers and plastic honoraria. From Vancouver to Osaka, apparently, Grafton Lodge was a home from home.

To be fair, Adam had no complaints about his small clean room overlooking the mews lane at the back. Everything worked: the Teasmade, the shower, the mini bar, the TV with its ninety-eight channels. Seamus and Donal were charming and helpful and solicitous about his every need, yet, as he turned up the street towards the hotel and saw its pink neon 'VACANCIES' sign flashing, he felt a small shudder of dread vibrate through him.

18

He stopped and forced himself to think: it was now well over an hour, nearly two hours, in fact, since he had fled from Anne Boleyn House. However, he had signed his name in the visitors' register that the porter had proffered to him – Adam Kindred – and had written down Grafton Lodge, SW1, as his home address. That was the huge, catastrophic mistake he had been worried about, that was what had been nagging at him . . . The last person to visit Philip Wang before his death had obligingly left his name and address in the guest ledger. He felt a sudden nausea, considering the implications of this guileless self-identification as he approached Grafton Lodge. All seemed well – through the decal-encrusted glass door he saw Seamus at the reception desk talking to one of the chambermaids – Branca, he thought she was called – and he could see a few customers in the residents-only lounge bar. Across the street a black cab was parked, its 'for hire' light off, its driver dozing at the wheel – no doubt waiting for one of the revelling businessmen in the lounge bar to eventually emerge.

Adam urged himself onward: go in, go to your room, change your bloodied clothes, call the police and go to a police station – bring the whole horrible business to a proper, decent conclusion. It seemed the only sensible way forward, the only completely normal course of action, so he wondered why he decided to walk down the access lane at the end of the street and try to look up at his window from

19

the mews behind. Something else was nagging at him now, something else he had or had not done, and that act, or non-act, was spooking him. If he could remember what it was and could rationalise about it perhaps he'd feel calmer.

He stood in the dark mews at the back of Grafton Lodge and looked at the back of the hotel for the window of his room and duly found it: dark, the curtains half-drawn as he had left them that morning for his interview at Imperial College. What world was that, he thought? Everything was still in order, nothing out of the ordinary, at all. He was a fool to be acting so suspic—

'Adam Kindred?'

Later, Adam found it hard to explain to himself why he had reacted so violently to hearing his name. Perhaps he was more traumatised than he thought; perhaps the levels of recent stress he had been experiencing had made him a creature of reflex rather than ratiocination. In the event, on hearing this man's voice so close, uttering his name, he had gripped the handle of his new, solid briefcase and had swung it in a backhanded arc, full force, behind him. The immediate, unseen impact had jarred his entire arm and shoulder. The man made a noise halfway between a sigh and a moan and Adam heard him fall to the ground with a thud and a clatter.

Adam swivelled round – he now felt a surge of absurd concern: Jesus Christ, what had he done? – and he crouched by the man's semi-conscious body. The man was moving – just – and blood was flowing from his mouth and nose. The right-angled, heavy brass trim at the bottom corner of Adam's briefcase had connected with the man's right temple and in the dim glow of the mews' streetlighting he could see a clear, red, L-shaped welt already forming there as if placed by a branding iron. The man groaned and stirred and his hands stretched out as if reaching for something. Adam, following the gesture, saw he was trying to take hold of an automatic pistol (with silencer, he realised, a milli-second later) lying on the cobbles beside him.

Adam stood, fear and alarm now replacing his guilty concern, and then, almost immediately, he heard the approaching yips and yelps of a police car's siren. But this man, he knew, lying at his feet, was no policeman. The police, as far as he was aware, didn't issue automatic pistols with silencers to their plain-clothes officers. He tried to stay calm as the logical thought processes made themselves plain – somebody else was also after him, now: this man had been sent to find and kill him. Adam felt a bolus of nausea rise in his throat. He was experiencing pure fear, he realised, like an animal, like a trapped animal. He looked down to see that the man had groggily hauled himself up into a sitting position and was managing to hold himself upright there, swaying uncertainly like a baby, before he spat out a tooth. Adam kicked his gun away, sending it sliding and clattering across the cobbled roadway of the mews and stepped back a few paces. This man wasn't a policeman but the real police were coming closer – he could hear another siren some streets away in clamorous dissonance with the first. The man was now beginning to crawl erratically across the cobbles towards his gun. All right: this man was looking for him and so were the police – he heard the first car stop outside the hotel and the urgent slam of doors – the night had clearly gone wrong in ways even he couldn't imagine. He looked round to see that the crawling man had nearly reached his gun and was stretching out an uncertain hand to grab it, as if his vision was defective in some crucial way and he could barely focus. The man keeled over and laboriously righted himself. Adam knew he had to make a decision now, in the next second or two, and with that knowledge came the unwelcome realisation that it would probably be one of the most important decisions of his life. Should he surrender himself to the police – or not? But some unspecified fear in him screamed – NO! NO! RUN! And he knew that his life was about to take a turning he could never reverse – he couldn't surrender himself, now, he *wouldn't* surrender himself: he needed some time. He was terrified, he realised, of how bad circumstances looked for him, terrified of what complicated, disastrous trouble the baleful, awful implications of the story he would tell – the true story – would land him in. So, time was key, time was his only possible friend and ally at this moment. If he had a little time then things could be sorted out in an orderly way. So he made his decision, one of the most important decisions in his life. It wasn't a question of whether he had chosen the right course of action or the wrong one. He simply had to follow his instincts – he had to be true to himself. He turned and ran away, at a steady pace, up the mews and into the anonymous streets of Pimlico.

What drew him back to Chelsea, he wondered? Was it the fig tree and his momentary dream of expensive riverside apartments that made him think that this attenuated triangle of waste ground by Chelsea Bridge would provide him with safe haven for twenty-four hours until this crazy night was over? He waited until there were no visible cars on the Embankment and climbed swiftly over the spear-railings and into the triangle. He pushed through the bushes and shrubs away from the bridge and its swooping beads of light outlining its suspension cables. He found a patch of ground between three dense bushes and spread his raincoat flat. He sat on it for a while, arms hugging his knees, emptying his mind, and feeling an irresistible urge to sleep grow through him. He switched off his mobile and lay down, resting his head on his briefcase for a pillow and folded his arms around himself. He didn't think, for once, didn't try to analyse and understand, simply letting the images of his day and night flash through his head like a demented slide show. Rest, his body was saying, you're safe, you've bought yourself some precious time, but now you need rest – stop thinking. So he did and he fell asleep.

CHAPTER 2

Rita Nashe was trying to explain to Vikram why she so hated cricket, why cricket in any form, ancient or contemporary, was anathema to her, when the call came through. They were parked just off the King's Road round the corner from a Starbucks where they had managed to grab a couple of coffees before it closed. Rita acknowledged the call – they were on their way to a 'cocktail party' in Anne Boleyn House, Sloane Avenue. She jotted down the details in her notebook, then started the car.

'Cocktail party,' she said to Vikram.

'Sorry?'

'Domestic. That's what we call them in Chelsea.'

'Cool. I'll remember that: "cocktail party".'

She drove easily to Sloane Avenue – no need for lights or siren. A woman had called the station complaining about loud thuds and bangings in the flat above and then small stains appearing in her ceiling. She pulled up opposite the entryway and headed for the front lobby, Vikram following some way behind – he seemed

25

to have become stuck in his seat belt – not the most agile of young men. Her mobile rang.

'Rita, I can't find my specs.'

'Dad, I'm working. What about your spares?'

'I don't have a fucking spare set, that's the point. I wouldn't be calling you if I had.'

She paused at the front door to let Vikram catch up with her.

'Have you looked,' she asked her father, her voice full of impromptu speculation, 'in the front bulkhead cupboard where we keep the tins?' She could practically hear his brain churning faster.

'Why,' he said, angrily, 'why would they be in the bulkhead cupboard with the tins? . . .'

'You left them there once before, I remember.'

'Did I? Oh . . . OK, I'll check.'

She closed her phone, smiling: she had hidden his spectacles in the front bulkhead cupboard, herself, to punish him for his general rudeness and selfish behaviour. Ninety per cent of the nagging irritants in his life were her responsibility – he had no idea – and he had never noticed how these irritants diminished as his moods became sunnier. He was an intelligent man, she told herself as she and Vikram pushed through the glass doors into the lobby, he really should have figured it out by now.

At the wide marble counter the porter looked surprised to see two police – a policewoman and a policeman – confronting him and, when told the trivial reason for their presence, couldn't understand why the complainant (difficult old woman)

26

hadn't simply called down to the front desk – that's what he was there for, after all. Rita said there was some mention of stains appearing on the ceiling – she checked her notebook. Flat F 14.

'What flat's above F 14?'

'G 14.'

She and Vikram travelled upwards in the lift.

'Wouldn't mind a little place here,' Vikram said. 'Studio apartment, Chelsea, King's Road . . .'

'Wouldn't we all, Vik, wouldn't we all.'

The door to G 14 was slightly ajar – Rita thought that was strange. She told Vikram to wait outside and she went in – lights were on and the place had been thoroughly ransacked. Burglary, she thought at once, though the widespread trashing seemed to say that someone had been looking for something specific and hadn't found it. TV still there, DVD player. Maybe not . . .

When she saw the dead man in the bedroom, lying supine on the soaking red sheets, she realised the source of the stains on the ceiling below – she had seen a few dead and injured bodies in her police career but was always surprised at the amount of blood the average human being could spill. She held her nose and swallowed, feeling a small swoon of light-headedness hit her. She breathed shallowly as she stood in the door, letting the sudden tremble in her body subside, and looked around quickly – again, everything turned upside down and the paned door to the small balcony was open, she could hear the traffic on

27

Sloane Avenue, and the muslin curtains stirred and filled like sails in the night breeze.

She walked carefully back through the flat to the main door where she clicked on her PR and called the station duty officer at Chelsea.

'Anything interesting?' Vikram asked.

CHAPTER 3

Underpants or no underpants? Ingram Fryzer pondered to himself, staring at the long rank of two dozen suits hanging in the cupboard in his dressing room. He was wearing a cream shirt with a tie already knotted at the throat and his usual navy-blue long socks, socks that came up to the knee. Ingram had a horror of showing white hairy shin between sock-top and trouser cuff when sitting down, legs crossed – it was in some ways the besetting and prototypical English sartorial sin. Sartorial sin, he smiled to himself, or should that be sartorial shin? No matter, when he sat in meetings with rich and powerful men and saw them shift legs, re-cross their thighs and expose two inches of etiolated shank, he found he immediately thought less of such people – this kind of lapse said something about them. However, the matter of underpants was an irreducibly personal issue – it was unthinkable that anyone in his company would ever guess that their chairman and chief executive officer was naked beneath his perfectly tailored trousers, that his cock and balls hung free.

Ingram deliberated further on this pleasant dilemma – underpants or no underpants – imagining the potential stimuli that awaited him that day. He loved the way the glans of his penis would rub against the material of his trousers, or snag itself for a second on a raised seam – at such moments you could never be sure that a semi-erection might spontaneously occur and of course this possibility raised the stakes, particularly if you were about to go in to an important meeting. The whole texture – every nuance – of the business day was immeasurably different if you were naked beneath your trousers. *Une journée de frottis-frotta*, as a French friend had termed it, and Ingram enjoyed the sophisticated pretension this title conferred on his little vice. He had made his mind up – no underpants it would be – and he selected a Prince of Wales check suit, pulled on the trousers, fitted his red braces to them and slipped on the jacket. He chose a pair of dark-brown, tasselled loafers and went downstairs to the full English breakfast that Maria-Rosa had waiting for him promptly at 7.30, Monday to Friday.

On the way to the office he asked Luigi to stop the car at Holborn Underground station. He often did this – rode the Tube to work for a few stops while Luigi took the car on – particularly on days he wasn't wearing underpants. He liked to mix with the 'people', look around him at the various types of human being on display and wonder what kind of lives they led. Not that he had any

contempt for them or felt any comfortable super-
iority – it was simply a matter of anthropological
curiosity, intrigued by these other members of his
species – and he thought that, as a person, he was
all the better for it, as no one else he knew in his
social and economic class did the same. For ten
minutes or so he became another faceless
commuter on the Central Line going to work.

He stood in the crowded compartment looking
around him, curiously, innocently. There were two
pretty-ish girls not far away, in suits, listening to
their music, plugged into their tiny earphones.
Smartly dressed, jewellery, quite heavy make-
up . . . One of them glanced blankly at him, as if
aware of his gaze, and then looked away. Ingram
felt his cock stir and he wondered if this might
be a day for Phyllis also. My god, what was wrong
with him? Did other men in their fifty-ninth year
think so constantly of sex? What was that expression, that term? Yes – was he an 'erotomane'? Not
the worst category of sexual offender in which to
be classified but sometimes he wondered if there
were something clinically wrong, or diagnosable,
about his obsessions . . . Then again, he reflected,
as he walked up the steps leading out of Bank
Station and saw the glass tower that contained his
company – CALENTURE-DEUTZ plc – on
several of whose floors some 200 of his employees
were settling down to their day's work, perhaps
such feelings, such urges, were entirely healthy
and normal.

He knew something was wrong as soon as he saw both Burton Keegan and Paul de Freitas waiting for him in the lobby. As he strode towards them he consciously began to run through the worst possible scenarios, preparing himself: his wife, his children – maimed, dead; an industrial accident at the Oxford laboratories, contamination, plague; some terrible stockmarket upheaval; a boardroom putsch – ruin . . .

'Burton, Paul,' he said, keeping his features as impassive as theirs, 'good morning. It can only be bad news.'

Keegan glanced at de Freitas – who would be the messenger? Keegan stepped forward on de Freitas's nod.

'Philip Wang is dead,' Keegan muttered in a low voice. 'Murdered.'

CHAPTER 4

Adam woke at dawn. Seagulls chanted and screamed in the air above him, flying low, swooping aggressively overhead, and for a brief moment he thought – oh, yes, of course, I'm dreaming, none of this happened. But the cold in his legs, the overall feeling of dampness and the itch of uncleanliness made him remember, forcefully, the fraught conditions he was in. He sat up, feeling depressed and almost tearful as he reflected on what had happened. He looked out at the river and saw that it was at full tide, brown and strong. He felt hungry, he felt thirsty, he needed to piss, he wanted a shave . . . The urination requirement was easily satisfied – and as he zipped up his fly he recorded bleakly that this was the first time in his entire life that he had 'slept rough'. It was not to his taste.

He pulled on his raincoat, picked up his brief-case and pushed his way through the dewy bushes towards the Embankment and watched the first commuters whizz by on the near empty road, beating the rush-hour. He jumped over the fence, snagging his raincoat on the railings and – once freed – wandered off. It was cool this early in the morning and Adam felt the chill, as he paused and brushed the leaves and grass off the skirts of his already stained raincoat. He had to eat.

In a café on the King's Road he ordered a 'Full English Breakfast' and quickly consumed it. He checked his wallet – notes and coins to the value of £118 38 pence. He thought that if he were going to turn himself in he should at least look presentable and so went to a chemist where he bought some disposable razors and shaving foam – now his hunger was satisfied he found he wanted to shave, more than anything – and rode the Underground from Sloane Square to Victoria Station where he paid £2 for admission to the new 'executive washrooms'. He shaved carefully and closely and combed his hair, sweeping it back from his forehead so that it sat thickly in place, the scores from the tines of the comb visible like corduroy – it already seemed unpleasantly greasy after his night in the open. On the station concourse he asked a transport official where he could find the nearest police station and was given directions to one close by on Buckingham Palace Road, a few minutes walk away.

Finding it easily, he paused a moment to gather his strength before confidently climbing the steps to what seemed a newish police station – all angular caramel brick blocks and bright blue railings. He had deliberately not thought about what was about to ensue – or what would be the immediate consequences of his inevitable arraignment. There was too much unhelpful, damning evidence against him, that was obvious, indeed that was why he had run away last night. He bleakly assumed he'd be arrested and kept in cells, before he was assigned a lawyer. He knew that he looked far too conveniently like the perpetrator – they wouldn't just listen to his version of events and let him go back to his hotel and wait for their call. And then, thinking of a telephone call, he suddenly remembered the job, the senior research fellowship, that he'd been interviewed for yesterday afternoon. They had promised to phone him . . . There had been no call on his cell-phone – rather, his 'mobile' – since the interview. He checked his phone for a second and saw there were no texts, other than spam messages from the phone company. His texting life had been more or less moribund since he had left the States – no banter or chatter from friends, colleagues or students any more – the silence of guilt . . . Still, he was curious to know about the Imperial College job. Had he been selected, he wondered, did they want him? He felt rueful, hard-done-by: whatever happened to him next was hardly going to look impressive on his curriculum vitae.

He stepped through automatic doors into a small lobby with a reception desk facing him, empty. A running red illuminated sign above it informed him that 'the station officer will be with you shortly'. A man and a woman sat waiting, also, staring silently at the floor. Adam stayed standing and turned to check his reflection in one of the glass-covered noticeboards – full of warnings, instructions about domestic violence complaints, job opportunities in the Metropolitan Police, legal notifications and photofit pictures of various villains. His eye swivelled instantly, uninstructed, to find his own name displayed there: 'ADAM KINDRED – WANTED. SUSPICION OF MURDER'. Even more alarming than seeing his name was seeing his face – a familiar image of himself, cropped from another photo (there was a stranger's shoulder in the bottom right-hand corner). Adam immediately knew where the photo had been taken as he contemplated his younger, smiling self – at his wedding to Alexa. He knew, also, that he was wearing a tailcoat, a grey waist-coat and a silver silk tie, in the English tradition, even though the wedding had taken place in Phoenix, Arizona, and all the other men present were wearing dinner jackets and bow ties. There had been some gentle mockery. He looked at his younger self: the smile was broad, his hair was considerably longer and a thick forelock, displaced by the buffeting desert wind, hung over his brow, rakishly. Self-consciously, Adam smoothed back his shorter, greasier hair. He looked different now – leaner and more worried. Then he thought: where in Christ's name had they found the picture so quickly? His father? His father was in Australia

36

with his sister. No . . . He stepped back, shocked – it must have come from Alexa, his ex-wife. He thought through the chain of events again, bitterly: no wonder they were on to him so fast – the name and address in the ledger at Anne Boleyn House led them straight to the Grafton Lodge Hotel (Seamus and Donal knew all about the job interview); then emails, telephone calls to his former employer, family members. A photo provided by the ex-wife ('Adam? Are you sure?' – he could hear her voice, just not quite protesting enough), then scanned and sent electronically to London in a fraction of a second. Maybe they'd contacted his father as well? . . . He began to feel sick. He could see it from the police's point of view – they were only looking for one man, the man who had signed himself in to Anne Boleyn House, the last man to see Philip Wang alive, the man whose fingerprints were on the murder weapon – an open and shut case. Find Adam Kindred and you have your murderer.

Adam felt his chest tighten and clench as he first outlined and then built the compelling circumstantial case against himself once more. He could be placed in the murder room at the hour of death – at the very moment of death. His fingerprints would be everywhere. His clothes were flecked with the victim's blood. He was the obvious suspect – anyone, everyone, would think he had killed Philip Wang. But where was motive? Why would he have wanted to kill this eminent immunologist? Why? . . . Crime of passion was the explanation that came unhappily to mind. Later, he reasoned that it had been the sight of his young guileless face that had made him act as he did. Something about his evident blame-lessness was enshrined in that photograph and he could not voluntarily sully it. He told himself to stop thinking and turned away from the image of this happy, smiling, carefree, younger Adam and walked through the sliding doors, back down the steps (past three uniformed policemen, ascending, who were talking animatedly amongst themselves) and headed west, turning right along Pimlico Road towards the notional safety that Chelsea offered.

As he walked away from the police station – brief-case in hand, raincoat flapping, feeling hot, almost feverish with alarm – Adam realised he had come to a crossroads. No, not a crossroads – wrong metaphor – it was a forking path and, moreover, as dramatic a forking path as anyone could encounter in their life. He could (a) turn himself in and submit himself to the due process of law – charged, held, bail refused, on remand, trial, verdict – or he could (b) not turn himself in. He was a naturally law-abiding person – he held in unre-flecting trust the legal institutions of the countries he had lived in – but now, suddenly, everything had changed. It wasn't 'respect for the law' that seemed to him paramount and fundamental, any more. No: it was freedom that governed this instinctive choice – his personal freedom. He had to stay free, at all costs, if he were to save himself, somehow. To remain free seemed the only course of action he could and should take. It was odd, this philosophical epiphany, but he was immediately aware that the individual freedom he currently possessed was unbelievably precious to him – precious because he now realised how tenuous and vulnerable it was – and he did not propose to surrender it to anyone, even temporarily.

And besides, he told himself, as he trudged along, feeling hotter with each pace, he was innocent, for god's sweet sake. He was an innocent man and he did not want to be accused of a murder he had not committed. How simple the situation, how clear the choice he had made – had to make – the only choice possible for him. He felt no dilemma, no doubt – anyone in his hideous, rotten position would have done the same. And there was this other factor, this 'X' factor, that had to be considered. Who was the man in the mews who knew his name and who had the pistol with the silencer? He must have been the killer, surely? The man on the balcony whom Adam had frightened off when he came into Wang's flat . . .

He passed a pub on his left and was tempted to go in and drink something but, along with his new belief in personal freedom, he was aware of how expensive everything was in this city – he had to hoard his remaining funds as he figured out what to do next while he waited for the real guilty man to be identified and apprehended.

He sat down on a bench in a small leafy square

and looked blankly at the statue of the boy Mozart. What had Mozart to do with this part of London? . . . Adam forced himself to concentrate: perhaps the best course of action would be to lie low for a while – a few days, a week – in order to see how the case was developing. What was that expression? Go 'underground' – yes, what if he went underground for a few days and let the other leads in the case receive their proper follow-up? He could cover events through the newspapers, or on TV and radio – then the thought came to him abruptly: what if Wang *had* been gay? Wang and Adam met in a restaurant, struck up a conversation and were witnessed there, Adam went to his apartment, Wang made a pass, they quarrelled, fought – everything got shockingly, terribly out of control . . . He felt a weakness come upon him again, looked at the boy Mozart and tried to summon up a Mozart aria, any tune to distract him, but the words that came into his head were of a rock song, from his youth: 'Going underground, going underground / Well the brass bands play and feet start to pound'.

The lyrics were prescient, he decided, he would go underground rather than meekly surrender himself at a police station and be accused of a crime he hadn't committed. Give it a few days, he told himself, other clues will emerge, the police will consider other scenarios and suspects. The Mozart came to him, finally, the overture to *Così Fan Tutte* – it always cheered him up. He rose to his feet, humming the overture quietly to himself: time to buy some essential provisions for his new life.

Later that day, as dusk was gathering, Adam threw his three bags of possessions over the railings of the Chelsea triangle and swiftly followed them. He sought out the area where he had slept the night before and examined it more closely: there were three large bushes here and some mid-sized trees, a sycamore, and some kind of holly, near the sharp apex of the triangle – the western end, furthest from Chelsea Bridge – forming a small clearing, and one of the bushes seemed almost hollow at its base, he could easily crawl in beneath its lower branches. He crouched down – yes, if he slipped in here he'd be effectively invisible from the Embankment's traffic, Chelsea Bridge and any passing boats on the river.

He emptied his carrier bags and contemplated what he had bought: a sleeping bag, a ground-sheet, a folding spade, a small gas stove with extra gas canisters, a torch, a metal cash-box, a knife-fork-spoon set, two bottles of water, a small saucepan and half a dozen tins of baked beans. He had been frugal in his purchases, buying only the cheapest items and those on sale – he had £72 left and some small change. He could hide here in the triangle during the day and venture out at night, as required, to scavenge – he could live, after a fashion.

He made a shelter in the hollow bush, breaking a few branches to clear a bigger space around him and draping the groundsheet over other branches in an inverted 'V', creating a squat, rough tent-shape. He unrolled the sleeping bag and pushed it in under the raised groundsheet – yes, he would be dry, protected from all but the heaviest rain. He looked round, suddenly, hearing a police car shriek by on the Embankment, siren whooping, and smiled to himself – all of London's police would be looking for him, CCTV footage would be being studied, further calls would be going out to his ex-wife and his family in Sydney, Australia, distant relatives and old acquaintances would be hunted down. Anybody seen anything of Adam Kindred? How they would laugh about this adventure once it was over! He was a wanted man but he was nowhere to be found. Having made his bed he lit his gas stove and heated up his baked beans. He spooned them into his mouth from the saucepan, hot and succulent – delicious. One day at a time, Adam, he said to himself: keep your mind as empty as possible. He had gone underground.

CHAPTER 5

Oil of cloves, Jonjo Case reflected: who would ever have guessed, who figured that one out? Picking up the small bottle, he dripped a few beads of oil on to his forefinger and massaged it on and around his damaged tooth – he felt the sharp pain dull, almost instantly. The big filling had fallen out when that cunt, Kindred, had hit him in the side of the head with the briefcase. The other tooth had shot out clean, as if a dentist had pulled it. When he came round fully he saw it there on the cobbles and picked it up and put it in his pocket – evidence.

Jonjo looked at his face in the mirror. He'd never liked his looks, as such, but Kindred's briefcase had given them a turn for the worse. His nose wasn't broken, at least, but it was swollen and he was going to have ear-to-jaw contusions. But what most upset him was the weal caused by some hinge or strengthening bracket of the briefcase that had stamped itself, in the course of the blow, on his right temple. He turned to find a better angle in the mirror. There it was, in the clear shape of an 'L', an angry blood-red weal. 'L for Loser,' Jonjo thought. It was bound to scab and he would probably be left with a white L-shaped scar there. No. No, that was not on, well out of order: he'd muck it up with a knife-point, later – disguise it. He wasn't going to spend the rest of his life walking around with an L-shaped scar on his forehead – no fucking way, mate.

He strode to his drinks table, pushing The Dog gently out of his way with his foot. The Dog looked at him, plaintively, as Jonjo searched the crowded bottles for his favourite malt whisky. What had possessed him to take a basset hound puppy off of his sister, he asked himself – taking a slug of whisky straight from the bottle – those big brown eyes, full of accusations? That face in a permanent anxious frown, the preposterously long velvet ears . . . It wasn't an animal, it was a toy, something to put on your bedspread, or block draughts coming in under the door. He grimaced as the malt mingled unpleasantly with the powerful taste of cloves in his mouth. Nasty.

He sighed and looked round his small house – the pain was definitely easing. He had to clear this place up – a week's dishwashing in the sink and four years'-worth of *Yachting Monthly* stacked behind the telly. He wondered what Sergeant-Major Snell would say if he could see the Jonjo Case abode. Air turned blue – air turned black, more like. I used to be the smartest soldier in the regiment, Jonjo reminded himself – what went wrong?

He scooped some clothes off the armchair and sat down. The Dog wandered over and stood there looking at him. He's hungry, of course, Jonjo realised: what with last night's shenanigans he hadn't fed the poor bastard in twenty-four hours. He searched and found, under a sofa cushion, half a pack of digestive biscuits which he scattered on the carpet. The Dog began to munch them up, his big pink tongue slapping them into his mouth.

Jonjo thought about last night, going backwards and forwards randomly in his mind. Thank Christ he'd found the tooth and the gun quickly, the police were everywhere. Then he thought about Wang, how he'd knocked him about a bit, then got him on the bed, choking him purple with the left hand, breadknife going in deep with the right. Must have missed the heart, somehow – Snell would have tortured him to near-death for that error. Then someone fucking *coming in*. Out on to the balcony in a jiff, but, all the same, knowing Wang wasn't dead . . . Bad, bad, bad. What had gone on while he was out there? he wondered, sadly. Sadly, because he knew he was losing it – two years ago he'd have simply taken out the other guy. Brutal but easy – way more efficient. Now this Kindred was alive, not arrested and somewhere out there, in London, according to the newspaper. He gave The Dog a Mars Bar. Jonjo helped himself to a slug of whisky and a few more drops of oil of cloves.

Kill Wang, make it messy and bring us every file in the place, they had said. He had done that, messed up Wang and his flat and he had all the files in a bin liner in the back of his taxi. They would know by now that things had gone wrong – well wrong – all he had to do was wait for the call.

Jonjo thought on, diligently: Kindred had gone out the emergency stairs at the back. Jonjo had followed, as soon as he'd stuffed all the files he could find into his bin liner, and the two smoking chefs had confirmed that a young guy in a rain-coat, carrying a briefcase, had just left, couple of minutes ago. Long gone then, Jonjo thought, going to his taxi and dumping the bin liner in the back. Then he had pondered for a minute before strolling round to the front of Anne Boleyn House. He took a book of matches out of his pocket – he always carried half a dozen on him, from different venues – and then folded out one match that he lit with his lighter and then dropped the whole matchbook in the half-full litter bin by the entryway. He heard the small hissing whoomph as the matches ignited and when the first waft-ings of smoke appeared he wandered casually into the lobby. The porter looked up with a false smile.

'Sorry to bother you, mate,' Jonjo said, 'but some kids just set fire to your litter bin.'

'Bastards!'

After the porter ran outside, Jonjo swivelled the guest-ledger round. There it was: G 14, visited by Adam Kindred, Grafton Lodge, SW1.

Outside, the porter had tipped the burning rubbish on to the roadway and was trying to stamp it out.

'Cheers,' Jonjo said, leaving. 'Little rascals, eh?'

'I'd castrate 'em.'

'Gas 'em.'

'Thanks, mate.'

Jonjo then drove his taxi to the Grafton Lodge Hotel in Pimlico and parked across the street, directly opposite. A young man in a raincoat with a briefcase ... It was a fine evening and there were few raincoat-clad men out and about. However, he had to wait longer than he thought – a couple of hours – before the person he assumed was Kindred appeared. Young, dark-haired, tall, wearing a tie, raincoat, briefcase – but he didn't go into the hotel, that's what threw him. The real, authentic Kindred would have gone straight into the hotel, surely? But this man turned down the narrow street that led to the mews behind. Jonjo eased himself out of his cab and followed him discreetly, turning the corner into the mews to see the man staring up at the back windows of the hotel. Was he lost? Was he an estate agent? Was it in fact Kindred at all? There was one easy way to find out so he asked the obvious question.

His tooth was throbbing again. With the palp of his forefinger he traced the L-shaped weal on his forehead. He hoped they'd ask him to kill Kindred. My pleasure, squire. The phone rang – three times. Then it stopped and rang again. Jonjo picked it up – it was them.

CHAPTER 6

Ingram spread the newspaper flat as Maria-Rosa hovered with the coffee pot.

'Just a drop,' Ingram said, his eyes not leaving the page. He was reading about the man who had killed Philip Wang and was both highly intrigued and somewhat astonished. Ingram read on.

'Adam Kindred, 31 (pictured right), was educated at Bristol Cathedral School where he was deputy head boy. He won a scholarship to Bristol University where he studied engineering. Mother died when he was fourteen, one older sister, Emma-Jane, father – Francis Kindred – a long-serving senior aeronautical engineer on the Concorde project . . .'

Ingram looked again at the picture of the smiling young man. A wedding photo. How did someone like this become a killer? This Kindred then won another scholarship to America – the Clifton-Garth scholarship – to Cal-Tech where he studied for a PhD in applied engineering. Was this a clue? Ingram wondered, suddenly suspicious – the US of A . . . At Cal-Tech Kindred became part of a team developing minute gyroscopes for NASA. Nothing there about drugs or pharmaceuticals, no

48

apparent involvement in the world of medicine, Ingram reasoned, nothing to suggest an interest in Calenture-Deutz and its business. He read on.

So, this Kindred fellow acquires his PhD and takes up a post as associate professor at the Marshall McVay University, in Phoenix, Arizona, where he helped design and build the world's largest cloud chamber at Painted Rock, the Western Campus of Marshall McVay University, in the Mohawk Mountains near Yuma. (What in god's name was a cloud chamber? he wondered. Ah, something to do with climatology.) Kindred became an associate professor and received tenure at the Faculty of Climatology and Ecology, Marshall McVay University . . . He skimmed a few lines. MMU was a private institution, 2,000 rich students, over half of them graduates, with a student–faculty ratio of 6:1, founded and endowed by a multi-billionaire who had made his fortune mining bauxite around the world. Ingram sipped the coffee Maria-Rosa had poured, calculating. So, Kindred had been away, living and working in America for eight, nine years, time enough for anyone to suborn him. He listed the four or five obvious rivals in his head, the big drug companies, the ones with vast amounts of money, time and, above all, patience. He should check to see if any of them were involved in this Marshall McVay University – an endowed professorship, a research programme. But it made no sense: why go for an engineer/climatologist? They would have wanted a doctor, somebody in the medical world. Why would they recruit an engineer turned climatologist to kill Philip Wang and thereby try to destroy Calenture-Deutz? Ingram read on.

'Kindred married – one Alexa Maybury, 34 (pictured left), a realtor with Maybury-Weiss in Phoenix, Arizona. The marriage ended in divorce some months ago. Kindred resigned his position at the university and returned to London where, on the very day after he had committed the murder, he had been offered the job of senior research fellow in climatology at Imperial College' (an offer that had been hastily withdrawn, apparently).

Ingram pushed Maria-Rosa's cooling coffee away. There was no sense in this – it must be blind chance. Why would this young, successful academic kill Philip Wang and ransack his flat? Was it sexual, perhaps? Drug-fuelled? (Ingram was still vaguely impressed at how many drugs young people consumed today, far more and far more effective than those of his youth.) What clues to the dark, vicious side of Adam Kindred's personality lay buried in this laudatory, blameless curriculum vitae?

He looked up. Maria-Rosa was hovering again.

'Yes, Maria-Rosa?'

'Luigi, he here. With car.'

On the way in to Calenture-Deutz, Ingram called Pippa Deere, head of public relations, and asked for the Adam Kindred profile in the newspaper to be copied and circulated to all board members prior to the extraordinary board meeting. Everyone had to know whom they were dealing with – the whole conspiracy clearly had huge and complex ramifications.

He rode the lift to the Calenture-Deutz floors of the glass tower, feeling – and he was happy to acknowledge the feeling – unusually important and strong. He had summoned all the board members to this extraordinary meeting because he had formulated a plan and wanted to make an important announcement that would have a bearing on the reputation of the company. He bustled around his office for a while making numerous enquiries of his personal assistant, Mrs Prendergast, on the whereabouts and presence of the other board members. Mrs Prendergast was an unsmiling, fifty-something, wholly professional woman. Ingram, after a couple of years, realised he could barely function – in a business sense – without her and consequently she was munificently rewarded with free holidays, stock options, unilateral salary rises. He knew her first name was Edith and thought she had two grown-up male children (photos on desk) but that was about all – and they were ineluctably Mr Fryzer and Mrs Prendergast to each other.

When she finally told him that everyone was present in the boardroom he slipped down the back stairway to the 'Chairman's dining set' as he fancifully called the small dining room off the boardroom (he had furnished it himself: a decent oak table and ten chairs, a long walnut dresser-base, some nice paintings – a Craxton, a Sutherland, a big vibrant Hoyland) where he planned to have a quick, covert brandy before he addressed the board, just to get his juices flowing. He felt a strange attack of nerves, as if there were some evil premonition about what was happening, what was in the air, not like him at all – a little Dutch Courage was called for – though he excused himself, simultaneously, by the knowledge that it was not every day that one of your closest colleagues is viciously murdered.

So he was more than a little annoyed to find his brother-in-law already there in the room, in the 'set', casually helping himself to a large whisky from the bottles grouped on a silver tray on the walnut dresser-base (under the vibrant Hoyland).

'Ivo,' Ingram said with a wide false smile. 'A little early, no?'

Ivo Redcastle turned. 'No, actually – I've been up all night, in a recording studio. I got your message at three a.m. Thanks, Ingram.' He took a large gulp of whisky and topped his glass up again. 'If you want me to stay awake this will have to do.'

It was impossible now for Ingram to pour himself a proper drink so he helped himself, with bad grace, to an apple juice. He glanced at his brother-in-law – downing his second whisky – and noted

52

for the thousandth time that Ivo, for all his silly debaucheries and pretensions, was still an absurdly handsome man. In fact, Ingram thought, there was something faintly creepy about how handsome he was: the thick, longish black hair swept off his forehead to one side, forever flopping down, the straight nose, the full lips, his height, his leanness – he was almost like a cartoon of a handsome man. Thank god he wasn't intelligent, Ingram thought, gratefully. And at least he had shaved and was wearing a suit and a tie. Everyone had to have a 'Lord on the Board' – so he'd been advised when starting out in business – and acquiring a brother-in-law that fitted the category seemed both ideal and simple but, as everything with Ivo, Lord Redcastle, there were endless complications. Ingram looked at his watch as Ivo set his glass down – it was not quite 9.30 a.m.

'I see the dyer's hand has been at work,' Ingram said.

'I don't follow.'

'The new lustrous blue-black sheen to your copious hair, Ivo.'

'Are you implying – insinuating – that I dye my hair?'

'I'm not "implying" or "insinuating" anything,' Ingram said evenly, 'I'm stating. You might as well hang a sign around your neck saying, "I DYE MY HAIR". Men who dye their hair can be spotted at a hundred yards. You, of all people, should know that.'

53

Ivo went into what Ingram could only describe as a brief sulk.

'If you weren't family,' Ivo said, his voice trembling, 'I'd actually punch you in the face. This is my natural hair colour.'

'You're forty-seven years old and you're going grey, just like me. Own up.'

'Fuck you, Ingram.'

Mrs Prendergast opened the door to the set.

'Everyone is ready, Mr Fryzer.'

The meeting went well, initially. The full board was there, executive and non-executive members: Keegan, de Freitas, Vintage, Beastone, Pippa Deere, the three Oxbridge professors, the ex-Tory cabinet minister, the retired senior civil servant, a former director of the Bank of England. They sat soberly and seriously as Ingram made his short speech about the tragedy of Philip Wang's death and the debt that everyone at Calenture-Deutz owed him. It was only as he moved on to speculate about the future and the new drug that Philip had been working on that the first interruption took place.

'Zembla-4 is unaffected, Ingram,' Burton Keegan said, raising his hand as an afterthought. 'I think everyone should know: nothing of Philip's work will have gone to waste. The programme continues – full force.'

Ingram paused, irritated: Keegan should have sensed he wasn't finished.

'Well, I'm delighted to hear that, of course. Still, Philip Wang's contribution to the success—'

'Actually, Philip had pretty much signed off on phase three, isn't that correct, Paul?'

De Freitas responded to Keegan's cue.

'Yeah . . . Effectively. I spoke with Philip two days before the tragedy. We were at the end of the third stage of clinical trials – and he was more than happy with everything. "Full steam ahead", were his precise words, if I recall. He was a happy man.'

'But he hadn't actually signed off, as far as I'm aware,' Ingram said.

One of the professors chipped in (Ingram couldn't remember his name). 'Philip was more than happy – the data was really superb. He told me himself just last week – superb.'

Now that Ingram had been interrupted so comprehensively a general buzz of conversation grew around the long, glossy table. Ingram leant towards Mrs Prendergast.

'Remind me of that man's name, Mrs P.'

'Professor Goodforth – Green College, Oxford.' She looked at her list. 'Professor Sam M. Goodforth.'

Ingram remembered him now, another new appointee to the board, simultaneous with the arrival of Keegan and de Freitas. Ingram cleared his throat, loudly.

'Good news, excellent news,' he said, aware of how bland he sounded. 'At least Philip's work will survive.'

Keegan had the grace to hold his hand up this time.

'Burton, do go ahead.'

'Thank you,' Keegan said, smiling politely, 'I'd like the board to know that we're flying Professor Costas Zaphonopolous in to take over the day-to-day supervision of the final stage of the trials before we submit our NDA to the FDA. Our New Drug Application,' he added politely for the benefit of any uncomprehending non-executive directors, 'to the Food and Drug Administration.' He turned to Ingram. 'Costas is Emeritus Professor of Immunology at Baker-Field.'

Reverential mutters of approval from the other professors round the table. Ingram felt a twinge of unease – who was this man they were flying in, and at what cost? Why hadn't he been consulted? He saw Ivo cleaning his fingernails with the sharp tip of the pencil that had been placed on the blotter in front of him.

'So much the better,' Ingram said, feeling that he had to reassert his authority – he still hadn't had the chance to reveal his *pièce de résistance*.

'Right, now—' he began and then stopped. De Freitas had raised his hand. 'Paul?'

'I should say, for the record, that there is some data missing from Philip's files.'

Ingram kept his face blank, authoritatively blank. 'Data missing?'

'We think,' de Freitas flourished his copy of the Kindred profile, 'that Kindred may have it.'

The professors gasped. Ingram felt that sick premonition again. Something bad was going to happen, he couldn't see it yet, but this awful death was just the beginning.

'What kind of data?' Ingram asked, in a quiet voice.

Keegan pitched in now. 'Data that is incomprehensible to anyone not wholly cognisant of the Zembla-4 programme. We think Kindred has it – but he doesn't know what he has.'

Ingram's instincts were hard at work – he felt high anxiety now: Keegan and de Freitas's insouciance didn't fool him at all – this was very serious. He was suddenly glad he'd had an apple juice and not a brandy.

'How do you know this data is missing, Burton?' he asked, carefully.

Keegan smiled his insincere smile. 'When we went through the material recovered from the London flat we became aware of inconsistencies. Stuff we expected to see wasn't there.'

Ingram eased himself back in his chair and crossed his legs. 'I thought the London flat was a crime scene.'

'Correct. But the police were most accommodating. We informed them of the importance of the Zembla-4 programme. They gave us complete access.'

'I don't get it,' Ingram said. 'Do the police know data is missing? Doesn't that provide motive?'

'They will know, in the fullness of time.' Keegan

paused as de Freitas whispered something in his ear. Keegan fixed Ingram with his dark, intense eyes, and then they traversed the table. 'For the sake of the Zembla-4 programme it's best that this knowledge is kept within this room.'

'Absolutely,' Ingram said. 'Absolute discretion.' There were mutters of agreement from around the table. Then he said 'Good' three times, cleared his throat, asked Mrs Prendergast for another cup of coffee and announced that he had decided that Calenture-Deutz should offer a reward of £100,000 to anyone who assisted the police in the capture and arrest of Adam Kindred. He put it to the board for a vote of approval, confident that it would be unanimous.

'I couldn't disagree more fervently,' Ivo, Lord Redcastle said loudly, casting his pencil down on his blotter where it bounced, impressively, twice and then skittered off the blotter to the floor with a thin wooden clatter, less impressively.

'Ivo, please,' Ingram said, managing a patronising smile but feeling all the same a surge of heartburn warm his oesophagus.

'Just let the police do their job, Ingram,' Ivo said, pleadingly. 'This only muddies the water. We offer this kind of sum and every money-grubbing loser will be deluging the police with spurious information. It's a terrible error.'

Ingram kept his smile in place, reflecting that it was rather rich for one money-grubbing loser to so denigrate his tribe.

'Your objection is noted, Ivo,' Ingram said. 'Will you note it, Pippa?' Pippa Deere was keeping the minutes. 'Lord Redcastle disagrees with the Chairman's proposal . . . Good, duly noted. Shall we vote on it? All those in favour of the reward . . .'

Eleven hands went up, including Keegan's and de Freitas's, Ingram noted.

'Against?'

Ivo raised his hand slowly, a look of disgust on his face.

'Carried.' Ingram basked in his insignificant triumph for a few seconds, knowing full well that this small revolution on Ivo's part was a misguided act of revenge for the hair-dyeing accusation – clearly it still rankled. Ingram wound up the meeting and everyone dispersed.

'Nothing personal,' Ivo said, as they left the room. 'I just think that rewards are iniquitous, corrupting. Why not hire a bounty hunter?'

Ingram paused and tried to look Ivo in the eye but he was too tall.

'One of your close colleagues has been horrifically murdered. You've just voted against the one thing we as a company, as his friends, can do to help bring his murderer to justice. Shame on you, Ivo.' He turned and walked into his dining set ready for his brandy. 'Have a nice day,' he said as he closed the door.

CHAPTER 7

As Sergeant Duke homed in for a farewell kiss, Rita took last-second avoiding action and ensured his lips did not meet hers – he would be allowed to kiss her cheek like everyone else at the station.

'Going to miss you, Nashe,' he said. 'Where we going to get our glamour, now?'

She knew he fancied her – Duke being a married man with three children – and he was very aware that she and Gary had split up: his commiserations had been both heartfelt and eager. She would have to watch him later, at the farewell party. Sergeant Duke, off duty, drink taken . . . She felt her heart heavy, all of a sudden: she didn't like goodbyes.

Duke was still talking. 'But you'll be back for the inquest, of course. And the trial.'

'What's that, Sarge?'

'The Wang murder. The limelight has sought you out, Rita. Chelsea, brutal death, eminent foreign doctor. The beautiful WPC Nashe gives her evidence at the Old Bailey. Press'll go ape.'

'Yeah. Well, let's catch Kindred first,' she said,

dryly. 'Or there won't be a trial at all. See you at The Duchess.'

'I'll be there, Rita,' he said, his voice heavy with lustful implications. 'Wouldn't miss it, love, not for the world.'

Shit, she thought as she picked up her bag and left the station, regretting the party idea already. Vikram was waiting at the main door, affecting coincidence badly.

'Going to miss you, Nashy.'

'Don't call me Nashy, Vik.'

He gave her a peck on the cheek. 'Sorry. Anyway, thanks for everything. Couldn't have done it without you.' Vikram had just been confirmed as a full-time police constable, his days as a special – a hobby-bobby – over.

'See you at The Duchess, eight o'clock.'

'Wouldn't miss it for the world.'

Rita stepped out of Chelsea Police Station for the last time and decided to take a taxi home to Nine Elms. This move was a triumph, even though of small order – maybe not in the 'dream-come-true' category but it was going to be a key change in her life, and one for the better, she hoped – so a small indulgence was called for and justified.

The taxi dropped her at the boatyard and she walked down the metal gangway towards TS *Bellerophon* with a light heart. The tide was rising and the sun was shining through the lime trees above her on the river bank, turning their leaves almost unbearably green and fresh – and she suddenly had the feeling that this change in her life was going to be a successful one. To her vague surprise she acknowledged what she was experiencing: she was happy.

Then she saw her father on the foredeck leaning on his arm-crutches. She climbed up the steps to join him.

'Hi, Dad.'

'I hate you coming home in uniform, you know that.'

'Too bad.'

'It freaks me out.'

'What a shame.' She stopped and put her bag down. 'What's wrong with you, then?'

'I had a fall, done my back in, again. Couldn't find my crutches so I had to call Ernesto.'

'You should have texted me. I know where everything is – no need to involve him.'

As they went below she noticed that her father managed to cope with the steep stairs with little fuss or effort. He eased down into his chair in front of the television, saying how knackered he was, thought a lumbar disc must be protruding, then flipped his ponytail over his shoulder and rummaged in the little chest of drawers beside the chair where he kept his things.

'You can't smoke skunk, Dad,' Rita warned him, going along the companionway to her room. 'I'll arrest you.'

'Pig!' he shouted after her as she closed her door.

She changed out of her uniform and into jeans

62

and a T-shirt. When she emerged she was pleased to see that her father wasn't smoking a spliff, though he did have an extra-strength Speyhawk lager in his hand.

'Medicinal,' he said.

'Enjoy.'

'So what's happening to you?' he asked. 'Becoming a detective?'

'You know.'

'It means nothing to me.'

'I told you: I'm transferring – to the MSU.'

'MSU, USM, MUS, USA, FAQ, AOL—'

'Marine Support Unit. We're having a farewell party at The Duchess. Why don't you come along?'

'To a pub full of policemen? You must be joking.'

'Suit yourself. Can't say you weren't asked.'

She started to climb the stairs to the upper deck.

'I don't want to know about your police life,' he said. 'It depresses me. What does the Marine Support Unit do?'

'We go up and down the river,' she said. 'I'll toot when we pass by.' She smiled at his discomfort. 'I'll be keeping an eye on you, Daddy-O.'

She went up on deck. The *Bellerophon* was an ex-Royal Navy, World War II mine-sweeper, 'Bangor' class. It had been refurbished in the 1960s and stripped of all its bellicose appurtenances – guns, depth charges, mine sweeps – to reveal a plain and sturdy ship and one that made a roomy, narrow home permanently, immutably moored on the Battersea shore of the Thames, by Nine Elms Pier.

Rita had created a sizeable container garden on the foredeck – where the main Bofors gun-mounting had been – and she fitted the coiled hose to the standpipe and watered her plants carefully – the palms, hydrangeas, tuberoses, plumbago, oleander. Beneath her feet she sensed the *Bellerophon* shift on its mooring as the tide rose, lifting the keel off the mud. She felt herself calming after the emotions generated by her departure and the endless farewells and looked around her, enjoying the silvery gleam of light coming off the river in this late afternoon. Downstream she could see the green glass blocks of the MI6 building and the gull-wing roofs of St George's Wharf. Over her left shoulder were the four chimneys of Battersea Power Station – one of the chimneys thick with scaffolding – and, turning her gaze upstream, she could see a train crossing Grosvenor Railway Bridge and beyond that the twin peaks of Chelsea Bridge's suspension cables.

Seeing Chelsea Bridge made her think of Battersea Park, and Gary and that day she had spotted him there. An old lady had been knocked flying by a cyclist in the park, some lad illegally cycling along the Embankment front. The old lady's dog had been injured in the collision and the police had been called. Once Rita had overseen both victims' departure in an ambulance and the cyclist charged, she went in search of an ice cream. It was a hot early May day and the sun shone with a fresh strength, clear and vigorous. She cut across the car park, heading for the tennis courts where she knew there was an ice-cream van parked in the afternoons and as she emerged from the trees she had seen Gary – her Gary, Gary Boland, Detective-Constable Gary Boland – lying on the grass with another girl.

They were lying head to toe, the girl – blonde, short-haired – leaning back against Gary's raised knees. Rita stepped behind the trunk of a plane and watched them talking. She didn't know the girl, didn't recognise her, but everything about their familiarity with each other told the story and nature of their relationship thus far, and its clear intimacy. Not even the most plausible and inventively persuasive Gary would have been able to convince her of its innocence. But what upset her most was the way Gary had his hand resting on her knee. She could see his thumb gently, reflexively beating out a rhythm against the girl's kneebone – the rhythm of some song in his head. This was something Gary did, on table tops, against the sides of coffee mugs, the arms of chairs, as if he were some frustrated drummer from a rock band – a sign of his nervous energy, she supposed, pent up. This is what Gary used to do to her when they lay in bed in the mornings, he would gently tap a rhythm with his thumb on her bare knee, on her shoulder. She had filed it unconsciously in her mind under his name – this was what Gary did with her – its banal intimacy was one of those factors that made their relationship uniquely individual. She looked at the girl and imagined her filing it away in her mind also:

Gary Boland, always beating out a rhythm, any knee would do. And now that it had lost its exclusivity for Rita she saw it suddenly as an irritating habit and her heart went cold and passionless. She watched him stop his drumming, change position and kiss the girl full on the lips.

She had confronted him that evening and broken off their relationship five minutes later – maturely, resignedly, sadly – she thought. They would see each other all the time, police business made their paths cross inevitably, so there was no point in becoming hysterical and accusatory about it. Maybe that was giving her the extra pleasure she was experiencing about her move to MSU: she wouldn't see Gary any more and she would stop continually thinking about that afternoon in Battersea Park, as indeed she was now . . . Angry, she forced herself to change the direction of her thoughts and she tried to imagine herself, in a day or so, powering up river in a Targa launch of the MSU looking over at the TS *Bellerophon* at its moorings as she cruised by. How strange that would be – but she liked the idea of policing London's river, rather than London's streets, and indeed the idea seemed to her to be somehow miraculous, given that she had lived on this boat on this river almost her entire life. She heard her father calling for her and ignored him – not wanting to spoil her mood: she felt suddenly blessed – no one could be this lucky. Then she thought of the party at The Duchess – just a few hundred yards away. Would Gary come? She'd asked him – they were grown-ups – no hard feelings and all that. What would she wear? Something to make him realise what he'd—

'RITA! For god's sake, I need you!'

She carried on watering her plants.

CHAPTER 8

'£100,000 reward for information leading to the arrest of Adam Kindred.' Adam regarded the full-page advertisement in the newspaper with frank astonishment and an obscure, though fleeting, sense of pride. Never had he seen his name written so large – and to be worth a £100,000 reward. Who would have thought it? There was his picture, also, and details of his height, weight and race. Adam Kindred, 31, white male, English, dark hair. His raincoat and briefcase were also specified as if he never wore or carried anything else. Then the reality of the situation struck him and he felt shame creep over him, imagining his family seeing this, imagining people who had known him, speculating. Adam Kindred, a murderer? . . .

He was sitting in his small clearing at the sharp end of the Chelsea Bridge triangle. The grass was well flattened now and the three thick bushes that protected him from the gaze of passers-by were like the familiar walls of his secret room. It was five days since his grotesque, brief encounter with Dr Philip Wang in Anne Boleyn House – five days that had allowed his beard to grow, dense and dark and, he hoped, all-disguising. He had never grown a beard before but was grateful for the speed with which his facial hair sprouted, however much it itched. The key thing was he looked nothing like the man in the newspaper's favourite photograph.

The itch around his jaw, throat and lips was just one amongst the many itches that dominated his waking life. He hadn't stepped under a shower or into a bath since he had prepared himself for his interview at Imperial College. And here was another admixture of pride and regret: to learn from the newspapers that it had been decided to offer him the job of senior research fellow was gratifying (he was the perfect, well-qualified candidate) but then only to have the offer withdrawn hours later – once he was a publicised murder-suspect – was a blow, however predictable. He had kept his phone switched off but wondered if anyone had called: Imperial College, offering the job, then withdrawing it? The police – urging him to give himself up? He was unwilling to use his phone in the triangle – uncertain whether it might give his position away and keen to conserve whatever juice was left in the battery – he was down to one bar. It had all gone quiet for the last forty-eight hours, however. But he found he didn't care as much as he thought he would about the job, such were the incremental complexities and disasters of his strange new life underground. He would rather have a thirty-minute soak in a hot bath, currently, than be a senior research fellow at Imperial College – it was some measure of the waking nightmare his life had become.

He washed as well and as much as he could in public lavatories – he could just about manage hands, face and neck – but his hair was now heavy and dull with grease (in his other life he had washed his hair every day – what a preposterous luxury that seemed) and his clothes were taking on that encrusted, creased look of the homeless, adhering loosely to the body-shape like a fabric integument, another skin. He slept and lived in the same shirt, underpants and trousers and he knew he was beginning to smell as he steadily acquired that unmistakable look – of poverty, of self-neglect.

As he roved around his triangle at night – easily avoiding the occasional drug-takers and the lovers who took advantage of its dark undergrowth for some moments of privacy – he had become aware that, at low tide, a long, thin sand and shingle beach appeared below the sheer embankment wall. Three looped rows of chains had been attached, one above the other, to this wall, as a safety aid, he supposed, something to grab on to if you found yourself in the river being washed up- or down-stream, depending on the powerful tides. These chains also allowed him to descend easily to his beach, a thing he had done twice now, and the first time he had done so, at about two in the morning, he had felt an overpowering temptation to strip off, immerse himself in the river and wash himself clean. But the tide was still ebbing and he could sense its tremendous flow and strength: he didn't yet know the river well enough, he realised. Perhaps the only minutes he could safely wade in would be when the tide was turning and the rush of water slowed or slackened for a few moments. As he clambered back up to the triangle, hauling himself up the chains, he was pleased to think that he would have a beach now, twice every twenty-four hours – the river was becoming a feature of his tiny triangular world.

He lay low in the day, stretched on his ground-sheet in the shade of the bush, listening to the traffic grind by on the four lanes of tarmac just a few feet away, thinking endlessly about what had happened to him and making plan after plan for any number of potential futures. He watched the clouds travel above the Thames, idly noting their types and transformations. One day he saw the sky cover steadily with a thin layer of altostratus translucidus, the sun a shrouded, nacreous disc, and, as the cloud-layer inevitably thickened to altostratus opacus, he sensed the rising moisture gathering ahead of an advancing warm front and, two hours before the inevitable rain began to fall, he prepared and waterproofed his sleeping quarters under his bush as best he could. He lay in his makeshift tent hearing the tapping patter of rain and felt, not pride at his expertise and manifest foreknowledge, but sadness. Clouds were his

71

business – he was a cloud-man who made clouds in his giant laboratory and stimulated them to deliver their moisture in the form of raindrops or hailstones . . . So what was he doing lying, filthy and alone, in this small triangle of ground on the bank of the Thames? Not for the first time the life that he had once so recently led seemed some kind of taunting chimera – the contrasts between his two existences, before and after, appeared too acute to seem real – as if the Adam Kindred he had been was a fantasy figure, a vagrant's dream, the fond imaginings of a desperate down-and-out.

These moods passed and when they did so, late at night, when it was dark and the tide was low, he climbed down the wall-chains on to his small beach and retrieved what bounty the river brought him: three rubber tyres that he stacked on top of each other and used as a seat, a battered wooden fruit box, in which he kept his cooking utensils, and a traffic cone – somehow he thought it better that it wasn't on the beach where it might draw attention to itself. When he was hungry he went out and, with his dwindling supply of money, bought sandwiches and hot drinks in cheap cafés and fast-food franchises where his shabby, dingy appearance attracted no surprised looks. With the aid of his small street-map paperback he familiarised himself with his neighbourhood in south-west London. He followed the progress of the Wang murder investigation in discarded newspapers and he sensed, even after a few days, how it was quickly ceasing to be a long-running story. The advent of the reward-announcement had changed all that, however, provoking another surge of interest in him and wild speculation on the uncanny 'disappearance' of the prime suspect: had he committed suicide, had he fled abroad, was he being sheltered by some misguided friend or family member? . . .

He had read of his father's emotional televised plea that he surrender himself to the police, hugely grateful that he hadn't actually seen it. 'Give yourself up, son, you're only making things worse. We know you're innocent. Let's sort out this horrible mistake.' He read that his ex-wife Alexa Maybury Kindred had declined to comment, though the details of his divorce (and its adulterous catalyst) were surprisingly accurate. As he read, and as each day went by, Adam was alarmed to note that no other suspect was listed, no other scenario of Wang's death mooted, and he began to ask himself if, by deciding to go underground, he had made not only the most important decision of his life but also the biggest mistake – a life defined, he now thought in his depressed state, by a catalogue of errors that had led him inexorably to this one. Only he, he realised, knew about the man on the balcony; only he could testify to the fact that Philip Wang had had a breadknife in his chest when Adam opened the bedroom door; only he had confronted the man with the gun at the rear of Grafton Lodge . . .

He had to do something, he thought glumly, looking at his watch. Crouching, he scurried over to a nearby laburnum bush and peeled back a rectangle of turf. This was where he had buried his cash-box, a dry, secure hiding place where he could leave his few precious possessions – his wallet, credit cards, his *A–Z* street map, mobile phone and the file he had tried to return to Wang. It was this dossier he was interested in now – an interest triggered and heightened by the announcement of the reward. He had looked at it before a couple of times, trying vainly to decipher what its importance was, but now the advertisement had appeared it seemed even more crucial, somehow. What was this firm Calenture-Deutz and why was Philip Wang so important to them? Why were they prepared to pay so much money to find Adam Kindred?

Adam sat and sifted through the few pages in the file, trying to muster up some real forensic or analytical intent. It was a simple list of names and ages (all young children, clearly) and beside each name, in small neat handwriting – Wang's? – was some form of shorthand that looked like the record of some kind of dose: '25ml i/v x 4 – 75ml b/m x 6'. Beside each name was the name of a hospital: one in Aberdeen, one in Manchester, one in Southampton and one in London – St Botolph's in Rotherhithe. Wang had told him he was an 'immunologist' – so perhaps some sort of clue might be found in St Botolph's Hospital.

★   ★   ★

Adam now leapt over the fence of the triangle on to the Embankment pavement as if it were the most natural, unconcerned thing in the world. Conscious of the new reward advertisements, he was not wearing his raincoat nor carrying his brief-case. He was wearing his tie, however – in an effort to look presentable – and he had his wallet, credit cards and mobile phone on him. His dense, growing beard made him look vaguely disreput-able but he hoped the suit and the tie would counterbalance this. He had a strange confidence in his invisibility in the city – he was already a long way from the man pictured in that wedding photo, so widely disseminated: nobody was going to connect this new version of Adam Kindred with that one. He was also aware that he had £18.78 on him – all his cash.

He had thought about using his card to extract more cash from the many cash machines he passed but he had sensed instinctively that the only way to avoid detection in a modern twenty-first-century city was to take no advantage of the services it offered – telephonic, financial, social, transporta-tional, welfare-related and so on. If you made no calls, paid no bills, had no address, never voted, walked everywhere, made no credit card transac-tions or used cash-point machines, never fell ill or asked for state support, then you slipped beneath the modern world's cognizance. You became invisible or at least transparent, your anonymity so secure you could move through the city – uncomfortably, yes, enviously, prudently, yes – like an urban ghost. The city was full of people like him, Adam recognised. He saw them huddled in doorways or passed-out in public parks, begging outside shops, sitting slumped and wordless on benches. He had read somewhere that every week in Britain some 600 people were reported as missing – almost 100 people a day – that there was a population of over 200,000 missing people in this country, enough to fill a sizeable provincial city. This lost, vanished population of Great Britain had just gained a new member. Nobody appeared able to find these missing people unless they themselves wanted to be found and gave themselves up or returned home – they just seemed to disappear, swallowed up – and Adam thought it shouldn't be too difficult to join their number, as long as he didn't make any foolish mistakes. He tried not to think how he was going to survive when his money ran out tomorrow or the next day.

He Tubed to Rotherhithe and, emerging from the Underground station, asked a mother with two young children where he could find St Botolph's Hospital.

'St Bot's?' She pointed. 'Just head down to the river. Can't miss it.'

And indeed it was unmissable, sitting like a great lucent cruise ship – like several, lucent cruise ships – on the Bermondsey/Rotherhithe shore, across the river from Wapping. At the centre of this modernist

76

conglomeration of buildings was the small red-brick Victorian hospital – 'St Botolph's Hospital for Women and Children' proudly emblazoned in blue and cream tiles across its ornate façade. On either side the glass and steel stacked floors of the new NHS Foundation Trust Hospital's buildings spread through its car parks and newly landscaped gardens, some of the blocks linked by transparent aerial walkways lit by red or green lights – like arteries or veins, Adam thought – no doubt this was the 'wit' that had won the architect his gold medal or his knighthood.

Adam followed signs to the reception atrium and stepped into a space that reminded him more of a huge convention hotel in Miami or an airport terminal. Great primary-coloured abstract banners hung from the cantilevered glass ceiling sixty feet above his head and fully grown trees – bamboo, weeping fig, palms – grew from small, walled islands here and there. He could hear the sound of plashing water (piped or genuine? – he couldn't tell).

People wandered to and fro in this vast transit lounge – in transit from health to ill health, Adam supposed, or vice versa – some, in dressing gowns, were clearly patients, others, in multi-zipped over-alls in differing pastel shades, with name-badges on their breasts and dangling ID photos hung around their necks, were orderlies or administrators of various kinds. There were also people like him in civilian clothes that must have been either visitors or else putative patients seeking entry into this self-contained, health-city. The mood was calm and unhurried – like an ante-room to heaven, Adam thought, as he wandered deeper into the atrium, his ear now picking up some inoffensive jazzy muzac. Nobody asked him who he was or what he was doing here; he imagined he could live in this building for days, unnoticed, as long as he drew no attention to himself. But then he saw the CCTV cameras everywhere – small and discreet, barely moving this way and that – nothing was that simple any more.

He went to a desk set beneath a superimposed blue neon 'i' where a girl in an apricot overall smiled welcome at him. The name badge on her breast read 'Fatima'.

'I'm looking for Dr Philip Wang,' he said, and she typed Wang's name into her computer. He watched carefully to see if any alarm or curiosity registered on her face but there was none. He might as well have asked for Dr John Smith.

'Felicity de Vere Wing, level six,' she said.

'Thank you, Fatima.'

Following Fatima's directions, Adam headed towards a cluster of glass and steel columns that contained the scenic elevators serving the nine floors of St Botolph's. As he rode upward, Adam felt he was in some kind of human hive, a hive dominated by signs and acronyms: everywhere there were signs, signs that made sense and others that didn't; signs that were welcoming and vaguely reassuring, others that provoked sudden dark fears – A&E, Radiology, Pathology, Cafeteria, GUM (what was that?), Neuroscience Centre, Teenage Pregnancy Clinic, Sigmoidoscopy Dept., car park 7, IBD clinic, Medicine Management Services, ENT and Audiology – signs that directed him to segments of buildings on this campus where every potential health need could be catered for – it seemed – in every functioning part of the human body and its glossary of maladies, from birth to death.

Emerging at level six he looked over the balustrade to the swarming life on the atrium floor below and marvelled, dizzily. He felt like a modern Dante in an antiseptic inferno – all he needed was his guide.

And his guide duly came to him in the form of a man in a pistachio overall and matching turban who asked if he could help. Adam said 'The Felicity de Vere Wing' and he was sent down a wide corridor that led to one of the vertiginous, aerial green-lit tubes linking him with another of St Botolph's many modules. As he walked along the tube Adam could see, through the smeared plexi-glass, the river to his left curving gently round Wapping. The first lights were coming on in the city as dusk set in but Adam sensed that in St Botolph's it was forever a fluorescent twenty-four-hour day, 365 days a year. Nothing stopped here: darkness and light, summer and winter solstices, heat and cold, the changing seasons meant nothing. People arrived, they were admitted, they were healed and sent on their way – or they were not and they died.

Arriving at the Felicity de Vere Wing – the sign writ bold above double doors, and some sort of ornamental, curtained plaque on the wall – Adam encountered a recognisable reception desk manned by a crisply uniformed nurse, not an overalled apparatchik. He saw a doctor with a stethoscope round his neck, he saw porters with a trolley – this was familiar. The atmosphere was hushed, as if people were whispering, 'illness', 'sickness' – and for the first time Adam felt he was in a hospital and recognised the need for some caution. Not a good idea to mention the name of the recently murdered Dr Wang here, he concluded.

'Hi,' he said to the nurse, improvising, 'I'm looking for Dr Femi Olundemi.'

She frowned. 'Olundemi?'

'Olundemi. Femi Olundemi.'

'We've no Dr Olundemi in this wing.'

She went and asked another nurse and they both came back shaking their heads.

'I must have the wrong information,' Adam said. 'This is the immunology department, isn't it?'

'No, no,' said his first nurse, smiling now that the error was confirmed as his, and whose name, he noticed, was Seorcha. 'Immunology's on level three – I think. This wing's for children with chronic asthma. Only children.'

'My mistake,' Adam said. 'Thanks for your help.'

★　★　★

Adam wandered out of St Botolph's wondering if he was any wiser – if this trip and the expenditure of a few valuable pounds had been worth it. He supposed so: Wang was on the main-frame computer but his death had yet to be registered, and the wing with which he was associated dealt exclusively with children suffering from chronic asthma. That Wang's death was so far unremarked in this vast sickness factory seemed to indicate he was not a familiar or regular presence. But chronic asthma? . . . What was the name of the company Wang worked for – the eager reward-givers? Calenture-Deutz – yes. Adam repeated the name as he walked away from the luminescent strata of the hospital buildings: Calenture-Deutz, children with chronic asthma . . . How had Wang described himself? An 'allergist' – maybe there was something there . . .

Adam had come out of a different lift and had left through a different door and, quitting the grounds of St Botolph's, he turned and walked along a street wondering where Rotherhithe Tube station was. Outside a kebab shop he asked directions from a young guy sitting on a small-wheeled bike, eating a kebab.

'You what?'

'Tube station,' Adam repeated. 'Rotherhithe.'

'You got Canada Water, mate. Close. Go up there, then down there.'

'What? Straight on, then right?'

The young guy looked blank. 'Yeah. Whatever.'

Adam set off thinking hard, thinking that maybe he had proved his point, that maybe it *was* time to turn himself in. He was dirty, bearded, almost penniless, sleeping under a bush on waste ground at night, living off baked beans and cheap sandwiches, defecating and washing in public lavatories. And yet, something at the back of his mind kept saying insistently – no, no, stay free at all costs. Only this way can you retain any vestige of control over your life. The minute he re-entered society all freedoms would be curtailed. Who was the man with the gun in the mews behind Grafton Lodge? And who was to say that he, Adam, would be any safer in police custody than he was on his own in London, living underground? That man had come to kill him and had doubtless killed Wang. Only while he was free and undiscovered was he safe – as soon as he was corralled, penned-in, then anyone could find him. Something very big was at stake here, something he had blundered in on – something currently unknowable, unimaginable. Adam Kindred standing up in open court protesting his innocence, testifying about a man on a balcony, a man with a gun, might draw down other fatal dangers on himself. And what, if anything, did it have to do with the Felicity de Vere Wing of St Botolph's Hospital and chronic asthma in children? It was all hideously complex and worrying – perhaps a few more days in the triangle wouldn't make any more difference now. He stopped . . .

He was lost. He hadn't been paying attention.

He looked about him. Tall, crude blocks of apartment buildings, concrete stairs, walkways. A few lights on. He walked up to a sign badly defaced with graffiti: 'THE SHAFTESBURY ESTATE – UNITS 14–20.' He peered around again: 1950s public housing – a few trees, a few functioning street lights, a few clapped-out cars and, fifty yards off, a group of kids sitting on the low wall around a playground – a slide upended, some rubber tyres hanging from chains, a roundabout. Looking up, he saw some people leaning on their elbows, gazing out from the zig-zag stairways that gave access to the higher terraces.

He turned and walked back the way he had come, purposefully but not with any sense of panic. Suddenly his three bushes in the triangle by Chelsea Bridge seemed like home to him – he wanted to be there, settling down in his sleeping bag under the inverted V of his groundsheet – and he felt tears well in his eyes as he realised how pathetic, how abject, this yearning was. No, it was becoming impossible: he had to go to the police, he had to go through whatever ordeal was waiting for him, there was no altern—

All Adam felt was a massive blow to his back – as if he'd been hit by a sledgehammer or a silent car – dropping him to his hands and knees, and then, almost immediately, another blow, to his head this time, provoking a spiralling supernova of light. And then everything went black.

CHAPTER 9

He was a regular that one guy, yeah, anyway said he was – she remembered. Then she thought, maybe not: fat, white, small moustache . . . One them guys just want tugging but no handkerchief no tissue nothing don't mind the mess. Mhouse was muttering to herself, goading her reluctant memory as she walked along the river from her usual beat. She couldn't remember: they all blurred into one generic punter – male. He was the one keep saying he was a regular, she continued to herself. What he wanting, discount? Fuck.

She breathed deeply, smelling the strange river smell. She liked working by the river, plenty of dark corners, very few passers-by at night. She didn't like getting into cars – not after that last time, no fucking way – plenty of quiet places by the river and there was always Margo's room – extra fiver to Margo – no problem. You get in a car they can lock the door – like that last time. Fucking hell. She paused and lit a cigarette, looking across the river to Wapping on the other side. A boat had gone by and the lights were dancing on the diminishing wake. Lights were pretty, she thought, like someone pulling them on rubber strings, always bouncing back . . . She unzipped her boot and slid her money in under her instep, zipped it up again, and headed up Southwark Park Road towards The Shaft.

When she saw him she thought at first he must be a junkie or a drunko, lying under the stair by the car park, half his clothes off. She wandered over, cautiously. He was wearing a shirt, underpants and socks – and there was a smear of blood on his forehead. He was moaning, trying to sit up. She walked a bit closer.

'Oi. You all right?'

'Help. Help me . . .'

His voice was different, like on the telly, not from The Shaft, surely? She took her lighter from her bag and clicked it on. He had a beard and drops of blood were trickling from a kind of pattern on his forehead. Like a grill mark on a hamburger, she thought. She knew what it was, now, from the reinforced cleated front of a trainer: three bars and the blurred indentation of a logo. He been jumped, this guy.

'You been jumped,' she said. 'They take you clothes?'

'I assume so.'

Mhouse didn't understand.

'You what?'

So he said, 'Yes, they did.'

'Where you live,' she asked, 'what unit?'

85

'I don't live here. I live in Chelsea.'

Chelsea, Mhouse thought . . . My lucky time, my lucky tonight.

'Wait here,' she said, 'don't move, I help you to home.' She gestured to the man, shooing him back, encouraging him to move further under the shelter of the stairs and watched him huddle up in the darkness, folding his white, bare knees with his arms. She walked quickly across the parched grass of the wide quad formed by the stern rectangle of The Shaft's many blocks, heading for her unit, and ran up the two flights of stairs to her flat. She looked in on Ly-on, but he was still fast asleep, spark out, and then rummaged in a cardboard box searching for some trousers that would fit the guy who had been jumped. Tall geezer, big man.

On her way back she called Mohammed on her mobile. Got one, Mo. You be at South Bermondsey Gate, five minute. Then she picked up speed, trotting back to find him, praying he hadn't wandered off somewhere. He was still there in exactly the same position; he looked up as she whistled. She handed him the pair of cropped cotton cargo pants and a pair of flip-flops.

'Best I got,' she said. Then she offered him a cigarette but he didn't want one. So she lit up herself, watching him pull on the trousers slowly, wincing. He took off his socks, stuffed them in the thigh pockets of the cargo pants and slipped on the flip-flops.

'You come with me, I take you to Chelsea.'

Mhouse led the man down the side of The Shaft – no one was about – to the South Bermondsey Gate where Mohammed was waiting in his Primera.

'You got any money?' she asked the man. 'Cash?'

'They took everything – my mobile, my shoes, my credit cards, jacket, trousers, even my tie . . .'

'No problem – we'll get sorted.'

She opened the rear door and helped him in – he was very stiff after his battering, she knew what it was like – then she slid in the front with Mohammed, who was trying to keep a broad smile off his face, unsuccessfully. She gave him a cigarette and he put it in his shirt pocket.

'Where we go?' he said.

'Chelsea. Where you live in Chelsea?' she asked the man.

'Just drop me at Chelsea Bridge Road, right by the bridge on the Embankment. That'll be fine.'

'I take you Parliament Square,' Mohammed said. 'You tell me after.'

They headed off through the dark city, Mhouse glancing back at him from time to time to see how he was coping. He kept dabbing with his fingers at the imprinted shallow cuts on his forehead, looking at the smear of blood on his fingertips.

'What happened?' she asked. 'You remember anything?'

'I was walking down the street – I was lost, I was looking for the Tube and then I felt this incredible blow on my back. I heard nothing.'

'Blow?'

'As if I'd been hit by a car on my back. I fell to the ground and then something hit my head. I don't know – maybe I hit my head on the ground.'

'No. They do like a drop-kick to your back – you know? Two feet. Bam. Then another bloke kick you head when you fall down. You never hear nothing.'

'It's very kind of you to take me back,' the man said. 'I'm most grateful.'

'You English?'

'Yes – why?'

'I thought you maybe come from foreign – like asylum.'

'No, I'm English . . . I was born and bred in Bristol.'

'Where's that then? London?'

'No, to the west, about 100 miles from here.'

'Right.' Mhouse smiled. 'What's your name?'

'Adam. What's yours?'

'Mhouse.'

She showed him the inside of her right arm: tattooed there, clumsily, unprofessionally, were the words 'MHOUSE LY-ON'.

'I'll be for ever in your debt, Mhouse – my good Samaritan.'

'Samaritan. I know that. I don't pass by. I do it for the Lord.' Mhouse stared at him: Adam – young guy, nice-looking guy. The way he talk – like a book, like Bishop Yemi. He talk like that. What was this Adam doing round The Shaft at night? Asking

88

for trouble and he got it. She turned and looked out of the window at the changing cityscape rolling by. They were all quiet in the car for a while.

'Good driving, Mo,' she said.

'I drive good, man,' Mohammed said.

When they got to Parliament Square, Adam directed Mohammed on towards Lambeth Bridge and the Embankment. Mhouse looked out of the window at the river – she found it hard to imagine it was the same river she worked beside at Rotherhithe, it looked different here. Mhouse closed her eyes, tired. Maybe she'd let Ly-on sleep until morning: she could smoke some chagga, yeah, call Mr-Quality-He-Delivers and smoke some chagga and sleep well, have breakfast with Ly-on.

'Here is Chelsea Bridge,' Mohammed said.

'Just go through the lights,' the Adam-man said. 'This is close enough.'

Mohammed pulled up and put his flashers on. A few cars whizzed by, it was getting late, quieter. Mhouse looking out of the window. Just trees behind pointed railings on both sides. She opened the door and stepped out on to the pavement. The Adam-man followed, awkwardly, stiffening up. Mohammed stayed behind the wheel, engine running.

'It's incredibly kind of you—' Adam began.

'Where you live?' she said, interrupting, suddenly cautious. 'Where you house, where you flat?'

She took in his rueful smile, unaware of the

ironies clustering around her innocent question. He gestured behind him at the triangular patch of waste ground between the roadway and the river.

'Actually, I live there,' he said, still pointing. 'I don't have a home at the moment.'

'You're joking me.'

'Alas, no.'

Every suspicion stirred in her and came sharply alive.

'You sleeping in there,' she said. 'You gone rabbit.'

'I'm . . . I'm in a bit of trouble. I'm hiding. Keeping out of sight.'

This made sense now – he was lying. 'I don't fucking believe you,' she said. 'You scatter my head.'

'Honest. Look, I'll show you if you like.'

He helped her over the fence and he followed – then Mhouse let him lead the way, pushing through bushes and ducking under branches as her eyes grew accustomed to the strange electric darkness, charged with the cold glow of the street lights from the Embankment. They came to a small clearing between three large bushes and the man – Adam – showed her his things: the sleeping bag, the groundsheet tent, his rain-coat, his briefcase, his stove. Mhouse walked around behind him as he explained, her brain going – yeah, typical, my fucking lucky tonight, yeah?

He turned to her, spreading his hands and said,

'Listen, believe me, if I had any money, you'd be welcome to—'

She punched him – two-fisted – in the gut and then kneed him in the balls. He went down with a high cracked-voice sigh, like a girl. She kicked him.

'You fucking gambling me, man. You fucking owe me.'

He kept groaning, holding his groin, as she went through his possessions: sleeping bag, saucepan, gas stove, folding spade. Nothing – homeless shit. She took the raincoat and the briefcase and stood over him, the folding spade in her right hand.

'You fucking gamble me, man, this is what you get.' She raised the spade.

Adam stopped moaning and shrank away from her. She thought about hitting him with the spade, do some real damage, but he had called her his Samaritan. And there was something about him – something nice – that she responded to. He was an animal and he needed help.

'You need help.'

'Yes. Yes, I do. You helped me. Please help me.'

'I help you one more time. I'm your Samaritan, man, though I can't not fucking think why after what you done, how you scatter me.'

'Thank you, thank you.'

'You go to the Church of John Christ in Southwark. They help you.'

The man said, 'You mean "Jesus" Christ.'

She hit him on the leg with the spade and he cried out.

'John Christ, you wanker! *John* Christ. You say Mhouse sent you.'

She threw the spade at his head but he managed to duck and it glanced heavily off his shoulder. She spat at him and pushed her way through the bushes to the road, climbed the fence and jumped into the Primera beside Mohammed. He sped away.

'Nice Bumberry raincoat for you, Mo. Leather and golden briefcase for me.'

'Safe. Super safe, Mhouse,' Mohammed said. 'Thanks.'

'Yeah, whatever. He was a wanker, he had no money. Homeless wanker. Let's get back to The Shaft.'

CHAPTER 10

Even though he drove a taxi, a black London cab, his motor vehicle of choice – ubiquitous, unremarkable and there was no law against it – Jonjo liked to steer clear of other black-cab taxi-drivers, particularly when they were present in significant numbers. He wanted no impromptu solidarity, no leading questions. So he parked up some distance from City Airport and its long line of taxis waiting for their clients and walked a good half-mile to the neat little terminal building.

Inside, he took a tour around, checking the available exits. He was an hour early for his meeting – he was always an hour early, just in case, you never knew – and he rode up the escalator to the first floor and selected a seat in the corner of the cafeteria with a view of the escalator and the small concourse and settled down with his coffee and croissant and his newspaper and contentedly did the puzzle for half an hour before deciding that the time was right for some more vigilance.

Fifteen minutes before the appointed time for the rendezvous – 10.00 a.m. – he saw his contact come in. He could spot them a mile off, other soldiers. He could go into a crowded pub and in three seconds could have picked out the men who were Tags or Blades, Crap Hats, Toms, Jocks, Squaddies, whatever they called themselves or each other. Funny that, he thought: like an instinct, like we give off a spoor, a smell. We're like Jews and Scotchmen, Roman Catholics and Freemasons, ex-cons and gays. They spot each other, they know in seconds, split seconds. Funny that – as if we've got some sign on us only visible to our kind.

He watched this young guy – thirty-something, short cropped fair hair, burly – come in and check the terminal as he had and then come up the escalator to the cafeteria. He stepped in and on his first sweep of the tables Jonjo knew he'd clocked him. He stayed bent over his puzzle: how many four-letter words could you make from the letters LFERTA? Tear, fart, leaf—

'Excuse me. Are you Bernard Montgomery?'

Jonjo looked up. 'No.'

'Apologies.'

'I'm often mistaken for him.'

The young guy sat down.

'We got news,' he said.

'From our friends in the Met?'

'Yeah.'

'About bloody time.'

The young guy seemed edgy, on the tense side.

'Kindred's phone has been used,' he said. 'Few seconds.'

'Not by Kindred, obviously,' Jonjo said. 'He's not that daft.' He leant back, putting down his pen as the word 'FERAL' came into his head. Must remember that.

'No . . . It was used only once, in Rotherhithe – someone on an estate: the Shaftesbury Estate. Then they must've changed the sim-card.'

'Someone stupid, then.' Jonjo thought for a second. 'So, his phone was stolen or he sold it. I suppose we don't know who made the call.'

'No.'

'Lovely-jubbley. I'll check it out.' Jonjo smiled. 'I'll need paying by the way. For the last job.'

The young guy pushed a thick envelope across the table. Jonjo scooped it up and stuffed it in the inside pocket of his leather jacket. The young guy was staring at him intently.

'You're Jonjo Case, ain't you?'

Jonjo sighed. 'You're breaking all the rules, mate.'

'I knew it was you,' the young guy persisted. 'You were a friend of Terry Eltherington.'

'Terrible Tel,' Jonjo reflected, bitterly. 'Great shame. Fucking shame . . .'

'Yeah . . . My brother-in-law. I saw you in his photos.'

'Those cunting IEDs. How's Jenny coping?'

'She killed herself. Couldn't face it. Three days after the funeral.'

Jonjo took this news in, sadly, sagaciously: he remembered Jenny Eltherington – blonde, big,

jolly girl. He nodded to himself: soldier's wife –
worst fate on earth.

'You must be Darren, then,' Jonjo said, stretching
his hand across the table. 'Blues and Royals.'

'That's me.' They shook hands.

'Tel and I were in the Regiment, went through
Hereford together. Fucking nutter, Tel.'

'I know. Yeah, he used to talk about you a lot:
Jonjo this, Jonjo that . . .'

They were both quiet for a few seconds thinking
about Terry Eltherington and his sudden violent
death in Iraq, victim of an unusually powerful
roadside bomb. Jonjo felt his neck stiffening and
eased it side to side.

'What happened to you?' Darren said, indicating
the now star-shaped but still livid scab on Jonjo's
forehead.

'You should see the other guy,' Jonjo chuckled,
then said, 'Anything you want to tell me, Darren?
On the Q-T? Off the record?'

Darren looked grim for a moment. 'This is as
hot as I've ever seen it, Jonjo, believe me. Blazing
hot. No idea why, but they're going train-wreck.'

'No pressure, then?'

'Find Kindred, priority "A". Call in any time –
you can have every resource: Metropolitan Police
database, back-up, tools, intel, Centurion tank.
Anything you need.'

'Good to know,' Jonjo said, feeling his guts squirm,
and becoming slightly worried, all of a sudden – not
like him at all.

'What happens when I find Kindred?'

'They need to know what he knows – first. Then they'll tell you what to do with him.'

'Cool.'

'I'd better get going.' Darren made as if to get up but Jonjo gestured him back into his seat.

'Nice meeting you, Darren. Do me a favour, will you?'

'Of course.'

'Keep me in the loop. Just you and me . . .' He paused to let Darren understand the full implications of what he was asking. 'Sorry to hear about Jenny – my condolences.'

Darren nodded.

'I better give you my number. Like they said – anything you need. Call me, twenty-four-seven.'

'Write it on the newspaper. I don't think I'll need you. Only last resort, yeah?'

'Anything.' Darren wrote down the number.

'You've obviously got mine. Call me if you need me. Terry Eltherington, one in a million – if his sixteenth cousin called me, I'd be there. If his step-sister's adopted son's mate's mate called me. Know what I mean?'

Darren nodded, visibly moved. Good to know someone in the chain of command, Jonjo thought, might give him a bit of time if it was needed. Darren wouldn't know any more about this Wang–Kindred thing than he did, but an ally was an ally, every little helped.

Jonjo stood. 'I'll leave first,' Jonjo said. 'You wait

here for ten minutes.' He picked up the newspaper. 'It was a pleasure, Darren.'

'Copy that.'

Jonjo walked back to his taxi-cab, his mind busy. These freelance jobs were usually so straightforward: you were told to slot someone, you did it and you were paid. You didn't know anything more. He took the envelope from his jacket pocket and briefly contemplated the packed, mint wad of 200 £50 notes. Ten grand on completion. At least they weren't punishing him for the fuck-up, though by rights he should have had a further 10K advance on the new Kindred job. Still, the full twenty grand would be all the sweeter once that was done and dusted. Wang was dead, he'd been paid his money, now on to the next one. Busy, profitable month.

He continued on his way, heading for his taxi, thinking about Wang for a moment, the last man he'd killed. Strange, that, he thought: he had no idea exactly how many people he'd killed in his life – thirty-five to forty, perhaps? It all started in 1982 with the Falklands War when he knocked out that bunker at Mount Longdon. He had been an eighteen-year-old paratrooper firing a Milan wire-guided missile, steering it right into the sandbagged sangar on the hillside. When he went to look after the battle all the dead were laid out in a row, like on parade – he looked for all the burnt and mashed-up ones and counted five.

Then he'd killed a Provo in a car on the outskirts of Derry but three other Paras had opened fire that night so they had to share the kill. It wasn't until he joined the SAS and went through Hereford that the tally began to climb. Gulf War I, after the Victor Two fire-fight when the prisoners ran off – he slotted three. Then in Afghanistan, in 2001 – his last operation – at the fort, Qala-I-Jangi. He lost count at Qala, all those rioting Taliban prisoners down below and our guys up on the battlements. Terry Eltherington had been there also. Shooting fish in a barrel, Terry had said. Jonjo could see his big, stupid, smiling face, chucking him ammo. Prisoners running around in the big overgrown courtyard, all the guys up on the battlements blasting away – SAS, SBS, the Yanks, the Afghans. Incredible. They just laced the whole courtyard, hosed it. He must have got a dozen or so, just picking them off as they ran around.

He opened the cab door and sat down behind the wheel, still computing. Christ – then there were all the jobs when he left the forces and joined the Risk Averse Group, one of the biggest private security companies. God knows how many Jacky-bandits he'd slotted on the Jordan–Baghdad run when he was a PSC – six? Ten? Then the five free-lance jobs – he'd started counting again, properly – and there was always the money in the bank to confirm the number. He had no idea who'd found him, who called him up, sent him the details, no idea who paid him, no idea who the victims were and no idea why they were victims. Solid, professional, efficient, discreet – he was damn fucking good. Wang was number six and it would have been perfect if bastard Kindred hadn't blundered in with his briefcase . . . His hand went reflexively to his new star-scab. Got rid of 'L-for-Loser' – got pissed, sloshed a bit of vodka on the wound and the tip of a hot knife had done the rest. Kindred had made a neat job messy – so now he would find Kindred, hand him over for interrogation, and then make sure that his last moments on planet Earth were very memorable.

His mobile rang.

'Hello?'

'Jonjo, it's Candy.'

Candy was the woman who lived next door. Divorcee, big woman, managed one of those flat-pack stores in Newham. Nice enough, friendly, looked after The Dog when he was busy.

'Yeah, Candy, what is it? I'm working, darling.'

'I don't think The Dog's very well. He's been sick all over your carpet.'

Jonjo felt his chest fill with air.

'I think we need to take him to the vet . . . Jonjo? Hello?'

'I'll be there in twenty minutes,' Jonjo said, his mouth dry. He started the engine.

CHAPTER 11

Adam was flying above a dense cloudfield of supercooled cumulus, high over Arizona, the grey packed clouds stretching to the horizon. A cloud desert. Somehow he was both piloting the plane and at the same time supervising the dry-ice dispenser in the rear. Running beneath the wings of the plane were plastic tubes with small, lipped vents set in them at regular intervals. The plane dipped to one side and descended close to the cobbled surface of the cloudfield, flying a few feet above its gently shifting mass. What time of day was it? In the rear of the plane Adam flipped the switch on the high-pressure pump and tiny granules of frozen silver iodide, like fine sand, began to stream from the plastic vents on to the clouds below. The plane flew a course of a long oval, ten miles long and two miles wide, like a giant racecourse, the trajectory of its passage and the dusting of silver iodide revealed by a wide deepening trench appearing almost immediately in the cloud surface as the frozen ice crystals coalesced into water droplets. Down below the clouds, standing in a dry arroyo in the

Arizona desert, Adam lifted his face to the sky as the first fat drops of the rain that he had made hit his brow and cheeks.

Adam woke. He felt cold, although the sun was shining, and he had horrible nausea. He eased himself out of his sleeping bag, crawled a few feet away and vomited. Concussion, he thought, wiping his mouth and spitting: I must be still, be quiet, drink lots of water.

He hauled himself back into his sleeping bag and lay there, shivering, now growing conscious of aches beginning to make themselves felt about his body. Curiously, his head wasn't sore but his balls hurt and so did his back and, worst of the lot, his left thigh and left shoulder were competing for first place in the throbbing-pain stakes. He remembered the dream, vividly, it was one of his recurring ones, but one he hadn't had in months. Why was he dreaming about his old life when his new one was so immediately and dolorously present? He shed his sleeping bag again and checked out his body. He had a long thin bruise on his thigh – a lurid purple-blue – the skin only slightly broken, and on his left shoulder was a clear gash: his dirty, greasy shirt was slightly ripped at the shoulder and the rip was fringed with dried blood. He remembered – both injuries caused by that Mhouse-woman wielding his entrenching tool. He touched his forehead gently, feeling the gridiron of scabs, crusty under his exploring

102

fingertips. He wondered what he looked like – a terrorist bomb casualty? A survivor from a car crash? Or a destitute, homeless person, victim of a brutal mugging? . . .

Back under his bush, he found himself recalling the dream. He had never seeded clouds from a plane – that was why they had built the cloud chamber. Plane trials and tests were too erratic, too easily disproved – that was why Marshall McVay himself had funded the building of the Yuma Cloud Chamber. They made their clouds, cooled them to the required temperature, then seeded them with dry ice or frozen silver iodide or salt or water droplets and measured the precipitation down below. All very straightforward and controlled.

He forced his thoughts to change – he had to stop thinking about his past, his old job, it was making him even more depressed – concentrating instead on the events of the previous night. He remembered the Mhouse-person bringing him clothes. He was still wearing her beige-grey, camouflage, mid-shin cargo pants and he could see the flip-flops a couple of yards away where he had kicked them off. And then the journey from the Shaftesbury Estate to Chelsea became patchy, something of a vague, troubled dream: buildings passing, car headlights and tail lights glaring, talking to Mhouse, her small cat face staring back at him, her body twisted round over the front passenger seat . . . Who was driving? He remembered her

103

showing him her name, tattooed on the inside of her right forearm: 'MHOUSE LY-ON'. What kind of name was that? 'Mhouse' pronounced 'Mouse', clearly. And then he had helped her over the fence of the triangle – a skinny little thing, with a pretty, snub-nosed, thin-eyed face. Yes . . . And then she had attacked him.

Why had she attacked him with such sudden violence? She had punched him and then kneed him in the balls – he winced at the pain-memory – then she laid about him with the entrenching tool. Why, for Christ's sake? Christ – John Christ, of course, the unlikely answer came to him. Go to the Church of John Christ in Southwark, she had said, his fiendish Samaritan, they'll help you.

Somehow he managed a laugh – it sounded cracked and strange to his ears – and he slipped out of his sleeping bag for the third time that morning to see what he had left in his campsite. The inventory did not take him long: she had stolen his raincoat and briefcase. The muggers had taken everything else, leaving him with worldly goods of three tins of baked beans, a gas stove, a saucepan, a knife-fork-and-spoon set, an entrenching tool and half a bottle of mineral water – non-sparkling. He sensed self-pity invade him and his eyes warm with tears. Yes, he felt sorry for himself – this was no sin, surely, under the circumstances? He had a dirty, torn shirt, underwear, a pair of socks, some tight, cropped camouflage cargo pants and flip-flops for his feet. Meagre assets. He thought of his new three-bedroom house in Phoenix, Arizona (now the property of his ex-wife, of course) – he could see its watered green lawns, the neat laurel hedge, the twin-car garage . . . It seemed like a parallel universe, or something that had existed aeons ago. Moreover, he had money in bank accounts in Arizona and in London – thousands upon thousands of dollars and pounds – and yet here he was crouched, hiding, battered, stinking, a fugitive hiding amongst the bushes and trees of a patch of waste ground by London's river.

Thinking of Arizona and his Arizonan life brought the cloud chamber back into his mind. Only days ago he had been showing the interview panel at Imperial College the abstract for his half-completed monograph: 'Hail suppression in multi-cell thunderstorms'. One of the panel (the woman) had been at the glaciation conference in Austin, Texas, and had heard him read his paper on 'Silver iodide seeding and the production of biogenic secondary ice nuclei'. He had described to them his last experiment in the Yuma cloud chamber (before he resigned his post) that had been a highly successful reduction of hail swath from a beautifully formed cumulonimbus cloud, its anvil head just brushing the plexi-glass roof of the chamber, nine storeys high. He had stood there on the viewing gantry watching the icy dust of the seeding crystals disperse and witnessed the near magical generation of a billowing warm updraft. Hardly any hail had fallen into the vast collecting trays below. His colleagues had broken into spontaneous applause.

Adam could taste the bitterness of frustration and disappointment in his mouth as he lit his camping-gas stove to heat a tin of baked beans. The smell of the gas and the odour rising from the cold beans as he tipped them into the saucepan made his gorge rise – but he knew he had to eat something.

Stop! he told himself abruptly, as he felt a scream of rage and anger building in him. Those days were gone, the cloud chamber was no more. All that was history, now. Adam Kindred, cloud-seeder, hail-suppressor, rain-maker was as real and tangible as a strip-cartoon superhero. He crouched on his haunches and concentrated on the here-and-now, spooning warm baked beans into his mouth and trying not to think about the life he had once led.

Two days later, Adam wondered if he was actually beginning to starve: he felt light-headed and, when he stood up, dizzy and unsure on his feet. It was twenty-four hours since he had finished his last tin of beans and he was now filling his plastic bottle with water from the Thames itself – brownish water with some sediment but the taste was acceptable and he needed to put something in his empty stomach. He felt oddly fearful since his attack – since he'd been jumped – frightened about venturing out from the security of the triangle – his small, known realm – into the pitiless, vast world of the city beyond. He had no money, for a start, not a brass penny, and unkempt hair and beard and his clothes – his torn shirt, stupid trousers and flip-flops – would draw curious glances, he was sure, and the last thing he wanted was people staring at him. He felt safe in the triangle: the near-constant traffic noise reassured him; the tide on the river rose and fell; boats and barges passed. No one came to the triangle and at night the strings of glowing bulbs on Chelsea Bridge seemed festive, almost Christmassy, and cheered him up.

The next morning, at the first glimmerings of dawn, he climbed down to the small beach to fill his water bottle. There was another rubber tyre half buried in the mud, numerous broken plastic bottles, some driftwood and a tangled coil of blue nylon string. He picked up the string – thinking vaguely that this was the sort of useful jetsam that a castaway might use – and estimated that it must be at least twenty foot long. What a waste and what irresponsible bargee or seaman had tossed this over the side? – sea birds could become tangled up in it, propellers snagged. He looked around him; the light was beautiful, peachy-grey, and the air was cool. Already the river birds were flying and soaring about: gulls, crows, ducks, cormorants. He saw a heron flap inelegantly by, heading for Battersea Park and its tall trees. There were Canada geese on the river as well, he knew, and, all of a sudden, the phrase 'cooked his goose' came into his head. He looked at the beach – the tide was on the turn – maybe he had half an hour before it would be too light and he'd be spotted. He clambered back up the chains to the triangle.

It didn't take him long – scouring his abandoned tins produced half a handful of cold beans. Grabbing his wooden box, he was down on the beach again in seconds. The trap he constructed was rudimentary in the extreme but he had faith that it would work: one end of the box was propped up on a driftwood stick to which his new acquisition of blue nylon string had been attached. He shaped a small cone of cold baked beans on a flat pebble and placed it under the propped-up box. Then he climbed back up the chains, holding the end of the string between his teeth and settled down out of sight behind a bush to wait. He wasn't seriously expecting a goose to take his bait but he was hoping for a duck – a small, plump duck would do nicely – though he'd happily settle for a mangy London pigeon. He waited, telling himself to be patient, to muster a hunter's calm and steadfast patience, if he could. He waited, and waited. Cormorants drifted downstream with the ebb tide, then dived under the water. A couple of crows flapped on to the beach and pecked around the pebbles at the water's edge showing no interest in his beans at all. Then he heard a dry whirr of wings, like an angel overhead, and a big white-and-grey gull swished past above him, banked steeply, stalled, and touched down, immaculately, delicately, with almost ostentatious care. The crows ignored it, methodically turning over their pebbles, pecking at bits of weed. The gull made straight for the baked beans, stooping under the propped end of the box ... Adam tugged his string, the prop clattered away and the box fell.

'Easier said than done,' Adam remarked to himself, out loud, as he contemplated his box, now shifting about agitatedly on the mud beach as the panicked gull flapped and skittered inside. Easier planned than executed. But he was hungry: he had caught his prey, he had fuel, a knife and roast flesh was what he craved. There was nothing for it – he reached quickly under the box and grabbed the gull by a leg. Its hard yellow beak stabbed viciously at his forearm, drawing blood, until Adam battered the bird senseless with the driftwood prop. He rinsed his forearm in the river – more wounds, who cared? – and went back to pick up his limp and lifeless gull, its broad white wings thrown wide. As he did so a big laden barge appeared under Chelsea Bridge heading upstream. There was a man standing on its prow staring over at him. Adam moved the gull behind his back and waved, casually. The man did not wave back.

Adam plucked the gull and somehow, with the knife from his knife-fork-and-spoon set, managed to gut it, throwing the intestines in the river. Then he cut slivers of greasy flesh from its surprisingly raw-boned body and, pronging them with the fork, held them in the blue flame of the gas jet until

109

they blackened. The taste of the hot meat was gamey but inoffensive, though the flesh was sinewy and required much chewing, washed down with draughts of Thames water. He ate as much as he could and flung the carcass into the river, the tide now beginning to surge upstream. Then he sat down on his seat of three rubber tyres and wept.

It had been good to cry, he told himself, later: it was a salutary release of emotions, very necessary after everything he had been through – the mugging, the trauma of that first surprise attack, the relief of rescue, then the trauma of the second attack. At the darkest hour of the night he left the triangle for the first time in days and went into Chelsea to scavenge. He felt better, calmer and more determined, as he rummaged in dustbins and scampered cautiously down empty streets, peering in basement wells. It was amazing what people left out in their rubbish. By dawn he had managed to acquire a newish, white denim jacket (one breast pocket disfigured by a stain of black ink, as if from a leaking biro), a pair of golfing shoes that had been left on a back step – a little tight but more tolerable footwear than the flip-flops. He had also eaten from the rubbish bins of fast-food franchises – cold chips, the end of a kebab, half-inches of cola and other fizzy drinks remaining in the bottom of tin cans. He returned to the triangle belchingly replete and newly attired – he almost looked normal, he thought. But what was uplifting him was the realisation that he could survive, now. It was as if the roasted gull-meat had strengthened and emboldened him in some way, had given him new resolve and heart. He had some of the squawking cheek and strutting arrogance of a big white seagull. Once the scab on his forehead had healed and disappeared he would venture forth with more confidence and range more widely. Perhaps, he thought, and this was a measure of his new frame of mind, he might even take Mhouse's advice and go to Southwark and see what help the Church of John Christ might offer him.

CHAPTER 12

Ivo, Lord Redcastle stood at his open front door wearing a T-shirt that read: 'FULLY QUALIFIED SEX INSTRUCTOR – FIRST LESSON FREE'. Ingram said nothing, affecting not to notice that anything was out of the ordinary.

'Ingram, baby,' Ivo said, 'you made it.'

'Is Meredith here?'

'She is indeed – *mi casa* – *su casa*.' Ivo didn't move, standing squarely in the doorway, clearly expecting me, Ingram thought, to comment on his stupid T-shirt. He could expect in vain.

'Do I have to push past you? Is that the idea?' Ingram said. 'Shoulder charge? Wrestle you to the ground?'

'Very droll. Come on in, you old wanker.'

Ingram entered the wide hall of Ivo's Notting Hill house – stripped pine floorboards, a huge stuffed grizzly bear in the corner wearing a pork pie hat and, on the wall, some erotic felt-tip drawings by Ivo's latest wife, Smika. Ingram glanced at them, noting breasts, vulvae and various types of penis, flaccid and erect. Climbing the stairs towards the drawing room, Ingram passed a series of black-and-white photographs – the usual suspects, Ingram thought: Bill Brandt, Cartier Bresson, Mapplethorpe, Avedon – astounding how they had managed to retain, in minds like Ivo's, the idea that these perfectly fine but over-familiar images were still 'cutting-edge'. His spirits declined further as he ascended, hearing the volume of the babble emanating from the knocked-through rooms on the first floor. Six was the ideal number for a dinner; eight at a pinch – anything above that was a complete waste of everybody's time. A young man in a shot-silk Nehru jacket stood at the door holding various coloured drinks on a tray.

'Any chance of a glass of white wine?' Ingram asked.

'No,' Ivo said. 'Pick a colour: red, yellow, blue, green, purple.'

'What's in them? I have allergies.'

'That's for me to know and your allergies to find out.'

Ingram chose a purple drink and followed Ivo into the reverberating room, seeing, and immediately changing course towards, his wife, Meredith, somehow absurdly, ridiculously pleased to see her – he was already hating this evening with unusual intensity – though as he approached her he noticed a roseate glow on her cheeks, always a give-away about her alcohol consumption.

'Hello, Pumpkin,' he said, kissing her. 'We can't stay long, remember?'

'Don't be silly, it's Ivo's birthday.' She squeezed

113

his bum and winked at him and Ingram thought, a little wearily, thank the gods for PRO-Vyril, one of Calenture-Deutz's more successful drugs. It treated erectile dysfunction – slogan: 'unmatched act duration' – not up there with Cialis or Viagra or Foldynon but a nice steady earner for the firm all the same. It worked very well for him, also, Ingram acknowledged, some sort of individual metabolic conformity with the chemicals occurring, he supposed. After a couple of PRO-Vyrils he felt he could take on anyone, or indeed anything, for an hour or so. He and Meredith made love fairly regularly for an old married couple with a grown-up family, he reckoned, though it was always at her behest. He had never figured out what made her randy – there was no discernible pattern, but she always contrived to give him a few hours' warning when the mood came upon her – like the phases of the moon, he thought: something, somewhere, triggered her off. They slept in separate bedrooms divided by their dressing rooms and bathrooms, but all with connecting doors. Ingram actually quite enjoyed the sessions – though it was more a matter of mechanics, thanks to PRO-Vyril, than passion, and was a distant world away from his Phyllis encounters.

He held Meredith's hand for a few seconds, reassured. She was a petite, slim woman with well-cut white-blonde hair and a slightly too large head for her body. This and her snub nose and widely spaced eyes made her seem, from some angles, a doll-like creature and, as if as a result of such a perception, she tended to affect, in company, a bubbly, nothing-gets-me-down, climb-every-mountain demeanour. But Ingram knew that she was a tougher and shrewder individual than the image she presented to the world. At moments like these – in the braying hell of Ivo's party – he felt very glad that he was married to her.

'It's been a long and trying day, my darling girl,' he said, in a low voice. 'So the sooner we leave, the sooner we can—'

'Message received, over and out,' she said, smiling warmly.

'Lady Meredith Fryzer!' a man in a black T-shirt (with the same inane message as Ivo's) shrieked at her, and took her in his arms. Ingram turned away, set his untouched purple drink down on a table and sought out the young waiter at the door and repeated his request for a glass of white wine, if that were possible, thank you so much.

He surveyed the room – no one was interested in him, a grey-haired, soon-to-be fifty-nine-year-old man in a dark suit and tie – and wondered who all these friends of Ivo were. Some of the men were clearly older than he (grizzled, bald, with patches of beard) but were dressed as adolescent boys in faded, ripped T-shirts, baggy low-pocketed trousers and unlaced trainers – he wouldn't have been surprised if they had been carrying skate-boards under their arms – still, as his gaze swung

115

here and there, he saw there were also quite a lot of slim pretty women in the room, but all with slumped and sullen faces, or with watchful, guarded expressions, as if they expected a cruel joke was about to be played on them and they were going to be mocked in some way.

His white wine was brought to him and he sipped it with unusual gratitude, standing against a wall by the door, feeling the fatigue leave him a little. He thought he recognised an actor and someone else who was on TV as the people milled around – and there was a clothes designer. Yes? No? . . . He had no idea. He hardly watched television or read magazines, these days. Idly, he picked up a little bronze maquette from a table and thought it might be a Henry Moore – quite pleased that the name came to mind – and wondered again how Ivo managed to live so well for someone with no visible means of support apart from the £80,000 a year Ingram paid him as a non-executive member of the Calenture-Deutz board. Ivo and Meredith's father, the Earl – the Earl of Concannon – had no money left and lived in a large modern bungalow outside Dublin. The family seat, Cloonlaghan Castle, was derelict and millions would be required to make it habitable. He suspected that Meredith gave Ivo money, on the sly, thinking he wouldn't know – she was very fond of her younger brother, for some reason, forgiving him every trespass and humiliation. Smika, Ivo's wife number three, had no money either (unless there was some trade in her erotic drawings). What had happened to Ludovine, the second, French wife? Tiny, feisty, with spiky orange-yellow hair – Yes, Ludovine, Ingram had liked her (he had paid for the costly French divorce, he now remembered). Ah, here was Ivo, heading towards him.

Ivo loomed up and Ingram dutifully registered his brother-in-law's preposterous good looks, once again. His blue-black hair was lightly gelled, and his stupid T-shirt was tight enough to demonstrate how lean his forty-something torso was.

'Having a good time?' Ivo asked. 'Chilling?'

'Fabulous,' Ingram said. 'Any chance of a bite to eat? I'm starving.'

'What do you think of my T-shirt?'

'I think it's hilariously funny. You should wear it all the time. People will fall over laughing.'

'You don't get it, old man.'

'It's as *old* as I am, you fool. I saw one of those at the Isle of Wight festival in 1968. It's so passéé.'

'Liar.'

'Why are you wearing it, anyway?' Ingram said. 'Aren't you a bit past it yourself?'

'I've had 100,000 printed up. We're going to sell them outside every club in the Mediterranean this summer. From Lisbon to Tel Aviv. Ten euros each.'

'Don't ever let anyone stop you dreaming, Ivo.'

Ivo's look was one of pure hatred for a second, then he laughed in a fake, hollow manner, Ingram thought, clapped him on the shoulder and walked away. Ingram found some hard, shiny, shardy crackers in a bowl and munched on them for a while until a chef in white kitchen regalia and a toque announced that dinner was served.

There were twenty-four around the large dining table at the front of the house on the ground floor. Tightly squeezed in, Ingram thought, but by now he was past caring, having quickly consumed his fourth glass of white wine as they waited interminably for the main course. This ghastly evening was finite, he told himself, it would end, he would leave and he would never accept an invitation to dine at Ivo's again for the rest of his life. This thought consoled and sustained him as he waited for the food with the rest of the guests, noticing he was as far away from Ivo as possible (Meredith was on Ivo's right), placed between a woman who spoke hardly any English and one of the sullen-faced, pretty girls. She had smoked three cigarettes since sitting down and they'd only been served an insufficiently chilled, over-garlicked gazpacho, thus far. Ingram glanced at his watch – ten past eleven – there must be a serious crisis in the kitchen. He was the only man at the table wearing a tie, he realised. Then he saw to his astonishment that Ivo had his mobile phone on the table beside his pack of cigarettes. In his own home, Ingram thought: that is *sad*. Tragic. He turned to the sullen faced, pretty girl – who was lighting her fourth cigarette.

'Are you a friend of Smika?' he asked.

'No.'

'Ah, a friend of Ivo, then.'

'Ivo and I went out for a while . . .'

Ingram saw she was growing annoyed at his failure to recall her.

'Ivo and I stayed with you and Meredith at your house in Deya.'

'Really? Right . . . Yes . . .'

'I'm Gill John.'

'Of course you are. Gill John, yes, yes, yes.'

'We've met . . . A dozen times?'

Ingram heaped his apologies on her, blaming his age, encroaching Alzheimer's, fatigue, hideous work crises. He remembered her now, vaguely: Gill John, of course, one of Ivo's old girlfriends, between Ludovine and Smika. He always went out with pretty girls, did Ivo – Ingram realising that it was one of the automatic benefits accruing to a preposterously good-looking man. And Gill John was indeed pretty, though her expression, posture and demeanour seemed to exude bitterness in some way, as if life had consistently let her down and she was expecting nothing to change.

'Oh, yes, good old Ivo,' Ingram said, not having a clue what to say to this young woman, simmering in her anger and bitterness. 'Great lad, good fellow, Ivo.'

'Ivo's a cunt,' she said. 'Not a "great lad" or a "good fellow". You know that as well as I do.'

Ingram wanted to say: then why are you here at his birthday party? But he contented himself with:

119

'Well, not a grade-A cunt. Grade-C, perhaps. Though as his brother-in-law I might be biased.'

She turned to look at him, squarely. Pale eyes, high forehead, lips a little thin, perhaps.

'You just prove my point,' she said.

'I don't follow.'

'About what unites all men.' She laughed to herself, cynically, knowingly.

'I can think of a few common factors,' Ingram said, wondering how the conversation had suddenly taken this abrupt swerve. 'But I suspect not the one you have in mind.'

'Internet porn.'

'Sorry?'

'Internet porn unites all men.'

Ingram accepted another refill of his wine glass from a patrolling waiter.

'I think your average Kalahari bushman might disagree,' he said.

'All right. All Western men with computers.'

'But what if you don't have a computer? Your "unites all men" claim has already lost some of its universal force. You might as well say . . .' he thought for a second. 'What unites all men who own golf clubs? Love of golf? I don't think so. Some men who own golf clubs find golf boring.'

Gill John lit her fifth cigarette. 'Get a life,' she said.

'Or,' Ingram persisted with his analogy, rather pleased with it. 'You could say: what unites all men who own umbrellas – fear of rain?'

'Fuck off,' Gill John said.

'In fact pornography *is* boring – that's its fundamental, default problem. Women should take comfort from that.'

Gill John slapped him – not hard – just a little sharp slap with her fingers that caught his chin and lower lip. She turned away. Ingram sat still for a moment, his lower lip stinging. Amazingly, no one seemed to have noticed. Ivo had just left the table to see what was going on in the kitchen and all hungry eyes were on him. Ingram turned to his other partner. She smiled broadly at him – what could go wrong here, Ingram wondered?

'*O Rio de Janeiro me encanta*,' he said, unconfidently. Then Ivo's mobile phone began to ring, with an annoying ring-tone taken from some heavy-metal guitar riff, and at that moment he reappeared.

'Sorry, guys,' he said to the assembled company, 'but the tagine has cracked. We'll only be another ten minutes or so.' He picked up the phone. 'Ivo Redcastle . . .' He listened. 'Yeah. OK.' He looked at Ingram with irritation. 'It's for you.'

Ingram left his seat and walked round the table thinking: who the fuck is calling me on Ivo's phone? Meredith looked at him in hazy, tipsy surprise. Everyone else was talking, indifferent.

Ivo handed his phone over. 'Don't make a habit of this, right, Ingram?'

Ingram put the phone to his ear. 'This is Ingram Fryzer.'

'Ingram. It's Alfredo Rilke.'

121

Ingram suddenly felt chilly. He stepped quickly out of the dining room and into the hall.

'Alfredo. How did you get this number?'

'I called you on your own cell. The man who answered said you were with your brother-in-law.'

'Of course.' Ingram's own phone was in his brief-case in the car outside with Luigi.

'I'm coming to London,' Rilke said.

'Excellent. Good. We—'

'No, not good. We have a serious problem, Ingram.'

'I know. Philip Wang's death has set us—'

'Did you find this Adam Kindred?'

'No. Not yet. The police haven't been able—'

'We have to find him. I'll call when I arrive.'

They said goodbye and Ingram clicked Ivo's phone shut. He felt small, suddenly, felt small and worried as he used to when a child, when events were too big and too adult to comprehend. That Alfredo Rilke should call him here at Ivo's party only betokened serious problems. That Alfredo Rilke should come to London only underscored how serious those problems were. His brain worked furiously but no explanation came – only other worries, coagulating. He felt for the first time that he was no longer fully in control of his life – it was as if events were being ordered by an outside force he couldn't master. Nonsense, get a grip, he told himself. Life is full of crises – it's normal – this is just another. He looked through the open door to the kitchen and, as if to confirm

122

his analysis, considered Ivo's current crisis as the chef spooned stew from a shattered tagine into an orange casserole dish. He strode back into the dining room and returned Ivo's phone to him.

'Any time, mate,' Ivo said, gracelessly.

'Meredith, we have to go,' Ingram said quietly and Meredith stood up at once.

'Aw, the party-poopers,' Ivo said in a bad American accent.

'Don't say another word, Ivo,' Ingram said, squeezing his shoulder very hard. 'You just carry on enjoying your lovely evening.'

CHAPTER 13

The 'new annexe' of the Marine Support Unit in Wapping, as it was rather grandly termed, consisted of four large Portakabins on a patch of waste ground off Wapping High Street, at Phoenix Stairs, where there was now a gleaming steel jetty, recently constructed. The Phoenix Stairs jetty was situated some 100 yards downstream from the MSU police station at Wapping New Stairs, almost equidistant from Wapping High Street's two pubs, the Captain Kidd and the Prospect of Whitby. The MSU had recently acquired four new launches, Targa 50s, slightly smaller, slightly faster but with the same custom-built roomy wheelhouse as the current fleet of older Targas. Hence this expansion to new premises and a new jetty, and hence, Rita supposed, her fast-track into the division. There was no point in having a bigger budget and the fleet increased by four new boats if there was nobody to man them.

She still felt something of the new girl at school – the MSU was small and close-knit, there was hardly any turnover of personnel (once you arrived at MSU you were there until retirement, more often than not) – and there were very few women police constables. So far in her few days at Wapping Rita had only met two other WPCs.

She stood at the end of the new jetty, pausing before she headed back along it to the Phoenix Stairs passage, and looked down river to the clustered towers of Canary Wharf, watching a jet soaring up from City Airport, and then turned her gaze across the river – it was high tide – to the vast modern blocks of St Botolph's Hospital. It was like a small, complete city, she thought, everything you needed – heating, food, transport, sewage, life-support systems, morgue, funeral home – was there: no need ever to leave . . .

Morbid thoughts, Rita thought – ban them. She wasn't in the best of moods, she knew. Her father had been aggressive over the breakfast cornflakes this morning and she'd snapped back at him. Then he had counter-accused her of sulking . . . They were beginning to argue like an old married couple, she thought, and she realised she wasn't happy being on her own – she'd always had boyfriends and lovers and being single didn't suit her. She hadn't enjoyed her party either, her mood had soured when – re-touching her make-up in the ladies' lavatory – she had heard two men in the corridor outside talking about her. She had recognised Gary's voice but couldn't place the other's – the music from the public bar was warming up, half obscuring it.

She heard Gary say: '– No, no. We, you know, broke up.'

Then the other man: 'Shame, yeah . . . (something inaudible) lovely girl, Rita. Just my type.'

'Yeah? What type would that be?' Gary said.

Rita was now at the door, ear to the jamb.

'Full breasts, thin frame,' the man said. 'You can't beat it. What a fool you are, Boland.'

They laughed and she heard them wander off. Rita came straight out of the ladies and went into the bar to see that Gary was standing on his own. She looked around: the place was full. Had it been Duke? She just couldn't be sure. But it aggrieved her and it cast a cloud over her farewell. Every man she greeted, chatted to, let buy her drinks, said goodbye to, swore to stay in touch with and kissed on the cheek might have been Gary's interlocutor. It made her wary and awkwardly self-conscious of the tightness of the T-shirt she'd chosen to wear. She'd drunk too much to little effect and woken up crapulous with a mighty day-long hangover.

Get a grip, she said to herself, disgusted with her self-pity, it's hardly the end of the world, girl. For god's sake – just blokes talking, nothing new there. Still, it was never nice to eavesdrop on conversations about yourself. Just as well she hadn't been able to see their faces or any gestures they had made . . .

Routinely, she checked that the mooring ropes were made fast on her boat, a brand new Targa

50, re-tightened one, and turned her back on the river and went briskly along the jetty through the passage, across the narrow cobbled roadway that was Wapping High Street and into the operations Portakabin. Joey Raymouth was already there, still diligently writing up his notes from that morning's intelligence briefing, and they greeted each other, perfunctorily but warmly – she liked Joey. He was assigned to her, seeing her through her first month on the river, 'mentoring' her. His father was a fisherman in Fowey, in Cornwall, and he had a West Country burr to his voice.

'You all right, Rita? Look a bit under the weather.'

She forced her face into a wide smile. 'No, no probs at all.'

He rose to his feet and together they went to receive their instructions from Sergeant Denton Rollins – ex-Royal Navy, as he constantly reminded his charges – with the heavy implication that he still could not understand how he had come down so low in the world.

Their duties for this shift were all very straightforward – checking mooring permits at Westminster and Battersea, investigating a fire on a boat at Chiswick and some thefts from pleasure cruisers in Chelsea marina.

Raymouth took more notes as Rollins read out the details. Rita looked round as more colleagues came in and the swell of banter grew.

'Oh, yeah,' Rollins said. 'One for you, Nashe. Reports of a man killing a swan at low tide by

Chelsea Bridge yesterday morning. Your neck of the woods.'

'A swan?'

'It's illegal. Don't die of excitement.'

'I'm in it for the glamour, Sarge.'

She and Joey went back out to their boat and put on their buoyancy vests. Joey went through the checklist and started the engines while Rita undid the moorings, cast off and then stepped aboard as the Targa pulled away from the jetty into mid-stream.

Because the tide was high the Thames looked like a proper city river – like the Seine or the Danube – the river broad and full, perfectly apt and proportional to the embankment walls and the buildings on either side and the bridges that traversed it. At low tide everything changed, the river fell between twelve and twenty feet, walls were exposed, weed draped the now visible piles of the bridges, beaches and mud flats appeared and the river looked like the Zambezi or Limpopo in times of drought. Correspondingly, the city suffered aesthetically, but this morning the river brimmed and Rita felt her moodiness begin to disappear and her heart quicken with pleasure. This was why she had transferred to MSU, she realised, hauling the fat rubber fenders on board as Joey accelerated off, the two big Volvo diesels firing up with a bass roar, heading up river, Bermondsey to the port side, Tower Bridge up ahead, the clear morning light making the windows

128

of the City's office blocks flash brazenly, the breeze whipping her hair. HMS *Belfast* coming up, then London Bridge, Tate Modern, the Globe Theatre. What a way to earn a living, she said to herself, widening her stance on the deck, gripping the guard-rail with both hands as Joey speeded up, the spume of their bow wave almost indecently white, drops of river water bouncing off her uplifted face. She held herself like this for a second or two, breathing deeply, feeling her head spin before she went down below to the forward galley to brew up two mugs of strong tea.

The Chiswick fire had been intriguing. A barbecue on deck of a Bayliner cruiser had been left untended, sparks from which had set small fires going on the boats moored alongside. Lawsuits for damages were pending. Joey and Rita interviewed angry boat owners and took down details – but there was no sign of the careless cook. His Bayliner was now semi-burnt-out, sunk to the gunwales from the weight of the water from the fire brigade's hoses. Piecing together the various accounts witnesses supplied, it seemed he had lit the barbecue, had a violent row with his girlfriend, she had run off and he followed, forgetting about their soon-to-be-chargrilled Sunday lunch. Joey was pretty sure it was illegal to have a barbecue on a moored boat anyway – no naked flames. Anyway, they had the man's details – the Chiswick police could track him down while they would serve notice to remove his burnt-out boat within seven days or face further penalties.

On the way upstream to Chiswick they had passed the *Bellerophon* and she had given the klaxon a toot but there was no sign of life on deck. In fact in the dozen or so times she'd passed her home since she'd begun at MSU she'd never seen her father. He was sulking below, she knew: somehow her new job with the river police irritated him more than when she'd been on the beat in Chelsea and elsewhere. She didn't care – she was happy, she was enjoying her new job too much – he'd come round to it one day, or not. Up to him.

As they motored under Albert Bridge, almost coasting downstream on the ebb tide, Rita remembered what Rollins had told her about a man killing a swan. She told Joey and he steered them over to the Grosvenor College stairs on the Chelsea shore.

'You check it out, Rita,' Joey said. 'I'll write up the great Chiswick barbecue fire.'

She strode along the Embankment, back on familiar ground, past the Royal Hospital (where the Flower Show marquees were now all but dismantled) and stopped at the gate of a small triangle of waste ground on the west side of Chelsea Bridge. How many times had she come past here, she thought, and never noticed this place? The man who had phoned in the complaint had come through under Chelsea Bridge before he had seen the man with the swan, so the beach, as such, had to be on this side. The gate was locked so Rita climbed over the railings and went down some steps that led towards the river. At the base of the bridge she found the usual graffiti, and a fritter of condoms, needles, beer cans and bottles. Peering over the edge of the Embankment wall she could see the small mud beach exposed by the ebbing tide. She looked downstream – if she went down to the beach she would almost be able to see the *Bellerophon* from here. Why would anyone kill a swan? Some junkie out of his skull? Some drunk waking up, showing off for his drunken mates? She moved away from the bridge, pushing through bushes and low branches towards the apex of the triangle. She noted how dense the undergrowth was, a little sliver of rampant waste-land in douce Chelsea. She ducked under the branches of a sycamore, eased carefully by a holly bush, shimmied through a gap between two rhododendrons – and stopped.

A small clearing. Trampled grass, flattened grass. Three rubber tyres set on top of each other to make a seat. She hauled a dirty sleeping bag and groundsheet out from under a bush, and from under another found a wooden orange box with a camping gas stove and a saucepan in it. She put everything back as she had found it. Kneeling, she found feathers and evidence of scorching on some of the longer grass stems. Gull feathers, not a swan's, she realised: to some people all large white

131

birds looked the same. She stood up: somebody had killed, plucked and no doubt eaten a seagull here in the last few days. She looked around – she was perfectly screened from the Embankment and from anything crossing over Chelsea Bridge. There was a view of the river between two of the bushes but no one looking back from a passing boat would see anything. She searched some more but found nothing except wind-blown litter – nobody ever came to this bit of the triangle, clearly. Whoever had been staying here would be perfectly safe from prying eyes.

She made her way back to the road, thinking: 'had been staying'? Perhaps, 'was still staying'? This site didn't suggest a homeless person dossing down for the night or two – this was more of a hiding place. Somebody was hiding on this triangle of wasteland at Chelsea Bridge, someone desperate enough to catch and eat a seagull at dawn one day. Perhaps it might be worth coming back one night and searching the place – see what or who they turned up. She'd run the idea by Sergeant Rollins. It was their case, after all, killing a 'swan' on the river was MSU business.

CHAPTER 14

The light over the western sector of the Shaftesbury Estate was a milky blue, the early morning sun brightening the brickwork of the topmost storey – the sixth – and beginning its slow creep down the façades of the remaining five, casting sharp geometric shadows as it moved, making the apartment blocks look stark, but at the same time austerely sculptural – exactly the aim and purpose that the architect, Gerald Golupin (1898–1969), had in mind as he had drawn up his visionary design for this complex of social housing units in the 1950s, until someone else, to his abiding chagrin, had named it the Shaftesbury Estate (Golupin had proposed something more Bauhausian – MODULAR 9, in reference to its nine apartment blocks and three wide quadrangles – in vain). The Shaft, in certain lights, could still appear severely impressive: hard-edged, volumetrically imposing, a triumphant melding of form and function – as long as you didn't look too closely.

Mhouse, of course, was thinking none of these thoughts as she plodded up the stairs to her

133

flat – Flat L, on Level 3, Unit 14. She was tired; she had drunk a lot of alcohol and had snorted many lines of cocaine over the last six hours or so as well as performing a variety of sexual acts with two men – what were their names? Still, she had £200 folded flat in the sole of her white PVC boot. It had been one of Margo's specials. She and Margo showed up at this hotel in Baker Street at midnight where two men were waiting for them in a double bedroom (nice bathroom en suite) – Ramzan and Suleiman, that was it – and so the long night had begun. Ramzan and Suleiman, that was them, yeah, old blokes, but clean – but which one was which?

Luckily, Margo had called her at lunchtime and so she had been able to park Ly-on with her next-door neighbour, Mrs Darling. She was always happy to look after Ly-on (Mhouse gave her a fiver) but it couldn't be done spontaneously, she needed a few hours notice, at least.

Mhouse rang the bell and, after a two-minute delay, Mrs Darling opened it. She was in her sixties, with a misshapen, lumpy body and a thin head of dyed auburn hair. She had no front teeth.

'Aw, hello, Mhousey, sweet,' she said. 'Tired out, eh?'

'Them late shifts is killers, Mrs D.'

'You want to complain – way that factory works you people. Why can't they pack veg at a proper hour?'

'It's the early markets, see?'

'Still: it's a living, I suppose – in these sad times of ours. Here's the little fella.'

Mhouse crouched and kissed her son's face – which was still blank and neutral with fatigue, roused from his bed so early.

'Hello, baby,' Mhouse said. 'You been a good boy?'

'Not a peep out of him. Slept like a log, little lambkin.'

Mhouse slipped Mrs Darling her fiver.

'Any time, dear,' Mrs Darling said, 'such a quiet, well-behaved little chap.' She paused and ruffled Ly-on's hair, then looked meaningfully at Mhouse. 'Haven't seen you down the Church, recent.'

'I know, I know. I need to go. Maybe tomorrow.'

'God loves you, Mhousey, never forget. He doesn't loves us all but he loves you and me.'

Mhouse led Ly-on along the walkway to their flat and unlocked the door. Inside she filled the kettle to make a cup of tea, then switched it off. She felt the urge to sleep encroaching on her like onrushing night, a tiredness so acute she could hardly stay on her feet.

Ly-on had turned on the television and was searching the channels looking for a cartoon.

'You want some happy-flakes, baby?' she asked, thinking: please say yes.

'Yeah, Mum.'

'Yeah, Mum, what?'

'Please happy-flakes me.'

Mhouse filled a bowl with sugar-frosted cornflakes,

added some milk and a few glugs of rum. Then she crushed a 10 mg Diazepam under the blade of a knife and sprinkled its dust over the flakes. She handed it to Ly-on, who was now curled up in a nest of cushions on the floor in front of the TV. She sat down beside him and watched him eat his happy-flakes. When he'd finished she took the bowl from him and stuck it in the sink with the other dishes. She slipped her £200 into the stash under the floor-boards in the toilet and, when she came out, saw that Ly-on was now fast asleep. She turned the TV down and settled him more comfortably on the cushions, then went into her room, took two Somnola and smoked a joint – she wanted to be out for twelve hours, minimum.

When she woke it was four o'clock in the after-noon. Ly-on was still sleeping but he'd wet himself.

That night, Mr Quality-He-Delivers knocked on the door at about 8.00.

'Who is it?' Mhouse said, through the letter-box.

'Quality coming,' was the reply.

'Hey, Mr Q, come on in,' she said, unlocking the door. Mr Quality was perhaps the most import-ant man in The Shaft, for all sorts of reasons, none of them particularly violent. No one who dealt with Mr Quality wanted him to be angry with them so he very rarely resorted to main force. He was very tall and thin and Mhouse knew that his real name was Abdul-latif. He stepped into the room, seeming twice as tall as Mhouse, and anyone might have thought he was about to go off running as he was wearing a dark maroon track suit and very new trainers, box-fresh. Only the fact that he had silver rings on all eight fingers and two thumbs made this supposition less than likely.

Mr Quality lounged against the kitchen wall, looking around him, proprietorially – it was his flat, after all. He was always lounging, was Mr Q, Mhouse thought, as if he supposed it made him seem not quite so embarrassingly lofty.

'Hey. Ly-on, man. How it hanging?'

Ly-on looked up from his TV. 'Good,' he said. 'I fit like new car.'

Mr Quality chuckled. 'Sweet-sweet. You keep chillin', man.'

Mhouse beckoned him away from Ly-on. 'Where we at?' she asked.

'Saktellite TV, rent, gas, water, electric . . .' he pondered. '£285, I say.' He smiled at her, showing small perfectly white teeth in mottled pink and brown gums. 'You dey get problem?'

'No, no,' Mhouse said, thinking thank the good lord for Ramzam and Suleiman. 'Everything working. Sometime the light he go out but I know it's not you fault.'

'The electric he go be difficult. We have many problem. Gas easy, water easy, but electric . . .' he winced, tellingly. 'We done get wahallah. They chase us – ah-ah.'

'Yeah. Bastards.'

She went into the bathroom for her stash, then pretended to rummage in the cardboard box beside her bed and opened and closed the cupboard doors before coming back with his £285. That left her with about £30 – and she owed Margo . . . she'd have to go out again tonight. Still, the good thing about Mr Quality was that he could provide you with anything – anything – as long as you had the money. In Mhouse's flat the gas, water and electricity had been cut off months ago but Mr Quality had reconnected her within hours. Every now and then Mr Quality paid to have sex with her – or rather, 'paid' in the sense that he always offered her money that she always declined.

She handed the £285 over and Mr Quality paced about the flat, checking it out as if he were a prospective buyer. Mhouse kept it as clean as she could – she had very little furniture, but she had a broom and she always kept the floors swept.

'You have spare room, here,' Mr Quality said, opening a door into the second bedroom. There was a mattress on the floor and a few cardboard boxes with clothes and old toys in them. 'I can get you lodger – £20 a week. No worry, clean nice person. Asylum, no speak English.'

'No, I'm fine at the moment. Keeping busy, business is good,' she said, trying to appear casual. 'Things are OK, going fine. Yeah, fine.'

'You go let me know.'

'Yeah, sure. Thanks, Mr Q.'

After Mr Quality had gone she gave Ly-on his supper – mashed banana and condensed milk with a slug of rum. She crushed a Somnola into the mix and mashed it further with a fork.

'Mummy's got to go out to work tonight,' she said as she handed him the bowl.

'Mummy working too hard,' he said, spooning the banana pabulum into his mouth.

'You go to toilet if you need pee-pee,' she said. 'Don't do it in you pants.'

'Mum – don't saying that.' His eyes were on the screen.

She kissed his forehead and went to change into her working clothes. No point in waiting, she thought, might as well get the cash as soon as possible. She put on a cap-sleeved T-shirt with a red heart across her chest, wriggled into her short skirt, pulled on her zip-up white boots, picked up the umbrella, checked her bag for condoms and fastened the keys on the long chain to her belt. She locked the door on a sleeping Ly-on – she'd be back in a couple of hours or so, she reckoned, no need to alert Mrs Darling, and headed along the walkway to the stairs.

As she was leaving The Shaft, heading out to the Rotherhithe shore and her usual beat, she saw a black taxi-cab pull up, its light off. No one got out while it sat for a minute or two at the kerb. Who's ordering a black cab at The Shaft? she wondered as she made towards it. Brave fool.

The driver stepped out as she walked past – big bloke, ugly face with a weak, cleft chin. She glanced back to see where he was going and saw him lock his cab and wander into the estate.

CHAPTER 15

The vet had been – what was the word? – contemptuous, yes, almost contemptuous when Jonjo had told him what The Dog's routine diet was. He was a young fellow with a square of beard under his bottom lip and a single dangling earring – something Jonjo didn't expect to see in a Newham veterinary surgeon.

'He eats pretty much what I eat,' Jonjo had said, reasonably. 'I tend to cook for two – scrambled eggs and bacon, curries, sausage rolls, pork pies – he really likes pork pies – biscuits, crisps, the odd bar of chocolate.'

'This is a pedigree bassett hound,' the vet said. 'Anyone would think you were trying to kill him.'

Jonjo sat quietly as the vet berated him for his neglect, then told him the sort of food The Dog should and must eat and wrote a list down on a piece of paper and handed it to him. Smug bastard, Jonjo thought.

He touched his breast pocket and felt the crinkle of the vet's folded list. The back of his cab was full of tins of special dog food and paper sacks of dog biscuit and fibrous additives; there were pills and suppositories and other types of medication should symptoms appear and complications occur. Bloody expensive too. He'd hand it all over to Candy in the morning. He wondered whether he should give The Dog back to his sister . . .

He stepped out of the cab and locked it, contemplating the tall blocks of the Shaftesbury Estate. He ran through his checks: the small Beretta Tomcat between his shoulder blades, snug in a rig he had designed himself; the larger 1911 .45 ACP holstered in the small of his back, one round in the pipe, cocked and locked; knife strapped just above the left ankle. He was wearing an extra roomy leather blouson jacket that perfectly concealed the small prints of his weapons. He had loose, pale blue, stone-washed jeans and yellow builder's boots with steel toecaps. He eased his shoulders and rotated his head, remembering the last time he'd experienced this adrenalin buzz – when he had knocked on Dr Philip Wang's door in Anne Boleyn House.

He walked into The Shaft completely unafraid, calm, ready for anything.

Jonjo could hear Sergeant Snell's voice in his ear. *'The Three O's, youse cunts!'* Over-arm. Over-react. Over-kill. Number one: you can never have too many weapons. Number two: somebody calls you a name – you knock him down and kick him senseless. Number three: – you don't just wound, you permanently disable. Somebody tries to hit you – you kill him. Somebody tries to kill you – you destroy his family, his house, his village. Snell always made sure you got the picture. True, these instructions were tailored for violent combat zones but Jonjo had always regarded them as pretty sound counsel for life in general and, by and large, adhering to the Three O's had served him well, only a few of his overreactions landing him in trouble with the police – but they tended to understand once they learned of his background.

Jonjo wandered across the cracked dry mud of a grassless central courtyard, looking around him. He was in a wide, two-acre quadrangle, surrounded by four of The Shaft's apartment blocks. He saw snapped-off saplings, a washing machine with its guts ripped out and its porthole window open, graffiti-ed walls and doors. A few people looked down at him from the upper walkways, elbows resting on the concrete balustrades, smoking.

These places should be razed to the ground, Jonjo thought, and houses built for decent people. Take all the scum who live here, put them down with humane killers, like cattle, incinerate their bodies and throw their ashes in landfill sites. Crime in the area would fall by 99 per cent, families would relax, kiddies would play hopscotch in the street, flowers would bloom again in front gardens.

Three little girls were sitting on a bench, sharing a cigarette. As he approached, Jonjo saw that they weren't so much little – just small. He looked at them: eleven? Or eighteen?

'Hello, ladies,' he said, smiling. 'Wonder if you can help me.'

'Fuck off, peedlefile.'

'What's the name of the main crew, round here? Who runs the area, you know? Number one gangsters. I'll give you a fiver if you tell me.'

One of the girls, with bad acne, said, 'Give me ten and I'll flog you off.'

Another, a fat one, said, 'Give me ten and it's the best blow-job of your life.'

They all laughed at this – giggling, silly, pushing at each other. Jonjo remained impassive.

'Who's the big guy in The Shaft, eh? I got a job for him. He'll be well angry you didn't tell me.'

The girls whispered to each other, then Acne said, 'We don't know.'

Jonjo took a twenty-pound note out of his pocket and dropped it on the ground. He turned away from them and put his heel on it.

'Let's do it this way,' he said. 'I didn't give you this, you found it. I just need a name and a place, then I walk away and I won't know who told me. No one will know. Just tell me – and don't play silly buggers, right? Because I'll come back and find you.'

He crossed his arms and waited. After about twenty seconds one of the girls said, 'Bozzy, Flat B 1, Unit 17.'

Jonjo walked away, not looking round.

Jonjo followed the signs to Unit 17 and found Flat B 1 – it was derelict, on the ground floor, the windows boarded up. For a second or two he wondered if those little bitches had conned him but then he saw that there was no padlock on the door and, peering through a slit at the edge of one of the boarded-up windows, he realised there were lights on inside.

He slid his 1911 out of its holster in the small of his back and held it loosely in his hand, butt first. Then he knocked on the door.

'Bozzy?' he said, in an anxious voice. 'I need to see Bozzy. I got money for him.' He knocked again. 'I got money for Bozzy.'

After a moment he heard bolts being thrown and the door opened six inches. A bleary, stoned face looked out.

'Give me money. I give it Bozzy.'

Jonjo smashed his gun, held flat, into this guy's face and he went down with a yelp. Jonjo was through the door in a second, gun in both hands and put his big builder's boot on the guy's throat. His nose was broken, askew, and he was spitting blood, feebly.

'Relax. I'm not the police,' Jonjo said in a level voice, 'as you can probably tell. I just want a word with Bozzy.'

The room was full of smoke and the strange smell of burnt rope hit Jonjo's nostrils. He saw a couple of sagging filthy armchairs, three stained mattresses, some empty bottles and a litter of food wrappers and foil containers and, to his vague surprise, halved lemons, squeezed dry. Three other dazed young men were slowly rising to their feet.

145

'Lie down on the floor,' Jonjo said, pointing his gun at each of them. 'Face down. Place your hands on the back of your heads. I just want a conversation with Bozzy, then I'll fuck off.' He smiled as the young men lay down on the floor. He lifted his boot off the sniffler's face and with a few prods of his toe encouraged him to turn over also. 'So . . . Which one's Bozzy?' Jonjo said.

'I am,' said a beefy guy with a hot, flushed face.

'You'd better be Bozzy, mate,' Jonjo said. 'Otherwise you're in deep shit.'

'I'm Bozzy. And you fuckin' dead, man. I know you face, now. You dead.'

Then, swiftly, Jonjo kicked the other three prone young men very hard in the ribs with his steel toe-capped bricklayer's boots, feeling ribs give way, stave, splinter, yield. The men shouted and rolled around in serious pain. Every time they coughed or sneezed for the next three months they'd remember this encounter, every time they crawled out of bed or reached for something they'd think of me, Jonjo acknowledged with satisfaction.

'Get out,' Jonjo said. 'Now.'

They left slowly, stooped, carefully, clutching their sides like old men while Jonjo covered them with his gun. Then he bolted the door behind them and turned to Bozzy. From the pocket of his jeans he took two plastic cuffs and first bound Bozzy's ankles and then attached Bozzy's left wrist to his ankles before heaving him into a sitting position.

'This is very simple, Boz, me old mate,' Jonjo said, taking his knife out from its ankle scabbard. He grabbed hold of Bozzy's free hand and very quickly cut the web of skin between Bozzy's third and ring finger – just a nick, really, about a centimetre deep.

'*Fuck!*' Bozzy cried out.

Jonjo dropped his knife and grabbed the pair of fingers on either side of the gash and gripped them fiercely in both fists. Blood was dripping now, welling up from the small cut.

'We used to do this a lot in Afghanistan,' Jonjo said. 'The Al-Qaeda guys say they'll never talk but they always do.' He could see Bozzy looked blank. 'You heard of Al-Qaeda?'

'No. Who they?'

'OK. They're tough fuckers. One thousand per cent tougher than you. We did this to them to make them talk: cut between their fingers, then rip their hands in two, down to the wrist.' He tugged – Bozzy yelled. 'It's like tearing a rag or a sheet. Only the wrist bone stops it, but you ain't got a hand any more – you've got a *flipper*. And they can't fix it, no doctor can. If you don't tell me what I want to know I'll rip this hand in two. And, if you still don't tell me, I'll rip your other hand in two. Then you'll be drinking beer through a straw for the rest of your life and someone will have to help you piss.'

'What you want to know?'

Jonjo smiled. 'I'm betting, I'm having a wager

with myself, that you jumped a guy last week on this estate. His name was Adam Kindred. You stole his phone and someone used it.'

'I stole ten phones last week, mate.'

'This one was different. You'd remember him.'

'We jack a lot of mims. I can't not remember what mim is like another.'

'You would remember this one. Not your usual mim. What happened?' Jonjo tugged gently on Bozzy's fingers.

'Yeah – *agh!* – yeah . . . We jumped him. Kicked him proper, took everything. Left him under the stairs. I thought he might of been fucked. But, when we come back, half an hour later. He gone.'

'Gone? Walked away?'

'We left him out cold, mate. Butcher meat.'

'Somebody must've helped him.'

'Prob'ly.'

'Where's the phone?'

'I sold it.'

'Get it back. Who could have helped him?'

'Must of been someone in The Shaft. It was late, like. Only Shaft people round and about. That's how I remember this mim. He was well lost.'

'Find out who helped him,' Jonjo said, letting go of Bozzy's hand, picking up his knife and cutting the plastic cuffs from his tethered wrist and ankles. 'Call me.' Jonjo gave him a piece of paper with his mobile number on it. 'Call me in a week. I'll give you a grand if you find the person who helped him. A grand – one thousand pounds.'

He tossed a couple of £20 notes on the floor. 'If you don't call me I'll come back and get you. Cut off your head and send it to your crack-whore mother. Got it?'

'Flat, bruv. Well flat.'

Jonjo unbolted the door and strolled out into the night.

CHAPTER 16

Adam walked from Chelsea to Southwark –
across Chelsea Bridge to Battersea and
then round the back of the power station
and along the river, most of the way. He had his
little street-map paperback but he still stopped
people – poor people, like him – to ask directions.
He was guided past Lambeth Palace and the
National Theatre, along Bankside and under
London Bridge to Southwark. Something was
leading him there, some unconscious urge – he
wasn't sure if it was wise but somehow he felt
obliged to do it. Perhaps it was because Mhouse
– his rescuer and tormentor – had suggested it.
He felt that she had blurted out this potential
sanctuary because, even as she attacked him, she
recognised how needy and desperate he was. The
scab on his forehead had finally fallen off, leaving
only the faintest pink tracery of the trainer sole
that had connected with his forehead. The time
was right – he knew it was something he had to do.

In Southwark Street he asked a few people if
they had heard of the Church of John Christ. He
was corrected a few times – 'You mean Jesus

Christ' – and was twice directed to Southwark Cathedral. Eventually someone told him there was a strange kind of church hall off Tooley Street, down on the river by Unicorn Passage and so he headed that way, realising he was leaving Southwark for Bermondsey.

In Tooley Street there were small signs with arrows attached to drainpipes and traffic signs – 'The Ch. of John Christ, straight on' – and he went further east, along Jamaica Road, turning left and then right, following the signs and arrows before finally arriving at his destination – on the edge of the river, he saw.

It looked like an old nineteenth-century brick warehouse with large sliding wooden doors and no windows on the façade. Behind it he could see the brown river flowing by. Above the doors in bright plastic lettering – blue on white – was printed: 'THE CHURCH OF JOHN CHRIST. Est. 1998'. And below that: 'Archbishop the rev. YEMI THOMPSON-GBEHO. Pastor and Founder.' And below that, again, the promises: 'NO SIN ENDURES' and 'ALL SINS FORGIVEN'.

There was a smaller door set in the large sliding one and Adam knocked on this, waited a minute, knocked again, waited another minute and was walking away when a woman's voice called after him, 'Was that you, dear?'

Adam turned. An elderly woman with thin, carroty-auburn hair and no front teeth stood smiling at the open small door with a steaming mug of tea in her hand.

'I was told I could get help here,' Adam said.

'God will provide, darling. Service starts at six, see you later.' She shut the door and Adam walked back to Tooley Street and asked someone the time – 4.30. He might as well wait, he thought. He was hungry, his feet were sore from his too-tight golf shoes and having walked all this way it would be as well to see what was on offer. He found a boarded-up doorway next to a newsagent's and sat on its step, settling down to wait until the church opened. He closed his eyes, hoping he might doze for a few minutes, happy to have put his faith in John Christ, whoever he might be.

But he couldn't doze: across the street was an estate agent's and he watched a plump girl in a pale grey suit and very high heels step out of the door and light a cigarette. She blew the smoke up into the air over her shoulder as if directing it away from an invisible someone – an invisible non-smoker, Adam supposed. Just like Fairfield Springer, he realised with something of a shock – that was how Fairfield smoked. And he felt a cold guilt creep over him and another feeling which he decided to call remorse, rather than self-pity. He saw Fairfield in his mind's eye – her thick, straw-blonde hair, her powerful, black-rimmed spectacles. She had a pretty face but somehow the mass of hair and the spectacles prevented you noticing that for a minute or so.

In their two intimate encounters – a sex act and a dinner three days later – she had smoked a cigarette exactly like that girl standing outside a Bermondsey estate agent's, blowing the smoke up and away over her right shoulder, out of consideration for the non-smoker she was with . . .

As he thought about Fairfield his memories inexorably drew him back to that night in the cloud chamber. In fact it was late afternoon/early evening but they were doing a night-simulation cloud-seeding run so it might as well have been night. The cloud chamber's lights had been dimmed and an artificial moonlight was glowing dimly. Fairfield was one of his graduate students, a promising, bright girl, a little overweight, short-sighted (hence the spectacles), serious, attentive. She had asked if she could accompany him to the very top of the chamber, nine storeys high – and he had said, of course, by all means, anyone else want to come? But none of the other graduates wanted to – they were more interested in seeing the rain falling. He supposed, now, with the bitter wisdom of hindsight, that she had planned everything. Adam and Fairfield had stood there, leaning on the viewing gantry, looking out over the grey, shifting cloud-mass, covering an area the size of two tennis courts, bathed in the bluey-white light of a notional moon. They were standing shoulder-to-shoulder, elbows resting on the safety railing, watching the clouds billow gently beneath the acrylic-glass roof of the cloud chamber. Adam pressed the button to release the huge feeder-arms and they swung out, circling clockwise, over the clouds, releasing their tiny granules of frozen silver iodide.

'It's so fucking beautiful,' Fairfield whispered. 'It's like you're playing god, Adam.'

He turned to face her, to correct her – this was a scientific, climatological experiment, not some proto-numinous ego-trip – and almost immediately they were kissing, her spectacles pressing hard into his cheeks and brow.

'I love you, Adam,' she said, breathing heavily, breaking apart to remove her clothing, 'I've loved you since the day I saw you.'

They made love on the viewing gantry at the top of the cloud chamber – above the clouds – with a quickness and urgency that did not inhibit his orgasm in the slightest. Adam came with a gasp of surprise at the unparalleled, animalistic sensation of release (the next day he found his knees scratched and his elbows and legs bruised). When it was over they replaced whatever clothing they had removed and sat beside each other on the metal floor of the gantry in silence, regaining their breath and thoughts, and Fairfield smoked a cigarette, blithely ignoring the no-smoking signs, blowing the smoke considerately away from him, up and away over her right shoulder.

Fool, Adam said to himself, now, bitterly – it had been an almighty risk; any one of the other students might have taken the elevator up to the viewing gantry and surprised them. Had that moment with Fairfield been the fatal catalyst that had led him here, to this doorway in Bermondsey – the throw of the destiny-dice that found him sitting on his arse on the threshold of a derelict shop, wanted for murder, penniless, bearded, filthy, hungry, wearing cast-off clothes? But no, he reasoned, get real, Adam – you could trace the causal chain back to the day you were born if you had a mind to. That way led to madness. But then why, as a relatively happily married man in a respected and secure job, with a growing academic reputation, had he chosen to have sex with Fairfield Springer, one of his graduate students? What had possessed him? Why had he not simply said, 'No, Fairfield, this cannot happen, please,' and pushed her gently away? Their lovemaking, if that was the correct expression for something so instinctive and unrefined, must have lasted barely a couple of minutes, before he collapsed, gasping, and rolled off her. They had adjusted their clothes, sat for a while in silence, then Fairfield had kissed him, her tobacco-y tongue deep in his mouth, and she had taken the elevator down to the laboratory to rejoin her fellow students. That was it – the act, the sex act, had never been repeated.

Damage control, Adam had thought the next morning over breakfast, sitting opposite his smart and pretty wife as they both prepared to go to their respective jobs. Yes, damage control, that was what was required: a meeting with Fairfield, sincere apologies issued, a moment of madness conceded, his fault entirely, affection expressed, a rueful comment on this unseemly breakdown in professorial–student relations. It would never, never happen again. But by then the first streams of texts – explicit, not obscene; passionate, not crazed – had already started arriving on his cell-phone.

'Fucking hell,' Adam said to himself and opened his eyes to see a man staring at him a few feet away. Big guy, burly, built like a forward in a rugby team, fifties, with a square, lived-in face, semi-bald, longish hair, wearing a blazer and grey flannels and carrying a small leather bag over his shoulder.

'You all right?' this man said.

'Yeah, fine, thanks,' Adam said, managing a vague smile. And the man smiled back and went into the newsagent's next door. He came out a few minutes later with an armful of newspapers and magazines and leant forward towards Adam, with something in his hand.

'Good luck, mate,' he said.

He gave Adam a £1 coin.

Adam watched him stroll away. Adam thought: what's going on here? He looked in some amazement at the small heavy coin in the palm of his hand, experiencing a kind of revelation. He had money now – and it had been *given* to him. He didn't need to steal, he realised – he could beg.

When the Church of John Christ opened its doors at six o'clock Adam was the only potential parishioner waiting. The small door was ajar so he stepped through it into a vestibule where the toothless woman sat behind a desk.

'Hello, dear,' she said. 'Welcome to the rest of your life.'

He noticed that she was wearing a plastic badge on her lapel that said 'JOHN 17'. She scribbled something with a broad felt-tip pen and handed Adam a small card. In fact it was a cardboard badge, with a securing pin on its back. On the front she had written: 'JOHN 1603'.

'You'll get a proper plastic one like mine the next time you come,' she said. Adam fastened the badge to his white denim jacket. 'Take a seat at the very front, John,' she said, indicating a door behind her.

Adam went through the door as directed and found himself in a large hall-like room with brick walls and an iron-girdered roof with skylights. Rows of simple wooden benches were set out – with padded prayer-stools in front of them – facing a dais with a lectern in the centre. The lectern had a microphone and wires from it led to a couple of loudspeakers on either side. On the wall behind was a richly embroidered, glowing cloth-of-gold banner depicting a stylised sun with long cursive rays emanating from it. There were no crosses to be seen anywhere. Adam took a seat in the front row, as instructed, and sat there patiently, his mind empty, hands clasped together on his knees.

Over the next few minutes a dozen or so other people – mainly men, mainly homeless men, as far as Adam could tell – shuffled quietly in and took their seats. All were wearing 'John' badges. The few women, similarly badged, sat at the very back, Adam noticed. He felt and heard his stomach rumble – his hunger was returning. At least it was all remarkably anonymous and discreet: no questions, no names required, no back story, nothing. Just become a member of the Church of John Christ and—

A man slipped in beside him. Adam saw he was wearing a cardboard 'JOHN 1604' badge. He had thinning frizzy hair – a small man in his forties with a big head and suffering from a condition Adam knew and recognised that was called, among other names, acropachyderma. The skin on his face was unnaturally coarse and thick, forming heavy, exaggerated creases, like elephant's skin – hence the condition's name. It was also known as Audry's Syndrome, Roy's Syndrome and, most exotically, Touraine-Solent-Golé Syndrome. Adam knew all about this as his father-in-law – his ex-father-in-law – Brookman Maybury also suffered from acropachyderma. There was no cure but it wasn't fatal, just unsightly. The most famous acropachydermic was the poet W. H. Auden. The man sitting beside Adam, John 1604, was not as bad as Auden but would run him close, one day. His naso-labial clefts looked an inch deep; four striations, so marked they looked like tribal scars, ran across his forehead, even with his face in repose; odd creases that seemed to have no bearing on any potential facial expression descended

158

vertically from below the swagged flesh bagging
beneath his eyes and his mangled chin looked as
if it had been mutilated by some childhood accident. He turned and smiled, showing long brown
teeth with large even gaps between them. He
offered his hand.

'Hello, mate. Turpin. Vincent Turpin.'

'Adam.' They shook hands.

'You get a decent meal, here, so they tell me,
Adam.'

'Good.'

'You just have to sit through the service, that's
all.'

Adam was going to say that it didn't seem too
onerous a price to pay but was interrupted by loud
rock music blasting out from the two speakers – rock
music with shrill, blaring trumpets and other brass
and many drums of varying types thumping out a
strident, addictively rhythmic dance beat. A man
in purple and gold robes came dancing down the
central aisle between the benches and a few of
the Johns began to clap in time. The man paused
in front of the dais and continued dancing for a
while, head wobbling, eyes closed. He danced well,
Adam thought: a good-looking man with a thick
neck and strong features and a boxer's broken nose.
This would be Archbishop Yemi Thompson-Gbeho,
patron and founder, he reckoned.

With a wave of his hand Bishop Yemi caused the
music to stop and he took his place behind
the lectern.

'Let us pray,' he said in a deep bass voice and everyone knelt on the cushions in front of them.

The prayer lasted, by Adam's rough calculation, almost thirty minutes. He ceased to follow it after the opening phrases, letting his mind wander, tuning back in from time to time, growing increasingly aware of Turpin's effortful breathing beside him – a kind of wheezing and whistling as if his nasal cavities were clogged with dense undergrowth – brambles and tough grass. What Adam heard of the prayer ranged widely through world geo-political events, touching many continents, happy outcomes to the various global crises being devoutly wished for. By the time Bishop Yemi had said, 'In the name of our Lord, John Christ, amen,' Adam wondered if his stomach's borborygmi could be heard at the back of the hall.

Bishop Yemi eventually requested them to be seated.

'Welcome, brothers,' he said, 'to the Church of John Christ.' He looked over his small congregation. 'Who, amongst you, has sinned?'

Glancing round, Adam saw that everyone had put their hands up. He and Turpin promptly, though a little sheepishly, did the same.

'In the name of John Christ your sins are forgiven,' Bishop Yemi said and opened what looked like a bible and continued. 'Our lesson this evening comes from the Great Book of John, Revelation, chapter 13, verse 17.' He paused, and then his voice grew theatrically deep. 'No man

160

might buy or sell, save that he had the mark or the name of the beast, or the number of his name.'

After the reading Bishop Yemi used the text to begin a free-associating and apparently improvised sermon. Adam now felt exhaustion creeping up on him and struggled to stay awake. As he drifted in and out of concentration, certain phrases, certain tropes, managed to imprint themselves on his mind.

'Would you stone your father?' Bishop Yemi bellowed at them. 'You say – no. I say – yes, stone your father . . .' Then, minutes later, Adam re-focussed to hear: 'You feel despair, you feel your life is worthless – cry out. CRY OUT! John, John Christ, John, the true Christ, come to my aid. He will come, my brothers . . .' Later still: 'John Christ would bless the European Union – but he would not bless the G8 summit . . .' And then, 'You eat chicken for supper, lovely roast chicken, you clean your teeth. In the morning you find a shred of chicken stuck between two molars and with your tongue – or a toothpick – you work it free. Do you spit it out? No: this is the chicken you chewed and swallowed last night. Why would you spit it out? No. You swallow it. These are the tiny blessings bestowed on us, the brothers of John Christ, like shreds of meat trapped between your teeth, small deliveries of nutrition, spiritual nutrition . . .' Then it all went hazy: 'Mao Tse-tung . . . Grace Kelly . . . Shango, God of Lightning . . . Oliver Cromwell . . .' The words became mere sounds, all meaning gone.

The sermon lasted two hours. Darkness clouded,

then occluded, the skylights in the gantried roof. Adam was sitting upright, his eyes half open, in a semi-conscious, zoned-out state, hearing the noise of Bishop Yemi's sonorous baritone, but comprehending nothing, when, all of a sudden, he realised it had stopped, There was silence: his brain re-engaged with the world. Bishop Yemi was staring at him and Turpin.

'Please stand, John 1603 and John 1604.'

Adam and Turpin rose to their feet as Bishop Yemi left the dais and approached them. He placed the palms of his hands on their foreheads.

'You are one of us now – we will never turn you away. Welcome to the Church of John Christ.'

There was a sporadic chatter of applause from the rest of the congregation before the rock music boomed out once again and Bishop Yemi danced enthusiastically out of his chapel.

John 17, the woman with no front teeth, took Adam to a room full of piles of clothes, clean but un-ironed, and asked him to help himself. He chose a cornflower-blue shirt and a pin-striped navy-blue suit that didn't quite match: the pin-stripes on the trousers were wider than those on the jacket. He asked if he might exchange his golf-shoes for some other footwear but John 17 said, regretfully, 'We don't do shoes, love.' Still he was glad to surrender his filthy white shirt – stained with Philip Wang's blood and his own – his white denim jacket and Mhouse's beige camouflage

162

cut-off cargo pants. John 17 turned away as he changed – the fit was perfectly acceptable.

'I suppose you're hungry,' John 17 said as Adam refastened his 'John 1603' badge to his pin-striped lapel.

'I am, rather,' Adam confessed, and he was led down a corridor to the small communal dining room where he picked up a plate and joined the end of the queue of other members of the congregation. They were being served rice and beef stew from pots bubbling over gas jets. Adam loaded his plate with rice and held it out to have the stew ladled over it. He looked up to thank the server and saw that it was Mhouse, wearing a plastic badge that said 'John 627'.

'Hello,' Adam said.

'Yeah?'

'You're Mhouse.'

'Yeah.'

'We met. I'm Adam. I was mugged – you took me back to Chelsea . . .' He was going to add, *and you beat me up with an entrenching tool*, but thought better of it.

'You sure?'

'You lent me some clothes. You found me at the Shaftesbury Estate. Remember? It was you who told me to come here.'

'Did I? This is my church . . .' She looked at him, head cocked, as if trying to place him, somehow. 'Oh, yeah . . . I remember. You finished with them clothes?'

'John 17 has the trousers – but I still have the flip-flops.'

'No prob. I wouldn't mind the flip-flops back.'

'I'll bring them to you.'

'Cool.'

He smiled at her and then helped himself to several slices of white bread and went to look for a place to sit. The room contained half a dozen Formica-ed tables with four seats set around them, like a small workman's café. Turpin was sitting at a table with two other men, the seat beside him empty, so it seemed logical for Adam to join his fellow convert.

'Wha-hey, city gent,' Turpin said, admiring Adam's new clothes, as Adam slipped into the seat beside him. Then Turpin said to the other two men, 'This is Adam.'

'Hi. I Vladimir,' the first man introduced himself. He had a perfectly shaven head – a gleaming oiled dome – and a small neat goatee. His eyes were darkly shadowed, he looked terminally exhausted. He extended his hand and Adam shook it.

'Gavin Thrale,' the other man said, in a middle-class accent, raising his hand – not offering it for shaking. He was an older man, in his fifties, perhaps, also bearded, but heavily, with an old salt's full grey shag, and had a long lock of matching grey hair swept across his forehead and tucked behind his ear like a schoolboy. He had said 'Gavin Thrale' with a subtle inflection in his voice that implied that it was a name that Adam

164

might possibly recognise, though he would prefer to remain incognito.

The four men ate their beef stew in silent concentration. Turpin ate like a porker at the trough, slurping, chewing with his mouth open, making small grunting sounds of pleasure as he swallowed. If Adam hadn't been so hungry he might have found it nauseating, but he shut his ears and concentrated, filling his belly with his first proper meal in two weeks.

Turpin finished first and pushed his plate to one side, expelling a soft belching whoosh of air.

'What're you doing in a place like this, Adam?' he asked, picking at his widely spaced teeth with a fingernail.

Adam had prepared himself for this question. 'I've had a series of nervous breakdowns,' he said, unemotionally. 'My life sort of fell apart. I'm trying to put it back together.'

'My wife chucked me out,' Turpin volunteered. 'The Birmingham wife. Turned very nasty. Got to lay low for a while, you know. Very angry and unhappy woman. Out for my blood, I'm sorry to say.'

'Hell hath no fury,' Gavin Thrale said.

'Sorry?' Turpin said.

'What you do to her?' Vladimir asked.

'Not so much to *her*, exactly,' Turpin said, unperturbed by the question. 'More a "family" matter – very delicate – other members of the family were concerned.' He went no further.

'I come to England, come to London for heart surgery,' Vladimir said, unprompted. 'In my village they collecting money for one year, send me for London to fixing my heart.' He smiled engagingly. 'I never be in big city like this. Too many temptings.'

'Temptations,' Thrale corrected.

'What happened?' Turpin asked.

'I come here. I go to hospital. Suddenly I feeling OK, you know? So I check out.' Vladimir shrugged. 'I have problem with heart valve – it fix himself, I think.'

'What about you, Gavin?' Turpin asked.

'None of your business,' Thrale said, stood up and left.

It became clear, once the congregation of the Church of John Christ had finished their meal, that there was to be no lingering. Mhouse and John 17 began to put chairs on tables and another John started mopping the linoleum floor.

As Adam, Turpin and Vladimir left the church they were bade farewell by Bishop Yemi himself. He shook their hands, then gave them a hug.

'See you tomorrow, guys,' he said. 'Tell your friends – six o'clock, seven days a week.'

Vladimir drew Adam aside. 'You like monkey?'

'Monkey? What's that?'

'Knack. Maybe you say "beak"? We call it monkey.'

'I've never tried it.'

'You come with me we go smoke monkey. You have money?'

'No.'

Vladimir shrugged and smiled, clearly disappointed. He seemed an almost innocent soul. 'I like monkey too much,' he said and wandered off, leaving Adam with Turpin.

'Where you headed, Adam?'

'Chelsea.'

'Great. I'm headed for Wandsworth. Got a wife up there I haven't seen for a year or two. Might put me up for the night.'

Turpin had some money and offered to lend Adam the bus fare to Chelsea – 'Now that we're brothers in John Christ, eh?' – an offer Adam accepted, promising to pay him back as soon as he could.

On the bus, Turpin, still exhaling soft gusts of beef-laden air from his gut, and every now and then pounding his breast-bone as if something were stuck there, said, 'What do you make of this John Christ story, then?'

'Pure mumbo-jumbo,' Adam said. 'It's all nonsense – this god, that god. Complete rubbish.'

'No, no. Hang on,' Turpin said, frowning, the deep pachydermous creases on his brow folding into an unnatural wave effect. 'You got to give credit to—'

He stopped, interrupted by the arrival on board of a fat harassed woman and a plump, placid child, a girl, carrying a balloon and eating a chocolate bar. Turpin pressed his elbow into Adam's side.

'Hello, hello. That's a nice little chicken,' Turpin said, admiringly. 'Very nice. You married, Adam?'

'I was. I'm divorced.'

'Kiddies?'

'No.'

'I love little kiddies,' Turpin said. 'You know, "proof of heaven", as they say . . . I've had a lot of kids myself, nine or ten. Eleven. I like little boys, little chaps, but I'm a little-girl man at heart. Sweet little darlings. What about you, Adam? Boys or girls?'

'I haven't really thought about it.'

'Girls for me, all the way. But after the age of ten it all changes,' Turpin said, ruefully, almost bitterly. 'Goes to the bad. Not the same. Nah.'

Adam looked out at the street as the bus pulled up at a traffic light. A policeman stood there, looking directly at him. Adam smiled, vaguely, confidently anonymous.

'Yeah, but listen: John Christ,' Turpin said, returning to his original argument. 'What if Bishop Yemi's right and John, disciple John, is the real Christ and like Jesus was the fall guy . . . The patsy. Like it was a cover-up.'

'I think I must have missed that bit.'

'The point being that the Romans think they've got the real guy – Jesus – but John, the true Christ, goes off scot-free. Clears off to Patmos, lives to be a hundred and writes Revelation. On his own Greek island.'

'It's all nonsense, I told you, raving nonsense.'

'Hold on, hold on. They were like freedom fighters, a cell. The guy they crucify – Jesus – isn't the real leader. It's John.'

168

'Why not sacrifice a goat to the sun-god Ra?'

'Say again? No, I mean – I think Bishop Yemi may be on to something, here. Makes a kind of sense.'

Turpin was still expatiating on the possibilities of this clever hoax when they both left the bus at Sloane Square and walked down to the river. They paused at Chelsea Bridge, leaning on the parapet, looking out at the ebb tide, the black flowing water lit by the hundreds of light bulbs positioned on the bridge's superstructure and suspension cables.

'Got a smoke?' Turpin asked.

'Sorry, no.'

'I'll cadge a smoke off of someone. You get off to your bed, Adam. See you tomorrow, mate.'

Adam said goodnight and wandered off, not particularly wanting Turpin to see where he dossed down, so he crossed to the other side of the Embankment, opposite the triangle, and dawdled along the railings of the Royal Hospital, glancing back to see Turpin accosting passers-by. When he eventually cadged a cigarette and lit up and began to cross the bridge towards the Battersea shore, Adam scurried across the road and climbed over the fence, secure in the knowledge that Turpin hadn't seen him.

In his small clearing Adam hung his new jacket and trousers carefully on a branch and removed his clean, un-ironed shirt, before sliding into his sleeping bag. He lay there, snug under his bush, feeling strangely confident. He hadn't enjoyed

169

such a sensation of unremarkable but genuine ease and pleasantness since the murder. He wasn't hungry, he realised, that was what was different, and now he had a place he could go to for hearty, sustaining food where no one was curious about him and no questions were asked. Everything was going to change, he felt sure: he had seen the way forward. His begging life was about to begin.

CHAPTER 17

The bath was ideally hot and full enough so that the bubbles came up to his chin. Ingram wallowed, ran his hands over his naked body and felt himself both relax and anticipate. Today was his birthday – he was fifty-nine years old – and he was about to enjoy his birthday present to himself: a most agreeable way, he considered, of entering his sixtieth year.

'Where are you going?' Meredith had said, appalled, seeing him in a suit and tie on a Saturday morning. 'I thought we were having lunch.'

'There's a crisis, darling,' he had said. 'Crisis meetings. One of those ghastly days. I'll be back by six, promise. Oh, and I have to see Pa, as well.'

'Don't be late,' she had said. 'Everyone'll be here at seven.'

Ingram picked up a floating sponge and squeezed hot water over his head. This was what he needed after the grim affair that had been Philip Wang's funeral last week. Putney Vale Crematorium, even on a summer's day, summed up everything in the word 'joyless', Ingram thought. Philip's mother – a tiny, frail woman, weeping and uncom-prehending – had flown over from Hong Kong with his sister. There had been a superb turn-out from the boys and girls in the Calenture lab at Oxford. Not such a good showing from head office but then Philip wasn't really known to them, other than by name and reputation. Ingram had written and read the eulogy himself, concentrating, natur-ally enough, on his own relationship with Philip. How, in the early days of Calenture-Deutz's growth, Philip had virtually single-handedly de-veloped the anti-hay fever drug Bynogol in pill form and nasal inhaler – Calenture-Deutz's first real earner – and the breakthrough discoveries made during that Bynogol process (Ingram was always a bit unsure about the chemistry) had led Philip directly on to evolve Zembla-1, and its subsequent derivatives, into what should prove to be the world's first truly effective asthma drug. How had he put it at the funeral? 'Philip's death was brutal and senseless but everything about his life was the exact opposite. We have lost Philip but the world's gain will be incalculable.' Quite nicely phrased, he thought – almost aphoristically balanced: death and life, loss and gain.

Ingram leaned forward and ran some more hot water into the bath. He remembered that day when Philip had come in to his office, had come up from Oxford to London at very short notice, wanting to talk, he said, about asthma. He was visibly excited and Ingram kept having to tell him

172

to slow down and repeat himself. He had been testing some antigens, he said, tiny spores that provoke the allergic response that is hay fever, with a view to improving Bynogol. In one of the tests he had used some pollen from a type of magnolia that he had collected on his last trip to see his mother in Hong Kong. To his astonishment, this antigen, meant to provoke a hay-fever attack – swelling, mucus, irritation and so forth – had instead produced the opposite effect. Rather than generating the secretion of toxic Th2 cells of a classic allergic attack, benign Th1 cells were secreted in their place. He started talking very fast at this stage about histamines, leukotrienes and IgE antibodies and Ingram told him to stop.

'Words of one syllable, please, Philip,' he said. 'I'm not a scientist. What's all this to do with asthma?'

Philip drew breath and began to explain. No one really knows why there is a worldwide epidemic of asthma, he said. There are 20 million sufferers in the USA, 5 million in Great Britain, tens of millions of others in the developed world (Ingram was impressed by these numbers). There was a line of thought that saw asthma, an inflammation stimulated by an allergy, as some kind of malfunction of our prehistoric immune system. The immune system defences of early man were meant to be triggered by ancient organisms that no longer exist – organisms that flourished in the primordial mud – but were now being activated by pollens, mites, feline dust, air conditioning, bright sunlight, newspapers, aerosols, cigarette smoke, perfumes, etcetera. Asthma sufferers, in other words, were victims of our malfunctioning, prehistoric immuno-defence systems.

'What is so intriguing,' Philip continued, his voice rising a register, 'is that the angiosperm—'

'Angiosperm?'

'Flowering plant. The plant that I used, the Zembla flower—'

'Zembla flower?'

'The magnolia from Hong Kong. Locally it's known as the Zembla flower. Anyway, this magnolia's pollen spores are present in the fossil records of the Cretaceous era.' He spread his hands – it was so obvious.

'Meaning?' Ingram asked his third question.

'Meaning that this magnolia was one of the very, very earliest angiosperms. That it, if you like, seems to produce a "memory" response in our immune system, the immune system "remembers" this trigger from the Cretaceous past, making it react properly. Nice Th1 cells not nasty Th2.' He paused and when he spoke again, his voice trembled. 'I think we may, just possibly, have found a way of controlling bronchial asthma.'

'So what do you want?' Ingram asked, carefully.

'Money,' Philip said, faintly apologetically, 'to see if there's some way of replicating the effect of this Hong Kong Zembla flower on asthma sufferers. Set up trials, start testing on animals. Go to phase one, in other words.'

174

Ingram thought: all those millions upon millions of asthma sufferers ... If Calenture-Deutz could fabricate a drug that they would be happy to use ... Anything Calenture-Deutz could do to alleviate their misery had to be worth pursuing. So he had provided Philip with his necessary initial funding and the Zembla development had begun in earnest. They applied to the FDA for an Inaugural New Drug Licence and it was granted. Then to his complete astonishment, about three months later, Ingram had received a call from Alfredo Rilke with an offer to buy 20 per cent of Calenture-Deutz stock and pump real investment into the development of Zembla. Ingram had never asked Alfredo how he had learnt of Zembla's existence but it seemed both a prudent and lucrative idea. So Calenture-Deutz and Rilke Pharmaceutical had become partners.

There was a polite rap on the bathroom door and Phyllis came in. She was wearing a lemon-yellow cardigan and chocolate-brown slacks.

'How are we doing, Jack?' she asked. She was a small, plump, full-breasted woman with a great quiff of reddish blonde hair swept up in a frosted, billow-effect around her pretty face. 'Out we get – turn into a jelly fish, you will.' She had a deep voice for a small woman – probably an ex-smoker, Ingram thought – one that he found made her cockney accent more raucous and agreeably lewd, somehow.

He stepped meekly out of the bath and she advanced on him with a towel and began to dry him.

'Someone's growing a little pot belly, Jack-me-lad,' she said, patting his stomach. 'Hello, hello, what've we got here, then?'

Ingram counted out the four 50-pound notes and laid them discreetly on Phyllis's dresser. It seemed unspeakably cheap for the thirty minutes or so of intense sexual pleasure he had enjoyed with her. He checked his hair in the mirror – he looked a little flushed, still – and adjusted his tie-knot.

'That was wonderful, Phyllis,' he said, adding another £50. 'Tremendous.'

'You can fuck me any day you want, Jack, darling,' she said, slipping naked out of the bed. She gave him a kiss and squeezed his balls, making him flinch, then laugh. 'Ta muchly,' she said, picking up the money. 'Close the door behind you, Jack dear, there's a love.' She put the notes in a large wallet. 'Give us a bell any time – don't forget, twenty-four hours notice.'

On the Tube back to Victoria, Ingram thought back, with nostalgic pleasure, over the various sex acts he'd performed with Phyllis that morning and marvelled, as he always did when he left her, that he'd found her at all. For five years before Phyllis he had enjoyed the professional services of Nerys, a Welsh woman, with a thick, singing Welsh accent, who had a couple of rooms in Soho. When she told him she was going back to Swansea to look after her grandchildren Ingram felt some key component of his life was being removed. 'Don't worry, lovely,' she had said, 'I'll find you a perfect substitute,' and it was Nerys who had introduced him to Phyllis. Networking, he supposed, everyone did it . . . He kept his Nerys name – 'Jack' – and the relationship, such as it was, flourished and endured – perhaps even better than it had been with Nerys.

How come? he wondered. He didn't want to delve too deeply into the reasons why he found the Neryses and the Phyllises of this world so sexually alluring. He wasn't a fool: he knew absolutely that on one level it was all about class. It was because they were working class – because they were 'common' – that he was excited by them: the terrible decor of their rooms, their funny names, their culture, their accents, their grammar, their language. He suspected also that it was something to do with his schooldays, his prep school, the onset of puberty and all that – not wanting to delve too deeply . . . Didn't someone say that what attracted you sexually as a thirteen-year-old haunted you all your adult life? A friend's mother, an aunt, a sibling's nanny, an au pair, an under-matron, a girl working in the school kitchen . . . What set these time bombs ticking in your sexual psyche? How could you know when and how they would detonate?

He stepped out of the train on to the platform – he took careful precautions on his journeys to and from Phyllis – Shoreditch not being somewhere he frequented, normally. Luigi parked in a square not far from the station. Ingram would say he had a meeting that would last a couple of hours and he wasn't to be disturbed. He'd walk to the Underground station on a circuitous route and always return to the car by a different one.

He paused on the station concourse for a second and briefly closed his eyes, remembering Phyllis's generous, well-padded body, her gentle mockery. Sex was fun, a bit of a lark, robustly uncomplicated – no need for PRO-Vyril's stealthy, chemical helping hand. He headed out of the station, wondering if she ever thought about him after he'd left – her 'Jack' – and if she ever speculated about who he really was (he took no ID with him, another precaution, just cash). No, he thought, this was the punter's typical, sad fantasy – all she wanted was her 200 quid because another 'Jack' was due. He wasn't that vain, that naïve – thank god! Still, sometimes he wondered . . .

Her husband, Wesley – he knew his name – was a despatcher for a minicab firm, absent about twelve hours a day, and Phyllis had decided to make the family home in Shoreditch generate some income while he was at work. Only once had he met another client, coming to the house as he was leaving – another man his age, grey-haired, in his fifties, his whole demeanour reeking of upper-middle-classdom: the dark suit and banded tie, the covert coat, the briefcase. A QC? A senior civil servant? Politician? Banker? Harley Street doctor? They had ignored each other utterly, as if they were both invisible – ghosts. But it was a jolt: a tangible reminder that Phyllis sold her time and her body to others. How did we find our Phyllises, he wondered? What led us to these accommodating professionals?

Luigi was waiting with the car in Eccleston Square.

'You have one call, signore,' he said, handing Ingram his mobile phone. 'Signor Rilke.'

Ingram called back. 'Alfredo, you're here – wonderful. I was expecting you on Monday.'

'Where were you?'

'I had a meeting,' Ingram improvised quickly. 'I had to see a doctor. About my son,' he added, taking the heat off himself.

'Is that your homosexual son?'

'Yes – my "gay" son. All very troublesome and complex.' Ingram rather wished he hadn't embarked on this lie.

'Has he got AIDS?'

'No, no – nothing like that. Anyway, let's—'

'I'm at the Firststopotel, Cromwell Road.'

'I'll be there in half an hour.'

Alfredo Rilke only stayed in chain hotels – Marriott, Hilton, Schooner Inns, Novotel – but he always took an entire floor and however many rooms that floor contained. When he arrived, Ingram was shown up to the fifth floor and one of Alfredo's youthful associates – a young man in jeans with an earpiece and a thin stick-microphone at his mouth – led him down a featureless corridor to one of the rooms and left him there with a smile and a small bow from the waist.

Alfredo Rilke opened the door himself before Ingram could knock. They embraced, diffidently, more a clasping of the upper arms and a leaning in to each other than anything else – their faces did not touch – Rilke patting him reassuringly on a shoulder blade and steering him into the dark room, curtains drawn.

Rilke was a tall, heavily built man in his early sixties, bespectacled, smiling, avuncular, bald with a neat semicircular ruff of unnaturally dark hair that started above one ear and circumnavigated the back of his head to the other. He moved slowly and deliberately as if he were on the verge of frailty. It was an illusion: Ingram had seen him playing energetic tennis in Grand Cayman and the US Virgin Islands, hitting the ball with real force. But off the tennis court he feigned this quasi-senility – a way of reassuring and disarming his colleagues, rivals and competitors, Ingram supposed. Alfredo Rilke seemed like a rapidly ageing man – exactly what he wanted people to think.

'Sit down, Ingram, sit down.'

Ingram did, noting that the bedroom had been converted, somewhat half-heartedly, into a sitting room – the bed pushed back to the side wall, some chairs and a coffee table added.

'Help yourself to a drink, Ingram,' Rilke said, opening the door of the mini-bar. 'I have to make one phone call. I'll be two minutes.'

Rilke went into the next-door room and Ingram poured himself a tonic water, and sat down, waiting. He knew a certain amount about Alfredo Rilke, but he always felt he knew only half of what he really should. He'd tried to find out more, had other people try on his behalf to find out more, but the story remained frustratingly the same, fundamentally unchanging, full of gaps and un-answered questions – over the years very little detail had been added to the Rilke biography.

Alfredo's father, Gunther Rilke, had arrived in Uruguay (from Switzerland, by all accounts, though all that was very vague also) in 1946. He almost immediately married a Uruguayan, Asuncion Salgueiro, the only daughter of the owner of a small company producing fungicides and fertilisers, servicing the Latin American coffee industry. Alfredo was born in 1947 and his brother, Cesario, in 1950. Alfredo Rilke took over his father-in-law's company in 1970, Cesario having died in a plane crash in 1969, and changed the name to Rilke Farmacéutico S.A.

He made his first fortune in the following decade with a cheap contraceptive pill and a powerful anti-depressant, surviving a series of lawsuits for patent infringement brought against him by Roche, Searle, Syntex and others.

Rilke himself left Uruguay and became perma-nently non-resident in 1982, choosing to live, henceforth, on board a series of large, regularly changed yachts that permanently cruised the Caribbean and the Gulf of Mexico, within easy two-hour reach of a dozen airports and the company jet. Rilke Pharmaceutical was born at that moment and a series of smaller pharmaceutical companies were steadily acquired in the USA, France and Italy. By the late 1990s Rilke Pharma was listed as one of the top ten pharmaceutical companies in the world.

And that was really about all he or anyone knew, Ingram thought, dissatisfied. Perhaps that was what happened when you lived 'nowhere' for a quarter of a century – you became very hard to pin down, in every sense of the expression. Except that the pharmaceutical world knew that patents on Rilke Pharma's big drugs, the blockbusters, that provided the massive cash flow for the continued acquisitions – the oral contraceptive, an ACE inhibitor, a retroviral and a new series of 'me-too' anti-depressants – were all coming to the end of their licence period. Rilke Pharma needed a new blockbuster drug and that was when they had approached Calenture-Deutz and offered to invest heavily in the clinical trials and research of Zembla-4 . . .

Ingram looked up as Rilke returned – he was apologising generously as he came through the door, carrying a file from which he spread documents on the coffee table. They were full-colour, mock-up, two-page advertorials. Each page had in bold type the message: 'AN END TO ASTHMA?'. Ingram scanned through them: the usual bland advertorial pap – 'Renowned scientists in our research laboratories'; 'The struggle to rid the

182

world of this debilitating disease' – and pictures of serious-looking men in white coats peering into microscopes, holding up test tubes, healthy people enjoying enviable lifestyles on ranches and at the seaside. The pages concluded with heartfelt assurances of the continued fight against these chronic ailments (money no object) threatening the good life. It was all subtext. Here and there the name 'Zembla-4' cropped up. No claims were made, but the promise was vaguely implicit: just give us time, we and our handsome, white-coated scientists are working on it.

'Very impressive,' Ingram said, 'but a little premature, no?' It had not escaped his notice that each advertisement featured the familiar logo: the red-circled, blue, scribbled 'R' of Rilke Pharmaceuticals. As far as Ingram was aware Calenture-Deutz still owned Zembla and all its derivatives, one through four. He decided to say nothing.

'You may be right,' Rilke said in his usual humble, non-confrontational manner. 'It was just that Burton told me that Zembla-4 was close to ready. Third stage clinical trials complete. The documentation ready to be sent in to the FDA at Rockville . . . We've found in the past that an early, vague, very vague, advertorial campaign – with the usual brief-summary caveats, of course,' he pointed to a dense inch-thick footnote at the end of each advertorial page, 'can make a significant difference. Everything seems to speed up, we've found.'

'Burton told you that, did he?' Ingram said, a little stiffly. 'Actually, I wanted to talk to you about Keegan and de Freitas – I'd like them off the board.'

'That won't be possible, I'm afraid, Ingram,' Rilke said, with an ingénue's smile of apology.

It was at moments like these that Ingram found it helpful to remind himself that Alfredo Rilke had enriched the Fryzer family to the tune of some £100 million. It made bitter pills very easy to swallow. He changed his tone.

'It's just that Keegan and de Freitas are assuming responsibilities no one gave them. It's not in their remit to—'

Rilke held up his hand as if to say, forgive me, stop, please. 'I asked them to assume these responsibilities after Philip Wang's death. You know, Burton Keegan has supervised four, no five, successful new drug applications for Rilke Pharma. He's the best: he knows exactly what he's doing. There's too much at stake here, Ingram.'

'Well, that's a different matter. If I'd known—'

'How are things going on the investigation, by the way? Has Kindred been found?'

'Ah, no. Not yet. He seems to have disappeared off the face of the earth. The police have lost all trace of him. Baffling.'

'We don't need to rely exclusively on the police, thank god,' Rilke said. What did he mean by that? Ingram wondered.

Ingram sighed. 'We ran our reward-advertisements

184

for two whole weeks. The police think Kindred may have killed himself.'

'What do you think?'

'I, ah, I really don't have an opinion.'

'A dangerous state of mind, Ingram. If you don't have an opinion, you can't function.' Rilke smiled.

Ingram smiled back: safer to say nothing at these moments.

'Here's what's going to happen,' Rilke said, standing, and hoiking his trouser waist up over his gut. 'We submit Zembla-4 to the licensing authorities in the US and then the UK. The advertorials will begin to appear, first in learned medical journals, then in selected high-class outlets of the global media – *New Yorker*, *Time*, *Economist*, *El Pais*, *Wall Street Journal*, *Le Figaro*, etcetera. Who can complain if a drug company declares that it is trying to eradicate asthma? Who can object to a mission statement? Then Rilke Pharmaceutical will offer to buy Calenture-Deutz at a moment of my choosing. But all this will happen only, I repeat, only after Adam Kindred is apprehended and dealt with.'

'Yeeessss,' Ingram said slowly drawing the word out, like a piece of chewing gum, his mind whirring like a malfunctioning clockwork toy. 'What's, um, your timescale? When will all this start to happen?'

'Maybe next month, all being well,' Rilke said. 'You'll be an even richer man, Ingram. And the world will have its first fully functioning anti-asthma drug. It's a no-lose situation.'

Ingram was told that Colonel Fryzer could be found in the rose garden, so he set off through the well-tended grounds of Trelawny Gables in search of his father. He wandered along the meandering pathways of this high-priced, private, sheltered housing, passing uniformed nurses, white-overalled assistants pushing trolleys laden with meals, dry-cleaning, vases of flowers, wondering vaguely if this were the sort of place in which he would end his days – a five-star ante-room to oblivion with cordon-bleu catering. He was also wondering vaguely about his meeting with Alfredo Rilke and what was its real import, its gravitas. Keegan and de Freitas were staying, that much was clear, but it appeared to him there was a near unseemly rush to have Zembla-4 licensed. Philip Wang had always advocated the slow-but-steady route, that was how the Bynogol licence had gone through so smoothly . . . Ingram paused to sniff at a flower: he was almost sure something was going on behind his back – that he was not in full control of Calenture-Deutz any more was both as clear as day and very troubling.

His father disliked Trelawny Gables with a calm but fierce intensity, Ingram knew, but he endured its customs and rituals with amused pragmatism. He didn't blame his son that he had ended up here – at least Ingram hoped not as he now saw

186

his father from a distance, spraying insecticide on rose bushes in a small arbour by the perimeter wall. He was a tall, lean, grey-haired man wearing an olive-green sleeveless fleece, a shirt and tie and neatly pressed blue jeans. Ingram had foresworn jeans at the age of forty – no mature or middle-aged man should be seen dead in them, he reasoned, but he had to admit they rather suited his father, now eighty-seven years old. Perhaps jeans were to be taken up again in one's eighties . . .

'Hello, Pa,' he said, kissing him on both cheeks. 'Looking well.'

Colonel Gregor Fryzer looked at his son closely – scrutinising me, Ingram thought, as if I were on parade. Ingram smiled at this old man's foible but then worried – absurdly, he knew – that some scent of Phyllis was emanating from him, some odour of sex that only octogenarians could sniff out.

'You seem a bit nervous, Ingram. Bit edgy.'

'Not in the least.'

'I've always thought there was something a little *fourbe* about you.'

'What does "*fourbe*" mean?'

'Look it up when you get home.'

They walked back to his small ground-floor flat – one bedroom with a sitting room, bathroom and kitchenette. The walls were covered with his father's watercolours – still lifes in the main. His father's pastimes were tying flies for fishing – that he sold – and painting.

The Colonel went into the kitchen and returned

with two gins and tonic, one ice cube in each, no slice of lemon. He handed one to Ingram and sat down and fitted a cigarette into a holder and lit it.

'What can I do for you, Ingram?'

'I just came to say hello – see how you were getting along. You know I pop up on a Saturday.'

'You haven't been here for two months. Thank god for Forty.'

'Has Forty been here?'

'He comes up twice a week. He's got some kind of a contract for the gardens.'

'Oh yes, of course.' This was news to Ingram. Forty was his youngest son. 'We've been very busy,' he said, changing the subject. 'Will you come to supper tonight? The whole family will be there. I thought it might—'

'No thanks.'

'I'll send a car, there and back.'

'No thanks – there's a documentary on Channel 4 I want to watch.'

Ingram nodded – at least he'd asked. Meredith would have had a seizure if the Colonel had accepted. He felt the usual cocktail of emotions when confronted by his father: admiration, irritation, affection, frustration, pride, distaste. It astonished him, more often than not, to think this difficult old bastard had sired him. But sometimes all he wanted from his father was a sign of affection – a squeeze of his shoulder, a genuine smile. They sat there sipping their warmish gins

188

and tonic like two strangers in a waiting room, bound only by their blood-line. He thought of his long-dead mother: time had transformed her – a diffident, neurotic woman – into something close to myth, a domestic saint. How he missed her.

'Actually, I wanted to ask your design,' Ingram began, carefully.

'Ask my design?'

'Sorry – advice.'

'Oh, yes?' The Colonel sounded surprised.

'Yes. I think I may be . . .' Ingram paused – suddenly having to articulate this intuition made it seem all the more real. 'I think I may be about to be the victim of a boardroom putsch. I think it'll look like I'm in charge, but I won't be.'

'I don't understand your nasty little world, Ingram – finance, banking, pharmaceuticals. Who are these people plotting against you? Get rid of them. Cut out the cancer.'

'I can't do that, unfortunately.'

'Then be cleverer than they are: second-guess them, pre-empt them, frustrate them.' The Colonel removed his smoked cigarette from his holder and lit up another. 'Get something on them, Ingram. Find a way of hurting them. Get some ammunition.'

Not a bad idea, Ingram thought, wondering if this were possible, if he had enough time . . . Perhaps there *were* things he could do . . .

'Thanks, Pa. I'd better be running along.'

'Finish your gin before you go.'

Ingram drank it down. Sometimes he disliked gin – he thought it made him depressed.

When Ingram arrived home he took down the French dictionary from its shelf in the library and looked up the word '*fourbe*'. Sly, shifty and crafty were the synonyms on offer. Ingram felt a little hurt, for a second or two – who did his father think was paying for Trelawny Gables? His army pension? – and then decided that it must have been the after-effects of his encounter with Rilke that had made him seem preoccupied and thoughtful. True, his brain had been working hard, his words of affection to his father had been token, insincere. Whatever quantities of guile he possessed were being summoned into action, like troops in reserve being called up, expelling his usual cultured, focussed politesse: typical of the Colonel to have sensed this.

He poured himself a large Scotch in his dressing room and drank it before coming downstairs to his birthday party. His three children were already present – Guy, Araminta and Fortunatus – and a stranger, he noticed, someone quickly introduced as Forty's boyfriend, Rodinaldo.

'Have you met him before?' he whispered to Meredith when he had a discreet moment.

'A few times.'

'He seems incredibly young.'

'He's the same age as Forty. They work together.'

Maria-Rosa served his favourite supper: cheese

soufflée, lamb shank with pommes dauphinoises, strawberries with champagne sorbet. The conversation around the table was banal, light-hearted, forgettable. Ingram looked closely at his children, rather in the way his father had looked at him: Guy, thirty years old, handsome, talent-less; Araminta, starveling-thin and, to his eyes, almost visibly twitching with nerves. Perhaps his father's ruthless objectivity was infecting him, but he realised anew, with no particular shock or guilt, that he didn't much like Guy and Minty – he cared for them, but he didn't much like them, to be honest, nor was he much interested in them. Only Fortunatus interested him – squat, muscley Forty, already seriously bald in his early twenties – gay, of all improbable things, the only one of his children who never asked him for anything, the only one he loved and the one who would not return it.

'I saw Gramps today,' Ingram said to him. 'You're working at Trelawny Gables, he said. What a coincidence.'

'He got us the job,' Forty said.

'Really? . . .' This required further thought. 'So, Forty, how's business?'

'Dad, please, it's Nate.'

'I can't call a child of mine "Nate", I'm sorry to say.'

'Then you shouldn't have called me Fortunatus.'

'"Fortunatus Fryzer",' Meredith said, 'it's a wonderful name.'

'It sounds like a medieval alchemist,' Forty/Nate said.

'You *know* why we called you that, darling,' Meredith continued, quietly.

'Yes. Why is so?' Rodinaldo said – his first words of the evening, Ingram realised.

'He nearly died when he was born,' Ingram said, remembering, his throat tightening as if by reflex. 'We thought we'd lost him.'

'And I nearly died too, 'Meredith reminded him, with some ferocity. 'We were both very lucky.'

After dinner, Ingram was drawn aside by Guy, who asked him to invest £50,000 in a classic car business he was starting up.

'What do you mean "classic cars"?'

'We buy them, do them up and sell them at a profit. You know: Citroën DS, Triumph Stag, Ford Mustang, Jensen Interceptor – modern classics, timeless.'

'What do you know about classic cars?'

'A bit – well, not much. Alisdair's the real expert. There's a huge market in these cars, huge.'

'Don't you need a garage, a warehouse?'

'Alisdair's working on that. We just need some seed money – get us going.'

'Been to a bank? They lend people money, you know.'

'They were very unhelpful, really negative.'

Ingram said he would think about it and excused himself and went off to his dressing room to drink more Scotch, he rather wanted to be drunk this evening, semi-lose control, for some reason. On his way back down the stairs Minty was waiting for him on a landing. She said she needed £2,000, cash, tonight.

'No, darling, it's impossible.'

'Then I'll go down to King's Cross and sell myself to someone.'

'Don't be silly and dramatic, you know I hate it.'

She began to cry. 'I owe this person money. I have to pay him tonight.'

Ingram went back up the stairs to his bedroom, opened the safe and returned with £800 and almost $2,000. Minty seemed suddenly calmer.

'Thanks, Daddy,' she said. 'I'd better go. Happy birthday.' She gave him a swift peck on the cheek. 'Don't tell Mummy, please, not a word.'

'Pay me back whenever you can,' he said to her as she trotted down the stairs, with more bitterness in his voice than he meant.

He followed her slowly down to the hall where Forty and Rodinaldo were putting on their jackets and rucksacks, not lingering either.

'Happy birthday, Dad,' Forty said and gave him a hug. For a second Ingram had his arms around his son before he broke free.

'All going well with the gardening?' Ingram asked.

'Yeah, fine.'

'I'd like to invest in it. You know: help you grow. Ha-ha.' Ingram realised he was finally a little drunk – the Scotches and all the wine.

'We're very happy as we are. Small is beautiful.'

Rodinaldo nodded. 'Nate and me, we can to be everything that we wan'.'

'Lucky you,' Ingram said. 'Remember the offer's on the table. New spades, new van, new . . .' He couldn't think what else a gardener might need, for some reason. 'Anyway, I'm here.' He felt drunken tears form in his eyes as he watched his youngest son pulling on some form of camouflage jacket. He wanted to hug him again, kiss him, but he stepped back and raised his hand in casual farewell. Meredith put her arm round his waist and squeezed discreetly. Ah, Ingram thought, just time for a PRO-Vyril.

As they went upstairs to their bedrooms the phone rang.

'I'd better get it,' Ingram said.

It was Burton Keegan.

'It's very late, Burton,' Ingram said, keeping his voice deep and calm.

'We need to meet – tomorrow.'

'Tomorrow's Sunday.'

'The world's still turning, Ingram.'

CHAPTER 18

Bozzy handed over Adam Kindred's mobile phone and his wallet containing his credit cards.

Jonjo fanned them out. 'They're all American – except one.'

'Yeah. We was going to come back to him – get the pin numbers. Zaz kicked him too hard, so we was a bit, you know, emotional. That's why we left him. When we come back – he gone.'

'Stop moving around like that. Getting on my nerves.'

'Sorry, bruv. Flat.' Bozzy tried to hold himself still.

'And don't call me "bruv". I'm not your brother – not in any sense of the word.'

'Safe. Check it, boss.'

Jonjo put the cards and the phone in his pocket and gave Bozzy a couple more twenty-pound notes. From another pocket he drew out a roll of printed copies of Kindred's wanted advertisement and handed them over.

'Go round the estate. Show this to people and ask if they saw him that night.'

Bozzy looked at Kindred's picture.

'That was the mim we jacked, yeah?'

'Yeah. He's wanted for murder. Killed a doctor.'

'*Cunt.*'

'Ask around,' Jonjo said, then looked at the soles of his boots – he had stepped on something moist and sticky. He wiped the mess off on one of the mattresses.

'You want to burn this place,' he said. 'I'm not meeting you here again, got it?'

'Got it, boss.'

'Find him,' Jonjo said. 'Somebody on this estate knows where Kindred is.'

CHAPTER 19

When you have nothing, Adam thought, then everything, the tiniest thing, becomes a problem. In order to begin his begging life he had been obliged to steal – steal a felt-tip pen from a stationery shop. Then on a rectangle of cardboard ripped from an empty wine case outside an off-licence he had written with the stolen felt-tip: 'HUNGRY AND HOMELESS. SPARE A PENNY. BROWN COINS ONLY.'

On his first day he had settled down outside a supermarket on the King's Road. He sat cross-legged on the ground outside the main entrance and propped his sign against his knees. Almost immediately, people began giving him their brown coins, as if relieved to get rid of their annoying small change, the near useless, purse-filling one-and two-pence pieces. Adam was pleased to see how logical his reasoning had been: there is nothing more irritating than heavy pockets and purses full of small-denomination coins. 'Buddy can you spare a dime' had been his inspiration. He took his jacket off and spread it in front of his knees so that potential donors could toss their

197

coins on to its material rather than risk contact with his grubby, black-nailed hand. In thirty minutes he had made £3.27. He filled his own pockets with pennies and tuppences – there was the odd five-pence piece as well – and someone had given him a pound, impressed by the modesty of his need and the politeness of his demand.

Twenty minutes later, when he had crossed the £5 margin, a man came up and squatted beside him. He was young, very lean, thickly bearded like Adam and just as dirty.

'*Mshkin n gsadnka*,' he said, or something that sounded like it.

'I don't understand,' Adam said, 'I only speak English.'

'Fucking off,' the man said and showed Adam the blade of a Stanley knife in the palm of his hand. 'I here. It belong me. I cut you.'

Adam left promptly and walked to Victoria Station where he found a patch of pavement between a cash-point and a souvenir shop. He made another pound or so before the owner of the souvenir shop came out and sprayed him with insecticide.

'Fuck off, you asylum scum,' the man said. And so Adam moved on, his eyes stinging.

He had made £6.13 his first day; he made £6.90 his second. Now, mid-afternoon on his third day of begging – situated between a newsagent's and a small twenty-four-hour supermarket called PROXI-MATE – he had garnered another £5 plus. At this rate, he calculated, say £5 per day, he would make £35 per week, almost £2,000 per year. He was both relieved by this and depressed. It meant he wouldn't starve – he could now afford to buy cheap un-nutritious food, and every now and then go to the Church of John Christ for a proper meal and, of course, sleep rough in the triangle by Chelsea Bridge. But it was early summer – what would he do in December or February? He felt ensnared, already – in a particularly impoverished poverty trap. He saw himself stuck in a barely tolerable circle of hell – underground, yes, undiscovered, yes – but something had to change. How was he going to recover his old life, his old persona? He once had had a wife, a nice, roomy, modern air-conditioned home, a car, a job, a title, a future. This existence he was living now was so marginal it couldn't really be described as human. He was like the London pigeons he saw around him, pecking in the gutter. Even the urban foxes were better off with their warm dens and families.

He went to banks and bureaux de change to change his handfuls of copper coins to brass pounds. The tellers were not happy, though they grudgingly obliged. He ranged further and wider, trying not to revisit banks and bureaux too often so as not to make a nuisance of himself and therefore become memorable.

He paid to have a shower in the executive suite at Victoria Station and washed his hair for the first time in nearly a month. He looked at the gaunt, bearded stranger staring out at him in the mirror, as he combed his hair back from his forehead, and was struck by the strength of the conflicting emotions inside him: fierce pride at his resilience and resourcefulness; bitter self-pity that he should have ended up like this. Yes, I'm free, he thought, but what has become of me?

Clean, in his mismatched pin-striped suit, with newly purchased, fairly shiny, black lace-up shoes (£1 from a thrift shop), he went back to the triangle and collected Mhouse's flip-flops. He wanted ordinary, civil contact with another human being (preferably female). In the last few days hundreds of people had given him tiny sums of money, some had even exchanged kind words, but he was more and more grateful to Mhouse for her suggestion of the Church of John Christ – the church had been his salvation, literally – even in her fury she had somehow been thinking of him, he thought, and he wanted to thank her and keep his promise to return her shoes. She would be surprised, he reckoned – and maybe even touched – that he had honoured it.

He took a bus to Rotherhithe – another small inching up the ladder of civilisation – and stepped out at The Shaft. He wandered around the estate's three quadrangles before he recognised the area where he had been mugged (the graffiti being the aide-mémoire) – he saw the trashed playground and the stairs beneath which he had lain uncon-scious. An old woman, trailing a shopping trolley behind her with a wobbly wheel, came slowly towards him and as she reached him he asked if she knew someone called Mhouse.

'What unit?'

'I don't know.'

'Then I can't help you, darling,' she said, shuffling off.

He wandered deeper into the estate. He felt inconspicuous – a shabby, creased, bearded presence in cast-off clothes, like most of The Shaft's male denizens. Two enquiries later secured Mhouse's address – Flat L, Level 3, Unit 14 – and he climbed the stairs to her walkway, feeling a little nervous and apprehensive, almost as if he were on a date.

He knocked on her door and after a pause heard her voice saying, 'Yeah? Who is it?'

'John 1603,' he said – and of course she opened the door.

He held up the flip-flops.

'Brought them back,' he said.

There were two bedrooms, a bathroom, a kitchen-diner and a living room in Mhouse's flat. There were no carpets or curtains and very little furniture: two mismatched armchairs, some cushions and a TV in the sitting room, two mattresses on the floor in the bedroom she shared with Ly-on. The kitchen had a stove but no fridge. In the other bedroom were some cardboard boxes filled with clothes and random possessions. Most odd,

Adam thought, was the rubber tubing and electric cables that were fed through an empty pane of the casement window in the kitchen. This provided running cold water in the kitchen but not the bathroom. There was electricity in every room, however, wires snaking out from a cuboid structure of stacked adaptors on the kitchen floor. Mhouse brought Adam a cup of very sweet tea – she hadn't asked him if he wanted it sugared.

'Ly-on, you sit on floor,' she said to the little boy who was watching the TV. He moved off his armchair obediently and sat on a winded cushion in front of the screen. He moved slowly, lethargically, as if he'd just been woken up. Adam took his seat and Mhouse sat opposite.

'That's my son,' she said. 'Ly-on.'

'Leon?'

'No, Ly-on. Like in the jungle. Like in lions and tigers.'

'Right.' Adam now remembered her tattoo: 'Mhouse' and 'Ly-on' on the inside of her right forearm. 'Good name for a boy.'

Ly-on was a small boy, almost a tiny boy, with a large, curly-haired head and wide brown eyes.

'Say hello to John.'

'Hello, John. You come mummy to take going?'

'We'll go for a walk tomorrow, darling.'

Adam noticed that although Ly-on was small and in no way fat he had a distinct pot belly, like a beer-drinker's.

'You still in Chelsea, then?' Mhouse asked.

'Moving around a bit,' Adam said, cautiously. Mhouse had been his only visitor to the triangle, as far as he knew.

'How you like the church?'

'I think it's . . . wonderful,' Adam said, with sincerity. 'I go there most nights. Haven't seen you for a while.'

'Yeah. I try to go, but, you know, it's difficult, what with Ly-on.' She scratched her right breast, unselfconsciously. She was wearing a cap-sleeved white T-shirt with 'SUPERMOM!' across the front and cropped pale-blue denim jeans. She curled herself up in the armchair and tucked her feet under her. She was also small, Adam realised, a tiny child-woman – maybe that was why Ly-on was so small himself.

He looked down at him and saw the boy was now stretched out on the floor as if he was about to go to sleep.

'You get to your bed, sweetness,' Mhouse said and the little boy rose slowly to his feet and weaved off to the bedroom. 'He's just had his supper,' she said. 'He's tired. And I've got to get off me bum and get working. No, no, you stay there. Finish your tea. I'll just go and get changed.'

Adam sipped his too-sweet tea and channel-hopped on the remote control. She seemed to have an interminable number of channels on her TV. When she came out she was wearing white shiny plastic zip-up boots, a mini-skirt and a red-and-black, tight satin bustier that pushed her small breasts up above the lace trim like round balls. Her make-up was vivid: red lips and black eyes.

'Going to a party,' she said. 'On a boat on the river.'

'Fabulous,' Adam said. 'You look great.'

She looked at him sideways, quizzically. 'Are you joking me?'

'No, seriously. You look great.'

'Thanking you, kind sir,' she said, rummaging in her handbag for keys. Adam looked at her hard cleavage and smelt the pungent chemicals of her scent, finding her suddenly extremely sexually desirable – recognising the simple efficiency of her outfit and the messages it was designed to send to people – to men. There was something impish, elvish about her – if you could imagine a sexually alluring imp, Adam thought – and her thin, hooded eyes added to this otherworldly effect.

She paused at the door. 'You signing on?'

'Ah, not yet,' Adam said. 'But I am making a bit of money, these days.'

'Tugging?'

'What?'

'On the game. Selling your arse?'

'No, begging.'

She thought, frowning. 'I got a spare room here, you know. If you want. Twenty a week. Seeing as we go to the same church, like.'

'Thanks, but I'm fine for the moment. It's a bit pricey for me, to tell the truth.'

'You can owe me.'

'Better not. Thanks all the same.'

'Suit yourself.' She opened the door for them both. 'Thanks for bringing back the flip-flops. That's kind, that is, that's well nice.'

'It was kind and nice of you to lend them to me. And to tell me about the church. I don't know what I would have done, otherwise.'

'Yeah, well . . . What's being a Samaritan for, eh?' They stepped out on to the walkway and she closed and locked the door.

'Will Ly-on be all right?' Adam asked, unconcernedly, he hoped.

'Yeah, he'll sleep to tomorrow lunchtime if I let him.'

They walked through The Shaft and then on to Canada Water Tube station. 'See you, John, god bless,' she said when they parted and she headed off to find her platform. Adam watched men turn to look at her pass by, saw their eyes swivel and their nostrils flare. He thought he'd pop into the Church of John Christ – he was feeling hungry.

'Soon I getting passport,' Vladimir said. 'When I getting passport, I getting job. I getting job then I getting apartment. I getting bank account. I getting credit card, I getting overdraft facility. No more problem for me.'

Adam listened to him almost as if Vladimir were a traveller returned from a distant, fabled land – a low-rent Marco Polo – telling of unimaginable wonders, of lifestyles and possibilities that seemed fantastical, forever beyond his reach. That he had once been a homeowner himself seemed laughable; that he'd had a wallet full of credit cards and several healthy bank accounts an intoxicated dream. He bowed his head and spooned a mouthful of chilli con carne into his mouth and chewed thoughtfully, thinking back. He was sitting at his usual table, Gavin Thrale also present, but no sign of Turpin.

'Where will you "getting" this passport?' Thrale asked, offhandedly.

Vladimir then began a complicated story about drug addicts and drug dens in European Community countries – Spain, Italy, Germany, Holland – where, if an addict looked close to death, on his or her last legs, he or she was encouraged by 'gangster people' to apply for a passport. When the addict eventually died, the passport was then sold on to someone in the same age-range who vaguely resembled the deceased junkie. No forgery was involved, that was the benefit, that was the absolute beauty of the scam: they were impossible to detect.

Thrale looked highly sceptical. 'How much do these passports cost?'

'One thousand euro,' Vladimir said.

Adam remembered he had once had a passport but he had left it in Grafton Lodge when he went for his interview. No doubt it had been impounded with the rest of his belongings.

'So,' Thrale continued, obviously intrigued.

'You get one of these passports but you might have to pass yourself off as . . . as a Dane, a Spaniard, a Czech—'

'Is no matter, Gavin,' Vladimir said, insistently. 'Most important thing is passport of European Community – we all the same now. Is no matter what country.'

'When do you get it?' Adam asked.

'Tomorrow, next day.'

'So you won't be back here again.'

'Absolutely no!' Vladimir laughed. 'I get pass-port, I get job, I finish with church. I was to training for *kiné*, you know.'

'Physiotherapist,' Adam added for Thrale's benefit.

'Of course. That was when your village in Ukraine collected all that money and sent you here for a heart bypass.'

'Not Ukraine, Gavin. Not bypass, new heart valve.'

Adam finished his chilli con carne – the serv-ings in the Church of John Christ were copious. Bishop Yemi's sermon that evening had lasted two and a half hours, expatiating further on this concept of John Christ as the leader of a small cell of freedom fighters struggling to liberate their people from the oppression of the Roman Empire. Jesus – loyal lieutenant – had sacrificed himself for John in order that the leader could disappear and the struggle continue. It was all there in the Book of Revelation if you knew how to decipher it.

Then he had dozed off for a while – only the hungriest could sit the sermons out with full concentration.

'Anyone see Turpin?' Vladimir asked.

'Probably loitering by some nursery school playground,' Thrale said.

Bishop Yemi appeared at this moment and beamed down at his Johns.

'How's life, guys?' he said, his smile unwavering, clearly indifferent to their reply.

'Fine, thank you,' Adam said. He felt a strange warmth towards Bishop Yemi: the man and his organisation had clothed and fed him after all.

Bishop Yemi spread his hands. 'The love of John Christ go with you, my brothers,' he said, and wandered off to the next table. The congregation had been sparse tonight, barely into double figures.

'Why does the word "bogus" suddenly come to mind?' Thrale said.

'No – he a good man, Bishop Yemi,' Vladimir said, standing. He looked at Adam and made a smoking gesture. 'Adam, you want come? I have monkey.'

'Ah, no thanks, not tonight,' Adam said. Vladimir routinely asked him to go and smoke monkey after their evening meal – he must like me, I suppose, Adam thought – and Adam routinely declined.

Later, at the church door, Adam and Thrale stood together for a second, both of them looking up at the evening sky. There were a few fine clouds, tinged with an apricot glow.

'Cirrus fibratus,' Adam said without thinking. 'Change in the weather coming.'

Thrale looked at him, curiously. 'How on earth do you know that?' he said, intrigued.

'Just a hobby,' Adam said quickly, but he felt his face colouring. Fool, he thought. 'Some book I read once ...'

'How come people like you and me end up here?' Thrale said. 'Hiding behind our beards and long hair.'

'I told you: I had a series of nervous break—'

'Yes, yes, of course. Come off it. We're both highly educated. Intellectuals. It's obvious every time we open our mouths – we might as well have "BRAINS" tattooed across our foreheads.'

'That's all very well,' Adam persisted. 'But I cracked up. Everything fell apart. Lost my wife, my job. I was in hospital for months ...' He paused. He almost believed it himself, now. 'I'm just trying to put my life back together, bit by bit, slowly but surely.'

'Yeah,' Thrale said sceptically. 'Aren't we all.'

'What about you?' Adam said, keen to change the subject.

'I'm a novelist,' Thrale said.

'Really?'

'I've written many novels – a dozen or so – but only one has been published.'

'Which was?'

'*The Hydrangea House.*'

'I don't rememb—'

209

'You wouldn't. It – I – was published by a small press: Idomeneo Editore. In Capri.'

'Capri? In Italy?'

'The last I heard.'

'Right,' Adam said. 'At least you were published. No small achievement. To hold a book you've written in your hand, your name on the cover: *The Hydrangea House* by Gavin Thrale. Great feeling, I would have thought.'

'Except I was writing under a pseudonym,' Thrale said. 'Irena Primavera. Not quite the same frisson.'

'Was it in English?'

'It wasn't called *La Casa dell'Ortensia*.'

'Got you. Are you writing another?'

They had wandered away from the church and were heading up Jamaica Road.

'I am, since you ask. It's called *The Masturbator*. Somehow I doubt it'll find a publisher.'

'Hasn't that been done already? *Portnoy's*—'

'My novel will make *Portnoy's Complaint* read like *Winnie the Pooh*,' Thrale said with some steel in his voice.

'But,' Adam said, 'if you're a published novelist, what are you doing at the Church of John Christ?'

'Same as you,' Thrale said, meaningfully. 'Lying low.'

Both of them went silent for a while. Adam paused to remove a sticky coin of chewing gum from the sole of his right shoe. Thrale waited for him.

'I used to make a fair living for years,' Thrale said, musingly, 'stealing rare books from libraries. Maps,

210

illustrations. All over Europe – posing as a scholar. Some of them extremely rare. Then I was caught and had to pay my debt to society.'

'Ah.' Adam stood up.

'My big mistake, once I was released, was to think I could bamboozle the ladies and the gentlemen of the DHSS – or is it the DWP now? Whoever. Anyway, I was signing on, but simultaneously working at various menial jobs. Somebody "shopped" me, I was spied upon – it's a nasty world out there, Adam – and my benefits were stopped. I am being searched for – charged with fraud. I don't intend going back to prison.'

'Hence—'

'Hence my enthusiasm for Bishop Yemi's fascinating conspiracy theory.'

They had arrived at Adam's bus stop.

'See you tomorrow,' Adam said.

'How are you getting by?'

'Begging.'

'Oh dear. Desperation.'

'What about you?'

'I've taken up my old trade. I steal books – to order, for students.' He frowned. 'I just mustn't get caught again.' His frown turned into a fake smile. 'I go this way. I live in a squat in Shoreditch with an intriguing mix of young people.'

Adam watched him saunter off, then he searched his pockets to see how much money he had left. It was a fine evening: he might as well walk home to Chelsea – save a few pennies.

CHAPTER 20

The Burberry trenchcoat lay on the cracked concrete of The Shaft's no. 2 underground car park. Mohammed stood looking down at it, concernedly.

'Don't get him dirty,' Mohammed said.

Bozzy picked it up and placed it on a gleaming oil spill and then stamped and ground the trenchcoat into the muck with the heels of his shoes. Then he tried to set it on fire with his lighter.

'All right, all right,' Jonjo said. 'Take it easy.'

Small flames burned palely on the familiar tartan lining of the trench.

'Fucking kill you!' Mohammed screamed at Bozzy.

'You already dead!' Bozzy screamed back. 'How you going to kill me? Suicide bomb?'

'SHUT THE FUCK UP!' Jonjo bellowed – and everyone calmed down.

Jonjo approached Mohammed, who flinched away from him.

'I'm not going to hurt you,' Jonjo said. 'Not yet, anyway . . . How did you get that coat?'

'Like I tell Boz,' Mohammed said. 'Three, four

212

weeks ago – I got minicab, right? I minicab driver, yeah? – it was late, I was just going down to the clubs, yeah? Then I sees this geezer, I thought he was pranged – but I see he got cut on his head, yeah?' Mohammed went on to tell his story: how this geezer said he lived in Chelsea and he needed to get back there, and Mohammed, liking the idea of a long journey and a big fare, told this geezer to step aboard. But, when they got to Chelsea, the geezer said he had no money, so he offered his raincoat instead as payment. Mohammed had been very happy to accept it.

'We drove to Chelsea, like. When he says he has to get his raincoat we was a bit suspicious – him being in the waste ground – thought he might be jerking us, thought he might do a runner. But he come back with it and I could see, like, it was a Blueberry raincoat. Class, man, no worries. One hundred quid, easy.'

Bozzy stepped forward and pointed his finger at the small space between Mohammed's lush eyebrows.

'Lying cunt.' He turned to Jonjo. 'We stripped the mim. He don't have nothing left but a shirt and his knickers.'

'He had cloves on, man. I don't take no naked man in my cab.'

'Lying cunt!'

Jonjo punched Bozzy extremely hard on his shoulder. Bozzy gave a sharp wheeze of pain and backed off, his arm dangling limp, dead.

213

'So you dropped him in Chelsea,' Jonjo said to Mohammed. 'At a house?'

'Nah. He was sleeping rabbit, next by a bridge.'

Now Jonjo grabbed Mohammed by his throat and lifted him off the ground, his toes just able to touch the stained concrete. Mohammed's hands gripped Jonjo's iron wrist, desperately seeking purchase.

'Don't lie to me, Mo.'

'I swear, boss,' he whispered, eyes bulging.

'Torture him,' Bozzy said.

Jonjo let Mohammed down. He coughed, raked his throat and spat.

'I drop him off. He go into this bit of like waste ground. He come out with coat and give it me.'

Jonjo felt a warmth spread through him. A patch of waste ground by a Thames-side bridge in Chelsea: Battersea Bridge, Albert Bridge or Chelsea Bridge – had to be one of those. Living rough, hiding out – no wonder Kindred had been so hard to find. He looked at Mohammed, still spitting as if he had a fish bone in his throat.

'So he was sleeping rough by a bridge, was he? . . .' Jonjo said, benevolence making his voice go ever so slightly husky. He wasn't going to hurt Mohammed any more. He didn't need to. 'Now, you tell me exactly what bridge you're talking about.'

Jonjo parked his cab in a small square and walked the half-mile back to Chelsea Bridge. He stood

214

for a while at the railings surrounding the thin triangle of overgrown waste ground, checking to see if there was any movement, any sign of somebody hiding. When he was sure there was no one there he waited for the traffic on the Embankment to slacken and then vaulted over the iron railings. He roved through the triangle quickly – it was bigger than it appeared from the road, and along the bridge side there was a huge old fig tree, of all things. Approaching the triangle's apex, moving away from the bridge, Jonjo found the undergrowth grew even thicker. He ducked under low branches and pushed through dense bushes and shrubs to find a small clearing. Three tyres were set on top of each other forming a rudimentary seat; under a bush he found a sleeping bag and a groundsheet; under another an orange box with a gas stove, saucepan, a bar of soap and three empty baked bean tins.

Jonjo prowled around a little further. Good cover from the road and the traffic on the bridge. The grass was bruised and trampled flat – someone had been living here for quite a while. He found an entrenching tool: there was no litter, faeces were presumably buried – quite impressive. He looked skywards, nearly dark, the light bulbs on Chelsea Bridge were glowing brightly against the purple-blue of the evening sky.

He checked the clips in both his guns and found himself a snug hiding place, a few yards from Kindred's clearing. Kindred would be coming back in an hour or so – or whenever. He didn't care how long he had to wait: sometimes in the regiment he'd hidden up for two weeks to slot someone. Kindred could take as long as he liked: now that he had found his secret home the Kindred chapter in Jonjo Case's life was about to be concluded – with extreme prejudice.

CHAPTER 21

London's vast size always surprised him – cowed him, almost – Adam realised, even though he'd tramped its streets endlessly these past weeks. To walk from the Church of John Christ in Rotherhithe to Chelsea Bridge took him well over an hour and a half, and yet on a map he would have covered no distance at all of the city's great sprawling mass – a tiny, meandering trajectory, crossing the boundaries of a few boroughs: Bermondsey, Southwark, Lambeth, Pimlico, Chelsea. True, he'd stopped to buy himself a cup of coffee and a bottle of water and an apple for his breakfast but he was feeling footsore as he arrived at the Battersea end of Chelsea Bridge, glad to see its glowing chains of light bulbs, noting that the tide was ebbing, traces of his beach beginning to appear. Perhaps he might have a midnight bathe, he wondered: shirt off, sluice a bit of chill Thames water over the upper torso – maybe even heat up a saucepan of water and wash his hair.

He crossed the bridge and turned left just in time to see four policemen, all wearing stab-vests, unlock the main gate to the triangle and go inside. He ran across the Embankment and waited, half hidden by the war memorial on the corner of Chelsea Bridge Road, watching and waiting – nerves on edge, suddenly alarmed, very alarmed. Nothing seemed to be happening. He looked at a non-existent watch on his wrist and paced to and fro a bit, as if he were killing time, for the benefit of anyone who might have been interested in his presence there – he could have been waiting for someone to come out of the Lister Hospital opposite – and needlessly re-tied both his shoelaces. Then, about ten minutes after the police had gone into the triangle, he saw the four of them emerge with a fifth man, a big guy, handcuffed.

He saw one of the policemen calling for support on his personal radio and about two minutes later two police cars – sirens going, blue lights flashing – pulled up outside the triangle and the fifth man was pushed inside one of them. Conveniently, the police car was under a street light and Adam was no more than fifty feet away so could see quite clearly. Just before he was bent into the back seat of the police car, the big guy paused and seemed to say something to one of the policemen.

With a spasm of pure surprise Adam recognised him. He felt his body lurch as the shock of familiarity hit him. The weak, cleft chin, the crew cut, the blunt features – this was the man he had knocked unconscious with his briefcase the night of Wang's murder.

The police car whooped off, one of the policemen stepped into the other car and it sped away, following. The three policemen left behind high-fived each other and clapped each other on the back before walking away down the Embankment. Adam watched them saunter off, following them discreetly a little way and saw them go through a gate in the Embankment wall and down some steps on to the river. Minutes later a patrol boat pulled away and sped downstream.

Questions yammered in Adam's brain. What was the big guy doing in the triangle? Waiting for him to come back? Jesus Christ . . . How had he known about the triangle? What were the police doing there? Why had the police arrested him? Had there been some new lead in the Wang case? Was this arrest going to vindicate him, finally? Question tumbled after question, a small slithering avalanche of questions. He felt quite weak, all of a sudden, and he realised at once that he couldn't stay in the triangle any more – the triangle days were over. He had to find somewhere else to hide.

Adam knocked on Mhouse's door: it was very late, about 3.00 a.m. and this was the seventh or eighth time he'd called back to see if she had returned from her boat-party on the river. He'd kept to the shadows, avoiding the few people around: The Shaft at night, as he knew all too well, was not a welcoming place. He saw a light go on behind the door.

'Who the fuck is that?'

'Mhouse? It's me – John 1603. I've changed my mind. I'd like to stay in the spare room.'

219

CHAPTER 22

The Targa cruised into the new steel jetty at Phoenix Stairs and Rita sprang ashore and figure-eighted the mooring rope around the big cleat on the jetty edge. Joey threw her the stern rope and she secured it. It had been a quiet day on the river. They had taken a diver from the Underwater Search Team down to a wharf in Deptford to investigate a potential submerged dead body – but it turned out to be three weighted sacks of rubbish. Then they'd intercepted a barge coming down river from Twickenham with inadequate paper work and passed on the details to the Thames Harbourmaster's office. Finally they had checked in with the RNLI station at Lifeboat Pier on the Victoria Embankment, collected the inflatable pathway they had borrowed and had a cup of tea. Almost a pleasure cruise, she thought: sunny day, out on the water, what could be nicer? She asked Joey if he could go to the end-of-day debriefing as she wanted an urgent word with Sergeant Rollins.

'Any news, Sarge?' she said, when she found him in his tiny office in Portakabin 3, next to the

humming, refrigerated mortuary in Portakabin 4.
You could hear the unit through the wall: she
wouldn't like her office next to a morgue, that's
for sure. She was trying to seem merely casually
interested, trying to keep the eagerness out of her
voice.

'Yeah. They let him go.'

'*What?*'

Rollins shrugged, spread his hands. 'That's all I
know. Kept him in overnight. Home free in the
morning.'

'Let him go? No charge?' Rita felt a strange
shock in her, an emptiness: this was the last thing
she expected.

'You'll have to go up Chelsea, Nashe. Find out
what happened. You're no longer required as
arresting officer. There is no case.'

'He was carrying, for god's sake. Two weapons
and a six-inch blade. No ID. What's going on?'

'An open-and-shut, I'd've thought, but there you
go. There must be a reason.' He smiled fondly at
her. 'You'll just have to arrest somebody else now,
darling.'

'Please don't call me "darling", sergeant.'

When she went off duty, Rita took the Tube up
to Chelsea police station to find out if she could
discover any answers. Sergeant Duke wasn't on
that night but she saw Gary going down a corridor,
called and went after him.

'Hey, Rita,' he said, looking her up and down.

221

'You all right? Looking lovely, as per. Great party, by the way.'

'What're you doing here?'

'Just popped up from Belgravia. Paper work.'

She looked around, making sure no one could overhear. 'We called in last night. Guy we arrested at Chelsea Bridge – two guns on him, no ident, wouldn't talk, not a word. I came up here with him myself, filled in the IRB, then we handed him over to CID. Job done. Now, I just heard they let him go. What the fuck's going on? Any idea?'

Gary looked up and down the corridor. 'Yeah, I heard . . .' He tapped the side of his nose. 'It was one of those calls, you know.'

'No, I don't know.'

He lowered his voice. 'Someone very high up in the Met rings up: "Let this bloke go now – I take full responsibility." That kind of number.'

'What's that meant to mean?'

'Some sort of covert surveillance thing you surprised. MI5. Anti-terrorist. I don't know. He's obviously well connected, your Chelsea Bridge bloke.'

'I'm not going to let this go.'

'OK – See that wall there? Just bash your head against it for an hour or two. You'll get the picture. Leave it, Rita – it's way, way over our pay-scale.'

She paced up and down the corridor, thinking.

'I miss you, Rita.'

'Tough.'

'I was a fool. Tosser. I admit it.'

'Too late, Gary.'

'We could have a drink, couldn't we?'

They went to a bar near the station – a pseudo-Spanish tapas place but with nice music. Gary continued his pleas to be forgiven and she half listened, still troubled by what had taken place, still angry in an unfocussed way, thinking back to what had happened the night before in that patch of waste ground by the bridge.

She'd gone straight to the clearing and had started searching, Joey and the other two shining torches here and there, when this man had reared up from behind a bush, giving her a shock, his hands raised above his head. 'You got me,' was all he said. She searched him, found the weapons, arrested him and officially cautioned him, cuffed him and called the Chelsea boys for a couple of area cars. The man never said anything more, had no ID on him, wouldn't give his name, was very calm. When she had pushed him into the back of the car he had turned to her suddenly as if he was about to say something before clearly stopping himself. Their faces had been close. Big, ugly bloke, weak chin with a deep cleft in it. Gary was still talking.

'Sorry, I was miles away,' she said. 'So, what's new? Any more Chelsea murders?'

'Not since your last rumble.'

'How's it going?'

'About to close it down, I reckon – nothing, *nada*.

Still got a murder room in Belgravia. Just a couple of DCs, a file and a phone line. For form's sake, you know.'

'No sign of Kindred?'

He shrugged. 'Kindred is either dead or being sheltered by friends and family.'

'I thought he had no friends or family in this country.'

'I reckon he topped himself.' Gary reached into his jacket pocket for a cigarette, then put the box back in his pocket, remembering he couldn't smoke in pubs any more.

'You put out a reward like that,' he said, 'that big – a hundred grand – you get a thousand calls. I think we got twenty-seven – all nutters. Then it dried up completely – he must be dead.'

'Or gone abroad,' she said. 'Fled the country.'

He wasn't interested, she could see. He reached for her hand. 'I'd like to see you again, Rita. I miss you.'

Rita climbed up the gangway to the *Bellerophon*, deliberately stamping her feet, and saw the glowing end of her father's joint arc out from the stern into the water. He had a can of Speyhawk in his hand.

'Hi, Dad – nice and mellow?'

'I've been mellower, but I'm not complaining. Ernesto's down below – you're late.'

They had supper together – pizza, salad, apple pie – a monthly date that Rita insisted on and that they mostly kept. Once a month, she said, they should meet as a family and have a meal, share food and wine. She and Ernesto never talked about their mother, Jayne – Jeff's ex-wife – now living, as far as any of them knew, in Saskatchewan, Canada, re-married, to an unknown man, but Rita liked to think that the very fact that the rest of the Nashe family gathered together like this meant she was a ghostly presence – their pointed not-mentioning her making her all the more there, somehow. Rita wrote her a letter from time to time but she never replied – but she knew that Ernesto always received a card on his birthday and an occasional telephone call. But nothing for Rita, though, because Rita had chosen Jeff – Ernesto had been too young so he was forgiven. It was all misunderstandings and bad feel-ings and it made her sad if she thought about it too much: still, at least here the three of them were, having a meal.

'Busy, Ernesto?' Jeff Nashe asked his son.

'I could work fourteen days a week,' Ernesto said. He was a small, burly young man, two years younger than Rita. He looked like Jayne, Rita thought. He disguised his intense shyness under a badly assumed air of untroubled placidity.

'How's the crane business going?' Jeff asked. 'Soaring? Overarching?'

'When they're building they need cranes. When they stop building we're in trouble.'

Rita could see her father's effort to feign interest. Ernesto was a tower-crane operator – he earned three times her salary.

'I arrested a man last night,' she said, keen to change the subject. 'Down by Chelsea Bridge. He had two automatic pistols on him and a knife.'

Jeff Nashe turned his semi-befuddled gaze on her, eyes widening. 'Are you armed-police, now?' he asked, accusingly. 'The day you carry a weapon is the day you leave the *Bellerophon*.'

She ignored his idle threat. 'He surrendered to me,' she said. 'Me and my fellow officers.'

'You want to be careful,' Ernesto said. 'Bloody hell, what's it all coming to, eh? Jesus.'

'London's been a violent city since it was founded,' Jeff said. 'Why should we be surprised that anything's changed.'

Fair enough, Rita thought, but, today, when we arrest a man carrying two unlicensed weapons on him we don't let him go twenty-four hours later. She thought she shouldn't just turn a blind eye and walk away – she really ought to do something about this.

CHAPTER 23

D arren brought their pints over and set them down on the table. They were in a large, loud bar off Leicester Square – the place was full of foreigners, all chatting away in their incomprehensible foreign languages, Jonjo thought, looking around him. Even the bar staff were foreign. He, Darren and this other bloke who'd been introduced as 'Bob' seemed to be the only true-blue English present. This Bob was another soldier, Jonjo had recognised instantly, though of higher rank – an officer, a 'Rupert' – but a Rupert who had seen some nasty business: two fingers were missing on his left hand and he had a fairly recent, wealed, crescent-shaped scar four inches long on his jaw.

'Cheers, dears,' Jonjo said and glugged three big mouthfuls of fizzy beer. He was in for a bollocking, or worse – might as well enjoy the free drink.

'You fucked up, Jonjo,' Bob said quietly, when he'd set his glass down. 'Big time. Do you know what we had to do to get you out? Any idea who we had to call? The special favours we had to ask of very important people? What favours we now owe?'

Jonjo didn't really care. Darren had told him he had every resource available so when he'd been arrested he made the call. What else was he meant to do? He smiled emptily back at 'Bob' and measured an inch of air between his thumb and forefinger. 'I was that close,' he said. 'I'd tracked Kindred down. I had him. Until that fucking police-woman showed up.'

'Malign fate,' Bob said. 'The one thing you can't calculate for.'

'Yeah, whatever.'

Darren said nothing, concentrating on drinking his beer – the message-boy.

'Trouble is,' Bob went on, 'now we can't even tell the police you almost had him. That would tie us in to the Wang hit – so we're taking it in every orifice.'

Jonjo ignored him. The worst was over. 'I know what Kindred's doing,' he said calmly, evenly, sitting back in his chair. 'I figured it out while I was waiting for him. He's been living there, by that bridge, for weeks . . . Just lying low. He's not stupid: he doesn't do anything, so there's no trail. No cheques, no bills, no references, no mobile phone calls – only payphones – no credit cards, only cash – nothing. That's how you disappear in the twenty-first century – you just refuse to take part in it. You live like a medieval peasant: you scrounge, you steal, you sleep under hedges. That's why no one could find him – not even the whole fucking Metropolitan Police murder squad.

He could be showing up on 300 CCTV cameras a day but we don't know. We don't even know what he looks like any more, we don't know where he goes, what he does. He's just a man walking on a city street. Big deal. Free as a bird.'

Jonjo paused, a little taken aback at his own eloquence. He decided that continued unapologetic belligerence was his best defence.

'But,' he said, 'but I found him. Me – Jonjo Case. I tracked him down. Not the police. Not your hundred grand reward advert. I had him – but fucking bad luck got in the way. So don't give me no bullshit about having to call in favours.' He measured his airy inch with his two fingers again. 'Nobody else got within a country mile.'

'You may well have a point,' Bob said. 'But one thing's for sure now – he's well and truly gone.'

'I'll get him, don't you worry,' Jonjo said, with more confidence than he felt. 'I got leads now – just give me a bit of time.'

'The one commodity we don't have in large supply, Mr Case,' Rupert-Bob said, his voice heavy with cynicism. Jonjo surmised that he'd been a smart-arsed sergeant with a clever tongue who'd been promoted. It made him relax a bit: he knew what these guys were like, knew their deep insecurities. He'd wager the accent was fake too – there was something Scouse, something North about him – the Wirral, Cheshire . . .

'That's not my problem, mate,' Jonjo said, fixing him with dead eyes.

229

'Yes, it fucking is. Time is short. You don't have much time. Got it?' He stood up. 'Come on, Darren.'

Darren drained his pint and gave Jonjo a wink round the side of his upended glass. What's that meant to mean? Jonjo wondered. He saw Bob hit his mobile as he left the pub – calling in, reporting back on the Jonjo Case meeting. Who could he be calling, Jonjo asked himself, who was higher up this chain? . . .

He wandered over to the bar, feeling disgruntled, put-upon, undervalued, and ordered another pint from a girl called Carmencita. What are they getting so excited about? he pondered as he stood there, sipping his beer. They now knew Kindred was alive and living somewhere in London. It was, in the end, as he had said, purely a matter of time. Time was Kindred's enemy. Time was Jonjo's friend, time was on Jonjo's side.

CHAPTER 24

'The sun is in the sky.'

'The sun is in the sky.'

Adam rearranged the big letters and spelt them out for Ly-on.

'The sky is blue.'

'The sky is blue.'

'Now you do it – do "The sun is in the sky" again.'

Ly-on began to shift the letters around to spell out the new words. Mhouse sat in her chair watching the two of them sitting on the floor in front of the TV – which wasn't on, she realised: that was what was odd – no TV. She liked the idea of John 1603 teaching Ly-on to read – it was important, reading and writing, and she wished she could read better than she did – she didn't need writing so much, but she had no time to spare.

'I'm go down shops,' she said. John looked up and smiled.

'What going to get Ly-on present?' Ly-on said.

'You just stick to your . . .' she couldn't think of the word. 'You just do what John tells you.'

She went into her room, took her leather jacket

out of the wardrobe and slipped it on. She liked having a man in the flat, even if he was just a lodger. Brought in extra cash too – three weeks now, sixty quid. She liked coming in from work, finding John and Ly-on at their . . . studying, that was the word. They was studying hard and Ly-on looked like he could nearly read. And Ly-on liked him, even better. Nice man, John 1603.

She walked through The Shaft, heading for the high street, saying hello to the few people she recognised. She *was* in a good mood, she realised, smiling to herself. There was some sun today, as well – 'The sun is in the sky', how hard was that? She could read that. 'The sky is blue today,' she said out loud, seeing the letters in her head, sort of – she could write that, almost. Just needed a helping hand from John and she'd—

'Hoi, Mhouse!'

She looked round. Mohammed sat in his Primera at the kerb, passenger door open. He beckoned her over and she stepped inside.

'Not seen you for ages, Mo. Been away?'

'Up north, seeing my cousins.'

'That's nice. Y'all right?'

'No. Not fucking all right. No way. I was keeping me head down.' Mohammed told her about his encounter with Bozzy and this other geezer in the car park, a ten-ton heavy, he said, fucking scary.

'Jeez,' she said. 'What's it all about?'

'They was asking questions about that night you and me took that mim to Chelsea.'

Mhouse felt a little creep of dread inch up the nape of her neck.

'So who was this heavy guy? Friend of Bozzy?'

'Nah. He wallop Bozzy. I don't know – I never seen him before. Thing was, I keep you out of it, Mhouse. I never say you name.'

'Thanks, Mo. That was good. I owe you.'

'That's the point, Mhouse. You do owe me – one raincoat. Fucking Bozzy stamps it in a oil, then he sets light it.' Mohammed's face registered his profound loss. 'My Blueberry raincoat – he set it on fire.'

Mhouse rummaged in her handbag and gave him a £10 note.

'It worth a hundred quid, Mhouse, easy. And I keep you name out of it.'

'I ain't got a hundred, Mo.'

'I'm well short, Mhouse. Couldn't work up north, could I? Need a hundred. Quick, like.'

'I can't give it you this week. What about next month? I have to pay Mr Q tomorrow.'

'What am I meant to do, Mhouse? I skint – my pockets is hungry. Maybe Bozzy give me some—'

'I'll get it for you next week.'

'Monday.'

'Monday. No prob.'

She stepped out of the car, shivering slightly, conscious of how lucky she had been. Mohammed wasn't lying because otherwise Bozzy and his crew would have come calling. Best to pay Mo his hundred, keep him happy. John 1603 was making a difference but it would take five weeks of rent to pay back Mohammed and she owed Mr Quality and she owed Margo – almost everything she made on the shore was going to them . . .

She walked down Jamaica Road in thoughtful mood. She could deal with Bozzy and his junkie pals – Mr Q would see them off – but who was this new bloke, the 'ten-ton heavy'? What did he have to do with anything? They must be looking for John 1603 – so maybe she should kick him out. Then she thought: he's been staying with me for three weeks – they don't know where he is or what he looks like, obviously. So why should she kick him out? – he brought in money, he bought food and drink, he was teaching Ly-on to read and Ly-on liked him. Fuck it – pay Mo his hundred, somehow, and that would be that.

At the check-out desk in PROXI-MATE she found Mrs Darling in front of her.

'Hello, love,' Mrs Darling said. 'You don't half eat a lot of bananas. Not in pod, are you?'

'No. No, it's Ly-on. It's all he wants. Mashed banana, please, Mum. Morning, night—'

'Little monkey, eh? Not seen much of him, lately. Don't need no babysitting, then?'

'I got this lodger now. From the church. John 1603.'

'John 1603? . . .'

'He's teaching Ly-on to read.' Mhouse stacked her goods on the rubber conveyor belt: rum, sugar,

234

bananas, white bread, milk, biscuits, crisps, chocolate, forty Mayfair Thins.

'Is that the bloke with the beard?' Mrs Darling asked. 'I seen him around.'

'That's him. "Blackbeard", I call him.'

'Yeah. And I seen him down the church. Must be nice for little Ly-on.'

'Yeah. They get on real good.'

'He's at church most nights.'

'Who? John?'

'Bishop Yemi's got his eye on him. He's devout.'

'What?'

'He *believes*. A true believer, and Bishop Yemi thinks he's well clever, also.'

'Oh, he's clever, all right. Clever-clogs.'

Mhouse paid for her provisions and bagged them up, amazed as ever at how much everything cost. That was her cleaned out again and John had already paid her this week in advance. How was she meant to find Mohammed's hundred when she was spending like there was no tomorrow?

That night Mhouse tapped on John's door – it was late, just gone midnight – tapped on his door, gently, with her fingernails. Ly-on was asleep, she'd given him an extra half Somnola at supper. She heard John say 'come in' and she pushed the door open.

'It's just me,' she said, needlessly, as he switched the light on. The mattress was in the middle of the room, surrounded by her cardboard boxes. John had bought a small lamp so he could read in bed.

'What is it?' he said, looking at her a little blearily. 'Everything OK?'

'I was a bit lonely,' she said, and pulled off her long T-shirt. 'Mind if I pop in beside you?'

She didn't wait for his answer, flipping back the blanket and sliding in beside him. He was naked – good. She put her arms around him and snuggled up against him. 'Lovely and warm,' she said. 'Warm like toast.' She kissed his chest. 'I was feeling a bit lonely.'

'Mhouse,' he said. 'Please. This is a bad idea. What about Ly-on?'

'Spark out,' she said, reaching down and finding him hardening fast. 'Somebody thinks it's a good idea.'

She found his mouth with hers and their tongues touched, she felt his hands on her breasts. He was trembling.

'Just one thing, John,' she said. 'Before we go any further. It's forty pounds, normal. But for you – twenty. And you don't need no condom.'

'All right,' he said, a kind of gasp in his voice. 'Yeah, anything.'

'Deal?'

'Deal.'

CHAPTER 25

There was a dark spot on his crisp, white, usually immaculate pillowcase. No – in fact there were two spots. Two dark red spots a little larger than pinheads. Ingram held his pillow up to the light. Blood. Two tiny spots of blood. Must have nicked myself shaving last night before dinner, he thought, fingertips caressing his jawline. Must have somehow rubbed the scabs off in the night. Anyway, no matter, he said to himself, rolling out of bed. He stepped out of his pyjamas and went for his power-shower.

Post-shower, in his dressing gown, he inspected his face in his shaving mirror but could see no tiny scab, nick or razor burn anywhere on his face. Could tiny drops of blood fall from your eyes? he wondered. Or your mouth – perhaps your teeth? Perhaps he'd bitten his tongue in the night. According to Meredith he ground his teeth while he slept – an unverifiable complaint – and the noise he made grinding his teeth had been the reason they had first decided to try separate bedrooms. Perhaps he had ground too hard last night and a little blood had ensued . . . Most odd, anyway.

He shaved and then opened the drawer in his dressing room that contained his ironed and neatly folded underwear. Was this a no-underwear day? He had a meeting with Pippa Deere at 10.00 and he always rather enjoyed his covert cock-chafing moments with her. Her nose shone, her lips shone, she wore rather too much gold jewellery: brassy, shiny Pippa Deere. But he thought not: the air of crisis in the company dictated full clothing and he slipped on a pair of red tartan boxer shorts. He could always take them off later, he reasoned, if the unclothed mood came upon him.

Once at Calenture-Deutz, he sauntered into his secretary's office with something of a spring in his step. Mrs Prendergast leapt to her feet, her face tense, making strange signs in front of her chest.

'Mr Keegan and Mr de Freitas are waiting for you, sir,' she said quickly, clearly as unhappy at this state of affairs as he would be. What the fuck were they doing in his office at 9.30 in the morning?

'I'll have a black coffee, Mrs P.,' he said, keeping his temper, 'one sugar today – and a couple of those custardy biscuits.' He opened his office door – Keegan and de Freitas were sitting on his leather sofa.

'Gentlemen,' he said, crossing the floor to his desk. 'What a surprise. Don't let this happen again, please.'

'Apologies, Ingram,' Keegan said, his tone deferential, 'but you had to be the first to know. The press release is going out in an hour. We didn't want you to hear it from anyone else.'

'Have you found Philip Wang's killer? Pinfold, Wilfred? What's-his-name?'

'No. It's about Zembla-4.'

'Oh. Why can't we find this man?'

'Ingram,' Keegan persisted, in a faintly, schoolmasterly pay-attention tone. 'Zembla-4 goes into the FDA and the MHRA this morning. We're announcing it. Officially, we're ready.'

Ingram said nothing. He thought he managed to keep his face very still.

'Since when did you become CEO of Calenture-Deutz, Burton? That is my decision and the board's to make.'

'Circumstances have changed,' de Freitas butted in, more emolliently. 'We had to move fast.'

'Well, move faster and rescind it,' Ingram said. 'This will not happen. Philip Wang died just a few weeks ago – his life's work is at stake. We are not ready. Philip would be spinning in his grave.'

Keegan held up both hands. 'Costas Zaphonopolous has been through all the trials, scrupulously, all the data. All the documentation from the other foreign trials – Italy, Mexico – is ready, immaculate. He gave us the green light, unequivocally.'

'I thought you said there was data missing from Philip's flat.'

'Not data that affects Zembla-4's launch.'

'I don't care what Costas says, I'm sorry. I make

239

this decision. I need to see the facts, the reports. Then the board must sanction the—'

'Ingram,' Keegan interrupted. 'Just watch your Calenture-Deutz stock treble – no, quadruple.'

Ingram said nothing. He paced around his office, hands in pockets, head down, giving, he hoped, a good impression of a man deep in thought. There was something about the nasal twang of Keegan's accent that he found particularly grating this morning.

'I'm sorry, Burton,' he said finally. 'This is my company, not yours. I make these decisions – not you. No, repeat, no.'

'It's too late,' Keegan said flatly, almost insolently, all deferment gone. Both he and de Freitas remained seated. Ingram went to his desk and sat down behind it, as if that restored his authority somewhat.

Now Keegan stood and reached into his brief-case. He fanned out three magazines on Ingram's desk. Not magazines – learned scientific journals, Ingram saw: *The American Journal of Immunology*, *The Lancet*, *Zeitschrift für Pharmakologie*.

'Three articles by independent experts in their field raving about Zembla-4,' Keegan said.

'How come? Where did they get their information?'

'We gave them the data and, of course, paid them extremely handsomely.' Keegan smiled. 'It's a slam-dunk, Ingram. And then, next month, wait till you see the advertorials. We're looking for a full licence well within a year. Six to nine months.'

He spread his thin fingers, blocking out the banner headlines: 'At Last A Cure For Asthma.'

'I've seen them,' he said, pleased to score a modest point. 'Alfredo showed them to me.' He smiled. 'Well, I'm going to rain on your parade, Burton,' he continued, 'very sorry, but the answer is still a loud and immovable "no". It's ridiculously premature and risky. Philip Wang himself told me a week before he died that he wanted at least another year of third-level clinical trials – he wanted more placebo comparisons – before he would confidently consider submitting for licence. No, no, no,' he smiled his cold smile. 'Call everything off.'

'I'm afraid not, Ingram. Don't go down this road, please.'

Ingram felt his stomach churn. He flipped the switch on his intercom. 'Any sign of my umbrella, Mrs P.?'

'Umbrella, sir?'

'I mean my coffee.'

Both Keegan and de Freitas were now standing in front of his desk.

'By the way, you're both sacked – fired – as of this moment. You have twenty minutes to leave the building. Security will escort you to your offices. You will take nothing with you apart from personal effects—'

'No, Ingram,' Keegan said, tiredly. 'We're not fired. I suggest you call Alfredo Rilke.'

'Alfredo will have your heads served up on silver platters.'

'This is Alfredo's idea, Ingram. It's his doing, not ours. We're just following his instructions.'

Mrs Prendergast came in with Ingram's coffee and biscuits. Ingram smiled warmly at her: 'Thank you, Mrs P.' She gave him a terrified, nervous glance and then hurried out, not looking once at Keegan or de Freitas.

'You can call Alfredo now,' Keegan said.

Ingram looked at his watch. 'It's five o'clock in the morning in the Caribbean.'

'Alfredo's in Auckland, New Zealand. He'll take your call – the usual number.'

'Kindly leave the room, gentlemen.'

After they had gone, Ingram sat there for a moment, still, taking stock, trying to come to terms with the whirling multitude of implications from this last conversation. It was as if a hundred invisible bats, or doves, were flying crazily round his room, his ears filled with rushing wing-beats signifying something bad, something doom-laden. He felt like the democratically elected president of a small republic that had just been the victim of a military coup. He had his office, his nice house, the limousine with the liveried chauffeur – but that was all.

'Alfredo? . . . Ingram.'

'Ingram. I was hoping to hear from you. It's all very exciting, isn't it.'

'It's all a bit sudden, that's for sure.'

'This is how it works, Ingram. Believe me. I think – if you'll permit – that I can say I've had more experience in this field than you.'

242

'Indubitably.' It was at moments like these that Ingram wished he had not abandoned property development for the baffling world of pharmaceuticals. It was all so simple, then – you borrowed money, bought a building, sold it for a profit. But Rilke was speaking.

'– Surprise is your best weapon. You build momentum, unstoppable momentum. You only get one chance. Zembla-4 is out there. We have to go now. Now, now, now. Go, go, go.'

'I just feel—'

'We estimate five to eight billion dollars in the first year of full licence. Ten to twelve billion per annum is very realisable, thereafter. This is another Lipitor, a Seroquel, a Viagra, a Xenak-2. We have our blockbuster drug, Ingram. A twenty-year patent. Global. We will die enormously, vastly, disgustingly wealthy men.'

'Yes, good . . . Well . . .' Ingram didn't know how to respond. He felt cowed; he felt that small-boy feeling again, out of his depth, not understanding. 'Onwards and upwards,' he managed to say.

'God bless,' Alfredo Rilke said, his voice crackling through the ether. 'And congratulations.'

'Good night,' Ingram said, reaching for one of Mrs P.'s custard crèmes.

'Just one thing, Ingram,' Rilke said, 'before I sign off.'

'Yes?'

'We have to find this Adam Kindred.'

243

CHAPTER 26

To steal from a blind man was almost as low as you could go. To steal a blind man's white stick surely condemned you to the most nether and excruciating regions of hell – assuming hell existed, Adam said to himself, which of course it didn't. This rock-solid secular rationality, however, didn't remove the feelings of guilt he experienced each time he took the stick out with him. But needs must, necessity the mother of invention, and so on, he told himself: there was no doubt that the acquisition of the white stick – the white-stick Damascene moment – and the introduction of the white-stick routine had transformed his begging life and his fortunes. On two particular days he had made over £100, most days he begged £60 to £70 with ease. He was going to clear £1,000 long before the end of the month.

He had seen the blind man – the partially sighted man – in a coffee-shop and had observed the almost visible currents of concern that emanated towards him from other people around him. It was as if he were a kind of care-magnet – chairs were discreetly moved out of his way, couples parted to let him by, a steering hand was laid gently on his elbow to direct him to the front of the queue. Adam sat, watching him order his cappuccino and muffin (a member of staff came out from behind the counter to place them on a table nearby), and the blind man haltingly came over and sat down. People's conversations quietened deferentially as he passed. He folded up his stick (it had a little plastic ball on the end) and slipped it into the canvas bag he carried and that he placed on the floor by his seat. Then he ate his muffin and drank his coffee and while he was doing so Adam had his revelation – his begging revelation – he saw, at once, his begging future.

He was scraping by perfectly well on his 'brown coins only' appeal – £5 to £6 a day – a smart idea in itself, but it was a *small* smart idea. He needed to take begging to new heights, he required a quantum leap in his begging imagination, and he saw in this blind man and his white stick the road he had to follow.

So Adam stole this blind man's white stick. He walked by his table, dropped his newspaper, bent down to retrieve it, picked the stick out of the bag and slid it up his jacket sleeve before strolling out of the coffee-shop.

The next day, Adam went to Paddington Station, wearing a shirt and a tie, his pin-stripe suit and a pair of cheap sunglasses bought from a thrift shop near The Shaft. With the stick unfolded, its white plastic ball-end grazing a zig-zag in front of him over the stone floor of the station concourse, he approached the big, elevated electronic display of departing trains. He chose an elderly woman to ask his question to.

'Excuse me,' Adam said in his politest, middle-class voice, 'but am I at Waterloo Station?'

'No. Oh, no, no. You're at Paddington.'

'Paddington? Oh my god, no. Thank you, thank you. Oh god. Sorry to bother you. Thank you.' He turned away.

'Can I help? Is there anything wrong?'

'I've been brought to the wrong station. I've spent all my money.'

The woman gave him £10 and paid for his Underground ticket back to Waterloo.

At Waterloo, Adam asked a young couple if he was at Liverpool Street Station. They gave him £5 for his Tube fare. Waiting half an hour, Adam then approached a middle-aged man, also in a pin-striped suit, and asked him if the trains to Scotland left from here.

'Bugger off,' the man said and turned his back on him.

But that was rare. In Adam's experience, for every 'bugger off', walk-away or blank ignoring stare he received four offers of financial aid. People thrust money on him, some were absurdly generous, offering to accompany him, buy him food, telling him to 'take care', pressing further notes into his hand.

On his first day begging as a blind man he made £53.

On his second day he made £79.

A routine soon established itself: he undertook a daily circuit of London's railway termini and larger Underground stations – King's Cross, Paddington, Waterloo, Victoria, London Bridge, Piccadilly, Liverpool Street, Earls Court, Angel, Notting Hill Gate, Bank, Oxford Circus. He also went to Oxford Street and shopping malls, farmers' markets and museums – anywhere that people gathered and where he would be inconspicuous. Wherever he was he simply asked if he was somewhere else. People were kind and attentive, people were helpful and understanding – his faith in the essential good nature of his fellow human beings was hugely reinforced. He never begged more than once a day at any one location and steadily the wad of notes in his pocket grew. He paid Mhouse's rent a week in advance; he went to the supermarket and came home with plastic bags full of food and wine for himself and Mhouse and treats for Ly-on. He bought a de-luxe Easy-Reading kit and began to teach Ly-on to read and write (it helped diminish the guilt, a little). In his second week of blind-man begging he purchased a new dark suit, three white shirts, a pseudo-club tie and a pair of black loafers in a sale.

And so when Mhouse scratched her nails on his door that night and offered him a lodger's discount for sex with the landlady he was both ready and happy to oblige – money no object. She came to his bed five nights in a row. On the third night he

247

asked her to stay – he liked the idea of them sleeping together in each other's arms but she said a full night was £100 so he demurred. Then suddenly, after five nights, she stopped coming. He missed her, missed her lean, quick body and her uptilted, dark-nippled breasts. He had not had sex with anyone since that ill-fated night in the cloud-chamber viewing gallery with Fairfield – and before that there was a distant, dimming memory of making love to Alexa – her tanned body, her white bikini-shadow, her lustrous blonde hair and perfect teeth. To have Mhouse in his arms, beneath him, to be inside her, to experience orgasm, was as close to happiness as he had known, recently – for the first time since the murder of Philip Wang he felt a sense of ease, of normality, of a stirring of human affection again – of need.

After a few days' abstinence he said to her: 'I'll give you a hundred, for a whole night.'

'I don't think so, John. It's not, you know, *proper*. Ly-on will know.'

'How come the other five nights were "proper"?'

'Well, sort of slam-bam-thank-you-Mam, you know. Quick as a flash. But I think he know something's happened.'

That was true. After the fourth night Adam had come up behind Mhouse at the sink, put his arms around her, kissed her neck and squeezed her breasts. She'd turned and slapped his face, hard. Adam recoiled and in spinning away was provided with an image of Ly-on looking up from his book, shocked and worried.

'Don't fucking never do that again,' Mhouse hissed at him in a fury. 'This is business. Pure and simple.'

But was it? Adam wondered. That first night she had come into his room she had said she was 'lonely'. He was lonely too – sometimes he thought he was the loneliest man on the planet. And he had so liked holding her small, lithe body, feeling the warmth of her breath on his neck and cheek, feeling her squirm and rub herself against him. As the days went by and nothing further happened, Adam – growing richer – began to find living in the flat a near intolerable frustration. He resumed his visits to the Church of John Christ, choosing to eat his evening meal there in the company of Vladimir, Turpin and Gavin Thrale, happy to endure Bishop Yemi's interminable sermons. But he still came back to The Shaft and lay on the mattress in his room, listening through the wall to Ly-on now reading simple stories to his mother. When all went quiet he would lie in the dark, willing Mhouse to slip out of bed and come and tap on his door, but it didn't happen again.

Adam thought – vaguely – about leaving: why torment himself in this way? But something kept him there. The flat in The Shaft was a kind of home, after all, and he felt safe, for once. And Ly-on liked him – strange, listless Ly-on who turned

249

out to be a quick learner – and if he left he wouldn't see Mhouse any more, wouldn't be in her company, watching television, eating bad meals together, laughing, talking. He wondered if he were becoming unhealthily obsessed with her . . .

Adam sat in his room counting out £500 and then looped a rubber band around the thick wad of notes. That left him a float of almost £300 but he was beginning to feel uneasy about carrying such a large amount of money around with him. Luckily he'd thought of somewhere secure where he could bank it.

On the way out of The Shaft he heard a call.

'Hey. Sixteen-oh-three.'

He looked round to see Mr Quality loping towards him, hand held out in greeting. They had met a couple of times before when he had called round at the flat, delivering small packets to Mhouse – pills for her problems, Mhouse said. They slapped hands and gripped thumbs.

'You still here, man?' Mr Quality said.

'Yeah, keeping busy.'

'Like little Mhousey, yeah?'

'We get on OK. And little Ly-on – nice little bloke.'

'You stay, you have to pay me rent. £100 a month.'

'I pay Mhouse rent.'

'Not her apartment, man. It mine.'

250

'I'll pay you tomorrow,' Adam said, 'OK?' The wad of notes in his pocket felt as heavy as a brick. 'You make me very happy, Sixteen-oh-three.'

Adam took the long bus journey to Chelsea, happy to have the chance to think. He thought about Mhouse and Ly-on and the strange new life he was living with them. And he rather marvelled at himself – at his ability to adapt, almost to thrive in this hostile and unforgiving world. He wondered what Alexa would have made of this new Adam; he wondered what his father and his sister would think. He deliberately didn't bring his family to mind, if he could help it – better to keep them parked on the rim of consciousness. He was sure he was never out of *their* minds; what must they imagine had become of him? Son and brother lost for ever. He could think calmly about this because he felt he had changed in some paradigmatic way: the old Adam Kindred was being ousted and over-whelmed by the new one – shrewder, more worldly and capable of survival. It was like *Homo sapiens* brushing aside the Neanderthals . . . This gave him pause, this notion: perhaps he wasn't quite so happy to wave goodbye to the old Adam, after all.

He shouldn't have thought of Alexa, he realised, as image after image of her came swimming un-invited into his mind, and he could hear her husky, throaty voice in his ear. In fact it had been her voice that attracted him initially – as if she were recovering from laryngitis – and was the first thing about

251

her he had become aware of when he had telephoned her office to enquire about an apartment for sale not far from the university in Phoenix. She had been the realtor when he eventually bought it. The physical presence of Alexa – the thick blonde hair, the tan, the briskness, the teeth, the glossy lips – almost contradicted what her vocal chords seemed to infer. It was as if he had been expecting some stout, heavy-smoking lounge-singer and instead had been presented with this glowing prototype of American pulchritude. But the disparate juxtaposition of voice and persona had its own telling appeal. There had been problems with the sale that necessitated further meetings, cell-phone numbers had been exchanged, and when the sale had gone through they had gone to a bar together to have a celebratory drink. They had shared a bottle of champagne, Adam walked her to her car, they kissed. That was the beginning: swift courtship, society marriage, the new house gifted by widower Dad, the talk of a family.

The end came, suddenly, unexpectedly, two years later, when Fairfield had called Alexa up, two days after the sex in the cloud chamber, sobbingly declaring her eternal love for Adam, begging Alexa to let her husband go free. Covertly Alexa had read the undeleted texts on Adam's cell-phone and printed them off. Brookman Maybury himself had stood beside the attorney when the divorce proceedings were initiated and when Adam learnt how the baleful course of events had unfolded.

Alexa was not present, her father acting as cold, stern proxy for his shattered, ill, medicated daughter, his eyes glowering at Adam beneath the folded strata of his acropachydermous brows. Adam tried to stop thinking – but the memory of his last meal with Fairfield elbowed its way remorselessly into his mind.

Three days after the cloud-chamber moment, they met on campus and had gone downtown in Phoenix to a large, anonymous mid-scale restaurant for supper. This restaurant had an open-air courtyard and was popular, therefore, with smokers. It served copious surf and turf, all the shrimps you can eat in a bucket, whole chickens with free fries – and, after they had eaten (Adam wasn't hungry, barely touched his food), Adam had tried to put his 'damage limitation' plan into first gear. The more he made the reasonable case – a moment of madness, inexcusable behaviour on his part, let's be friends – the more Fairfield said she loved him, wanted to spend her life with him, bear his children.

'You've got to stop sending me these texts, Fairfield,' he said. 'I keep deleting. But you keep sending.'

'Why should I stop? I love you, Adam, I want to declare my love to you, all the time, every moment of the day.' She lit a cigarette and blew the smoke considerately over her right shoulder.

'Why? Because . . . Because they can be traced . . . They, they, they, you know, might be used against me by Alexa.'

253

'But I've already spoken to Alexa.'

Adam knew it was all over then and he felt a kind of shrinking in him, a withering of his spirit. One stupid mistake – one lapse, one near-unconscious answering of an atavistic sexual instinct – that was all it took to put a perfectly secure life, a fairly happy and prosperous life, in free fall. Tell Adam and Eve about it, he thought, with some bitterness, some self-reproach. And he was sure nemesis was just around the corner – merely a matter of time. So he put his mind in neutral as Fairfield ordered ice cream and he watched her eat it, watched her lick her spoon provocatively, smiling at him, talking of their next date – a motel? A whole night? – their future, before a small commotion at the restaurant's door made him look up to see Brookman Maybury and some officer of law beside him striding across the courtyard, advancing on their table. Adam was served with a restraining order and told that he would never see his wife again: Alexa was filing for immediate divorce.

He left the bus at Sloane Square and walked soberly down Chelsea Bridge Road to the river, thinking back, gloomily. The divorce and potential scandal had obliged him to resign his associate professorship (Brookman Maybury was a major donor to MMU, there was an athletics scholarship in his late wife's name). Brookman had made it absolutely, unwaveringly clear: resign or you'll be charged with gross moral turpitude – you'll never

254

work in any educational institution again, let alone an American university where you'd be free to prey on your young women students. So Adam had resigned his associate professorship and thought – go back to England, start again, and had applied for the job at Imperial College. And look where that had landed him, he thought with renewed bitterness . . .

It was a cloudy, breezy day and the river was low, the tide beginning to flow back upstream. From the middle of the bridge Adam had a good view of the triangle – the long thin beach was exposed and there was the fig tree and all the familiar components of what had been his small three-sided world. He checked that nobody was watching the place, waited a few more minutes, walked back round to the Embankment and climbed quickly over the fence, pushing his way through the branches and the bushes to the clearing. Someone had flung the tyres here and there and his sleeping bag and groundsheet had gone – maybe the police had taken them?

He checked his bearings and found the spot, ripping back the turf – the grass was rooting again – to expose his buried cash-box. Inside was Philip Wang's dossier, the instructions he'd been sent on how to reach the interview room at Imperial College, a taxi receipt, his small *A–Z* paperback street-map of London, a Grafton Lodge memo pad with some phone numbers jotted on it, a list of flats for sale from an estate agent that he'd visited

– all that remained of the old Adam, he realised, the meagre documentary residue of his former life that he'd been carrying in his coat and jacket pockets that fateful night . . . He deposited his £500 wad of notes, closed the box and stamped the turf down. This was how all banks and banking began, he supposed, a simple store for excess money. And look how far we've evolved . . .

By coincidence, Bishop Yemi's sermon that night took as its starting point a text from 'The Book of John', Revelation chapter 14, verse 14 – 'Use your sickle and reap because the harvest of the earth is fully ripe' – one that he employed as a vehicle for exploring, at great length, some of the merits of globalisation.

Mrs Darling was serving the food that evening – a surprisingly good Lancashire hot pot – and she greeted him with particular warmth.

'Lovely to see you, John,' she said. 'Bishop Yemi would like a word after supper.'

What did this mean? Adam wondered, suspiciously, as he took his plate over to the table to join Vladimir, Thrale and Turpin. Turpin had been absent for over a week and was very vague with his replies. He'd been 'out west' to see a wife of his in Bristol. It hadn't been an enjoyable experience – one of his daughters had gone to the bad – and his mood was correspondingly morose and taciturn.

In strong contrast to Vladimir, who was in a state

of high excitement, having finally been provided with his passport, an object that was passed discreetly round the table. Turpin wasn't interested. It was Italian, Adam saw, and noted that Vladimir's new name was to be 'Primo Belem'. The photograph, over-lit, slightly blurry, did look remarkably like Vladimir: the original Primo Belem – the late Primo Belem – also had a shaven head and a goatee, a fact that made them generically identical. All men with shaven heads and goatees look vaguely related, even like brothers, Adam realised.

Thrale was particularly interested, however, asking if such passports could be had for less than 1,000 euros – Adam could see a plan forming – and Vladimir promised to ask his contact. There was something valedictory and unsettling about this last meal together. Vladimir/Primo was about to leave and re-enter the real world as a legitimate member of society. He had found a small one-bedroomed flat on an estate in Stepney; he had been interviewed for a job as a hospital porter; he had opened a bank account and applied for a credit card. He shook hands with everyone as he left, accepting their empty wishes of good luck and responding with equally empty promises that he'd stay in touch.

But he drew Adam aside before he left and handed him a slip of paper – on it was written his mobile phone number. Adam found this depressing: he wondered if his own circumstances would ever allow him to own and operate a mobile phone again – it was a pang-inducing reminder of how basic and circumscribed his life was.

'Call me, please, Adam,' Vladimir insisted. 'You come to my flat, we smoke some monkey, yeah?'

'That would be great,' Adam said. 'Take care.'

Their farewells were interrupted by Mrs Darling, who led Adam away up a staircase at the back of the hall to Bishop Yemi's offices. There, Adam found the bishop wearing a dark three-piece suit and bright amber silk tie, his cornflower-blue shirt sporting a contrasting white collar – the effect was detabilising: he looked like a prosperous, if slightly flash, businessman. In his lapel buttonhole Adam saw a tiny gold pin that said 'John 2' – the pastor had kept his badge of office.

'John 1603,' Bishop Yemi said, clasping Adam's hand in both his. 'Sit down, my brother.' Adam sat, noting the river view from the office windows, the tide flowing in and, across the brown water, the prospect of the expensive apartments on Wapping High Street.

'I have chosen you, John,' Bishop Yemi said. 'You are my chosen one.'

'Me?' Adam said. 'What for?'

Bishop Yemi explained. The Church of John Christ had recently been endowed with charitable status – they were now a registered charity with all the tax benefits that ensued from that. Moreover, they had been awarded a large grant from City Hall's 'Outreach for Kids' programme, sponsored by the Mayor of London himself. The Church of John was opening a crèche, a pre-nursery infant school, an office to provide free legal and medical counsel, an agency for fostering the disadvantaged young and, the jewel in the crown, an orphanage in Eltham for under-twelves.

'Congratulations,' Adam said. 'But what's this got to do with me?'

'I need an executive, a right-hand man, someone who knows the church, knows its doctrinal inclination.' Bishop Yemi smiled modestly.

'No crucifixes,' Adam said.

'Precisely. Our Lord did not die on a wooden cross. The radiant sun of Patmos is our new logo.'

'I'm afraid I—'

'I cannot forsake my pastoral duties entirely.' Bishop Yemi ignored him. 'I need someone to represent the church – my proxy – to all these new administrative bodies. And I have chosen you, John 1603.'

Adam repeated that he was very sorry indeed – hugely flattered, honoured, even – but the answer had to be a reluctant no. He blamed his fragile mental health, the numerous recent breakdowns, and so on. It would be impossible: he would hate to let down the church.

'Never rush to judgement, John,' Bishop Yemi said, 'I refuse to take "no" for an answer – it's my guiding principle in life. Think about it, take your time, my brother. We could be a great team and the rewards – spiritual and financial – will be considerable.' He hugged Adam at the door, warmly.

'I need intelligence, John, and this you have in copious supply. I have searched among the other brothers and I know you are the one. The starting salary is £25,000 a year. Plus car and expenses, of course.' He smiled. 'Use your sickle, John.'

'Sorry?'

'Use your sickle and reap because the harvest of the earth is fully ripe.'

That night, when he returned to the flat, Mhouse was waiting up for him. She kissed him on the lips – just a smack – but she never kissed him any more, since that first time she had slid into bed beside him.

'What's going on?' he said.

'Fancy an all-nighter?'

After they had made love they both felt hungry; Mhouse found some prawn-cocktail-flavoured crisps and Adam opened one of his bottles of wine – a Californian Cabernet Sauvignon. Mhouse sat on the mattress, cross-legged, facing him, munching crisps and drinking wine from the bottle. It was like a midnight feast, Adam thought – then, a second later, the school analogy seemed absurd. There were no naked midnight feasts at school, Adam realised: young women did not sit opposite you, naked, cross-legged, during school midnight feasts.

He placed his finger on her 'MHOUSE LY-ON' tattoo.

'When did you do that?' he asked.

She had other, more conventional tattoos: a jagged, two-pronged, lightning bolt on her coccyx; a multi-petalled flower on her left shoulder; a constellation of stars (Orion) on the instep of her right foot. They had been done professionally in tattoo-parlours: 'MHOUSE LY-ON' was all her own work.

'It was when Ly-on was born. Like to show we one person, you know . . . I did small one on him, on his leg when he was baby. Boy, did he crying. But,' she smiled, radiantly, she believed it, 'no one can separate us, now. Never.'

'Why are you called Mhouse?'

'My real name is Suri,' she said, spelling it for him slowly. 'But I never like being Suri – so many bad things happen to Suri. So I change it.'

'To Mhouse.'

'Suri means "mouse" in French language – someone told me.'

'Of course. But why do you write it like that?'

'I can write a bit. I can write "house", yeah? I learn that. So,' she smiled. 'House – Mhouse. Easy.'

Adam touched her breasts, kissed them, dragged his knuckles across her nipples, let his fingers trail down her flat stomach.

'Somebody offered me a job today,' he said. '£25,000 a year, and a car.'

Mhouse's laughter was loud and genuine.

'You a funny one, John,' she said. 'You know

how to make me laugh.' She put the wine bottle down and pushed him gently, rolling him over on to his back so she could straddle him. She leant forward, twisting her body, letting her breasts touch his lips, his chin, a nipple grazing it, one then the other, and she kissed him, taking his bottom lip between her teeth and biting gently.

'I kiss you for free,' she said.

'Thank you,' Adam said.

Adam ran his hands down her lean back to cup her tensed buttocks. One hundred pounds to Mhouse, he thought, and a hundred to Mr Quality – worth every begging penny.

CHAPTER 27

Luigi himself put the thick envelope on his desk.

'Thank you, Luigi,' Ingram said. 'I'll see you at six, as usual.'

He was about to open the envelope when he experienced one of these new virulent itches again – this time on the sole of his left foot. He kicked his shoe off. Removed his sock and scratched vigorously. 'Itch' was far too inert a word to describe these potent irritations: it was as if someone had inserted a red-hot acupuncture needle beneath the skin and had wiggled it around. Moreover, they seemed to occur anywhere on his body – armpit, neck, finger-joint, buttock – and yet there was no sign of a bite or an incipient rash. Some sort of nerve-ending playing up, he supposed – though he was beginning to worry that they might have some strange connection with his nightly blood-spotting: every two or three mornings his pillow was imprinted with these tiny blood spots coming from somewhere on his face and head. Anyway, the itches had started a week or two after the blood spots – perhaps there was no

connection (perhaps this was a natural conse-
quence of ageing – he was no spring chicken, he
reminded himself – and, once scratched, these
itches went away immediately) but when they fired
up they were unignorable.

He replaced his sock and shoe and returned his
attention to Luigi's package. It contained Philip
Wang's appointment diary. Ingram, acting on a
hunch – acting on a need to outflank Keegan and
de Freitas – had sent Luigi down to the Oxford
Calenture-Deutz laboratory to retrieve it from
Wang's PA. He opened it and started at the beginning of the year, working forward. Nothing very
dramatic, the usual daily round of a busy head of
a drug development programme, boring meeting
after boring meeting, only some of which were
directly to do with Zembla-4. Then, as he drew
closer to Wang's last day on earth, the pattern
begins to change: a sudden concentration of trips
in the last week or ten days – 'out of office' – trips
made to all four de Vere wings where the clinical
trials were taking place, in Aberdeen, Manchester,
Southampton and, finally, St Botolph's in
London, the day before he was killed. Turning the
page to the last day, Wang's ultimate day, Ingram
saw there was only one appointment: 'Burton
Keegan, C-D, 3.00 p.m.'

Ingram closed the diary, thinking hard.

None of this was out of the ordinary – which
was why the police had given it no thought, he
supposed – a research immunologist going about

his business in an entirely typical way. Unless, that is, you looked at it from a different angle – the Ingram Fryzer angle.

He asked Mrs Prendergast to connect him with Burton Keegan.

'Burton, it's Ingram. Do you have a moment?'

Burton had.

'I've just been called by the police about Philip Wang, trying to pin down his movements in his last day or two. They seem to think he came into the office the day he was killed. I told them that wasn't possible – I never saw him in the building, did you?'

'No . . .' Keegan kept his voice expressionless.

'Exactly. Philip always popped in when he was here . . . So you never saw him, either.'

'Ah, no. No, I didn't.'

'Must be some mistake, then. I'll let them know. Thanks, Burton.'

He hung up and went straight to the lift and down to the lobby, trying to seem casual, unhurried. He had the daily security manager bring him the signing-in book for the previous month and flicked back through the pages to the day in question. There it was: the shadowy carbon copy revealing that Philip Wang had signed in at 2.45 and signed out again at 3.53. A few hours later he was brutally murdered.

Ingram rode the lift back to his office in deep thought. Why had Keegan lied? Of course, Wang could have come to the office and cancelled his

Keegan meeting – but then Keegan would have said so, surely? No, everything pointed incontrovertibly to an afternoon meeting with Keegan at three o'clock on the day of Wang's murder. What had it been about? What had been said? Why hadn't Philip Wang come to see him?

'What the hell's it got to do with me?' Colonel Fryzer said impatiently, as he rearranged – ever so slightly – the vase of peonies, subject of his current still life.

'Nothing, Pa,' Ingram said, suppressing his own impatience, 'I'm just using you as a kind of sounding board . . .' He decided to try flattery. 'Get the benefit of your vast experience of the world.'

'Flattery doesn't work on me, Ingram – you should know that by now. I detest it.'

'Sorry.'

'Your number two – what's-his-name—'

'Keegan.'

'Keegan has lied to you. Ergo: he has something to hide. What could your Doctor Wang have said to him in that meeting? What would scare the shit out of Keegan?'

'I don't know yet.'

'What was this Wang chappie working on?'

'He'd spent the previous four days visiting the various hospitals where the clinical trials for a new drug we're developing are taking place. Nothing unusual in that. The drug's about to go for validation – here and in the US.'

'Is this Keegan involved in this validation process?'

'Absolutely. Very involved.'

The Colonel looked balefully at Ingram, then spread his hands. 'This is your ghastly world, Ingram, not mine. Think. What could your Wang have said to Keegan that would upset him? There's your answer.'

'I haven't a clue.'

'At least you're honest.'

There was a rap on the door and Fortunatus came in. Ingram felt almost shocked to see him.

'Dad, what're you doing here?'

'Came to pick Pa's brains. What about you?' Ingram kissed his son, who was wearing his usual infantryman-just-returned-from-combat outfit and, he noticed, had shaved his thinning hair to the shortest stubble.

'I'm taking Gramps to lunch.'

'I'll be two seconds,' the Colonel said and disappeared into his bedroom.

The unoffered invitation hovered in the air, like a rebuke, Ingram thought, wondering if he should boldly suggest that he join them. He felt a strange emotion: three generations of Fryzers in the one small room but he realised neither his son nor his father wanted his company. He felt one of his burning itches start up on the crown of his head. He pressed hard on it with a forefinger.

'I'd love to join you,' he said, managing a rueful smile. 'But I've got an exhibition.'

'You're going to an exhibition?'
'No. I mean I've got an appointment.'
'Oh, right.'
The Colonel reappeared. 'You still here, Ingram?'

CHAPTER 28

Sergeant Duke paused at the door.

'I wish you wouldn't do this, Rita. Believe me—'

'I've got no choice, Sarge. Nobody will tell me anything. I can't just walk away.'

'That's exactly what you should do. Things are going on here you don't understand.'

'Do *you* understand?' She confronted him, hands on hips, looking him in the eye, and he seemed to quail slightly.

'What would you do if you were in my position?' she said, forcefully, not letting him off the hook.

'It's not my problem. I'm not meant to understand.'

He pushed the door to the meeting room open and Rita sensed she had won a small victory. She stepped in and Duke closed the door behind her. She exhaled, thinking – Chief Inspector Lockridge wouldn't see me in his office. OK. He's confining me to the meanest meeting room in Chelsea police station. Why?

The room was almost worthy of some paradigmatic status as 'ROOM' in a typological dictionary: a table, two chairs, a battered plastic Venetian blind, a blazing strip light in the ceiling, bare walls. She sat down and waited.

Lockridge bustled in, after a couple of minutes, some sort of cardboard file in his hand that, she knew, had nothing to do with her complaint, but was an indication of the business he had waiting after he had peremptorily dealt with her. They shook hands.

'Good to see you again,' he said, sitting down, not mentioning her name, then raised his hand as if she was about to interrupt (which she wasn't). 'This is off the record, by the way. I'm only doing this because of your good service here.'

'I don't want any favours, sir,' Rita said, bravely. 'I'm just looking for some answers.'

'Fire away,' Lockridge said with his uneven smile. His face looked as though it had been kicked askew in his youth by a horse or a bull, his jaw bent right, making him talk out of the side of his mouth. He was known in the station as 'Twisted Kisser'. Rita banished this nickname from her mind as she detailed the events of her arrest of the unnamed man at Chelsea Bridge, and outlined the reasons behind her asking for this interview.

Lockridge sighed: 'This was a matter of the highest security. Word came down to us. You stumbled in on something –something even I know nothing about. I was told that this man should go free. These things happen. Particularly in the current climate. Terrorism, insurgency, etcetera.'

'We're all on the same side,' Rita said. 'Fighting the same fight. Why can't we share information – even of the most basic sort? If this man had shown me some ID, we might have been able to assist him. Even if he had told me, in so many words, what he was doing, what he was up to – then you and I wouldn't be sitting in this room, sir.'

Lockridge smiled, patronisingly, Rita thought. 'There are some operations that are so secret that . . .' he said, shrugged, and then left his sentence unfinished.

'So that's your answer, sir?'

'What do you mean?'

'It was an ultra-secret security operation. This man I arrested was some kind of security operative.'

'So to speak, as it were.'

Rita drew a breath, inwardly, summoning her reserves of self-confidence, trying to quell her nervousness and keep any tremor out of her voice. 'Because I'll have to report this to the Borough Commander,' she said, unaggressively, she hoped. 'And if he won't help me I'll have to go to the DPS. I arrested a man with two handguns on him. He was freed within twelve hours – no records, no statements, no prints, no DNA samples, as far as I can tell. The DPS will need to know where you stand.'

Lockridge's twisted face seemed to contort further. Rage, she presumed.

'Our meeting is completely off the record,' he said.

'But I'm afraid you may have to speak to the DPS – *on* the record. Once I make my complaint.'

Lockridge stood up and picked up his prop-file. Mr Busy, trying to keep his rage under control.

'That would be extremely unwise, Constable.' There was a tremor in his voice now as he empha-sised her rank.

'What happened to the weapons, sir?' She didn't know what made her ask this. It was the first time she had thought about them.

Lockridge looked at her – suddenly very uncom-fortable.

'What are you talking about?'

'Did they go to Forensics? They might help us.'

'We're not looking for help. You don't seem to have grasped that fact.'

He hadn't answered her question. She knew she was beginning to anger him beyond countenance.

'Did they go to Amelia Street, sir? His two auto-matic pistols? Or did we let him take his guns away when we released him?' This was her killer blow, she knew. 'We didn't just give them back to him, did we, sir? . . .'

'Where are you now, Constable Nashe? Since you left us?'

'The MSU, sir.'

'Lucky for you. And I'm sure they'll be the first to tell you – don't rock the boat. Excellent advice – I would take it.'

He left the room at the same brisk pace that he had entered.

Rita stood across the road from the triangle of waste ground on the west side of Chelsea Bridge, wondering what answers to her many questions this forgotten, tiny corner of London might have offered up. Two hundred square yards of over-grown river bank, she reckoned, yet a place that she had visited twice in a week. How unusual was that? And what could possibly be the connection between a man killing a seagull at dawn and eating it and that big ugly bastard hiding in the bushes with his two handguns? Was she going too far? Was it just strange, bizarre coincidence? Was she simply making life difficult for herself, as Sergeant Duke had implied? What had happened to those guns? But she knew the answer from Lockridge's shifty evasions – they'd just been handed back, like personal effects, a watch, a wallet. Surely that was inexcusable? She had no other clues to follow, no way of making any link other than her own vaporous, woolly intuition . . .

She walked slowly across Chelsea Bridge towards the Battersea shore, wondering what she should do next. She could try and set up an audit trail on the guns . . . And what did the custody record say about the disposal of the prisoner? She laughed at her naïvety: dream on, girl. She knew a firewall when she saw one – and this was being built higher and thicker as each hour went by – and she thought hard about what she should do, whether she *could* do anything. Maybe it was all pointless, maybe it was something 'bigger', security-related . . . She flipped open her mobile and called her father.

'Yes?'

'Hello, Daddy-O, it's me. What do you want for supper?'

CHAPTER 29

The dog shat easily and copiously, then did his little, funny, paw-scratching jig on the pavement before stepping away. He looked up at Jonjo – tongue out, panting – seeking approval.

'Good lad,' Jonjo said, patting his back. 'Good boy. That's my boy. Who's a clever boy?' He was pleased to note the firm consistency of this morning's deposit. The new diet was working like a charm, clearly. Beautiful.

'Disgusting.'

Jonjo looked round to see a woman staring at him, contempt and fury on her face.

'You got a problem, lady?' he said, pulling himself up to his full height.

'Yeah. That's disgusting, that is,' she said. 'You should pick it up and take it away with you. Absolutely disgusting.'

'You pick it up, darling,' he said. 'Be my guest.'

She glared at him, said 'disgusting' again and stomped off.

Jonjo twitched The Dog's lead and they walked away. He would rather rot in hell than follow his dog around with a plastic bag, picking up dog shit. Come off it, Jonjo said to himself, humans – *Homo sapiens* – did not crawl out of the primeval swamp and evolve, after millennia and millennia, into sentient beings that went around following their pet dogs and picking up their excrement. That was anti-Darwinian and, anyway, it was more a medicinal thing as far as he and The Dog were concerned – he needed a clean patch of pavement so he could verify how the new foodstuffs were being processed. Anybody who didn't like it was, of course, free to express their opinion. He was more than happy to argue his side of the matter – more than happy. Nothing he couldn't handle.

He walked The Dog down to the river, turning under the high elevation of the Dockland Light Railway and into the neat precincts of Thames Barrier Park. The grass had been recently mown, the saplings were coming along, in full healthy leaf, and a few people sat out on the decking of the small café, mums with their strollers, the usual joggers panting by. A few other dog-walkers were out and about and they nodded to each other and civilly said 'good morning'. For a brief moment Jonjo felt he was part of a community of sorts – decent people united in their affection for and care of a dumb animal. It gave him a comforting glow inside, Jonjo admitted, as he looked out over the wide river and saw the sun flashing off the huge, burnished silver humps of the Thames Flood Barrier. Like thick gleaming shark's fins: they were a symbol of the river's end, he supposed – beyond the barrier the river widened into the estuary and beyond that was the sea. He had always liked living close to the river but now the Thames brought with it unwelcome associations of Adam Kindred and his own arrest and humiliation. Now he came to think of it, Kindred had spoilt the river for him – another reason for violent retribution – and he turned his back on the Thames and headed for home, his benevolent mood dissipating fast.

It had all gone annoyingly, frustratingly, worryingly quiet. Nothing, not a sign, not a peep – as if Kindred had vanished, somehow disappeared off the face of the earth. And there were other troubling signs. After two weeks of silence Jonjo had contacted the Risk Averse Group, not because he was short of money – he had plenty of money – but because he didn't enjoy sitting at home on his arse doing nothing. He'd asked specifically to have an appointment with Major Tim Delaporte, the top man himself. He knew Major Tim – he had briefly been adjutant of 3 Para before he left the army and set up the RAG. A good man, Major Tim – tough but fair.

The appointment had been confirmed and Jonjo had travelled into the City, to the new RAG offices in a shiny glass and steel block off Lower Thames Street with a view of the Tower of London. Jonjo had suited up, polished his shoes to parade-ground brilliance and had a savage haircut. He felt both at home and out of place in the RAG offices – it was full of soldiers – men he had worked with or fought beside – but there were also many middle-class young women executives and secretaries with clipped accents that made him feel self-conscious and gauche.

He took a seat in the lobby, sitting upright on the edge of the hardest chair, keeping the creases out of his jacket. There was greenery everywhere – miniature trees and bushes and palms – and abstract paintings on the wall. Girls with long hair and high heels walked briskly across the lobby from time to time to fetch cappuccinos and espressos from the coffee machine and music – classical-lite – played softly from hidden speakers. The magazines on offer while you waited were all concerned with luxury resorts or foreign properties, full of advertisements for watches and speedboats. This was what felt wrong to Jonjo: most of the men in this part of the building were professional soldiers – between them they were responsible for hundreds, possibly thousands, of violent deaths. He thought the place should reflect this, somehow – be honest about the nature of the business transacted here – not dressed up like the office of some travel agent or poncy stockbroker or high-class dentist.

And they kept him waiting nearly an hour. The young woman on reception didn't know who he was, either. Then he was told that Major Tim had been called away and he was to see someone called Emma Enright-Gunn. As he was led to her office his mood worsened with every step: his collar seemed suddenly to be chafing his neck, he felt uncomfortably hot, his shirt sticking to his back, his armpits flowing with sweat.

The Enright-Gunn woman was brisk and professional – she looked like the headmistress of a smart school or one of those lady politicians. Her accent sounded brittle and alien to Jonjo's ears and he began to feel absurdly nervous, his saliva drying up in his mouth, his normal articulacy leaving him.

'Yeah – no – it's, ah, more a question of, you know, what's' – he'd forgotten the bloody word! – 'um, on offer, like.' Available, he remembered instantly. 'What's available,' he added more meekly than he meant.

'We're over-subscribed, Mr Case. Too many soldiers leaving the army. Everyone wants to be a private security consultant.'

'Maybe, but there's no way I'm going back to fucking Iraq. Apologies, excuse me.'

She smiled. Coldly, Jonjo thought.

'There's a CP bodyguard role available in Bogotá, Colombia.'

'No, no thanks, no. Not South America.'

She flicked through the folder on the desk in front of her. 'Small-arms training in Abu Dhabi – a sheik's private security team.'

'I don't do training, Miss—'

'Mrs—'

'Mrs Enright-Gunn. Major Tim will tell you what I—'

'I've all the information on you, Mr Case, all of it.'

He left with nothing, only the promise he'd be on the top of the list for anything 'exciting'. He paused in the lobby and drank three paper cupfuls of water in quick succession. As he tossed the cup in the waste-paper basket he saw Major Tim himself amble down the corridor, jacketless, lime-green braces on show, some papers in his hand. Jonjo reflexively came to attention, then stood at ease, thinking – what the fuck is going on here?

'Jonjo. How're you?'

'In the pink, thank you, sir.'

Tim Delaporte was tall and lean, taller than Jonjo. He had Scandinavian blond hair, oiled back from his forehead, like a blond slick cap set above a sharp-featured, alert face with pale-grey eyes. When he spoke his lips hardly moved.

'Sorry I couldn't see you. Emma's handling placements these days.'

'No worries, sir.'

'Keeping busy?'

'Getting itchy feet. Looking for something inter-esting. That's why I came in.'

'As long as you're behaving yourself, Jonjo.' Major Tim wagged his finger at him and saun-tered away.

'Good as gold, sir,' Jonjo said to his back.

Everything had been wrong about that meeting, Jonjo was thinking as he walked back home from Barrier Park with The Dog, everything. All the various subtexts he could discern were troubling. First, being fobbed off to that posh bint; second, being offered those piss-poor jobs – fourteen years in the SAS: who did they think he was? And then, third, that encounter with Major Tim, having been told he wasn't even in the building. And what was this 'behave yourself' stuff? . . . Not for the first time he wondered what the Risk Averse Group knew of his freelance work; not for the first time he wondered if they were in fact his secret facilitators. If you wanted somebody discreetly slotted wouldn't you go to an organisation that employed exclusively ex-special forces professionals, highly trained in lethal mayhem? . . .

If only he could find fucking Kindred, Jonjo thought angrily, approaching his house, then we'd be fine, home and dry. He searched his pockets for his keys. His house was only four years old, part of a row of detached and semi-detached 'executive homes' built on a landscaped tract of once derelict ground in Silvertown, close to Barrier Park. Every house had a garden and a garage built in to the ground floor. Jonjo had knocked through a door from the hall so he could access the garage from inside – it was where he kept his taxi-cab – as he often needed to move stuff in and out of his vehicle without his neighbours seeing him.

'We'll be fine,' he said out loud to The Dog.

He froze. The banal pronoun had unlocked something in his memory. 'We' . . . Who had said 'we' in such a way that it could trigger this memory twitch? . . . He thought back, and his mind returned quickly to his interrogation of Mohammed – he'd been distracted by that tosspot Bozzy and hadn't picked up on it at the time. What had he said? 'We drove to Chelsea, like. When he says he has to get his raincoat we was a bit suspicious – him being in the waste ground – thought he might be jerking us, thought he might do a runner.' *We was a bit suspicious*. Might be jerking *us*. But according to Mohammed it was just him and Kindred in the car. Why say 'we', then? The royal 'we'? No fucking way. Somebody else had been in that car apart from Mohammed and Kindred. Time for another visit to our friend Mo, Jonjo thought, his mood lifting – he had always reckoned the answer lay in that sink, that stew that was The Shaft.

He heard his name called and looked up. It was Candy, his next-door neighbour. She crossed the lawn and knelt and fussed over The Dog and they talked about how well he was looking and the new diet.

'Day off, Candy?'

'Yeah,' she said, standing up. 'I got a few days' holiday owing.' She smiled. 'All work and no play makes Jill a dull girl.'

'Too right.'

She was a fair-looking woman, Jonjo thought, nose a bit too lumpy, bit on the chunky side as well, you had to admit, but she had nice streaky blonde hair, clean nails.

282

'Fancy a bite of supper tonight?' she said. 'I'm doing a moussaka, profiteroles. Got some DVDs in.'

'No war movies, I hope.' They laughed – she knew a little about his military past. 'Yeah,' he said, 'that would be smashing, Candy, love. Smashing.'

'Don't forget to bring The Dog.'

Jonjo smiled, but he wasn't thinking about the bite of supper or what was bound to happen afterwards. He was thinking about his next visit to The Shaft and what methods he would employ to make sure Mohammed told him everything that he wanted to know.

CHAPTER 30

The steam was amazingly opaque, like watery milk, almost, like slowly shifting watery milk, stirred by currents of air as people walked to and fro. A real pea-souper fog of steam, Adam thought.

'This is buzzing,' Ly-on said.

Adam turned. He could see Ly-on because he was sitting right beside him. His little pot belly swagged over the edge of his towel, his curly hair damp with moisture, flattening against his skull.

'I never be in a place like this,' he said.

'Tell me when you get too hot.'

Mhouse had gone out early that morning, for some reason, and Adam had been alone with Ly-on in the flat. He had washed up the dishes in the sink (boiling a kettle for hot water) and had taken a bucket through to the lavatory to flush and then refill the cistern. Living with one cold water tap to provide for a household had its disadvantages – very Third World, he thought. When he returned to the kitchenette Ly-on was cleaning his teeth in the sink. Adam felt suddenly unwashed, smirched – and consequently began to itch – he needed, he realised, a hot bath. A Turkish bath. Someone had handed him a flyer for the Purlin Nail Lane Baths when he'd been begging at London Bridge Station – this was what had set the notion in his head: words like 'Sudatorium' and 'Tepidarium' made the simple process of cleaning yourself seem both timeless and exotic. He slipped out, found a functioning pay phone on Level 1 and called Mhouse.

'You taking him where?' she said.

'To the baths in Deptford. The Purlin Nail Lane Baths.'

'He can't swim, you know.'

'We're not going for a swim.'

It was surprisingly expensive at the baths – £10 for an adult, £5 for a child – but he supposed you could be there from morning to night if you had a mind to. It was a men-only day and, it being a Thursday morning, the place was tranquil. He showed Ly-on the swimming pool.

'It's a lake, man,' he said, intrigued. 'Buzzing.'

'Would you like to swim in it?'

'You bet, John. You teach me? I like that, John.'

'Yeah – one day.'

They changed out of their clothes in the Frigidarium and, wearing their towels round their waists, went into the steam room. From the odd cough and creak of wooden benches, they knew they weren't alone. He and Ly-on took their seats and waited for the sweat to flow.

When Ly-on said he was well roasted they went

out to the plunge pool. They hung up their towels and Adam lifted Ly-on into his arms: he was surprisingly light. Ly-on put an arm around Adam's neck as they stepped down the tiled steps into the icy water.

'Cor,' Ly-on said as the cold water hit his flushed body. 'I'm dreaming this. Peas, man – green, green peas.'

Adam let him float away from him a little, holding his hands.

'How old are you, Ly-on?' Adam asked.

'I'm two, I think,' he said.

'No, you're older than that.'

'Maybe seven. Mummy don't tell me. Maybe I'm four.'

'I think you're probably about seven. Where's your dad?'

'I never had no dad. Just Mum.'

'Do you go to school?'

'No. Mum says we do home-teaching.'

After the plunge pool they went into the hottest room, the Laconium. The heat stunned – anaesthetised them both: it was enough simply to breathe, conversation was impossible and they could only stand it for a couple of minutes. Lyon whispered, 'I'm dying, I'm burning,' so they went back to chill down in the plunge pool before they opted for more steam in the Sudatorium. But it worked, Adam felt he had never been cleaner in his entire existence: every pore void and pink, every sebaceous crevice purged and purified.

286

Under a hot shower he shampooed his hair and beard, washed Ly-on's curly mop for him. They dressed and stepped out on to Purlin Nail Lane.

'You hungry?' Adam said.

'Drinking,' Ly-on said. 'I need drinking.'

They went to a pub where Ly-on had two pints of lime and lemonade with ice and Adam drank two pints of lager, immediately replacing the weight he had lost in the steam room. He ate a baked potato with beans and grated cheese and Ly-on had spaghetti for the first time in his life. They went to Greenwich and Adam took him into the Maritime Museum and then they wandered down to the river bank where Adam bought him a sweatshirt with the word 'LONDON' written across it.

'What's that?' Ly-on said. 'Lon-don?' Reading the word, Adam was pleased to note.

'That's where you live. London.'

'I live for Shaft.'

'The Shaft's in London.' He gestured at the river, at the far bank, at Millwall and Cubitt Town opposite and, towering beyond them, the glass and steel alps of Canary Wharf. 'All this is part of London.'

They rode the Dockland Light Railway back to Bermondsey and walked to Rotherhithe. As they made their way along the pitted pathways of The Shaft, through its various bedraggled, worn quadrangles, hand in hand, Ly-on quizzed him about the city he lived in.

'So if somebody say – hey, Ly-on, man, where you come from? I say – I come from London.'

'Yes.'

'So, I say: I'm a London, I'm a London, me.'

'London*er*. You're a Londoner.'

'Londoner . . .' He thought about that. 'That's fit, John. Green peas.'

'Say it with pride. It's a great city, the greatest city in the world.'

'You a Londoner, John?'

'No, I'm not.'

'Why?'

'I don't live here, I'm not from here. I'm just visiting.'

They were almost level with the big guy coming towards them when Adam saw who it was. He let him go past and then changed course so he could get an oblique view. He stopped and looked back. It was the man from the triangle, the man from the mews at Grafton Lodge, the man he'd knocked unconscious. The man was walking purposefully, briskly, as if late for a rendezvous. He hadn't seen Adam, had walked right by him without a sideways glance – but, of course, he wasn't looking for a bearded man holding the hand of a small boy.

'What's knocking you, John?' Ly-on asked in a worried voice. 'What's freezing you?'

Adam eased his grip on Ly-on's hand.

'Nothing. Let's get home.'

★   ★   ★

In the flat – Mhouse was back – Adam gathered up his few possessions as Ly-on tried to explain to her what spaghetti was. ('Strings, Mum, like soft strings. Fit like new car.') Adam shoved his old pin-stripe suit and his various shirts into two plastic bags, checking his room thoroughly to make sure there was nothing left that would associate him with the place.

'What you mean, you leaving?' Mhouse said, with disgruntled surprise, when Adam offered her two weeks' rent in advance.

'I told you I've been offered this job. In—' He thought quickly. 'Edinburgh.'

'Where's that?' she said, taking the notes.

'Scotland.'

'Near Manchester?'

'Nearish. If anyone asks, say I've gone to Scotland. Got that? Scotland.'

Ly-on was lying on cushions in front of the TV, watching cartoons.

'I'm going away for a few days,' Adam said, crouching down beside him.

'OK.' Ly-on's eyes stayed on the screen. 'When you come back can we go to the mist again?'

'Sure.'

'Green, green peas.'

At the door Mhouse now seemed breezy, unconcerned.

'Mind how you go,' she said. 'Take care.'

'I'll be back,' Adam said, knowing he wouldn't and suddenly found himself completely incapable

289

of articulating his feelings, understanding only that he had to remove himself permanently from this small family that had sheltered him.

'I liked being here, you know,' he said. 'With you and Ly-on.' He touched her arm, letting his fingertips follow the swell of her bicep. 'Especially you.'

She brushed his fingers away.

'I'll have to get me another lodger now, won't I?'

'I suppose so.' He swallowed. 'Can I kiss you goodbye?'

She turned her face so her cheek was presented to him.

'On the lips.'

'No kissing.'

'Please.'

She looked at him. 'It'll cost you.'

He gave her a £5 note and pressed his lips to hers. He breathed in, smelling her particular odour and its superimposed layers of perfume – hair spray, talcum powder, cheap scent, trying to remember it, trying to store it away in his memory bank for the future. He felt her tongue flash against his teeth for a second – and their tongues touched.

'You'd better go,' she said blankly, unfeelingly, pulling back. 'Now.'

Was that a spontaneous sign of affection or a deliberate rebuke? Adam wondered as he walked out of The Shaft with his two plastic bags, not looking left or right. Will she miss me a little – or am I just another man, in the long list of men, who've disappointed her and cut and run? All he knew was that he had been tracked down and, if he didn't leave, he would inevitably lead his hunter to Flat L, Level 3, Unit 14. It had been no malign, extraordinary coincidence – the ugly man was in The Shaft for one reason only: he knows I'm here, somewhere, Adam said to himself, experiencing a surge and shudder of retrospective fear that made him stop for a second. What if he hadn't seen him? What if he and Ly-on hadn't crossed his path? . . .

He quickened his pace, heading south, wanting to be in a crowd. An Underground station – Canada Water – that would do fine. He'd make his phone call from there.

'Hey, Adam. I don't believing. Fantastic, fantastic.' Vladimir embraced him like a brother, Adam thought, almost tearfully: like a brother who'd been away at a war and had been presumed missing in action.

'You my first visitor,' Vladimir said, stepping back from the front door and beckoning him into the flat.

Vladimir's single-bedroom flat was in Stepney, in a building erected by a charitable trust housing project from the 1920s – Oystergate Buildings, off Ben Jonson Road. It was grimy and grey, built entirely of white-glazed bricks – that gave it an eerie monochrome appearance, almost like a ghost building – glazed bricks that were now cracked and stained. The façade was fussy with open landings, narrow balconies and wrought-iron railings everywhere, a far cry from the austere angles of The Shaft. Vladimir had a bathroom, kitchen, bedroom and sitting room. In the sitting room was a new, black, three-seater, leather sofa and a flat-screen TV. The rest of the small apartment seemed entirely unfurnished – no towels in the bathroom, no kitchen utensils – only a mattress and some tangled blankets on the floor of the bedroom.

'You sleep on sofa,' Vladimir said.

'Where did you get this stuff?'

Vladimir flourished his credit card. 'You have wonderful country.'

They went out and ate chicken burgers and chips in a Chick-'N'-Go. Adam paid, it was the least he could do, he thought, and Vladimir seemed to have no cash on him – he was living entirely on what his credit card could provide. They bought a six-pack of beer and returned to Oystergate Buildings. Adam gave Vladimir a month's rent in advance – £80. Vladimir said that everything would change once he started his job on Monday as a hospital porter at the nearby Bethnal & Bow NHS Trust hospital. He would be earning a starting salary of £10,500 a year. He showed Adam his uniform – blue trousers and a white shirt with blue epaulettes and a blue tie – and his necklaced 'proximity' ID badge with his photo in the name of 'Primo Belem'. Then Vladimir asked if he could borrow a further £50 – he would pay him back with his first pay cheque. Adam handed it over – he was running low on cash himself now, he'd have to visit his bank in the triangle.

'I get some monkey,' Vladimir said. 'We party this weekend before I starting work. We smoke monkey – best quality.'

'Great,' Adam said.

That night he lay on the creaking leather sofa (Vladimir had lent him one of his blankets) thinking about Mhouse and Ly-on. He was feeling sorry for himself again, conscious of the precarious nature of his life, his particular, unique plight and this new threat that, through swift response, was now neutralised, he assumed and hoped. He missed Mhouse and Ly-on, he had to admit, missed his life in The Shaft with them. But he consoled himself: despite the bleak realities he faced – his rare situation – he had done the only thing possible. He had had to leave The Shaft: at least Mhouse and Ly-on would be safe now, that was all that was really important, all that mattered.

CHAPTER 31

What is it about doctors' waiting rooms in this country, Ingram thought? Here he was, about to pay £120 for a brief ten-minute consultation with one of the most sought-after and exclusive general practitioners in London and he might as well be sitting in a two-star provincial hotel in the 1950s. Chipped, bad reproduction furniture, a worn, patterned carpet, a job-lot of dusty hunting prints on the wall, a couple of parched spider plants on the window sill, and a two-year-old pile of magazines on a coffee table with a spavined leg. If this were New York or Paris or Berlin it would all be clean, new, solid, glass, steel, lush greenery – the decor saying: I'm very, very successful, I'm high tech, cutting edge, you can trust me with your health concerns. But here in London, in Harley Street . . .

Ingram sighed, audibly, causing the other waiting patient in the room – a woman with a veil up to her eyes and a head-scarf down to her eyebrows – to look up at him. She had a small boy with her, his arm in a sling. Ingram smiled at her – perhaps she smiled back: he thought her eyes crinkled slightly, acknowledging the absurdity of the situation, but he couldn't be sure, that was the problem with veils – indeed, that was the purpose of veils. He picked up a copy of *Horse and Hound* and flicked through it, tossed it down and sighed again. Perhaps he should simply leave – he felt a bit foolish – just a few tiny drops of blood and these potent, fearsome itches: why bother the doctor at all?

'Ingram, old chap. Come away in, laddie.'

Ingram's doctor, Dr Lachlan McTurk, was a Scot, through and through, but a Scot who did not have a Scottish accent, except when he decided to affect one from time to time. He was very overweight, not quite clinically obese, had a head of thick, unruly grey hair and a flushed, ruddy face. He wore tweed suits in various shades of moss-green, winter and summer. He was married with five children and, although Ingram had been his patient for some thirty years now, he had never met Mrs McTurk or any offspring. He was a cultured man whose keenness to explore and consume every art form available was undiminished. Ingram sometimes wondered why he had bothered to become a doctor at all.

'Will you have a "wee dram", Ingram? It'll soon be noon.'

'Better not, thanks. I've got a rather important meeting.'

Lachlan McTurk had done all the obvious physical tests: blood pressure, pulse, palpation, reflexes, listened to his heart and lungs and could find no sign of anything wrong. He poured himself a generous three fingers of whisky and topped it up from the cold tap at his sink. He sat down behind his desk and lit a cigarette. He began to scribble notes down in a file.

'If you were a motor car, Ingram, I'd say you've passed your MOT with flying colours.'

'But where's this blood coming from? Why? What about these infernal itches?'

'Who knows? They're not symptoms I recognise.'

'So I've nothing to worry about?'

'Well, we've all got plenty to worry about. But I would say you could push your health to the back of the queue.'

'I suppose I should be pursued.' Ingram put his jacket on. 'What am I saying? I mean relieved. I should be relieved.'

'Do you smoke?'

'Not for twenty years?'

'How much do you drink, roughly?'

'Couple of glasses of wine a day. Approximately.'

'Let's say a bottle. No – you're in pretty good nick, in my professional opinion.'

Ingram thought. 'Perhaps I will have a small Scotch.' He might as well get something for his £120, he calculated. McTurk poured him his drink and handed it over.

'Have you seen the new production of *Playboy of the Western World* at the National?' McTurk asked.

'Ah, no.'

'It's a must. That and the August Macke at Tate Liverpool. If you do two things this month do those. I beg you.'

'Duly noted, Lachlan.' Ingram sipped his Scotch. 'I have to admit I've been a bit tense, lately. Lot going on.'

'Ah-ha, the Dread Goddess Stress. Stress can do the strangest things to a body.'

'Do you think stress might be the answer?'

'Who knows? "There are more things in heaven and earth than are dreamt of in your philosophy, Horatio".' McTurk stubbed out his cigarette. 'So to speak. Do you know what?' he said. 'I'm going to run some blood tests. Just so you sleep easy.'

This is what happens, Ingram thought, a simple visit to the doctor and suddenly you discover medical conditions, health problems, you were completely unaware of. McTurk took a good syringe-full of blood from the vein in his right elbow and made a series of samples from it.

'What tests?' Ingram asked.

'I'll just run the gamut. See if any flags are flying.'

Oh good, Ingram thought, another £500.

'You don't think,' he began, 'I mean, these couldn't be, I mean, symptoms of a – what would you say? – sexually transmitted disease . . .'

McTurk looked at him, shrewdly. 'Well, if there was blood dripping from your back-side and your cock was itching – or vice versa – I might have my suspicions. What *have* you been up to, Ingram?'

'Nothing, nothing,' Ingram said quickly, instantly

regretting this course the diagnosis had taken. 'Just wondering, perhaps, if a misspent youth was catching up with me.'

'Oh yes, the pox. No, no – we'd sort that out immediately. No mercury baths for you, laddie.'

Ingram left feeling weak and considerably iller than he had when he arrived. He also had a mild headache from the whisky. Fool.

CHAPTER 32

The Targa circled the small dinghy once and then Joey accelerated past it, downstream. The tide was ebbing and Rita heard the throaty change in the engine noise as the screws reversed and the Targa held itself immobile in midstream, stern to the tide, waiting for the flow of water to carry the dinghy down towards them. Rita took up position on the aft deck with a boathook poised. She saw a length of the painter that was attached to the bow of the dinghy trailing in the water and reached forward quickly to fish it out. She secured it to a cleat, hauling the dinghy in tight to the Targa's side, making it fast.

They had been about to go off duty when they were alerted to the abandoned dinghy – it had been spotted floating past Lambeth Bridge – and they had cruised upstream, Rita in the bow with the binoculars, looking for it. She saw it emerging from the shadow cast by Waterloo Bridge – it was barely eight feet long, a stubby, beamy pram tender made of dirty pale-blue fibreglass, with low freeboard, designed for short ship-to-shore journeys or jetty-to-jetty work, with one thwart, two rowlocks but no oars, as far as Rita could see as she tied her final half-hitch. In the well was a bundle of grey polythene tarpaulin and two inches of brown water slopping about.

'Give me a second,' she shouted to Joey, picking up a length of dock rope. Feed out a little extra line, she said to herself, we can tow it in, don't want this dirty old pram scraping our neatly painted sides. She knelt on the deck, reached down, slipped the end of the rope through the shackle in the bow and was about to knot it when the tarpaulin moved and she gave a short scream – more of an instinctive yip of alarm – but to her intense annoyance, all the same.

Something, somebody, was stirring under the tarpaulin and in a second it was flipped back to reveal her father.

It took only another split second to register that it wasn't Jeff Nashe, at all – just another stubbly, gaunt-faced, elderly man with a frazzled grey pony-tail.

'What the fuck—' the man mumbled, in a daze, rising to a kneeling position, looking across the water at Somerset House, as if suddenly struck by the austere classical geometry of its river faççade. He swivelled round to stare at her and Rita caught the half-deranged gaze of a man near the end of his particular road. Rita stretched out her hand and helped him aboard, smelling that unique sour reek of the long-unwashed, the foetor of poverty.

'Thanks, darling,' he said, as she steadied him. Now she was close to him she saw that he wasn't that old, really – late thirties, early forties – but toothless, the lower face squashed, jaws unnaturally close, lips making that unreflecting pursing and pouting that you see in very young babies. She sat him down in the cabin and re-rigged the towing-line, signalling Joey when he could safely move off. She took a blanket out of a locker and draped it round his shoulders, sitting down opposite him.

'I didn't nick it,' he said. 'Just crawled in for a kip. Stone the crows, got a shock when you woked me up.'

'Where was that, then? Where you started your kip.'

'Ah,' he thought, pouting his wet lips, rubbing his chin with the knuckles of his right hand. 'Hampton Court.'

'You've come a long way,' she said. 'Let's save it for the station, shall we?'

'Ain't done nothing wrong,' he said petulantly, hurt at the implication. He looked away from her, sniffed and tightened his blanket round his shoulders, freeing the rope's-end of his pony-tail with one hand as he did so, a gesture that brought her father's face back to her again. She felt a sudden worry-tug of melancholy in her chest, thinking of Jeff, old and vulnerable, then immediately consoling herself with the thought that she would always be there to look out for him, make sure he was safe and well. But that was no consolation, she realised, pondering the nature of this situation, as it spoke of a future she didn't wish for in the slightest.

She stepped out on to the aft deck and needlessly resecured her towing-rope, looking at the tender lurching and sliding in the Targa's wake. She didn't want to think of herself getting older, still living on the *Bellerophon*. Thirty, forty . . . The longer she stayed the harder it would be to move out one day, however much she routinely threatened to do so when her father made her angry. Not being with someone, not having a relationship, inevitably brought these thoughts on. When she'd been with Gary she never fretted morbidly or fearfully about her future. Gary had asked her out on a date and she wondered whether she should go – things between them could start up again, she realised, as easily as she had brought them to a stop.

She turned and looked at the toothless man, now berating Joey with his troubles, a dirty finger jabbing at his back from between the blanket folds. Gary wasn't ever going to be right for her, she realised, that much was clear, and she would make a big mistake going back to him just for some temporary security and confidence. She was young and attractive to men, she knew. Some lucky bastard was out there waiting for her and she would know it when he showed up – wasn't there a song about that? She searched her memory for the words and the melody and the prospect of her inevitable future happiness cheered her up, suddenly. She looked at the toothless man with pity, now – what brought a person down to that kind of state? He had been somebody's sweet little baby, once, dandled on a loving knee, repository of maternal and paternal hopes . . . What terrible mistakes had he made? What tricks had fate played on him? How had he fallen so low and helpless?

She turned away and looked back at the river as they swept under Blackfriars Bridge. Shakespeare had had a house in Blackfriars, she remembered, someone had told her that. Only one bridge across the Thames in those days – lots of boats, though, packed with boats. She smiled to herself, glad that her spirits were lifting again, happy to be part of the river and its timeless traffic.

CHAPTER 33

When Adam woke on Saturday morning, the smell – the smell of stale monkey smoke – almost made his stomach turn. Vladimir had found himself incapable of waiting until the weekend to party, especially with rocks of high-grade monkey in his pocket, and so Friday night had been designated the moment to celebrate his new name, his bank account, credit card, his sofa and TV, his salaried employment as a hospital porter at the Bethnal & Bow NHS Trust – and his new flat-mate and lodger, it went without saying. Adam hadn't joined him in smoking monkey but had drunk a lot of powerfully strong lager in an attempt to show willing, to demonstrate that he too was happy to get shit-faced on intoxicants. They had watched TV in an increasingly bleary, verbose and incoherent daze (they both added free-associating commentary, simultaneously) – they were watching a documentary about mountain climbing, as far as he could remember – Vladimir smoking and drinking, Adam drinking and drinking – until Vladimir roused himself somehow and lurched off to his bedroom, pipe in hand.

Now Adam turned over, the leather sofa squeaking beneath him like a nest of fledglings, and he saw that the TV was still on, though soundless. Groomed, smiling people relaying news of world events. He sat up, immediately aware of his foul mouth and dull headache, and went through to the bathroom to wash his face and clean his teeth. He pulled on his jacket and put on his shoes before knocking on Vladimir's door to let him know he was popping out for a spot of breakfast. He thought he heard Vladimir give a muted groan in reply, but couldn't make out if anything intelligible had been said. He didn't want to even try to imagine how Vladimir must be feeling this morning – he suspected there had been a few more pulls at the monkey-pipe before unconsciousness had claimed him.

Adam bought a newspaper, found a caff and ordered tea, toast and a Full English breakfast (two fried eggs, bacon, sausage, beans, mushrooms, tomatoes and chips) and duly consumed it. Replete, and feeling marginally better, he wandered off to Mile End Park and thought he might just lie down on the grass for a minute or two. Three hours later he woke up and staggered home to Oystergate Buildings.

Vladimir still wasn't up and this time he didn't reply when Adam knocked. Adam watched horse racing on TV for a while and made himself several cups of tea. The kitchen was marginally better furnished: Adam had bought a kettle, saucepan, two mugs, two plates and two sets of knives and forks – like an impoverished young couple setting up their first home, he thought. There was no fridge, as yet, so the milk was kept on the window sill.

He sipped his fourth mug of tea wondering, thinking about what to do. He could live on here in Oystergate Buildings, he supposed, certainly for a while, and continue his profitable begging life. He was earning more as a part-time beggar than Vladimir would in gainful employ as a hospital porter and, moreover, he had plans for some more audacious variations on the 'lost blind man' sting that served him so well.

Or perhaps he should leave the city and go north, as he had told Mhouse – actually go to Edinburgh, to Scotland. They had blind people in Scotland – he could beg as well there as here. But there was something about London that he needed, he realised, something basic and fundamental: he needed its size, its great sprawling scale, its millions of denizens, the utter and protective anonymity it provided. He thought about the 600 people a week that went missing in this country, the boys and girls, the men and women, who walked out of their front doors, closing them behind them, knowing they would never return, or who climbed out of back windows and ran off into the night to join that vast population of living ghosts that were The Missing. Two hundred thousand missing people – and most of them would

306

be in London, he reckoned, subsisting, like him, under all the categories of social radar – living underground, undocumented, unnumbered, unknown. Only London was big and heartless enough to contain these lost multitudes, the vanished population of the United Kingdom – only London could swallow them up without a qualm, without demur.

No, he thought, he would take it – in line with the cliché – one day at a time. As long as Vladimir kept his monkey habit under control (no police raids, thank you) he was safe enough in Oystergate Buildings. Life could continue in its reliably haphazard way. Thinking of Vladimir, he made him a cup of sweet tea and knocked again on his door.

'Vlad? I've made some tea, mate.' He pushed the door open. 'Let's go and buy some—'

It was immediately obvious that Vladimir was dead. He was lying on the mattress, twisted round, one arm flung wide as if reaching for one last time for his monkey-pipe and smoking gear. His eyes were open and so was his mouth.

Adam stepped back out of the room and closed the door. He was trembling so much that tea was sloshing out of the mug. 'Fuck, no,' he groaned out loud, 'no, no, no.' Cursing his misfortune, his stinking bad luck – and then guilt overwhelmed him: the horrible thought came to him that he might have saved Vladimir. When he'd gone out for breakfast he was sure he'd heard Vladimir moan something. Perhaps he had been alive then, *in extremis*, but alive and was calling for help. If he'd gone in at that point he might have been able to help – summon a doctor, call an ambulance. But all this retrospection was pointless, he realised. He set the mug down and went back into the room. He knew he should leave Vladimir's body untouched but, all the same, he closed his eyelids with a fingertip, pushed his mouth shut and straightened him out, positioning him supine on the mattress with his arms by his side. Now he looked as if he were sleeping – sort of. The complete and total inertness was the give-away: the absence of even the tiniest movement, the chest rising and falling, nostrils flaring, the little physical tics of vivacity we all produce unreflectingly, inadvertently, that show we are alive.

Adam supposed that Vladimir must have monkey-smoked his way to a massive cardio-vascular trauma: his weak heart succumbing to an attack brought on, perhaps, by one hit of the pipe too many, one final, dizzying, drug-buzzing, adrenalin surge that had overwhelmed him. The faulty heart valve that his kind, generous neighbours and fellow villagers had thought they had paid to have replaced, now fatally malfunctioning. And so Vladimir in his beatific drug-stupor had passed on. Maybe it wasn't such a bad way to go, Adam thought, as he covered him with a blanket and went out for a long reflective walk.

★ ★ ★

It should have felt stranger living in a flat with a dead friend lying in the next-door room, Adam considered, but once Vladimir had been 'laid out', discreetly covered and the door firmly closed, Adam found that hours could pass without him once thinking about the corpse in the bedroom.

He had decided not to do anything hurriedly or rashly – just wait and think, plot and plan, take his time – in order to see if he could come up with a course of action that would allow Vladimir's body to be properly removed and buried and, at the same time, not draw anyone's attention to the fact that he, Adam Kindred, on the run and wanted for murder, had been staying in the flat. Not easy. He thought all through Sunday and the only notion he developed was that of simply walking away and later making an anonymous telephone call to the authorities. Vladimir knew none of his neighbours in Oystergate Buildings, not even in the two flats on either side of his – he hadn't been there long enough, so no one would miss him or come unexpectedly calling. Adam himself reckoned that 'community spirit' in Oystergate Buildings was on the low side, anyway, not to say moribund. Sunday passed by, slowly. Adam walked the streets of Stepney, went to the cinema and saw a bad film, bought a pizza and took it back to the flat where he ate it while watching television.

On Monday morning, having come up with no new bright ideas, he decided to leave and packed up his few possessions again in their plastic bags. He wondered where he should go: he was tempted to return to the familiar security of the triangle by Chelsea Bridge but was immediately aware that however familiar the place was, its security was no longer on offer: the police had raided it; the ugly man from Grafton Lodge mews knew about it. No, he would simply have to find somewhere similarly secure – there must be somewhere else in London where he could hide up.

He shut the front door behind him – thinking: maybe Hampstead Heath? Wide open spaces – and had just turned the key in the lock when a postman in shorts, heavy boots and a dusty blue turban stamped wearily up the stairs.

'Brilliant, got you. Mr Belem?'

Adam turned. 'Mmm?' he said, in a neutral voice.

'Sign and print here, please.'

Adam signed and printed 'P. Belem' and was handed a registered envelope with the crest of Bethnal & Bow NHS Trust on one corner.

'Have a good one, Mr Belem,' the postman said and wandered off along the walkway.

Adam unlocked the door and went back into his flat.

CHAPTER 34

It had taken nearly a week to find Mohammed, much to Jonjo's intense frustration. The guy seemed to be living at about five addresses and he had been obliged to pay serious money to Bozzy and his cohorts to track him down.

They caught up with him eventually in a terraced house in Bethnal Green, lodging with an uncle. Jonjo decided that this next encounter would run more smoothly without Bozzy being present so he drove alone to Bethnal Green and parked up some twenty yards or so from Mohammed's temporary residence. Jonjo watched him come and go – with cousins and friends – before he finally left the house alone and headed for his Primera, presumably to start minicabbing and earn some money. Jonjo followed him for only a couple of minutes, Mohammed abruptly pulling up the Primera at the kerb – hazard lights flashing in the afternoon's sunshine – and running into a twenty-four-hour supermarket to buy something. Jonjo double-parked his taxi so that it was impossible for Mohammed to drive away and settled down to wait.

There was a brisk rap on the window.

' 'Scuse me, mate. But you've parked—'

Flinging the door open abruptly, Jonjo knocked Mohammed to the ground. He helped him up, dusted off his denim jacket. Mohammed recognised him at once.

'Listen, man, no way you can—'

'Step into my office, Mo.'

They sat in the back of Jonjo's taxi, Mohammed on the jump seat, Jonjo sprawled grandly at ease, opposite. The doors were locked.

'I got a big family,' Mohammed said. 'Uncles, brothers, cousins – anything happen to me, they know Bozzy. He's dead meat, yeah?'

'So do us all a big favour.' Jonjo leant forward and placed his hand on Mohammed's knee to quell its spasmodic jumping. 'I want to give you money, Mohammed – not hurt you.' He counted out £200 and handed them over. 'Take it.'

Mohammed did. 'Why?'

'Because you're going to tell me who else was in your car that night you took the mim to Chelsea. And then you're going to show me where I can find that person who was with you. And then I'll give you another £300.' Jonjo reached into his jacket and produced his big folded wad of notes.

'I was on me own, man.'

'No, you weren't. You said the mim went into the patch of waste ground to get his raincoat – while you sat in the car.'

'Yeah, right – so what?'

312

'So why didn't he do a runner if you were sitting in the car like a muppet?'

'Ah – 'cause I'd threatened him, like. Said I break his fucking leg if he don't not pay me.'

'He must have been shit-scared.'

'He was. That why he do what I say him.'

'So you *trusted* him. You just sat in the car and waited, trusting him to bring you his raincoat.'

'Ah . . . Yeah.'

Jonjo wrested back the £200.

'Even the most fucking useless, thick-as-shit, minicab driver in the world wouldn't do that. If you sat in the car who went with Kindred?' Jonjo waved the notes in front of Mohammed's face. Mohammed looked at the money and licked his lips. His knee started jumping again.

'It was someone called Mhouse.'

'A man called "Mouse"?'

'Woman.'

Jonjo's face registered no surprise at this information, even though he was very surprised.

'Do you know where she lives?'

'Yeah.'

'Take me there and you get the rest of your money.'

Jonjo waited until it had grown dark before he went back to The Shaft. He climbed the stairs and walked quickly along the walkway to Flat L. In his pocket he had a small thick jemmy that he wedged in the door-frame above the lock and

313

threw his full weight on it, levering at the same time, hearing the screws that held the lock ease and give under the pressure, the wood splintering. He slid the jemmy to the top and bottom of the door – no bolts. He paused, looked around to see that no one was looking, and with one powerful kick of his mason's boots blasted the door open. He stepped in quickly, swinging the door shut behind him and stood still in the entryway. There was no noise – the flat was empty. There was a light burning in the kitchen and he walked quietly into the sitting room and saw a TV, cushions, two chairs. In the kitchen he noted the power cable and the rubber water pipe coming through the window and allowed himself a small righteous sneer of taxpayer's disgust. These people will steal the bread from your mouth, he thought to himself. What kind of a world—

'Hello.'

Jonjo turned, very slowly, to see a small boy with curly hair, wearing a stained T-shirt that fell to his knees, standing in the doorway to a bedroom.

'Hello, little fella. Don't worry, I'm a friend. Where's your mum?'

'She working.'

'She asked me to get something for her.'

He moved past the boy into the bedroom – mattress on the floor, dirty sheets, wardrobe, a few cardboard boxes. He opened the wardrobe and rummaged through the clothes hanging inside, reaching into the back recesses to see what might have been stashed there. He pulled out shoes, a plastic bag full of sex toys, dildoes. The chemical smell of cheap perfume made his eyes smart. Then he pulled out a heavier box – no, a briefcase. He knew it well – solid locks, polished leather, brass trim at the corners. He clicked it open, empty. But this was Kindred's – pieces were beginning to fit together and he felt his excitement rise. The little boy was looking at him sleepily but curiously, leaning against the door-frame, scratching his thigh.

'Whose is this?'

'My mum's.'

Jonjo checked the other room – a bare mattress, bare floorboards, more boxes filled with crap. The state some people lived in – disgusting. He strode to the door, briefcase in his hand.

'Cheerio, mate.'

'You a friend of John?' the little boy said.

Jonjo stopped, turned. 'Who's John?'

'He live here but he gone now. You tell him to come back – say Ly-on want him to come back.'

'Does Mummy know John?'

'Yeah. She like John very too much. Green, green peas.'

'Whatever.' Jonjo patted him on the head, said good night and closed the door as best he could behind him.

Bozzy was waiting by the trashed playground. He pointed to the briefcase in Jonjo's hand.

'Where you get that?'

'The Mouse-woman. Kindred's been living there.'

'Fuck me. All this time?'

'Yeah. Where does she work?'

Bozzy grinned. 'Work? She's tugging sad bastards down Cherry Garden Pier.'

'She's a gas-cooker? . . .' This confused Jonjo – what was Kindred doing living with a whore? 'You sure?'

'Do dogs lick their bollocks? Twenty quid a go, mate. Thirty, no condom. Very high class, know what I mean?' He chuckled to himself.

'How do I get to Cherry Garden Pier?'

CHAPTER 35

The river was beautiful tonight, she thought, and very high, right up. It was the moving blackness, the beginning of the turn, the great mass of water beginning its journey back to the sea: the black river flowing strongly and the reflected lights on its moving surface staying still. Mhouse saw the power and the entrancement – not that she would have articulated it that way – but the river distracted her and she dwelt on it for a while before she remembered how fucking pissed off she was.

A quiet night – not half. She'd been trolling around Cherry Garden Pier for a couple of hours, up the side streets, down the lanes, looking for customers, for men. She'd met one girl who was thinking of heading up to King's Cross, it was so dead down here in Rotherhithe. She even wandered back into Southwark Park but it was all gay boys there, although one bloke asked her to follow him to the lake, said he had some kind of shack they could use, but she told him where he could shove his lake and his shack, no way.

She lit and smoked a cigarette. She could see

317

the big hospital, St Bot's, downstream, every light shining. Some electricity bill that one. It was a shame John 1603 had left – it was like living with a money tap, you just turned it on when you needed a bit more. Short of a £100? – Spend a night with John. He was a nice enough geezer (she wasn't that keen on men with beards, to be honest) – gentle, kindly, helped out – and he liked her. Well, he liked fucking her, anyway, she knew that, that was as obvious as the nose on his face. Ly-on liked him as well – and he seemed to like Ly-on. So, she let him fuck her from time to time, she got some ready money and he had a roof over his head with satellite TV, so why did he have to clear off like that all of a sudden? Now she owed Mr Quality and Margo and they were bugging her hard to repay. Lot of money. And you didn't want to end up on the wrong side of Mr Q . . .

She wondered if she could track down John 1603, offer him his room back, maybe reduce the rates across the board. How you going to do that, silly bitch? I could try the church, she thought – he was always at the church, and they might know where he was. Maybe Scotland won't work out for him. Maybe he'll come back to The Shaft, to Mhouse and Ly-on – his little family. Maybe he really wanted to be—

'Evening, darling.'

She turned to see a man standing on the river pathway. Where had he come from? She moved towards him slowly, hitching up the top of her bustier so her cleavage was more defined. Cleavage always worked – funny, that.

'What you after, my lovely?' she asked.

'I got a car back here,' he said, gesturing with his thumb. 'We could go for a nice drive.'

'I don't go in cars, dear – sorry. You follow me – you'll have the time of your life.'

She set off towards the King's Stair Gardens and she could hear his footsteps behind her. There was a blocked-up doorway she used in a kind of water-pumping station, deeply recessed, very dark – people could walk right past and not see what you were up to.

She stepped into the doorway and sensed rather than saw his bulk fill the space. Big bloke. She reached for his fly – whip it out and get your hands on it, that was her routine. Don't even let them have a second to think. All over before you knew it – before they had a chance to get specific.

She felt his strong hand on her wrist.

'Hold on, sweetness, not so fast. I got a few ideas myself.'

'It's forty pound,' she said. 'Fifty, no condom. If you want a room it's a hundred – half an hour.'

She clicked on her cigarette lighter. It freaked them out if they knew you'd seen their face clear – stopped them getting any nasty little notions. The flame lit his big face and she saw the pale-lashed eyes, the weak chin with a big cleft down the middle, the dancing flame making the cleft look even deeper than it was. He seemed familiar to her, somehow.

'Don't I know you?' she said. 'Ain't I done you before?'

'No. Not unless you work down Chelsea way.'

'I never been to Chelsea, darling.'

'Oh, yes you have.'

Then he grabbed her by the throat and lifted her almost off her feet, ramming her into the wall, driving the breath from her lungs.

'Where's Adam Kindred,' he breathed into her face. 'Tell me that and I won't have to mark you.'

She couldn't speak, so she made a choking, gagging noise. She had both hands on his wrist – it felt like the thick branch of a tree – and her toes were just touching the ground. He relaxed his grip slightly, let her down a few inches.

'I don't know the name,' she said.

'How about "John"?'

And, now, for some reason, she remembered him. He was the guy she'd seen getting out of the taxi outside The Shaft, one night a few weeks ago. It was the taxi she'd noticed and then she'd walked right past this man – this big ugly bastard with the cleft chin who now had his hand round her throat. But what did he have to do with John 1603?

'John who?' she said. 'There's lots of Johns in this world.'

'How about the John who was staying in your flat? Let's start with him.'

This chastened her – and she felt weak being

caught out so quickly. How the fuck did he *know*? Who had told him? And she experienced a horrible premonition: she was suddenly aware that she was going to have to fight this big powerful man, fight him for her life – like that last time she'd got in the car with that evil bastard punter. You turned into an animal – you just knew.

'Tell me about John,' he said.

'Oh, that cunt,' she said, bitterly. 'He fucked off to Scotland last week.'

'What? Scotland?'

She sensed his genuine surprise and his grip on her slackened again and she knew this was her moment. She drove her knee into his balls, full force, and heard his bellow of pain as she ducked beneath his arms and ran.

But he was after her in a second, it seemed, and she couldn't run fast in those fucking high-heeled boots. He caught her just before she got to the river and its lighted walkways, grabbed her hands in some kind of a lock and frogmarched her back up into the darkness of King's Stairs Gardens and there he did something strange to her neck – fingers digging deep in at the side, a thumb pressing hard behind one ear – and she felt one whole side of her body going limp, and pins and needles in her left hand.

She punched him in the face with her right hand, got her nails in his cheek and raked downwards, feeling his skin tear. She saw his whirling back-hander too late and tried to duck but he hit her so hard that the last thing she remembered was the sensation of flying through the air – Mhouse was flying, off the ground, flying in the air like a little birdie.

And then – nothing.

CHAPTER 36

Goran, the duty head porter, came into the porters' restroom, looked around at the half dozen porters sitting there – reading newspapers, texting, sleeping – and checked his clipboard.

'OK . . . Is Wellington and Primo, going for to ward 10 – Mrs Manning for surgery.' He paused. 'Hello, calling Primo, come in, Primo. Home base to Primo . . .'

Adam didn't react at first even though he was looking directly at Goran, forgetting for the briefest instant that in fact *he* was Primo, now, but – remembering – quickly stood and gave a thumbs up. Wellington heaved himself out of the armchair and rubbed his grey hair with a palm and looked over at him.

'Come on, Primo, man, this he going to be fun.'

Waiting for the service lift to arrive and take them up to ward 10 Adam caught a glimpse of his reflection in the scratched stainless steel of the lift-door surround, noting the ceiling lights bouncing off his bald pate, creating the effect of a refulgent skullcap on top of his head – like some kind of incipient halo. He ran his hand over the new stubble growing already on his lucent dome, feeling the rasp against the palm of his hand, keeping a vague, bemused smile on his face. This was his second day at work but he thought he had now finally figured out what to do with Vladimir's body. He was surfing the tide of experience, as he put it to himself, free-floating on the turbulent river of events that was carrying him along. Just do it, he said to himself – there would be time enough for calm reflection later.

It was only after the postman had left him and after he had re-entered the flat that Adam had seen – in a visionary flash – the simple beauty, the pure genius and potential of the plan that he had spontaneously and almost inadvertently conceived at the front door – that had allowed him to sign 'P. Belem' on the post office docket without his hand shaking. He had gone straight to the bathroom where it had taken him a surprisingly lengthy time to remove the hair from his head and radically trim his full beard into a Vladimir look-alike goatee. Staring in some shock at his reflection in the mirror – confronting his new appearance – Adam saw the clear generic resemblance: he now looked approximately like thousands of men in London, possibly tens of thousands: head completely shaved and a trimmed short beard around the lips and on the chin. No one looking at Vladimir/Primo's photo on his ID card would have any hesitation in identifying him. The eyes were a bit different, the nose was straighter but, by the standards of a passport photo-shot sealed under plastic, Adam Kindred had, with a bit of strenuous scissor and razor work, to all intents and purposes, become 'Primo Belem'.

And so it had proved: he had put on Vladimir's uniform and had reported to the administration at Bethnal & Bow hospital, apologising for being a little late, and had been sent down to the portering control room where he showed his ID to Goran, had it validated, filled in a form, delivered the form that had been in the registered letter, was led to the porter's call point and was assigned to one Wellington Barker for induction and general training. It was as straightforward as that. There were twenty porters on duty in the day at the hospital, half a dozen at night. A more polyglot group was hard to imagine: nobody was interested in him, nobody had any personal questions beyond asking him his name. 'Primo' came off his tongue as easily as John.

In ward 10 Adam discovered the reasoning behind Wellington's 'fun' prediction. Mrs Manning was a morbidly obese thirty-five-year-old woman who weighed a stone for every year of her life and who was due in surgery to have her stomach stapled. Her thin husband and three extremely plump children were gathered anxiously around her card- and lucky-mascot-strewn bed. Wellington showed Adam how to work the winch (portering

in Bethnal & Bow was an on-the-job learning experience) and together they hoisted Mrs Manning off
the bed and lowered her on to the creaking trolley
before taking her down in the lift to theatre.

She kept up a cheerful banter as they travelled
– 'I'll come back and you boys won't recognise
me' – but beneath the chirpy spirits Adam could
sense her fear of the future, of the new Mrs
Manning she was trying to become, in the same
way as he could also discern a once pretty face
beneath the triple chins and the bulging,
dewlapped cheeks. He wanted to reassure her –
don't worry, Mrs M., it's not too bad being
someone different – but he just smiled and said
nothing.

'Amazing what they can do these days,' Adam
said, once they had parked her in the queue of
patients waiting for the anaesthetist, and were
walking back to the lift.

'Yeah, but you know . . .' Wellington made a face.
'She lose the weight but it don't end there, man.'
Adam listened – Wellington had been a porter at
Bethnal & Bow for eighteen years and he knew
what he was talking about – in his time the hospital
had developed a renowned special unit for the
treatment of morbid obesity.

'The fat go, you see, but instead you flappin'
around everywhere – all that stretched skin empty.
You like a collapsed washing-line. Then you got
three year of ops cuttin' it away.' Wellington looked
balefully at him. 'Think of the scarring, man. It not

going to be nice.' Maybe Mrs Manning had every right to be fearful.

Adam felt tired at the end of his shift. Amongst general fetching and carrying and trundling of patients here and there with Wellington, they had also moved and set up ten trestle tables in a screened-off area of the cafeteria for a presentation/lunch party for area NHS junior managers, taken blood samples to the pathology lab, delivered clinical notes to the medical secretaries, removed decomposing bags of human tissue waste from the operating theatres to the furnaces, and, in a kind of electric golf-buggy, had made a series of runs transporting empty oxygen cylinders to waiting lorries and returning full ones to the on-site store.

On his way back to Oystergate Buildings he went into a discount electrical warehouse and ordered a fridge. He said to the salesman that he didn't care what brand it was as long as it could be delivered the next morning. He paid with Vladimir's credit card (Vladimir had obligingly kept his pin-number on a slip of paper in his wallet) signing 'P. Belem' for the second time. Then, in a builders' merchants, he asked a burly man for a delivery-trolley-thing and was told – tiredly, disdainfully – that what he actually was after was a long-toed, folding sack-truck. This was duly provided and he bought it and an all-in-one blue overall with a zip up the front, an acid green high-visibility waistcoat and a base-ball-cap with a hammer-and-nail logo on the front.

He was on night shift the next day and so had the morning and afternoon free. He reasoned that what he was about to do was, paradoxically, safer in broad daylight than darkest night. He would attract no attention in the day – by night he would look hugely suspicious.

His fridge arrived around 10.00 a.m, conveyed by two cursing men – 'Why no lift? What building this?' – who grudgingly helped him remove the fridge from its sturdy cardboard box and fit it in the window embrasure in the kitchen and plug it in. He liked its reassuring hum. He said he'd prefer to keep the box if they didn't mind.

When they had gone he took the empty box into Vladimir's room and flipped back the blanket from the body. Vladimir didn't look as though he was sleeping any more – he looked very dead: his skin pale, his face grimacing slightly, cheeks sunken, his eyeballs bulging behind the lids. This was the hardest part, Adam knew, as he put on his latex gloves, feeling queasy as he bent Vladimir into a rough foetal position. He was surprisingly supple – he had been expecting extreme stiffness – but then he remembered that rigor mortis disappeared after twenty-four to thirty-six hours, or there-abouts, and the musculature of the body became limp again. Thank god. He rolled Vladimir's skinny frame into the up-ended fridge box, lifting it back upright to seal it with yards of gaffer tape. Then with a knife from the kitchen he cut flaps and slits in the cardboard around the base. Then he put

328

on his blue overall, hi-viz waistcoat and baseball-cap and with the box secured on his sack-truck trundled it out of the flat. He bumped it down the four flights of stairs and wheeled it out of Oystergate Buildings.

He stuck to back and side streets, taking a meandering course towards Limehouse Cut, a mile or so away, a canal that ran from Bow River into Limehouse Basin. He looked completely normal, he knew – an ordinary delivery man on an ordinary weekday morning, trundling a new fridge in a cardboard box towards some domestic destination. Nobody he passed even glanced at him.

It took him half an hour to wheel Vladimir to the area he had scouted out the previous day. His hands were raw and his shoulders were hurting, but this access road to a light industrial estate led to the canal and there was a gate to the towpath that ran along the canal side for several hundred yards until the canal linked up with Bow Creek by the gasworks. It was not overlooked by any houses or other buildings, just the blank gable ends of warehouses and the razor-wired truck and lorry parks, shredded with the greying remains of polythene bags. It seemed little used, this path – great clumps of buddleia sprouted from crevices in the low wall built along the canal side, butterflies playing among their bright purple flowers. He paused to let a van go by – again unperturbed: the nearby warehouses explained his presence, with his sack-truck and his big cardboard box.

When the van was out of sight he carefully eased the laden sack-truck on to the towpath and pushed it some yards away from the access gate. He slipped the toe of the sack-truck out from beneath the fridge box and then manoeuvred the box itself to the very edge of the stone coping that ran along the canal-side path.

He looked around: some fleeting midday sun shone between the fair-weather cumulus clouds lighting the scene, the butterflies exulting in the glare and dazzle. He heard children shouting in the playground of a nearby school and some sort of motorcycle testing or rally seemed to be going on somewhere close, the air suddenly loud with the throaty rip of powerful engines. He had a final look and then casually kicked the box into the canal. It fell with a heavy splash and bobbed there for a while, buoyantly, before the water began to fill it, flowing in through the flaps and slits he had cut. Slowly it semi-righted itself and then settled lower and lower before, with some erupting bubbles, it slipped beneath the surface.

He thought he should say something – something for Vladimir. 'Rest in peace' seemed a bit crass so he contented himself with a *sotto voce* 'Goodbye, Vlad – and many thanks,' before tossing his new long-toed, folding sack-truck into the water also, letting it join the crowded debris on the canal floor, the rubber tyres and supermarket trolleys, the cast-iron bedsteads and the defunct cookers, the burnt-out chassis of joyriders' cars.

As he walked away, he wondered how long it would be before Vladimir's body would be discovered. The new box would hold for a good while, he reckoned, before the cardboard began to deliquesce and shred. A week? A month? It didn't really matter, he knew. The final, generous benefaction that Vladimir had bestowed on him was his total anonymity. *Vladimir who?* Even Adam didn't know his last name or what part of the former Soviet Union he had come from. And even if they found him and were able to identify him – oh, yes, that's him: the missing cardiac patient who had gone on the run from his village's mercy mission – no one was ever going to connect this sad drug addict's fatal overdose with Primo Belem, hospital porter at Bethnal & Bow, alive and well.

Adam walked back to Oystergate Buildings, feeling more calm and confident than he had since this whole crazy affair had begun. Now he had a name, he had a flat, he had a job, he had a passport, he had money, he had a credit card – soon he could acquire a mobile phone . . . It struck him that now he really could say that Adam Kindred didn't exist any more – Adam Kindred was redundant, superseded, obsolete. Adam Kindred had truly disappeared, truly gone underground, deep underground. He had a new life and new opportunities before him, now – the future really did belong to Primo Belem.

CHAPTER 37

Candy's face was a parodic mask, a bad cari-
cature of shock, eyes wide, mouth formed
in an 'O'.

'No,' she said.

'Yes.'

'No.'

'Yes, 'fraid so.'

'The Dog? Never.'

'I can't explain it either, Candy-babe,' Jonjo said,
trying to look both mystified and hurt. 'I bent
down to put his bowl of Bowser Chunks in front
of him and he just snapped – caught me.' Jonjo
was extemporising, attempting to provide a
convincing reason as to why his left cheek was
covered by a three-inch square of gauze held in
place by strips of sticking plaster. He felt a bit
guilty blaming The Dog – there was no more
placid creature on earth – but it was all he could
think of on the spur of the moment. Candy had
wandered into the garage as he was loading his
golf clubs into the back of the taxi and, on seeing
him, had gone into her oh-my-god-what-happened
routine.

'He's never snapped before,' she said. 'I mean, I kiss him—'

'Shouldn't kiss a dog, Cand.'

'Just a little peck on the nose. No, no – something must have triggered it, something must have spooked him. Poor old Jonjo.' She reached out and ran her hand over his cropped hair and nuzzled up against him, kissing his unplastered cheek. 'You come round to me tonight – I'll make you a nice bowl of soup.'

She kissed him again on the lips and Jonjo flinched, as though in pain. Everything had changed since their intimacy the other night – since their supper *à deux* and the sex that had followed, as predictable as the postprandial brandy and box of chocolates. She had moved into his life with all the tact of a suspicious social worker, he thought: calling, texting, popping over without warning, buying him presents he didn't want – clothes, food, drinks, little ornaments.

'Busy tonight, love. Sorry.' Don't have it off with your neighbour – he'd remember that in his next life.

'Shall I take The Dog? Where is he? I'll take him for a walk, give him a right talking to – biting his daddy, well I never.'

He delivered The Dog to her and drove off to Roding Valley golf course for a calming round. He took a nine at the first hole, five-putted the short par-three second and then shanked his drive off the third tee into the Chigwell sewage works.

He walked straight back to the club house, abandoning his round, tense and angry, wondering what had made him think golf was the palliative to the swarming can of worms that was currently masquerading as his life.

He sat in the members' bar with a gin and orange, trying to calm down and take stock. His scratched cheek was throbbing as if it were infected. *Bitch*. Bitching whore bitch. He would have just left her lying there and walked away but he knew she had four fingernails crammed with his skin, blood and DNA – so she had to go in the river.

He ordered another gin. He should have just stayed at home today, drinking medicinally, that would have helped. But then Candy would still have come round . . . He took out his score card and wrote down the words 'KINDRED = JOHN' in the hope that this might get his brain working. He hadn't meant to kill the little tart – she would have told him everything in the end – but he'd overreacted, following Sgt. Snell's rules, when she'd punched and scratched him like that. He just hadn't thought – it was a reflex – and had given her the old backhanded haymaker (they never see it coming) and she went flying, head first into the brick wall. He thought he'd even heard her neck snap but, whether he did or not, there was no doubt from the funny way she fell limp to the ground and lay there that she was dead, or as good as.

He had paced about cursing for a while, staunching the blood from the scratches with a tissue, and then strolled casually out to check what was going on riverside – nothing. So he picked her up and held her as if she were an unconscious drunk and walked with her to the embankment wall. He leant her up against it and slapped her face gently, talking to her, making it seem as if he were trying to revive her in case anyone was looking, all the while searching for CCTV. No sign – and there was no one about. The tide was high and ebbing fast, he saw, so he just threw her over the wall into the water and she was gone in a second.

Jonjo sat on a park bench with Bozzy and a tall thin man he had been introduced to as Mr Quality. They were in a small public square not far from The Shaft – Bozzy had brought Mr Quality there and Jonjo had been obliged to pay him £50 for this 'consultation'. A few tired young mothers and their wailing toddlers were gathered at the far end and an old bloke was methodically searching the rubbish bins.

'I no go charge you VAT,' Mr Quality said, pocketing the notes and then he laughed wheezingly to himself as if at a private joke.

'I'm looking for a man named John,' Jonjo said, keeping his temper. 'He was staying with a hooker called Mhouse in a flat that belongs to you, I believe. Stayed with her for some weeks.'

'I know Mhouse,' Mr Quality said. 'We are good friend.'

'Wonderful – so who is this bloke, John, then?'

'John 1603.'

'Say again?'

Mr Quality did.

'What does that mean? 1603 is not a surname. It's a date. A number.'

'This is how Mhouse introduce him me: John 1603.'

Jonjo looked over at Bozzy for confirmation that Mr Quality was one sandwich short of a picnic.

Bozzy shrugged. 'I don't know nothing, man.'

'Then you might as well fuck off.'

Bozzy left as haughtily as he could, offended.

Jonjo turned back to Mr Quality, who was lighting, as far as Jonjo could tell, a very thin spliff. This country had gone to the dogs, and the dogs were welcome to it. He kept his temper.

'What did he look like, this John 1603?'

'A white man like you. Thirty years. Long black hair. Thick black beard.'

Ah, thick black beard, Jonjo thought – that explained a lot.

'Do you know where he is?'

'If he no be for Mhouse – I don't know.'

Mr Quality ambled off, £50 richer. He deserved a good kicking that one, Jonjo thought, arrogant bastard, laughing at him, smoking weed like that, middle of the day, public park, little kiddies playing on the lawn. Jesus. This place needed hosing out, pest control. He told himself to calm down. John 1603, he said to himself, what does that mean? There must be a clue here somewhere . . . Why would Kindred choose such a weird name? But as he thought on, he began to feel better and thoughts of local Armageddon receded: he was getting somewhere, he had one more piece of information – bland 'John' had turned into intriguing 'John 1603'. He had a description now, he had met someone who had known Kindred, had seen him very recently, spoken with him. So much for the Metropolitan Police. He felt he was getting closer, drawing nearer.

He went back to The Shaft and wandered around the muddy square that Mhouse's flat overlooked, watching The Shaft's inhabitants come and go. He climbed the stairs to Flat L and knocked on the door, for form's sake. He thought he might have another sniff around, see if he'd missed anything, but the door had been fixed: it was locked and firm again. Maybe Mr Quality had a new tenant—

'She's not there. She's gone.'

Jonjo turned to see an old woman in an apron leaning out of the front door of the next flat along. She had no front teeth.

'Sorry, Madam,' Jonjo said, smiling politely. 'I'm looking for a friend of mine called John. I believe he lived here.'

'He's gone too. I think the two of them run off – she's gone off with him and left the little boy. Disgusting. Immoral.'

Jonjo approached. 'Did you know John?'

The woman bridled. 'Not "know" exactly. I was what you might say acquainted with him.'

'Somebody told me he called himself John 1603.'

'Well he would, wouldn't he?'

'Why would anyone call themselves that?'

'Because he was a member of the church,' she said with some defiance. 'Though they've both gone and let us down something shocking.'

Jonjo smiled: he couldn't believe his luck. What had seemed like a pig of a day was turning into a peach.

'And what church would that be? If I might ask.'

'The Church of John Christ, of course.'

CHAPTER 38

Typing 'itch' into half a dozen search engines, as he had surfed the Web that morning, had been no help at all. In fact it had been the very opposite of helpful, Ingram thought. Extremely unhelpful was a more accurate description, not to say creepily terrifying. A simple search for a piece of information, for an answer, had swamped him with massive over-information, provided tens of thousands of potential answers. He wished he'd kept away from the infernal computer and simply called Lachlan again and asked his advice – one human being to another. Now he was aware of having, maybe, one of a hundred nasty diseases – some of them flinchingly unpleasant, especially the sexually transmitted ones. He had had no notion that illustrations were so readily available online, either – it was appalling what could become of the diseased human body. He had no idea there were people wandering around with these degrees of purulence, pustulence, rash, swelling, decomposition . . .

Too much information – it was the curse of our modern times, most disturbing. But his itches seemed to be increasing – half a dozen biting, burning points of brief excruciation on his body per day, he now reckoned. Easily soothed with a bit of pressure, a quick and vigorous scratch, but with no discernible pattern at all. Head and foot, abdomen and elbow, earlobe and testicle. What was wrong with him? Could this be simple stress – could stress be tormenting him in this way?

Ingram tried to banish these unpleasant reflections as he prepared himself for his meeting with Burton Keegan. He had asked him to be in his office at 10 o'clock – at 10 past 10 Mrs Prendergast buzzed to say that Mr Keegan had phoned and was running a little late. He finally arrived at 10.40, full of apologies – something to do with his son and the special needs school he was at, the boy having had a hysterical reaction to a new teacher. Ingram was surprised to discover that Keegan had a handicapped child with severe Asperger's Syndrome and his simmering anger at being kept waiting quickly disappeared.

Keegan took a seat, coffee and water were ordered and served, chit-chat ensued about the company, the weather, Keegan's forthcoming trip home to the US, then Ingram moved into attack mode.

'Something's bothering me, Burton, that's why I wanted to see you, face to face.'

'I thought there might be an issue.'

'It's not an "issue", it's a simple question and it is this: did you have a meeting with Philip Wang

340

at 3 o'clock on the afternoon of the day he was murdered?'

Keegan almost managed to disguise his surprise and shock. 'Yes. I did,' he said.

'Yet you never told the police or me or anyone. Why?'

'Because it wasn't important – the meeting was completely routine.'

'Why did you lie to me?'

Keegan looked at him. 'I'd forgotten about it.'

Ingram could see him regaining his composure after the initial stumble. 'What was the meeting about?' Ingram asked.

Keegan cleared his throat. 'As far as I remember, Philip had been on a tour of all the UK hospitals we're using for our third-phase clinical trials of Zembla-4. He was delighted with our progress and he just wanted to urge me to bring forward the FDA and MHRA submissions.'

In every good lie, Ingram thought, there must be an element of truth. That was what they taught spies, wasn't it? His knowledge of Philip Wang's visits to the hospitals was no longer ammunition, now that Keegan had referred to them.

'How curious,' Ingram said. 'That's the complete opposite of what Philip told me two days previously.'

Keegan smiled. 'I guess he must have changed his mind. He was very upbeat, very adamant that we move quickly.'

'We'll never know, now, will we?' Ingram said, thinking that at least he had learnt what all this was about, finally. Keegan and Wang had obviously totally disagreed with each other, diametrically opposed. 'Strange to think you were the last person to see him hungry.'

'What do you mean – "hungry"?'

'I said "alive".'

'You said: "the last person to see him hungry". I'm sorry but I heard you.'

'All right. Slip of the tongue. You were the last person to see him alive.'

'Not so – his killer, Adam Kindred, was the last person to see him alive,' Keegan said with quiet logic and looked at his watch. 'I'm sorry to break this up, Ingram, but I really have to go.' He stood.

'The meeting's not over, Burton. I have more questions.'

'Send me an email. We have very important business today. All this talk about Philip advances nothing.'

Now Ingram stood up. 'This isn't going to be brushed aside—'

'If you're not happy with anything I suggest you call Alfredo. Thanks for the coffee.' He walked out of the office.

Ingram felt a burning itch spring up on his left calf that he banished by rubbing his leg against the sharp glass edge of the coffee table. It must be stress after all.

CHAPTER 39

Burton Keegan poured some more Scotch into Paul de Freitas's glass.

'I really shouldn't,' de Freitas said, 'but I think I should.'

'You ready?'

'Let's go for it.'

They were in Burton's office on the top floor of his Notting Hill town house, under the eaves with a good view down dusky Ladbroke Grove. This was where he kept the scrambled phone line. Both men's wives were downstairs in the kitchen clearing up the remains of supper.

Burton dialled Alfredo Rilke's private number, feeling his mouth go dry, and his shoulders tighten. It never became any easier – there was always that element of apprehension, of the unforeseen, when you talked to Alfredo – even after ten years of experience of working with him, working with him closely. He was twenty seconds early from the appointed time to call.

'Burton,' Rilke said, 'good to talk to you. How's the weather in London?'

'Surprisingly good.' Burton felt his hands begin

to sweat – banter was always a bad sign. 'I've got Paul here with me. Can I put you on speaker?'

'Sure. Hi, Paul. How's the beautiful Mrs de Freitas?'

'She's excellent. How are you, Alfredo?'

Too familiar, thought Burton, anxiously.

'I'm still waiting, actually – waiting for news from you guys,' Rilke said, the tone of his voice changing. Burton made a zip-your-lip sign to de Freitas.

'We have a slight problem with Ingram,' Burton said. 'He knows about my meeting with Philip Wang on that last day. I think he thinks he's on to something.'

There was a long pause from Rilke and Burton began to massage his neck.

'Does he have any idea what was discussed at that meeting?' Rilke asked.

'No. I told him Philip was delighted, was pressing for accelerated approval from both agencies, US and UK.'

'I want you to be extremely nice to Ingram until this is all over. Got that?' There was real edge in his voice now. 'What made him suspicious? Is it something you did?'

'I'm *always* extremely nice to him,' Burton said, not answering the question. 'I just don't think he likes me.'

'Then make him like you. Apologise, keep him sweet. What's happening your end?'

'Things are good,' Burton said. 'We have our

guys talking up Zembla-4 to all the important people. We're arguing compassionate use.'

'We're confident we'll get priority status,' de Freitas chipped in. 'Did you see the latest WHO report on asthma? People need Zembla-4. Couldn't be better timing.'

Burton was regretting pouring him that extra Scotch – you just didn't become garrulous with Alfredo Rilke.

Burton jumped in. 'We think the compassionate use, accelerated approval principle is unanswerable. Some of those AIDS drugs were approved in months, weeks.'

'What about post-marketing studies?' Rilke said. 'Funded by us. You should have all that in place.'

'We have,' Burton lied. He forgot, very rarely, that Rilke knew more than anyone when it came to pharmaceuticals. He made a note on a pad: 'post-marketing studies'. He should have thought of that himself. It was obvious – compassionate use, accelerated approval, licensee-funded post-marketing studies. It all fell into place – in theory.

'Children are dying,' de Freitas said, ignoring Burton's finger held to his lips. 'The data is enormous, exemplary, Alfredo, magnificent. Everything's ready.'

Rilke was silent again. Then he said: 'Run out the first advertorials next week.'

'Should I tell Ingram?'

'I'll tell him.'

345

'What about the FDA?' Burton asked. 'Are they happy with the European trials?'

'I think so,' Rilke said. 'Our people are very close – close to people who are close to people: though nobody knows how close anyone else is to the other. The word is that they seem happy. So,' he paused. 'Submit for approval, simultaneously, after the ads have run for a month.' Burton and de Freitas looked at each other, eyes wide. 'Then we want the opinion pages.'

'Consider it done.' Burton saw the logic, clearly. 'Everybody's ready.' Announce the impending wonder drug, have people start talking about it, have journalists write articles about it, then asthmatics will start asking their doctors for it. There are millions upon millions of asthma sufferers out there – a powerful lobby, exerting a lot of pressure. Nobody will want to be seen dragging their feet, no bureaucratic impediments, niggling rules and regulations preventing relief from awful suffering, saving children's lives.

'We'll get right on to it,' Burton said. 'Have a good even—'

'Just one thing.'

'Sure.'

'Did they ever find this Kindred guy? It's the one factor that disturbs my peaceful sleep. He could ruin everything.'

'We're closing in, is my latest report. He was seen in London a matter of days ago. We have a new description. A new name he's been using. It's just a matter of time.'

Now Rilke's silence grew ominously long.

'This is just not good enough, Burton.'

The rebuke was devastating even though Rilke's tone was mild. Burton felt the air leave his lungs and his guts contract. Somehow he managed to say, 'I'm sorry. We just can't explain how Kindred—'

'How many times do I have to ask for this? Prioritise it. Call your people.'

They said their goodbyes. Burton felt nauseous. He knew his hands would shake if he held them out.

'Why's he so obsessed with Kindred?' de Freitas asked, oblivious, with all the confidence of the nearly drunk. 'What can he do to us? It's all too late now, isn't it?' He put on a bad cockney accent: 'Kindred is toast, mate.'

'Yeah,' Burton said vaguely. But he was thinking: that's the first time in ten years I've heard Alfredo Rilke sound worried. That was serious. 'I'll see you downstairs, Paul,' he said. 'Take the Scotch with you.'

De Freitas left and Burton thought back to that afternoon's meeting with Philip Wang . . . Nice, mild, clever, plump Philip Wang in a shivering incoherent rage, his voice shrill, threatening to bring everything down on their heads – the deaths of children, cover-up, manipulation of research data. The trials would end, he'd go to the FDA himself, he didn't care. Philip Wang's fury as he had listed the abuses was almost as if it were driven by the death of one of his own children. Burton had stalled, but it was alarmingly clear to him that Philip Wang had independently figured out almost everything that had gone on in the Zembla trials – indeed, he was even impressed by Wang's detective powers, in an unhappy, panicky way, feelings that he managed quickly to control.

Philip had said that it was certain aspects in the 'adverse event reports' that had first alerted him: compulsory reports that logged patients dropping out of the trials because of certain seemingly mild side effects: shortness of breath, temporary fever. This appeared odd to him – Zembla-4 being so benign – so he had decided to investigate further, personally, and when he had visited the four hospitals and looked through the clinical records in detail he had discovered to his intense shock that of the several dozen drop-outs (perfectly normal figures in a trial of this size) fourteen had later died in intensive care.

'Those deaths were unrelated to Zembla-4,' Keegan had said at once. 'They were very, very sick children in the first place, remember. We've treated thousands of children with Zembla-4 over the last three years. There is no statistical significance.'

'I know what's happening,' Philip had said. 'This is Taldurene all over again.'

'Those Taldurene deaths are still disputed,' Keegan said, hoping he sounded convincing.

348

He knew the case – everybody in the Pharma world knew the case: five out of fifteen patients had died from renal failure in a particular phase-three Taldurene trial – everyone assumed that, because the patients already had hepatitis, the deaths were nothing to do with the drug they were testing. Turned out they were wrong.

Wang would not be appeased, reminding Keegan that the de Vere Wing children's trials had not been his idea. 'It's not just children who suffer from asthma,' he said, 'I wanted across-the-board population studies. I'm not developing a drug that's just for children.'

'And you got them. The Italian and Mexican trials are exactly that,' Keegan said. 'We just thought that in the UK we might—'

'You just thought you'd go flat out for accelerated approval, priority status of Zembla-4. Choose a niche group – children. Show genuine medical need. What can the FDA do? I know how it works.'

'I'm surprised you're so cynical, Philip.'

Wang had lost it again at that stage and had begun to detail, very skilfully, the components of the cover-up, explaining how parents, nurses and doctors in the de Vere wings could never have made the connections, how they would think, even in the face of these rare individual deaths, these particular family tragedies, that nothing was untoward. The de Vere staff were just administering, supervising and supplying data. Calenture-Deutz was analysing, collating and categorising it. A very sick child became ill and was logged as a drop-out from the trial, not a death. The deaths were part of any hospital's inevitable, grim body-count. The trials continued unaffected.

'What were the signs?' Wang had taunted him. 'What gave you those four or five days' notice? Something was telling you. How could you move them out of the de Vere wings so quickly? That's what I want to know. What was Zembla-4 doing to them?'

'I haven't a clue what you're talking about,' Keegan had said. However, he had conceded that there might have been some bureaucratic foul-up and feigned his own quiet outrage.

'Look, I'm as unhappy as you, Philip. We'll investigate, we'll triple-check again, we'll get to the bottom of this . . . Everything goes on hold from this second, everything, until we discover what's happening . . .' He had spoken on, continuing to reassure, praise, to promise retribution if there had been any sign of manipulation until he saw Philip calm down, somewhat mollified. They had left each other, not exactly as firm friends once again, but with a handshake at the door.

He had called Rilke immediately Philip had left. Rilke had listened and had told him, quietly, emphatically, what had to be done, now, with no delay – who to call and what precise words to use.

Burton now experienced a sense of déjà vu as he picked up the scrambled phone and punched out the number.

'Hi,' he said to the woman who answered, 'I'd like to speak to Major Tim Delaporte, please . . . Yes, I know it's late but he'll want to talk to me . . . My name's Mr Apache. Thank you so much.'

CHAPTER 40

Plane, oak, chestnut, ginko – Adam noted the trees on his way to work as if he were strolling through his own arboretum. High summer now and the sun on the dense leafage this early morning made him feel moderately exultant – if such a state of mind could be imagined. The exultance he owed to sunshine and nature – the moderation arose from the nature of the job he was walking towards, its disadvantages and inadequacies, especially given the profession he had previously occupied. But he shouldn't complain, he knew. He had woken up in what was his own flat, showered in hot water, breakfasted on coffee and toast and was going to work, however relatively underpaid that work was. It was a routine, now, and one should never underestimate the importance of routine in a person's life: routine allowed everything else to seem more exciting and impromptu.

He checked in with the duty head porter, Harpeet, and wandered through to the 'common room' as he privately referred to the porters' restroom – a small personal reference to the life he had once led in academe. A trio of other sleepy porters lounged there, the remains of the night shift coming off duty. Adam glanced at the clock on the wall – twenty minutes early – Mr Keen. He had received his first pay cheque and banked it; he had been sent his first utility bill (water) and had paid it – his life, to anyone looking on from the outside, would seem almost normal.

'Hey, Primo. How you do?'

It was Severiano, a young guy whom he liked, who had joined Bethnal & Bow around the same time as he had, and who claimed to have taken up portering to improve his English. They gripped hands briefly, in a kind of high slap, like tennis players across the net at the end of a match.

'So, how was weekend?'

'Quiet,' Adam said. 'Just stayed in, watched TV.' He kept all answers to all questions as bland and banal as he could manage.

He poured himself a styrofoam cup of tea from the tureen, picked up a discarded tabloid and began to flick idly through it, heading towards the back pages for the sport, but curious to see on the way what else was going on in the tabloid world. It was summer, the football season was over, but he still felt himself at a serious social disadvantage with his colleagues. Apart from work and its travails all anybody seemed to want to talk about was football – last season's football and the coming season's football. He knew a little about English football but he'd lost touch during his many years in the USA – the game had changed beyond all imagination since he'd left the country and he knew he had to learn more if he wanted to converse more naturally with his fellow porters, if he were indeed to become one of them. In his first week someone had asked him idly which team he supported and, not thinking, he said the first name that came into his head at that moment – Manchester United. The shouts of derision and cries of pure hatred that greeted this choice astonished him. But now it was if he came to work every day in a Manchester United strip for he found himself the constant butt of crude anti-Northerner jokes and obscene remarks about the members of 'his' team (names that meant absolutely nothing to him). One porter had shouted in his face: 'You live in Stepney and you support Manchester United – you WANKER!' Adam had smiled blankly back at him – what hideous sporting faux pas had he committed? So he was teaching himself more about English football against the day when he would publicly switch allegiance to a London club that would be found more acceptable.

As he turned the pages a photo caught his eye – a flicker of unconscious recognition occurring in the same way as you will recognise your own name in a list of a thousand. He turned back – it wasn't a photo, it was an 'artist's impression'. He stared at it – the eyes were drawn closed but there was no doubt the portrait had a look of Mhouse about it – a clear look of Mhouse. He read the text beneath it with a cold, creeping sense of foreboding that brought out goose-bumps on his body. 'Young woman – early twenties – unidentified – accidental death most likely . . .' Adam felt light-headed. Then he read about the tattoos on the body and saw, printed bold in capital letters: MHOUSE LY-ON.

He went outside to the staff car park to inhale some fresh air, the newspaper still in his hand, his head a shouting racket of plots and possibilities. No, not Mhouse, surely – he said to himself – not Mhouse. He re-read the article. The body was found in the Thames by Greenwich . . . Some decomposition, obviously in the water for many days. Unidentified woman. Anyone with information . . . There was a number to call.

He paced around for a while, bad feelings accumulating, a scenario building in his head that involved a big ugly man with a weak, cleft chin. How, though? He had left The Shaft within minutes of seeing him there – minutes – there could have been no trail . . . But Mhouse was dead, that much was certain. But what about Ly-on? He realised he owed it to Ly-on to make the identification – nobody in The Shaft would do it – perhaps that would allow his mother to rest in peace, after a fashion.

He went to the payphone in the lobby and picked up the phone. He put it down. He had to think this through – serious risk might be involved. So he outlined all the reasons why he shouldn't call and identify Mhouse's body and he had to acknowledge they were firmly sensible and anyone in his situation would have been well advised to heed them. But he realised that he wasn't going to act in a thoughtful, logical way. He thought of Mhouse, dead, cold, lying in some kind of steel drawer with a brown label tied around her big toe and a number written on it and his very being seemed to contract and shudder. He knew he couldn't leave her like that. So what if there were risks – everything in his life was risky, and once you accepted that risk element then another kind of strategic, worldly, impromptu thinking came into play that had nothing to do with reason but everything to do with the person you were and the life you were living. Nobody knew who he was, Adam told himself. Adam Kindred wouldn't be making this identification, no, it would be Primo Belem, a casual acquaintance of the nameless victim. He could confidently give his name and address – he'd done it a dozen times now – even to the police. There was no mention of foul play in the paper so perhaps a simple identification was all that was required. Mhouse would have her name back and Ly-on would understand, one day, what had become of his mother. More importantly, Adam knew he would feel he had done his duty by Mhouse. His wild, crazy Samaritan would have been repaid. There was no other way. He picked up the phone again.

'Marine Support Unit,' a voice said.

'Hello . . .' What did one say? 'I've just seen the paper. The body of the young woman found in the river at Greenwich. I think I know who she is.'

He took a pen from his pocket and noted down the details of what he should do and where he should go. He said he would be there when his shift ended in the evening and hung up.

Mhouse was dead. He had to face that fact – there was no escaping it and no escaping the equally appalling fact that, one way or another, he had inadvertently brought death to her. Whoever was leading this desperate hunt to find him had killed Mhouse in pursuit of information. Guilt overwhelmed him, gathered in his throat like bile. It was bile. He managed to make it outside to the car park before he vomited.

CHAPTER 41

The setting sun had turned the river orange – basting the brown waters of the Thames orange, like a Fauvist painting. Rita paused to log this miraculous effect and marvel for a second before she moved on and the vision was erased as she walked from the Annexe to the MSU headquarters building. Emerging from the narrow passageway that led to the main entrance was a tall young guy, looking around him as if lost, with a slip of paper in his hand. He wore a pin-stripe suit, an open-necked shirt, his head was shaved to a dark stubble and he had a dark neat beard.

'Can I help you?' she asked.

He turned. 'I've come to identify a body,' he said. 'I'm not sure where I should go.'

Their eyes met – it was an event that happened dozens of times a day: why should one be more intriguing, Rita thought, why do you register that particular interlocking of two gazes as more significant? All Rita knew was that this meeting of eyes was somehow different, as far as she was concerned, from the dozens of previous ones that had happened that day. Something had been triggered, some neural spasm registering alertness, a change in feeling, a concentration of interest. It must be deep, deep instinct, she thought, something beyond our rational control – the beast in us seeking a suitable mate.

'We've got a temporary morgue here now,' she said. 'It's back this way. I'll show you.' They turned and she led him back towards the Annexe and Portakabin 4.

'Was this the one in the paper?' she said as they went.

'Yes.'

'I'm very sorry. Family member?'

'No. Just a . . . Just somebody I knew.' He couldn't keep the catch out of his voice, she noticed, and she glanced back, seeing how nervous he was, how hard all this was for him.

They paused outside Portakabin 4, its refrigerating unit humming audibly from its rear.

She introduced him to the medical attendant and explained that he had to fill in a form.

'Name?' the attendant said.

'Belem.' Then the man gave his address and contact details. Then he was handed a white plastic coat and plastic overshoes.

'Tell you what,' Rita said, feeling sorry for him as she watched him put them on, his face set as if realising for the first time where he was about to go and what he was about to do. 'I'll get you a cup of tea, have it waiting for you.'

'Thank you,' he said and stood up as the attendant swung open the door to the mortuary.

It wouldn't be easy for him in there, she knew. They had decided to establish a temporary holding mortuary here because every year at Wapping the MSU removed fifty to sixty corpses from London's river, an average of one a week. Bodies decomposed fast once out of the river and if there had been no identification within a week they were moved to one of the larger city mortuaries where they were kept until the inquest. Some congruence of the tides and the river's swerving course meant that more than half of all the bodies were found in or around Greenwich, by the big southern loop that the river took around the Isle of Dogs. Often the dead had been in the water for a long time and were bloated and disintegrating, or else they had been disfigured by brutal contact with passing boats and barges, or were eyeless, eyes pecked out by gulls – not to mention any violence that might have been visited on them before they were dumped in the water.

The one body she and Joey had found had been that of a careless drunk. He had walked out at low tide on a sandbar at midnight by Southwark Bridge to urinate and found himself sinking in soft mud, trapped at mid-thigh. He remained stuck there remorselessly as the tide rose, covering him, no one hearing his desperate shouts or seeing his waving arms. He was still there the next morning at low tide when the waters receded, face down. But this one, the one that had been in the papers – DB 23 (the twenty-third body this year) – was different, she knew. She had been knocked about by river traffic – she had a fractured skull and a broken neck, half a leg was missing, raked by a propeller. She thought of the man – Belem – standing by the sheeted body waiting for the face to be revealed. It would not be nice.

She punched the button on the tea and coffee maker and watched the water flow into the plastic cup. She picked up a little cardboard rhomboid of milk, a stirring stick and two sachets of sugar and went back out to Portakabin 4. He was coming out, his face pale, a hand to his lips, looking as if he might faint.

'Come and have a seat for a minute,' she said. 'We can sort out the paperwork later.'

They went back into the restroom where he milked and sugared his tea and stirred it with the plastic stick – not saying anything, completely in his own head, eyes staring at the melamine table top. He began to sip his tea and looked up.

'That was her, was it?' Rita asked.

'Yes.'

'Known her long?'

'Not really.'

'Do you know her name? Where she lived?'

'Yes, she was called Mhouse.' He spelt it out and gave her address. 'Her son is called Ly-on. A seven-year-old. That explains the tattoo: their names.'

'Right. Mhouse what?'

'Actually, I don't know . . . I don't know what her last name was.' This admission seemed to trouble him, she saw.

'We'll get all this to the duty officer. He'll take all the details. Just leave the cup there.'

She walked back with him to main reception where she handed him over for more form-filling and statement-giving. While the duty officer searched for the right documents she held out her hand and he shook it.

'I'm sorry for your loss, Mr Belem.'

'Thanks for your help, you've been most kind. I really appreciate it,' he said.

'You're welcome.'

Then he asked her what her name was – she thought he might do that. It was one of her tests.

'Rita Nashe,' she said, smiling at him, thinking: he's a fit-looking guy – tall, slim, nice eyes. Obviously intelligent. Usually she didn't like that buzz-cut, close-bearded look, but it sort of suited him.

'I'm Primo,' he said, 'Primo Belem.'

'Nice meeting you, Primo,' she said. 'I'm off duty now – better run.'

'Just one second, Miss Nashe—' He looked troubled again.

'Sure, what is it?'

'Do they think she was killed?'

Rita paused. 'Killed? You're asking if she was *killed* – murdered? It could have been a fall. She could have been drunk—'

'I don't know,' Primo Belem said. 'I just don't see how she could have wound up dead in the river. It doesn't make sense.'

'She could have killed herself. We get dozens of suicides—'

'She would never have killed herself.'

'How can you say that?'

'Because of her son. She would never have left Ly-on alone. Never.'

Rita and Joey walked into The Shaft, heading for Unit 14, Level 3, Flat L, caution informing their every step. Rita had never felt so self-conscious. It was three o'clock in the afternoon but the few people they passed either took off in a different direction or else stopped and stared at them as if they had never seen uniformed police officers before.

'Wow,' she said to Joey. 'What country are we in?'

'We don't want to hang around, Rita.' He looked nervously over his shoulder. 'We should call in the Rotherhithe boys.'

'It's still an MSU case.'

'We're *river* police, Rita. What're we doing here?'

'Thanks, Joe. I owe you. It's a hunch – just have to check something out, for my own satisfaction.'

They had reached the bottom of the stairs. She looked around her – boarded-up flats, a strew of filth, rubbish, graffiti everywhere. Apparently, Rita had learnt, the Shaftesbury Estate was due to be demolished in a year or two – despite its listed status, its twentieth-century architectural heritage.

As a little septic, ulcerous dystopia in rapidly gentrifying Rotherhithe its days were numbered. A naked child came round the corner, a little girl, completely naked. She saw the two policemen, screamed and ran off.

'You stay down here, Joey,' she said. 'Let me check the flat.'

'I'll come running,' he said. 'Don't be too long.'

She climbed the stairs to the third floor walkway, looked over the balustrade, saw Joey and gave him a wave.

She knocked on the door of Flat L. Knocked again.

'Who dey be?' came a voice.

'Police.'

The door was unlocked and a tall thin guy in a maroon tracksuit stood in the doorway, smiling broadly. She noticed he had silver rings on all his fingers and his two thumbs.

'Praise the good lord. At last the police. We never see police for here. Welcome, welcome.'

She said she'd like to ask him a few questions. He said, no problem. In the dark flat beyond she could see women and children moving about, and heard a baby crying. Two men appeared in white ankle-length dishdashas and quickly went into another room. The conversation was going to take place on the doorstep: clearly he was not going to invite her inside.

'I'm making enquiries about a woman called Mhouse. This was her flat.'

'She rent it from me. Then she run away. She owe me five month rent. Lot of money.'

'You're the landlord?'

'Yes, madam. I am also chairman of the Shaftesbury Estate Residents' Association – SERA.'

'And your name is?'

'Mr Quality. Abdul-latif Quality. This is my apartment.'

'Who is living here now?'

'They are asylums. I am registered for the council. You can check me.'

'Do you know where this Mhouse went?'

'No. If I know, I go find her. I want my money.'

'She's dead.'

Mr Quality's expression did not change. He shrugged.

'God is great. Now I never get my money.'

'We believe that her death may not have been accidental. Do you know anyone who might have threatened her, might have wanted to cause her harm?' Rita drew her palm across her brow, finding it damp. Why was she sweating so much? 'Do you know any person who might have had a grudge against her? Anybody loitering, watching her?'

Mr Quality thought, pursed his lips, exhaled. 'I never see anybody like this.'

Rita frowned. When she had told Primo Belem that she was planning on going to The Shaft he had also asked her to find out about the boy, Ly-on.

365

'Do you know where her son is?'

'I think she take him when she run away.'

Rita looked about her. An old woman came up the stairs to the walkway, saw her, smiled nervously but broadly enough to show that she had no front teeth, immediately turned and hurried down the stairs again.

'Who's that woman?'

'I never see her before.' He smiled. 'In The Shaft people dey come and they dey go. Are you finished with me, officer?'

'I may want to speak to you again.'

'Very happy to speak to police. Plenty, plenty.'

'Where do you live?'

'I live for here.' He gestured at the dark interior of the flat. 'You can always find me here.'

Rita felt a strange impotence run through her; everything, good and bad, that she routinely expected that her role as a police officer and her uniform would confer – status, respect, disrespect, disdain, suspicion, lazy assumption, knee-jerk reaction – simply did not apply here, here in The Shaft. She was the alien, not the 'asylums'. She was out of kilter – they were in kilter. She wanted to run away from Mr Quality and that was not the sort of attitude, the state of mind, she should be experiencing, she knew: she was a public servant, paid to uphold law and order. She had never felt so redundant in her life.

'Thank you, Mr Quality.'

'My pleasure.'

He shut the door and she went down the stairs to rejoin Joey.

'Let's get out of here, Joe.'

Rita and Primo Belem sat in a coffee shop cum French delicatessen called Jem-Bo-Coo not far from MSU in Wapping High Street. She was out of uniform and her hair was down. He had been waiting at a table at the back by the ranked wine bottles for sale, already there when she arrived, and she had seen his almost comic double-take at her 'civilian' persona. He was wearing his pin-stripe suit and she noticed for the first time that the jacket and the trousers didn't quite match. She'd checked the contact details he'd provided to the duty officer and knew where he lived – a flat in the Oystergate Buildings, Stepney – and she knew that he worked as a porter at the Bethnal & Bow hospital, a job he'd only been in for a few weeks. Everything about his demeanour, accent and vocabulary, however, spoke of someone unused to menial, manual work. There was some mystery here – she looked forward to attempting to solve it.

She ordered her coffee, sat down and told him about her visit to The Shaft and what she had found when she'd gone to Mhouse's flat.

'There was a man there, said he was living in it – Mr Abdul-latif Q'Alitti.'

Primo nodded. 'Yeah, I've heard about Mr Quality. Mr Fixit.'

367

'Chairman of the Shaftesbury Estate Residents' Association. I checked him out – they know all about him at the council. Nothing gets done in The Shaft without Mr Quality.'

'Any sign of the boy?'

'No. I'm afraid not. Mr Quality said he knew nothing.'

This seemed to perturb him. 'I wonder—' he began and then stopped. 'Are you hungry?' he said. 'Can I get you a muffin?' She *was* hungry, in fact, so they went back to the counter and agreed to share a blueberry muffin. They took their seats again.

'Why do you think,' she said, picking the fruit out of her half of the bun, 'that this Mhouse may have been murdered?'

'I don't know,' he said, vaguely. 'The Shaft is a dangerous place. I lived there for a while,' he added, 'which is how I got to know Mhouse . . .'

'Do you think Mr Quality might have had something to do with it?'

'No, I don't think so. Not him.'

'Anyone else?'

'No . . . No. It just seems suspicious to me.'

'We need something to go on.'

'I know . . . I'm sorry . . .'

She smiled and leant back in her chair, taking a bite from her half-muffin. 'You look like you've seen a ghost.'

'I think I'm still a bit in shock, you know. The other day, getting the news, seeing the body . . .'

She leant forward now and pointed the remains of her muffin at him. 'Explain this to me: what motive could anyone have to kill this Mhouse person?'

'I don't know.'

'What did she do?'

'Odd jobs.'

'Sex industry? Drugs?'

Primo pursed his lips and exhaled. 'I don't know.'

'If she was a prostitute she might have a record.'

'Why do you think she was a prostitute?'

'Are you telling me she wasn't?'

He gave her a baffled, weak smile. 'I'll leave all that stuff to you,' he said. 'I can't figure it out.'

'Primo,' she said, her voice changing, a little sterner, smiling then frowning. 'Are you telling me everything you know?'

'Yes, of course. God – look at the time. I'd better go, my shift starts in forty minutes.'

They both stood up and dumped their paper cups and the remains of the muffin in the bin.

'You've been a fantastic help,' he said. 'Perhaps I'll see if I can track down the boy.'

'There'll be a post mortem and an inquest,' she said. 'We might learn something more.'

'I doubt it,' he said with some bitterness, then added, apologetically, 'of course, you never know.' He held out his hand. 'Thanks a million, Rita.'

She took his hand and held on to it for two or three seconds longer than she should.

'Listen, Primo,' she said, a little astonished at her own audacity, but she didn't want their new association to end there and then: she wanted it to have a little more life, see where it might lead. 'Do you fancy meeting up for a drink? We could have supper – curry or a Chinese or something. I could give you a progress report.' She sensed him thinking fast – she let his hand go – could see him mentally running through implications, complications, problems, possibilities.

'It's not compulsory,' she said.

'No, I'd like that,' he said with a grateful smile. 'Very much. That would be great.'

CHAPTER 42

The Italian restaurant was still there – why wouldn't it be? – sitting in its Chelsea side street with its yellow awnings. A man in an apron – a waiter – was hosing down the pavement outside as Adam walked past and inside other waiters were setting up the tables for lunch. Adam goaded his memory, thinking back to that evening. It seemed to him as if it had taken place in another century, or in a parallel universe. But everything had started then – the fact that he was standing here now was all to do with that encounter with Philip Wang, his fellow diner. He had seemed preoccupied, ill at ease; he remembered him dropping things, at one stage dabbing his perspiring forehead with a napkin. And of course he left his file, hidden under the adjacent table. He had looked like a man with a lot on his mind. But what kind of stress – how acute? Had he done something wrong? Stolen something, perhaps? And yet when he'd called up to say he had the file and was bringing it round Wang had sounded relieved but relatively calm, had even asked him up for a drink . . .

Adam turned away and walked through the back streets towards the river. If it all began with Wang then he needed to find out more about the man and what he did. Did he work for the government? Was he some ministry whistle-blower? Perhaps he was linked to the secret services himself and had found out something he shouldn't? Was he selling state secrets? Adam shook his head: conspiracy theories multiplied incrementally. Start with the facts: Philip Wang was a consultant at St Botolph's Hospital – perhaps the trail began there.

Adam took a seat on the bench on the wide section of the pavement at the beginning of Chelsea Bridge, checking to see if there was any activity in or around the triangle. He wandered past the gate a couple of times, waiting for a gap in the traffic. All seemed quiet. A power-walking couple engaged in intense conversation marched by, and when they were well past, he climbed over the gate and pushed his way through the bushes to the clearing.

He felt strange being back, acknowledging the huge changes his life had undergone since he had first camped out there. So much had happened to him: it was as if he were packing years of living into fraught, dense weeks; determinedly racing through a whole life's catalogue of experiences as fast as possible, as if time were running out. He stood for a while, hands on hips, taking things in, slowly, deliberately. There was more litter scattered around and he felt a sense of proprietorial outrage, picking up a piece of blown newspaper before crumpling it up and letting it fall. He knelt down and ripped back the turf that covered his cash-box and removed £200 and the Wang dossier. He paused for a moment, looking at the list of names and the incomprehensible jottings beside them. There was no doubt in his mind – this was where he should start next.

Sitting on the Tube heading back to Stepney, he found himself thinking about the policewoman, Rita Nashe. She was tall and rangy with a lean face – pretty, but one that looked almost mannishly strong when her hair was up. When her hair was down she seemed quite different – he remembered the frisson he'd felt when she came into the coffee shop – she didn't look like a police-woman at all. And at this he rebuked himself: as if there were a generic template of looks that applied to policewomen. You might as well say he looked like a typical hospital porter. No, he realised, it was because he had seen her in a uniform first, that day at the MSU morgue – he had to remove the uniformed Rita from his memory bank and replace it with the image of the pretty, tall young woman in jeans and a fleece, with her brown hair down on her shoulders, sitting opposite him in the coffee shop, picking the beads of fruit from her muffin, leaning back and smiling. It had all seemed very normal and easy – being Primo Belem changed everything, the risks that he had worried about never materialised. He brought her face back into his mind – Rita's face. Hard to tell what her figure was like under the fleece . . . He was glad she'd been the one to ask him for a drink – he wouldn't have had the nerve, however much he might have liked the idea.

CHAPTER 43

City Airport did not improve on further acquaintance, Jonjo reckoned, as he took his seat as close to the stairs down from the cafeteria as possible, had a sip of his cappuccino and began to do the puzzle in the newspaper. SREIBGMAR. Four-letter words, and longer, all with an 'R' in them; GRIM, GRAB, RAGE . . . He looked up to see Darren approaching. Jonjo's smile of welcome was not warm and he noticed that Darren ventured no smile in return – more of a wince, a frown – the bearer of bad news, Jonjo guessed.

'Better make it quick, Dar, I got a lot on. I'm getting close.'

'This has nothing to do with me, Jonjo, you have to know that.'

'Yeah, of course. Spit it out.'

'You're off the Kindred case.'

This was a real shock – he hadn't been expecting this – just more bollocking, more pressure. He kept his face still, somehow, though he felt his guts loosen. This was serious: no way he could go to the toilet now.

'You must be fucking joking me.'

'No, Jonjo. I told you: the heat on this one is massive. They can't understand how some poxy university bloke is still out there. Why can't you find him?'

'Because he's *clever*, precisely because he's a poxy university bloke and not some wanking loser,' Jonjo said with controlled vehemence. Then he added: 'Who's "they", by the way?'

'I don't know,' Darren said, pleadingly. 'I never know – haven't a fucking clue.' Jonjo believed him, but Darren went on, 'There's layer upon layer upon layer above me. I don't know who's sending me these messages, these instructions. I get paid – I just do what I'm told.'

'OK, OK. Cool.'

Jonjo sat for a while, thinking, letting his anger build. Then he said, 'Well, the upshot is you'll let Kindred go. I told that Rupert-arsehole, "Bob", that I was close. Now, I'm even closer. You take me off of this and Kindred walks free. You tell "them" that.'

'There's another plan. Hold on.' Darren took out his mobile phone and made a quick *sotto voce* call.

'I told him to wait outside,' Darren said, apologetically. 'I wanted to see you myself, first.'

A minute later Jonjo watched as a big bloke came up the escalator to the cafeteria: dark hair shaved close and a big drooping moustache, like he was in a 1970s western.

'This is Yuri,' Darren said.

Jonjo looked at Darren incredulously as if to say – *what?*

'Yuri was in Spetznaz for twelve years. Chechnya, counter-terrorism—'

'Fanbloodytastic,' Jonjo said. 'Does he speak English?'

'I speaking English,' Yuri said.

'Just tell him everything what you know,' Darren said. Jonjo could feel how uncomfortable and embarrassed he was. He looked down at his puzzle – the word AMBERGRIS formed mysteriously in front of his eyes. What the fuck was that? He looked up and told Yuri all he was prepared to let him know.

'Kindred was living on the Shaftesbury Estate, Rotherhithe – Flat L, Level 3, Unit 14 – for some weeks with a prostitute who went by the name of "Mhouse". Kindred now has long hair and a beard and he goes by the name of "John". He isn't there any more and the prostitute,' he paused, 'has run away.'

'Thank you,' Yuri said slowly. 'I go to this Shaftesbury. I asking questions – I get answers.'

'Good luck, mate,' Jonjo said coldly, standing. 'Nice to see you, Darren. Good luck to you too.'

Darren looked a little hurt, unhappy with the guilt-by-association. He rose to his feet and slipped Jonjo a packed envelope.

'Half your fee. There are no hard feelings—'

'Yeah, yeah, I know. Move on.'

Jonjo strolled out of the cafeteria without looking back.

Bishop Yemi paused and looked out at his sparse congregation as if searching for some encouragement, some zeal.

'Imagine – imagine you are John, the true Christ, and the Romans are closing in, with their swords and their spears. What do you do? And then your disciple, Jesus, the carpenter's son, steps forward. Lord, he says, let me pretend to be the Christ – I do it for the cause. While they arrest and torture me you can escape to continue the struggle, to spread the word.' Bishop Yemi paused. 'It's a superb plan, John says. Jesus is taken, he dies on the cross, the Romans think they have their man. Meanwhile John escapes to the sunny island of Patmos where he writes Revelation. It's all there – read the book of John. Only the true Christ could have written this book. Only the real son of God!'

It's a very interesting point, Jonjo thought, sitting in the front row with a 'John 1794' badge on his chest. Makes a lot of sense. Brave man, that Jesus bloke, sacrificing himself like that. Jonjo thought further: it must have helped you, also, while you were hanging on that cross, with nails through your hands and feet, knowing that your leader had escaped and outwitted everyone. The words 'escaped' and 'outwitted' chimed unhappily with his own recent preoccupations. He sneaked a look

378

at his watch – the bishop had been going for forty minutes already. He felt a little exposed sitting in the front row – the only new 'John' that evening. He glanced behind him at his fellow Johns, a small congregation of scumbags and halfwits, so he thought, but was encouraged to think that Kindred had been here, in this very room – that Kindred had been a John also, only 191 places ahead of him in the John-queue. He was on to him, people here must have known him, must know where he lived – where he was living. He smothered a yawn with the back of his hand. The bishop had now moved on to the evils of short-selling and of risky speculation on global stockmarkets, quoting from the Book of Revelation to support his argument and bolster his scorn. He could certainly talk, that Bishop Yemi, Jonjo conceded – but bloody hell, how much longer?

They were served steak and kidney pudding for supper and remarkably tasty it was, Jonjo thought. Excellent grub for a hungry man. In his pocket he had Kindred's reward poster with a heavy beard shaded on to the photograph with a felt-tip pen. He showed it to the other three junkies sharing his table but they claimed not to recognise him.

'Never seen him,' one of them said.

'He's a John like us. Friend of mine,' Jonjo said. 'He used to come here – I'm trying to find him.'

'Never seen him,' the junkie repeated.

'Nah,' said another.

As the meal ended and, as people began to leave,

Jonjo mingled with the departing Johns, showing the picture to as many as he could, but had no success, just shrugs of apology and shaken heads. He stepped outside the church: there had only been twenty or so in the congregation that night; if he was the 1794th John then he was canvassing only a tiny number. He strode off, unbowed – he'd just have to come back and try again.

He sat behind the wheel of his taxi-cab and started the engine. He was still feeling anger, he realised, a sense of betrayal, shocked at the peremptory way he'd been removed from the Kindred case, a case that should belong to no one else but him. A clear vote of no confidence – he was a failure in their eyes – whoever 'they' were . . .

And what was that mustachioed berk, Yuri, going to achieve? He might tip Bozzy off that Yuri would be prowling round The Shaft. Bozzy and his mates could lead him a merry dance while Jonjo Case, in the meantime, quietly and thoroughly followed his nose and brought them Kindred. In the same way, it struck him, that Jesus had taken the heat for John. A nice analogy, he thought: then gratitude would follow, certain reinstatement, a significant cash bonus. He smiled to himself as he pulled away from the kerb – he should just firm up, the Kindred trail was warm and getting warmer and one day one of these arsehole Johns would recognise him. It was simply a matter of time.

CHAPTER 44

The purply-taupe, all-in-one, zip-up 'action suits', as they were known in St Bot's, were a great improvement on the 1980s-style commissionaire look of the epaulettes and matching ties of Bethnal & Bow, Adam considered. In his action suit Adam felt like a paramedic, someone empowered, who might have sprung from a hovering helicopter or a skidding 4 x 4, ready to administer first aid, give help, rescue, save a life. The fact that he was going up to the de Vere Wing to pick up a file of invoices to deliver to the medical secretaries in Accounting didn't diminish his vague sense of himself as a significant, albeit minor, cog in the great machine – the medical Leviathan – that was St Botolph's. All the staff secretly liked their funky jumpsuits, whatever shade they were. The design guru who had come up with the scheme clearly understood human psychology better than most psychologists. Even the cleaners took more pride in their work, thanks to their acid-green overalls, as they fought the good fight, the unending battle, against MRSA, *C. difficile* and other bacterial infections.

As the lift approached the de Vere Wing's floor, Adam told himself to concentrate. This was his sixth or seventh visit to de Vere in the two weeks he'd been at St Bot's – Philip Wang's domain – and he was beginning to be recognised by the staff and develop the bantering relationship with them of a familiar, even though there were over a hundred porters at St Bot's – theatre, departmental and outpatient – on duty at any one time. 'Hey, Primo,' people were starting to say; 'Primo's here.' He'd been offered a cup of tea on his last visit. The aim was to become a routine presence, part of the transient furniture, someone that no one was surprised to see.

The transfer from Bethnal & Bow had been surprisingly easy to effect. Rizal, one of the senior porters, had a brother, Jejomar, who worked at St Bot's. It was one of the facts of British medical life that all hospital portering services were understaffed, hence the reliance on agencies to make up the shortfall. Primo Belem had been warmly welcomed: as a trained porter with good references and a CRB clearance he had already benefited from a marginal salary rise (another £200 per annum) and hints had been dropped by management that there was a clear promotional route available to him, should he wish to pursue it. A few evening courses to follow, some basic administrative training in human resources and he could move up several levels with ease – the portering world was his oyster.

There was an unusual and noticeable excitement on the de Vere Wing when he arrived to pick up the documents – nurses chatting loudly, laughing, showing magazines to each other. One was scissoring out a page which was then stuck on the wing's notice board along with the 'get well' cards, the health and safety warning notices and the holiday snaps and postcards from grateful former patients.

'Hi, Corazon,' he said to a nurse he knew. 'What's going on?'

She showed him a two-page advertorial in *Nursing Monthly*, headlined 'A CURE FOR ASTHMA?' And followed by a vague impassioned mission statement about a search for a drug to end this modern curse on the lives of so many.

'We are running the clinical trials here,' Corazon said, emotionally. 'For three years. Finally we are there.'

'What clinical trials?'

'For Zembla-4.'

She pointed out the references in the advertorial.

'Here? Zembla-4? Congratulations,' Adam said, disingenuously. 'Amazing. My niece has terrible asthma. Sometimes she can hardly breathe.'

'This drug can helping her,' Corazon said with real sincerity. 'I have seen it working. Incredible. Tell her to ask her doctor.'

'Maybe she could even come here,' Adam said. He knew the wing well now: twenty comfortable rooms with en suite bathrooms off a wide carpeted

383

corridor, a bright toy-crammed playroom at one end.

Corazon shrugged ruefully, as if to say – don't get your hopes up. 'Is private, you know. Expensive.'

'You mean all these are rich kids in this wing?'

'No, no,' Corazon said. 'They ordinary kids – the de Vere Trust pay for everything. But they choose. If you niece very sick maybe she can get in.' She lowered her voice, confidentially. 'You go to doctor, you say you niece very, very sick with asthma. You say, what about St Bot's? He send you here, to de Vere Wing – for free.'

'Free?'

'Yes. The doctors they send us the sick children. It's a wonderful thing. They getting Zembla-4. Only here.'

'Yeah, amazing. Maybe I'll try . . . Who runs this wing, anyway?'

'We have many doctors. Dr Zeigler is the last. He's in USA now. For FDA submission.'

'Of course. So he must work for Calenture-Deutz.'

'Yes. All our doctors are paid by Calenture-Deutz. We all get bonus from Calenture-Deutz. That's why we so happy.'

Adam left with his file of clinical records and invoices and duly delivered them to Accounting in the Main Building, third floor.

Back off duty in the porters' restroom Adam took out the document with Wang's list. He had had several copies made and had replaced the

384

precious original back in its buried safety deposit box in the triangle by Chelsea Bridge. There were five names listed under St Botolph's: Lee Moore, Charles Vandela, Latifah Gray, Brianna Dumont-Cole and Erin Kosteckova. Five children who had been in the Felicity de Vere Wing in the three years before Philip Wang's death.

He went to the payphone in the corridor, slotted in his coins and dialled Administration.

'Hello,' he said, when the phone was eventually answered, 'I wonder if you can help me. I've just got back from South Africa. My god-daughter is a patient in the hospital. I want to find out what ward she's in. She's—' he read a name off the list – 'Brianna Dumont-Cole.'

'One moment, please.'

There was a longish pause. He was asked to repeat the name. In the background he could hear the dry bony click of a computer keyboard.

'There seems to be some mistake, sir.'

'No, no, I just want to pay her a surprise visit. I've been out of the country for months. I haven't seen her for nearly a year . . . Hello?'

'Brianna passed away, sir. That was four months ago. I'm terribly sorry. Her family will know all the details.'

Adam hung up without saying anything.

It took him two days and many pound coins to work through the names on Wang's list, calling the four hospitals around the country: Aberdeen,

Manchester, Southampton and St Botolph's. It turned out that all the names on Philip Wang's list were those of dead children. After he had logged the first five he changed tack – when he telephoned he now let it be known from the outset that he was aware the child was deceased. He had a variety of excuses ready in his search for information – a memorial garden was being planned, or a headstone, a charity auction, a celebration of the child's short life at her primary school. Can you confirm the date and time of day? No problem. We want to donate money to a charity of the hospital's choice. Thank you so much. My uncle would like to speak to the doctor in charge at the time. I'm afraid that will not be possible, sir. Whatever the excuse, the pretext, the sentimental lie he proffered, the answers he received all confirmed that the fourteen names Philip Wang had noted down on his list were those that had died in Felicity de Vere wings in four hospitals in the British Isles where expensive and thorough clinical trials were being undergone over several years to test the efficacy of a new anti-asthma drug, Zembla-4.

Zembla-4 . . .

Adam went to an internet café. He typed 'Zembla-4' into a search engine and all the other relevant information came up, swiftly, obligingly, on the screen. Zembla-4. Calenture-Deutz plc. The Calenture-Deutz website had not yet been updated – there was a photograph of a beaming

Philip Wang, Head of Research and Development, with no news or date of his sudden demise. Adam looked at the picture feeling very strange, thinking of their last encounter. There too was an image of the Chairman and CEO of Calenture-Deutz, one Ingram Fryzer, even-featured, grey-haired, above a tendentious declaration on behalf of the board and the team detailing his company's ambitions and overall integrity. There was a list of other board members and a series of high-minded texts – with modern graphics superimposed (test tubes, computers, clean-cut men in white coats, laughing children in meadows) and mood music over – a major-key electronic ostinato – about the high ideals espoused by Calenture-Deutz as they searched for ever more efficient pharmaceutical products.

Adam exited the site theoretically wiser, he supposed, initially – but, really, after some reflection, none the wiser. He decided to concentrate on the five deaths at St Botolph's. What he needed now was access to some of the hospital's computers.

He walked into the pub in Battersea, The White Duchess, and saw Rita sitting at the bar with a bottle of beer in her hand. He kissed her on the cheek – they could kiss each other on the cheek now, having ended their first date (after a Chinese meal) with this polite embrace. She was wearing jeans and, seemingly, three loose T-shirts one on top of the other and her hair was tied casually back in a pony-tail. Out of uniform she seemed to dress with studied unconcern – almost like one of his students on the McVay campus, Adam thought. Adam found the style alluring – he did not think anyone would guess that she was a policewoman.

In the corner a small band were setting up for their next session – this was the 'LIVE MUSIC' advertised on the pub windows.

'Been to a meeting?' she said. 'Very smart.' Adam was wearing his other suit. He only had two suits, he realised, he would have to vary his wardrobe now he was seeing Rita.

'They want to promote me,' he said. 'I'm resisting.'

What was the difference about a second date? Adam asked himself. The difference was that all bets were off, he supposed . . . The first date was always exploratory, cautious, uncertain – however much you might seem to be enjoying yourself that was its essential purpose: exit doors were left ajar at every turn in case some terrible miscalculation had been made. On their first date they had talked vaguely about their jobs. Adam had alluded to a period of mental instability, a sustained period of hospitalisation, in order to explain his current lowly status in the medical food-chain. 'Finding himself,' he said. Rita had been equally vague about her own background, skilfully avoiding certain questions – Adam had no idea where she lived, for example. But, once the second date had been mooted (by Adam) and agreed upon, all the

388

prudence and tentativeness fell away. Now as they sat at the bar talking, listening to the jazz trio strike up, Adam could sense the change in mood, palpably. The subtext was clear to them both: full-on sexual attraction. As he ordered more drinks, swivelling to gain the attention of the barman, his knee connected with her thigh and stayed there. They clinked their bottles of beer.

'Primo,' she said. 'I like that name. But you don't have an Italian accent.'

'Because I was born and brought up in Bristol,' he said. 'I can't speak a word of Italian. OK – I can speak a word or two.' He shrugged. 'I'm a third-generation immigrant.'

'So where are your family originally from, then?' she asked, and Adam thought – this had better be the last question about my background, for both our sakes.

'Brescia,' he said, plucking the name from the map of Italy in his head. 'And before you ask, I've never been there.'

'Do you want to eat something?'

'Yeah,' he said. 'I'm starving.'

They stepped out of the pub into the soft night – it was dark, but not dark, some lingering luminescence in the sky making everything strangely though nebulously visible.

'Hang on a sec,' Rita said, and rummaged in her bag for her mobile phone, on which, once retrieved, she quickly sent a text. Adam stepped away,

389

listening to the band finish their set with a roll of drums and a shivering bash of cymbals. He felt slightly drunk, but was aware of another layer of light-headedness, of excitement, that had more to do with emotion than alcohol – he sensed the evening had longer to run.

'Do you want to come home and have a coffee or something?' she said.

'That would be great.'

'I live two minutes away,' she said. 'Which is why I lured you to sunny Battersea.'

Adam said nothing.

'We go along here,' she said, gesturing down river, and they headed off. After a few paces she slipped her hand in his.

'That was nice,' she said.

'It was.'

'Better than our Chinese.'

'That's the problem with a first date, you see – too much at stake, too many unknowns. Everything changes on the second . . . At least that's my experience – my theory.'

She glanced at him. 'You must tell me about your theory some time.'

He wondered if this was the moment to kiss her, but she was leading him across the road towards the river.

'I live on a houseboat,' she said.

'Amazing,' Adam said, now acknowledging that he was definitely drunkish and thinking: a houseboat, sex on a houseboat.

'I live on a houseboat with my dad.'

Adam said nothing.

'He said nothing.'

'No, good. I think that . . . You know, cool.'

'I'd like you to meet him, which was why I texted him.'

'Ah-ha. Excellent.'

She unlocked a metal gate and they walked down a sloping metal bridge to a substantial mooring area. There seemed many different types of vessel berthed here in the dark, some with lights shining from their windows, and Adam supposed this was a sort of floating village. They walked along shifting metal gangplanks between the boats.

'Where are we?' he asked.

'Nine Elms Pier,' she said. 'Apparently there used to be a row of nine elms round about here in the middle of the seventeenth century.'

'Really? Amazing . . .'

'Hence the name.'

'I think I got that.'

'Not just a pretty face, then.'

Adam said nothing. He could tell she was a bit tense.

They were heading towards a small inlet at the end where some larger vessels were berthed. He saw what looked like a deep-sea trawler and a modified barge and, at the end, what appeared to be a reconditioned naval vessel, still with its battleship-grey paint.

'Here we are,' she said, stopping in front of it. 'The good ship *Bellerophon*. Home sweet home.'

She unlocked another gate and they climbed some steep metal steps on to the deck. Sizeable, Adam thought, looking around him, some sort of minesweeper or large patrol boat, perhaps. Rita opened a bulkhead door and light streamed out. Steep stairs led down.

'Go down backwards,' she said. 'The Navy way.'

Adam did as he was told and heard a deep voice saying, 'Welcome aboard, matey.'

He found himself in a dark sitting room, with a few low lights burning, narrow with low ceilings but fitted out with an assortment of armchairs on a shaggy dark-brown carpet. One wall was all bookshelves. There was a lingering smell of joss sticks and in one corner was a TV set, the sound turned down.

A gaunt-faced man in his sixties with long, thinning grey hair tied back in a pony-tail heaved himself out of his seat and reached for an arm-crutch before coming over to greet them. Adam noticed there was a wheelchair in the corner of the room. The man moved towards them with obvious difficulty, almost as if he were walking on artificial limbs.

'Dad, this is Primo. Primo, this is my dad, Jeff Nashe.'

'Good to meet you, Primo,' he said, extending and twisting round his left hand in greeting. Adam gripped it and shook it briefly and awkwardly, but Nashe held on to it. 'First question: you're not a fucking copper, are you?'

'I'm a hospital porter.'

Jeff Nashe turned incredulously to his daughter. 'Is that true?'

'Yes.'

'At last,' Nashe said. 'One with a proper job.'

Adam decided Nashe was a bit stoned as he finally let go of Adam's hand. He was a strong-faced man with high cheekbones and a sharp, hooked nose, but wasted – he had bags under his eyes, his hair was thin and grizzled in its summer-of-love 1960s pony-tail. But Adam could see from whom Rita derived her bone structure.

'Coffee, tea or a glass of wine?' Rita asked.

'I wouldn't mind a glass of wine, actually,' Adam said.

'Same here,' Nashe said. 'Bring the bottle, darling.'

They settled themselves on chairs in front of the mute TV – a twenty-four-hour news channel, Adam noticed – Nashe kept glancing at it as he rolled himself a cigarette, as if he were waiting for a specific item to come up. He offered Adam his tobacco pouch and roll-up papers. Adam said no thanks.

'You can see I'm semi-crippled,' Nashe said. 'Victim of an industrial accident. Seventeen years of litigation.'

'Sorry to hear that.'

'No, you're not. You don't give a toss.'

He hauled himself out of the chair again and,

not picking up the arm-crutch, crossed the room to the bookcase, at a fair pace, Adam thought, and returned with a book that he dropped in Adam's lap.

'That was me before the accident,' he said.

Adam looked at the book, a large softback with the title *Civic Culture in Late Modernity: the Latin American Challenge*, and the author's name, Jeff Nashe.

'Fascinating,' Adam said.

'Forty-two universities, polytechnics and colleges had that book on their reading lists in the 1970s.'

Rita came through at this point with the bottle of wine and three glasses. She switched off the TV and replaced the book in the bookshelf.

'Sorry,' she said. 'He always does that.'

'Because it's important to me,' Nashe said petulantly. 'I know he thinks I'm some kind of saddo, has-been loser. I don't want your boyfriend's pity.'

'He's not my boyfriend and he doesn't pity you,' Rita said with some heat. 'OK? So sit down and have a glass of wine.'

He complied and Rita poured the wine. They all had a sip and Rita topped them up.

'So, Primo,' Nashe said. 'Who did you vote for at the last election?'

Up on deck there was a breeze coming down the river from the west. The leaves in Rita's deck-garden stirred and rustled, the palms clattering drily, clicking like knitting needles. Rita and Adam were sitting in the middle of this makeshift shrubbery, up by the forward gun-emplacement, smoking a joint. The tide was rising and below him Adam could feel the *Bellerophon* beginning to heave herself off the mud.

'I don't usually smoke,' Rita said. 'And I shouldn't let him wind me up like that. But I wanted you to meet him – just to let you know, put you in the picture. He was behaving fairly badly tonight – a bit too bloody pleased with himself – mostly he's much easier with guests.' She inhaled and passed the joint to Adam, who puffed dutifully at it and handed it back. He couldn't tell if it was having any effect.

'Sometimes I just need to get out of my head for a few minutes.' She exhaled and looked over at him. 'Lovely evening.'

'I won't tell anyone,' Adam said. 'Don't worry, officer.'

'Thank you, kind sir.' She smiled at him and inclined her head in a little bow of acknowledgement.

'What happened to your father?' he asked.

'He was a lecturer in Latin American studies at East Battersea Polytechnic,' she paused. 'And one night he fell down the stairs to the library and badly hurt his back.'

'That's it?'

'That's it. He sued, they appealed, he won. He hasn't worked since. That was the industrial accident.' She took a big hit on her joint.

'Latin American studies. So that's why your brother's called Ernesto.'

'Ernesto Guevara Nashe. I'm called after one "Margarita Camilo" – she was in the Sierra Maestra mountains with Castro's rebel army. Margarita Camilo Nashe at your service.'

'Right,' Adam was thinking. So it's Margarita . . . 'So there's a strong Spanish, Latin American connection in the Nashe family.'

'No, no, he's never been to either Central or South America.'

'But he taught Latin American studies. And the book.'

'Let's say there was an opening in academic life in the late sixties. A career opportunity. He was a historian who couldn't find employment anywhere. They set up a Latin American studies department at East Battersea and they offered him a job . . .' She shrugged. 'Suddenly he became a Latin American expert. To be fair he loved it – he was a kind of virtual revolutionary until he fell down the stairs.'

'Does he speak Spanish?'

'Do you?' She laughed loudly at the idea. '*Habla español, amigo?*' she said. The drug was beginning to work its narcotic magic. Adam was beginning to understand why Rita became a policewoman.

'I'd better go,' Adam said and stood up – and staggered as the *Bellerophon* heaved herself free from the Thames mud and was buoyant. Rita caught him.

Their kiss was, for Adam, a great, heady release – of pleasure, of desire for Rita. He felt a kind of fizzing through his gut and loins as her tongue searched deep into his mouth and he held her to him strongly. But at the same time as he was thinking this is wonderful – another part of his brain was saying: this is a bit sudden, all a bit rushed.

They broke apart.

'This is all a bit sudden, a bit rushed,' Rita said. 'But I'm not complaining.'

'I was sort of thinking the same.'

'You could come back down below,' she said. 'I'm a big girl – do have my own room.'

'Maybe not tonight, I think.'

'That is sensible, Primo Belem, wise man. Thank you. Yes.' She was high.

She walked him back through the marina along the gangways to the shore, holding on to his arm with both hands, her head on his shoulder. They kissed again, with more deliberateness, a more conscious savouring of their lips and tongues in contact. What was it about kissing? Adam thought. How could it seem so important, this meeting of four lips, two mouths, two tongues? Sometimes those first kisses can turn your head, Adam realised, recognising the absurd weakness in himself that made him want to have his head turned, to say something declarative to her, to register the emotion he was feeling. After two kisses? – ridiculous, he thought. He resisted.

CHAPTER 45

There was no doubt that the new advertorial was impressive, Ingram thought – and well designed, and classy, and highly effective. Two smiling, adorable, blonde children, a boy and a girl, looking up fondly at a really incredibly attractive – not to say stunningly beautiful – young mother, looking down equally fondly at them. The colours were lambent, radiant: golds, creams, the palest yellows. 'AN END TO ASTHMA?' was the heading in bold, writ large, confident in dark forest-green. There was a sententious quotation from him, something about being a force for good in a dangerous world, signed Ingram Fryzer, Chairman and CEO of Calenture-Deutz, and even his actual signature underneath it. Where had they taken that from? he wondered. Then he recalled it was routinely reproduced on all the brochures the company sent out. Yes, everything about the advertorial looked big, caring, a brighter future almost within our grasp. This could be the life we all could lead, the pages said, implicitly: let's not waste any more time, for the sakes of pretty children and beautiful mothers like these. We don't want them to suffer.

Ingram closed the magazine. He should feel proud, he supposed – this drug had been developed by his company, his team (with help from Rilke Pharmaceuticals, of course) and its success would rebound hugely in his and Calenture-Deutz's favour . . . He flicked back to the ad – interesting, no Rilke logo, just Calenture-Deutz's. In the proof he'd been shown by Rilke that day the inference was that this was a fight being led by Rilke Pharma. Perhaps Alfredo was shrewdly hedging his bets, waiting for the submissions to go through, get the rubber stamp before he re-directed the limelight.

Ingram sighed audibly – he was always sighing in Lachlan's waiting room, he realised, but this time he was alone. He should feel proud, yes, dammit – years of work and toil, millions of pounds of investment and the drug was perhaps only a few weeks, some months or so, away from licensing. Good would be done in the world, suffering would be eased, mankind's lot would be more bearable, this vale of tears less burdensome – and yet he felt unhappy, morose, powerless, even angry. How had he allowed this to happen? How come Burton Keegan and Alfredo Rilke were calling all the shots? . . . He knew immediately the simple, brutal answer to his outraged question – money. Maybe that was what was affecting his mood. Guilt. They had given him so much money that he had allowed himself to be neutered. That's what he was: a eunuch. A eunuch chairman, a testically challenged CEO—

'You'll have had your tea, Ingram,' Dr Lachlan McTurk said in the quavering voice of a Scottish miser, beckoning him with one finger into his consulting room.

Ingram showed him the pages in the magazine. 'Have you seen this?' he asked.

'Not until now – but half a dozen of my patients have already asked me for your wonder drug. There have been articles in the press hailing it. Congratulations – it looks like being a monster.'

'Thank you. Yes, I suppose . . .' Ingram waited for the warm glow of pride, that little kick of self-esteem, but it resolutely would not come. He felt flat, depressed.

'And I suppose you're going to make truly disgusting amounts of money,' Lachlan said, rummaging among his notes.

'Possibly,' Ingram said. 'But the question is: will I live to display it?'

'Display your money?'

'I meant to say "enjoy" . . .' Ingram said, frowning.

'Enjoy it *and* display it – conspicuous consumption.' Lachlan laughed, genuinely, a surprisingly girlish giggle from such a large man. 'There's nothing wrong with you. Cholesterol's a bit high – join the club. Gamma-GT's at the top end of the range – cut down a tad on the booze. You're not overweight for a man of your age. Nothing showed up in the tests. Clean bill of health in my book.'

'I still get these frantic itches. This blood-spotting on my pillow. Very unsettling, you know,' Ingram said, more plaintively than he meant. He didn't feel a stoic today. 'Also, I keep making these slips with words. I think I'm saying one word but I'm actually using another.'

'Ah. Catachresis.'

'Is that what I have?'

'No, no,' Lachlan said, quickly. 'That's just the linguistic term for the phenomenon: a paradoxical use of words, you know, in error. A kind of innocent mixed-metaphor effect. "Display" for "enjoy" is rather good, in fact.'

'But sometimes I've meant to say "conversation" and have said "temperature". There is no logic.'

'Everything's connected, particularly between words. Perhaps you were unconsciously recalling a particularly "hot" conversation.'

'If everything's connected, do you think this "catachresis" is connected with the blood-spotting and the itches?'

Lachlan looked at him closely, almost suspiciously. 'What I could do, of course, is give you a very powerful anti-depressant. You'll be walking on air.'

'No thanks.' Pull yourself together, man, Ingram told himself. 'I'm relieved. Thank you, Lachlan. Very grateful.'

'Let me know when your wonder drug's about to hit the market. I'll buy some shares.'

★   ★   ★

Ingram tugged on his socks, aware that his low mood had returned, if in fact it had ever left him. Maybe he should have taken Lachlan up on his offer of some happy pills – a little bit of chemical euphoria might be what he needed. He stood up and slipped his feet into his loafers and reached for his tie. Even this session with Phyllis hadn't really cheered him up. She came into the room now, wearing a long silk dressing gown, red with snarling, scaly golden dragons. She had a clinking glass in each hand.

'Large vodka and tonic, squire,' she said, handing his over. 'Cheers, Jack.' She blew him a kiss. 'No extra charge.'

They touched the rims of their glasses and Ingram took two large gulps, enjoying the hit and the clear dry taste of the vodka.

'Phyllis,' he said, feigning spontaneity, 'I was just thinking: would you ever contemplate – I mean, do you think we might be able to arrange a little holiday together?' He started putting on his tie. 'Short break. Four or five days. Somewhere far away, sunny.'

'I have done holidays with some of my gents, yeah. Nice change of scene for us all.'

She sat down on the bed and allowed her dressing gown to fall open so he could see her left breast.

'Where are we thinking about, love?' she asked.

'Morocco, I thought, there's a super hotel—'

'Nah – don't do the Med.'

'Florida? The Caribbean? South Africa?'

'More interesting.'

'I'd already be at the villa—'

'Hotel. Not villa holidays, darling. No room service.'

'Yes, hotel. And you fly in separately—'

'Business class,' she pulled the lapels of her dressing gown together.

'Goes without saying. We spend three or four blissful days together. You fly out.'

'I don't think so, Jack. I lose money on these holidays. And it's never really that enjoyable for me, to tell the truth. Thanks, but no thanks.'

'We could go radio if you prefer – I mean east: Sri Lanka, Thailand.'

'No. Best forget it.'

She stood and came over to him, frowning, pretending to show concern, rubbing his cheek with her knuckles.

'What's brought this on, Jack-me-lad? Thought you wasn't quite your old perky self.'

Ingram made up some story about pressure of work – he had told her once he was a pharmacist, he remembered. He said he was going to sell the shop – that was it, sell the business, he improvised – treat himself to a holiday.

'You built it up – you deserve the rewards,' she said. 'You save your money. You earned it. You couldn't really afford me on one of these trips. Wouldn't like to take it off you.'

'Fine, no problem. You're probably right.'

On the Tube train back to Victoria, Ingram felt

his spirits lifting somewhat, even though Phyllis had quashed his plans. The idea had come to him a few days ago, and he wondered exactly why. Maybe it was just the simple need for change – a temporary change in his life with a new, very short-term, complication-free partner (he knew Meredith would suspect nothing – he was always flying off abroad to conferences and meetings). Bit of sea and sun, good food, good wine, vigorous uncomplicated sex on demand . . . Maybe it wasn't such a bad idea – there were other 'Phyllises' out there in the world . . .

He looked about him, at his fellow passengers: shabby, slumped, expressionless, glum Londoners, a few reading, many plugged into their head-phones, one pretty blonde girl seemed to be watching a miniature TV – was that possible? – and he sensed his mood lightening further as he projected forward to potential holidays with other Phyllises, wondering at the same time how much more money Zembla-4 was going to make for him. 'The eunuch billionaire' – he could live with that. Perhaps his new Phyllis could fly in on a private jet after the Zembla-4 launch – personally, he wouldn't be setting foot on a commercial airline again for the rest of his life. He thought about that little trick she'd done with her scarlet dragon robe, letting it fall open like that. She knew what buttons to push, knew how to excite him. That would be the problem with someone new – it just wouldn't be the same.

He strode up the platform, heading for the exit, feeling stronger, more emboldened, as he always did after a Phyllis-session. Stop whingeing, man, he said to himself, let Keegan and Rilke run the show, do the leg work, the lobbying, the complicated dance with the licensing authorities. Don't make a fuss, just pick up the cheque at the end of the day.

Thinking about Keegan turned his mind to their last unsatisfactory meeting. He was pretty sure he knew, broadly, what had happened when Philip Wang went to see Keegan that afternoon. Philip must have discovered something about the Zembla-4 clinical trials that had enraged him and he had confronted Keegan about the matter, that final afternoon. Keegan had lied, not at all convincingly, and the opposite of the lie – 'Philip was delighted' – contained the truth: Philip was disturbed, Philip was suspicious, Philip was furious, possibly. He thought further: Philip was about to go public? Could that be what was mooted? . . . And how extraordinary that he had been murdered that very evening by this Kindred fellow, this sinister climatologist . . . No, no, no, Ingram upbraided himself – don't go there. It was just one of these hideous, terrifying, dark coincidences. Impossible . . .

Still, he didn't yet know what Philip had discovered, what had made him confront Keegan. That was the key issue. Perhaps he might call Keegan in again and bluff it out, make it seem as if he knew what Wang had come up with, what had disturbed him. He thought further: Keegan had taken that meeting, therefore it was one hundred per cent sure that Alfredo Rilke knew as well what Wang had unearthed. So Keegan *and* Alfredo knew what had gone wrong with Zembla-4, what had so troubled Philip Wang . . . He shook his head as if a bothersome fly were buzzing around him. But it couldn't be that serious because Alfredo himself had authorised the submission process. No, just a terrible, terrible tragedy.

Luigi was waiting for him in Eccleston Square, walking around the car with a chamois rag removing the odd smear of city grease or dusty water-spot from the Bentley's gleaming body-work. Ingram slid into the back and Luigi paused before closing the door on him.

'You have one call from your son, signore. He is going to be a few minutes late.'

'What about some pudding, Forty? – Nate?' he added quickly. Ingram offered the menu for him to see.

'I'd better be going, Dad, we've a job at—'

'Some coffee, then. You've only been here half an hour.'

'All right.'

Ingram signalled over a waiter and they gave their orders, Ingram sensing Fortunatus's discomfort coming off him like a force-field. He had given the choice of restaurant a lot of thought – nothing too grand, expensive or formal – but still something of a treat. This was their first lunch together since . . . He couldn't think when. Since Forty was at school? Surely not? Anyway, he had decided it was to be the inauguration of a regular series: he and his son were going to see a lot more of each other.

This restaurant was famous: customers, ordinary common folk, had to book six months in advance and yet – on his previous visits – Ingram had noticed many young people, extremely casually dressed, not to say scruffy, some of them reputedly with famous names. Even today, at lunchtime, he could spot the TV presenter, the knighted ballet dancer, the flamboyant actress with her irritating laugh. Ingram quietly pointed them out but Forty knew none of them. And the restaurant, despite its fashionably elite renown, still provided the consolations and comforts of solid tradition. Its multicoloured stained-glass windows would have been familiar to theatrical stars of the 1930s. Its napery was thick and impeccably starched, its silverware heavy and un-modish in design, its menu a comforting blend of English nursery food and the latest fusion cuisine. Yet for all this, Forty was so ill at ease that Ingram could feel his own shoulder muscles beginning to contract and spasm in sympathy.

'Look, isn't that the chap from that TV quiz show?'

'We don't have a television, Dad.'

'How is Ronaldinho?'

'Rodinaldo.'

'Of course.'

He looked at his unshaven, bald son, hot in his heavy combat jacket, his fingernails black with leaf mulch or compost and he felt a sob well up in his throat. He wanted to reach out and hug him, he wanted to bathe him, make him clean and pink and dry him in thick white towels.

'Forty – Nate – I'd like you to call me Ingram. Do you think you could?'

'I can't do that, Dad, sorry.'

'Could you try?'

'It won't work, Dad. I just can't.'

'I respect that. No, no, I do.'

They sat in silence for a while, sipping their coffee. Ingram had to accept this though he had thought that if they moved on to first-name terms there would be a concomitant loosening, a chance for a real friendship developing, without the tired old father–son relationship intervening.

'How's business? You know I want to invest.'

'We're fine. We've more work than we can handle.'

'Then take on more people. Expand. I can be useful with all this stuff, Forty. Capitalisation, new plant—'

'We don't want to expand, don't you understand that?'

Something about the jut of Forty's jaw and the stubborn way he looked at him in the eye stirred Ingram in ways he had forgotten he could be stirred. He felt his throat thicken with pure emotion and he said softly to his youngest son, 'I love you, Forty. I want to spend more time with you. Let's meet every week or so, get to know each other properly.'

'Dad, please don't cry. People are looking.'

Ingram touched his cheek with a knuckle and found it wet. What was happening to him? He must be having some kind of nervous break—

'Hey. Family! Who let you riff-raff in?'

Ingram looked up to see Ivo Redcastle standing there, looming over the table. Ivo was wearing a snakeskin jacket and tight jeans, sunglasses were pushed up into his dense blue-black hair.

'You all right, mate?' Ivo said, peering at Ingram.

'Bit of a coughing fit.'

'Forty, good to see you, man. Flat.' Ivo tried to give Forty a soul handshake, but Forty didn't know what to do. Ivo settled for a high-five.

'Hello, Uncle Ivo. I've got to go, Dad. Thanks for lunch, bye.'

And he was gone that quickly, almost running out of the restaurant, and Ingram could have happily eviscerated Ivo for denying him his farewell embrace. He stood up, face set, left three fifty-pound notes on the table and walked to the door, Ivo striding beside him.

'Where were you?' Ingram said. 'Didn't see you when we came in.'

'Down the far end with the grockles,' Ivo said. 'More discreet.' He glanced again at Ingram. 'If I didn't know you better, you heartless bastard, I'd say you'd been crying.'

'It's an allergy thing. Can I drop you somewhere?'

They stepped outside the restaurant: the usual small gaggle of paparazzi were unimpressed.

'No thanks,' Ivo said. 'I've got a meeting in Soho. Film producer.'

'How did the T-shirts go?'

'Well . . . Funny you should ask, but things are looking up. I just had a really interesting phone call.'

'Summer's lease hath all too short a date, Ivo.'

'What?'

'Time marches on.'

'Actually,' Ivo began, and Ingram recognised the change in tone – his wheedling, begging voice – 'I might possibly need to speak to you about that. Bit of a cash-flow problem. If this bloke doesn't come through. Which he will, I'm sure.'

There was the buzzing sound of a scooter starting up and its insect-noise increased as it sped up to the restaurant, slowing almost to a halt as it drew opposite them.

'Hey, Ivo!' the driver shouted through his helmet visor and Ivo of course looked up. Ingram thought it strange that this paparazzo should be taking a photo with a disposable camera. Ivo put his shades on, looking pleased.

'Fucking nightmare,' he said. 'If only they'd leave me alone.'

'Good to see you,' Ingram said and headed for Luigi and the Bentley.

410

'Oh yeah. Great ads, loved them!' Ivo shouted over his shoulder as he sauntered off, up West Street towards Cambridge Circus and the cramped purlieus of Soho beyond.

CHAPTER 46

It was all coming together fairly nicely, Adam thought, as he leant over Amardeep's shoulder and looked at the computer screen. They were correlating the porters' work log with the CCTV record of the same day.

'There she is,' Amardeep said, pointing to the screen. 'Trolleyed out of de Vere into intensive care on the 4th.' He pointed at the log. 'By OPP 35.' He checked the outpatient porter number against a name. 'That was Agapios. Then . . .' he flipped a few pages and searched the CCTV images. 'Then she coated on the 7th. Look.'

'Quoted?'

'*Coated.* That's what we say at St Bot's. She coated – she died . . . So we move her to the morgue.'

'What about the next one?'

Amardeep scrolled down to the next name on Adam's list, then flicked through the CCTV images. It was the same result – trolleyed out on the 17th of the month, coated on the 23rd. All five of the St Botolph names on Philip Wang's list had died in intensive care.

'Can we find out cause of death?'

'This is just the porters' work log,' Amardeep said, his voice vaguely offended. 'You need the clinical files. Why you want to know all this stuff anyway?'

Adam noticed that Amardeep's eyelashes were about an inch long. 'They just wanted some data at de Vere,' he said vaguely. 'Bit of a pain – but thanks a lot.'

Back in his flat at Oystergate Buildings that night, Adam spread out his accumulating material on the floor in front of the flat-screen TV. He took out the relevant documents and printouts from what he found himself calling – though very aware of its thriller-esque pretensions – the 'Zembla File'. The key item was his photocopy of Philip Wang's list of the fourteen names of the dead children from the clinical trials. Then Adam had his own certificate for the purchase of ten ordinary shares in Calenture-Deutz (460 pence each) that he had bought online when he'd moved to St Bot's and with it the glossy Calenture-Deutz brochure he had been sent as a new shareholder. He flipped it open to the usual euphuistic preface (who actually wrote this guff?) by Ingram Fryzer, Chairman and CEO, both photograph of the man himself and his flamboyant signature provided, the horizontal dashes of the 'I' of 'Ingram' distinctly separated from the vertical downstroke – more like a mathematical symbol than a letter. With the brochure had come an invitation announcing a press conference open to all share-holders to be held early next month at the Queen Charlotte Conference Centre, WC2. Adam had also cut out one of the Zembla-4 advertorials from a glossy magazine and alongside it printouts of articles from learned journals eulogising Zembla-4's curative powers – culled from the internet – and a colour photograph of Ivo, Lord Redcastle, that he had snapped the day before outside a Covent Garden restaurant.

He had opened a sub-dossier on Ivo, the lord, containing the paragraph devoted to him in *Burke's Landed Gentry of Ireland*, a magazine article about his house in Notting Hill, and a sarcastic and abusive gossip piece about his new, third wife's art exhibition. Adam had been looking for a weak link in Calenture-Deutz and he had decided fairly quickly, after searching the backgrounds to the names of the other executives and board members, that Lord Redcastle would be the most promising target.

As far as he was concerned his prime motive was only to end this pursuit. He wanted to stop being hunted by this man – whoever he was – a chase, he was now sure, that originated with Calenture-Deutz and this new drug, Zembla-4. He wanted, if at all possible, to have his old life back, insofar as that was feasible. Somehow, by grotesque happenstance, he had been drawn into a deep and complex conspiracy and he had to extricate himself – guile, tenacity and privileged information were his key weapons. But behind this first objective was the desire, also, to somehow avenge innocent Mhouse's violent death, and it seemed to him that the only way he might achieve both aims was to attack Calenture-Deutz itself, rather than confront its homicidal agent. If Calenture-Deutz felt itself wounded or severely threatened, then perhaps it would back off. Philip Wang had unwittingly placed in his hands the information that might work as potent leverage on the company. He didn't know – yet – what the precise details were behind these fourteen deaths but he was more than sure they constituted some sort of massive cover-up. He had in his possession fourteen potential smoking guns. Something had gone very, very wrong in the clinical trials of Zembla-4: so wrong that the rapidly, fatally sickening children had been rushed from the de Vere Wing to intensive care. Whatever it was, whatever rogue reaction the drug stimulated, was what had ensured Philip Wang was killed, and had brought about the death of Mhouse. In all likelihood, if circumstances had been favourable, he should have been killed also in order to keep this secret – whatever it was – secret.

He went into the kitchen and made himself a cup of tea. These thoughts always shook him up. The stark reality intruding behind the patient, deductive reasoning – unwelcome, disturbing. Danger signs suddenly present in a young child, some Calenture-Deutz doctor realising the inescapable consequences, porters hurriedly summoned to remove the evidence to intensive care, a quiet blurring of the data and the record. Seriously ill children: hundreds, thousands, had received and benefited from Zembla-4, but fourteen had perished . . . Statistical inevitability. But why such violence and ruthlessness? Was there some governmental, security issue in play here? Were these clinical trials cover for something else more devious and, on a national dimension, embarrassing to the government or the security services? What was at stake? What would happen if these fourteen deaths were made public? And then he stopped himself – go no further down that road. The deaths of chronically ill children were in themselves not enough, there had to be something more. It had to be highly significant that the dead children in St Botolph's had been moved to intensive care from the de Vere Wing some days before they had eventually died. The de Vere connection was obscured if not ruptured. How many children died in St Bot's in a given week? Ten, a dozen? Dozens? It was a huge hospital, its paediatric wing was enormous. Five children dying in the de Vere Wing where clinical trials for a new drug were in progress would have set scandalous whispers flowing. He would bet his life that all the other deaths logged by Wang had also occurred in intensive care. So there must have been something about the symptoms that first appeared that set warning lights flashing. Some doctor or whoever was supervising the trial must have known. Get them out of here – they'll be dead in a matter of days . . . He sipped his tea. He needed to talk to someone who knew about drugs, who knew about Big Pharma.

He went back into his sitting room and opened another file. He had been routinely collecting articles for the past couple of weeks from broadsheet newspapers and serious news magazines that dealt with the manufacture of drugs and the machinations of the pharmaceutical industry, trying to gauge if there was one journalist he might go to who would be able to interpret his patchy evidence. He had narrowed it down to a shortlist of three names: one in *The Times*, one in the *Economist* and one in a small specialist journal called *Global Finance Bulletin* that he had found abandoned in a Tube train carriage. Dry and fact-laden with no illustrations apart from graphs and diagrams, it seemed aimed at governmental policy makers, lobbyists and financial institutions – the subscription was an impressive £280 per year for the four issues. It was based in London and there was one journalist, called Aaron Lalandusse, who wrote in every issue on the pharmaceutical industry. Adam sensed that this Lalandusse was his man.

His mobile phone rang and Adam started – he was still not fully accustomed to the thing, symbol of his new, though modest, upward mobility in society. It was either the hospital or Rita.

'Hello, stranger,' Rita said. 'You avoiding me?'

'Sorry,' he said. 'I've been very busy, ridiculously busy. I was going to call you.'

'Where are you?'

'At home.'

'I get off duty at six. What about you?'

'I'm not on till tomorrow. Shall we have a drink somewhere?'

'Where?'

'I can come to you. I've got a scooter now. Bought one yesterday.'

'Hey. Wheels.'

'It'll work out cheaper.'

'That's what they all say.'

'Anyway, I could whizz over to Battersea.'

'Why don't we meet halfway,' she said, and told him the name of a pub she knew on the river. He said he'd see her there at seven.

'Don't bring your scooter,' she said.

'Why not?'

'Because I haven't got a helmet.'

CHAPTER 47

Something had gone seriously wrong with the cooking, Jonjo thought. Curried eggs? Who'd invented that? He took his plate from the server, looking dubiously at the three white, shifting eggs, rolling in an olive-green, lumpy pool of gravy with a ladleful of rice on the side. He avoided the junkies and found a place at a table occupied by a bearded man – looked like a wizard from a comic, Jonjo thought: pointed grey beard, long grey hair parted in the middle. Jonjo grunted hello, sat down and began to eat. The lumps in the gravy were sultanas, he noticed – god knows what this lot would smell like coming out the other end. He mashed the eggs into a pulp and mixed the whole caboodle together. He'd sat through another ninety-minute Bishop Yemi sermon and he wasn't going to miss his free meal, no way.

He took his folded photograph of Kindred out of his pocket, smoothed it on the table and pushed it over so Greybeard could see it.

'Do you know this bloke? Used to be a John, like us.'

Greybeard looked at the image and back at Jonjo. 'Why do you want to know?'

'I'm looking for him. He's a friend of mine.'

'Never seen him,' Greybeard said. 'If you'll excuse me, I feel a bit nauseous.' He stood up and walked briskly away, leaving his unfinished curry. Jonjo added the remains to his plate and mashed the new eggs into the mix. Weren't that bad, actually, these curried eggs.

Another John sat down beside him – nasty-looking bloke with thining frizzy hair and something wrong with his skin, like thick plastic set in heavy folds, like a tarpaulin or oil-cloth or something.

'Old Thrale got the hump, has he?' he said, extending his hand. 'Turpin, Vince Turpin.'

'John 1794,' Jonjo said, not offering to shake.

'Pleased to meet you, John,' Turpin said smiling, unperturbed, as if he were used to all manner of slights, his smile revealing his gap teeth. He began to cut his eggs up into small pieces.

'You a married man, John?' Turpin asked, amiably.

'No.'

'Then you must be either very lucky or very sensible. I'm a much married man myself and I don't mind telling you that ninety-nine per cent of my troubles have come from my wives.'

'You don't say.' Jonjo shovelled mashed curry into his mouth. He took it back – this was well tasty.

'The kiddies are a blessing, I have to say. They make up for all the woe.'

420

'I've got a dog,' Jonjo said. 'More than enough to keep me occupied.'

Jonjo finished his curry quickly – time to get away from this weirdo, elephant-man creep. He stood up and then sat down again, remembering his Kindred photo. He spread it beside Turpin's plate.

'D'you know this bloke? Used to come here.'

Turpin frowned, pointed his fork at the picture and slowly circled the tines around Kindred's face.

'Looks very much like John 1603. We joined the same day.' He pulled aside the end of the scarf he had around his neck to reveal his badge. John 1604, Jonjo saw.

'That's the man.'

Jonjo told himself to stay calm, but he could feel his heart beating faster already – a step closer to Kindred.

'He's a mate of mine,' he added. 'I'm looking for him.'

'Hasn't been here for weeks. Used to be in most nights. Nice bloke, well-spoken, like Thrale.' He pointed at Greybeard with his fork. 'Posh.'

'He's come into some money,' Jonjo said, carefully, lowering his voice. 'Do you know where he lives?'

'Money, eh? . . . No, haven't a clue.'

'Shame. Because anyone who can help me find John 1603 will get a two grand reward.' Jonjo smiled and repeated: 'Two grand. Two thousand quid.'

'Let me have a think,' Turpin said, 'ask around. Perhaps someone will have an idea.'

Jonjo wrote his mobile number on a slip of paper and handed it over.

'Give us a tinkle if you see him. Two grand, remember, cash.'

He took his plate back to the serving counter and handed it over. Don't get over-excited, he told himself: the tosspots and nutters that made up the congregation of the Church of John Christ couldn't be relied upon, that much he knew. Still, there was something sly and calculating about that Turpin and his eyes had widened with sly and calculating anticipation when the sum of money had been mentioned. He wandered out of the church, the curried eggs beginning to repeat on him unpleasantly, and headed for his parked taxi. He didn't want to rely on a scumbag like Turpin but at the moment he was his best and only hope.

CHAPTER 48

Rita woke and saw Primo looking at her, his face a foot away on the pillow. She stretched and groaned with semi-conscious pleasure, flinging a leg over his thigh.

'Good morning,' she said. 'Hello, there.'

He kissed her gently and she smelt and tasted toothpaste: thoughtful man. She felt his hands on her breasts, then on her back. She reached down and touched his cock, gripped it.

'I've got to go to work,' he said. 'Nobody's sorrier than me.'

'I am.'

'Take your time. Just pull the door behind you.'

He kissed her again and slid out of bed, Rita turning to watch him dress. She recalled, in her drowsy, morning-after euphoria, the night before, remembering them sitting on the terrace of the pub looking over the river as the dusk gathered, feeling the almost intolerable anticipation of the lovemaking that she knew was coming. They had chatted about her job, about her family – she had done most of the talking, she realised – their fingers intertwined, kissing from time to time and drinking just a little too much before they bussed back to Stepney and the Oystergate Buildings.

He leant into the doorway of the bedroom.

'I'll call you,' he said. 'I'm on late tonight.'

'Bye, Primo,' she called after him, raising her voice. 'Thank you!'

She heard the front door close and then a minute later the distant popping noise of his scooter starting. She turned over, wondering whether she should doze off again. It was a kind of bliss she was experiencing, she realised, and she thought that if she went back to sleep she might not wake again for hours.

So she washed her face and dressed, made herself a cup of coffee in the small kitchen and then ate some buttered toast, speculating – could she live here in Stepney with Primo? . . . Then she mocked herself – slow down, girl, don't let your heart run away with you, you barely know him.

Which was true, she thought, as she wandered around the small flat, but somehow it didn't seem to matter with him, for some reason. She stood in the living room – it was as if he had moved in yesterday. There was a bed, a TV, a black leather sofa. He seemed to keep his few clothes in cardboard boxes: some shirts, a sweater, a suit, a pair of jeans and some trainers. Another box contained underwear and socks. The flat was clean, the kitchen barely stocked – a few tins, a pint of milk, cornflakes. It was a place that could be abandoned in minutes, she thought: no books, no pictures on the wall, no ornaments, no mementoes, none of the personal detritus that someone accumulates in life without even trying. What sense of Primo Belem, she wondered, would you retrieve from these four rooms?

In the sitting room there was another cardboard box, full of newspaper clippings, printouts and, the first thing that came to hand, some kind of advertisement for a drug company. She felt a little guilty sifting through these papers but then again he was the one who had left her the run of his flat – he must have suspected some casual snooping would take place. She riffled through the documents in the box – they all seemed to be about medical matters, and there was a glossy brochure for a pharmaceutical company, Calenture-Deutz – the name seemed familiar, somehow. All to do with his hospital work, she supposed, and put everything back as carefully as she could. She glanced around the flat again, spotting a small picture that she had missed, propped behind a chopping board – an image cut from a magazine: a congregation of oddly shaped clouds in a blue sky over some parched desert landscape. In the middle of this mountain range rose some kind of obelisk. She looked closer – no, it was a building, a thin skyscraper in the middle of a desert. What was left of the caption said, 'The world's largest, tallest cloud chamber. Part of the western campus of—' The scissoring had removed the rest of the words. She put it back carefully. Take him as you find him, she said to herself – you like him, he likes you, end of story.

She closed the door behind her. Primo Belem was either a man who had nothing to hide or a man who had everything to hide. She was in no hurry to find out what category he fell into.

It turned out to be one of those hazy days on the river, with a layer of thin, high clouds partially screening the sun, turning the light thick and golden, blurring the hard edges of buildings, making the trees on the Chelsea shore seem dreamily out of focus. Rita stood on the deck of the *Bellerophon* watering her plants, thinking back to the previous night, remembering and registering that they had made love three times – a record for her – and wondering when they had fallen asleep. Four o'clock? Later? Not surprising that she felt so tired, as if she'd been in the gym for some endless workout.

'So why have you got a stupid smile on your face?'

She turned round to see her father step stiffly on to the foredeck. He seemed to be walking more easily today – or else he'd forgotten he was meant to be using a crutch.

She said nothing, just smiled more broadly.

'Enjoy yourself last night?'

'Yes,' she said. 'I had a nice time.'

'Off with your Italian porter.'

'As it happens.'

He began to roll himself a cigarette.

'He doesn't look Italian to me.'

'He's a third-generation immigrant. You don't look English to me, come to think of it.' She turned off the tap and coiled her hose neatly beneath it, ship-shape.

'Dad,' she said, thinking, as she uttered the words, that this was becoming ridiculous, 'what would you say if I moved out?'

'About bloody time.'

CHAPTER 49

There were three neat stacks of pound coins on top of the telephone and his pockets were heavy with more.

'That will be fourteen pounds,' the operator said.

Adam duly slotted in the coins.

'You know it's so much easier with a credit card,' the operator said.

'My credit card was stolen, I'm afraid.'

'Oh, sorry. Thank you. I'm connecting you now.'

Adam was in a phone booth in Leicester Square. It was ten o'clock at night but the next day had already dawned in Australia. He heard the phone ringing in his sister's house in Sydney.

'Hello, yeah?' It was his brother-in-law, Ray.

'Can I speak with Francis Kindred please?' He kept his voice deep and flatly businesslike.

'What's it about, mate?'

'About a money transfer from the UK to his bank.'

'Hold on.'

There was a silence, then he heard his father's reedy voice.

'Hello? I think there must be some mistake.'

Adam felt the tears brim in his eyes.

'Dad – it's me, Adam . . .' Silence. 'Dad?'

'Are you all right?'

'Yes, I'm fine. I didn't do it, Dad.'

'I know you didn't.'

'I had to hide out for a while. They thought it was me – the evidence was pretty overwhelming.' The phone beeped and he pumped in more coins.

'Go to the police, Ad. They'll sort it out.'

'No they won't. I have to sort it out myself. But I just wanted to tell you I was OK.'

'Well, it's a relief. Emma and I – we were going to come back. See if we could help find you. Go on television again, if we could, make another appeal.'

Adam swallowed. He tried to sound composed. 'I heard about the first one,' he said. 'No need for another, now, Dad.'

'People came to see us out here. Police – and other investigators. Secret service, we think. Asked us all sorts of questions. And they're still tampering with our mail – we can see letters have been opened.'

'That's what I mean. It's too big – there are other forces at work, other interests. Listen, I'll call you from time to time – and I'll let you know when I've sorted everything out.' The beeps came and more coins went in. 'They'll probably trace this call – you can tell them that we spoke. But I'm alive and well, Dad.' This statement made him feel like weeping, also, as he registered its poignant truth and its contingency.

'Well, take care, son. Oh, and thanks for calling.'
'Send my love to Emma and the boys.'
'Will do.'
'OK, Dad – bye.'

He hung up and wiped his eyes, swearing at himself under his breath. He should have said, 'I love you, Dad,' or some such declaration, but that wasn't the Kindred family way. He gathered up his remaining coins, wiped the mouthpiece of the phone with a tissue and stepped out of the booth. He took off his surgical gloves and dropped them in a bin before heading off towards the Tube station. He was tempted to hang around and wait to see how long it would be before the police arrived looking for him – it would have been a useful measure of their vigilance – but he had other more pressing tasks to occupy him.

It was a calculated risk calling his father, he knew, but it was something that he had been wanting to do for weeks. The fact that he had felt able to do it now seemed symbolic: it was a sign that matters were coming to a head, the slow crescendo was becoming louder and more agitated. He tried to imagine what his father's reaction would be – he would have been pleased to have his son's safety confirmed, proof that his son was alive, or so Adam supposed. Perhaps he hadn't been that worried – his voice hadn't sounded surprised or emotional – maybe he had practically forgotten that Adam was a wanted man, half a world away. Francis Kindred was enjoying his retirement with his daughter and his grand-children – what could he do about it if his miscreant son had decided to go to hell in a hand-cart? He was not an easily perturbed man, Francis Kindred – still, Adam was pleased, he felt he had done his duty: it was a small step in his rehabili-tation as a normal human being. He felt, in an absurd way, that he had his family back again.

At the end of the afternoon of the next day Adam watched the man he now knew was Ingram Fryzer walk across the small piazza in front of the glass tower that contained the Calenture-Deutz offices and slip into the back of his parked Bentley. Adam was fifty yards away, sitting on his scooter and, spotting Fryzer, he started the engine. He had been waiting almost two hours – it was now just after 6.00 p.m. Earlier, he had called Calenture-Deutz, saying he was a journalist from *The Times*, and that he wanted to speak to Ingram Fryzer about Zembla-4. He was brusquely told that Mr Fryzer was unavailable, in a meeting, please contact Pippa Deere at Calenture-Deutz public relations. Now he knew Fryzer was in the building he had been happy to settle down and wait. Then he saw the glossy Bentley slide to a halt in the reserved parking bay and, moments later, Fryzer emerged. He looked an innocuous man – tall, in a dark suit with a thick head of grey hair – Adam found it hard to stir up any emotion against him.

Adam followed his car across London to Fryzer's

large house in Kensington, saw the Bentley pull into the drive and the chauffeur leap out to open the rear door. Adam accelerated away, heading for Notting Hill. He needed to know where Fryzer lived and to see how close he was to his brother-in-law, Lord Redcastle. It turned out that they were reassuringly far apart.

It had been hard to gain much useful information on Fryzer, he seemed to keep himself to himself, and the details available about his life were bland: a semi-smartish public school, a second-class degree in PPE at Oxford, a brief stint at a merchant bank in the City before he moved into property in the 1980s Thatcher boom. The most interesting fact that Adam had gleaned was that Fryzer's mother's maiden name was Felicity de Vere. Fryzer had married, in his mid-twenties, Lady Meredith Cannon, the daughter of the Earl of Concannon. Three children blessed the union. Then in the 1990s Fryzer had transferred, bizarrely, out of property development into phar-maceuticals, buying a small company called Calenture, whose main asset was a highly successful anti-hayfever treatment (pill and nasal inhaler) called Bynogol. Shortly after, the company became Calenture-Deutz (Adam couldn't see where the 'Deutz' name originated: he suspected it was cosmetic, an ad-man's clever branding notion: it had more of a ring to it than plain old Calenture. Calenture-Deutz suggested an aura of Teutonic thoroughness) and the company had steadily grown to a reasonable size – a comfortable mid-table player in the Big Pharma leagues. There was nothing there that would arouse suspicion; nothing that would hint at any more sinister ambitions.

On the other hand, information on Ivo, Lord Redcastle couldn't have been more easily forthcoming. Ivo was readily unearthed on the internet where there was a badly designed, malfunctioning website for RedEntInc.com that managed to provide an address of an office in Earls Court and a telephone number. He had called the office from a phone booth and a girl called Sam – 'Sam speaking' – had told him Ivo was at lunch.

'It's not about the T-shirts, is it?' she asked, her rising voice betraying her excitement.

'Actually, it is,' Adam lied spontaneously and Sam had immediately given him Ivo's mobile phone number – 'He'll want to talk to you, I know.' When Adam called, Ivo himself answered. He could hear the clatter of silverware on crockery and the babble of a restaurant's conversation. Ivo had told him where he was lunching as if the address conferred on him some kind of instant status.

'It's about the T-shirts,' Adam said.

'Are you interested?'

'Absolutely.'

Adam said he wasn't free in the day and so Ivo invited him to his house that evening, giving the address, and post code, and home phone number in Notting Hill. Adam agreed to meet him there at 8.00 that evening, having not the slightest intention of showing up. All he wanted was the address, but he decided, now that he knew where Ivo was, to confirm that he had indeed got his man. All that he knew of Ivo's appearance was from a small photo in the Calenture-Deutz brochure. He bought a disposable camera and waited outside the restaurant until someone similar appeared. He had buzzed past in his scooter, calling Ivo's name just to be sure and, when he looked up, taken a snap. It all went into the Calenture-Deutz file. And now he knew also that the man Ivo had been with that day was Fryzer. Perhaps they had been discussing Calenture-Deutz business . . . The success of the clinical trials . . . The upcoming press conference . . .

Adam smiled to himself as he turned off Ladbroke Grove looking for the number of Ivo's house – there it was, tall white stucco, off-street parking. Two men were carrying a large abstract painting in through the front door. Adam pulled up across the street and pretended to be checking his *A–Z* street map. There seemed to be a CCTV camera mounted above the front door – he would have to be careful. He accelerated off – he was on the night shift at St Bot's again. He needed his days free at the moment, the only disadvantage being that he hadn't seen Rita since their night together . . . He would call her – they had spoken every day – and he beguiled himself as he motored east through London with images of her naked body flashing pleasingly through his mind's eye. It was time for another date. She didn't realise it yet but he had some need of the Nashe family in his emerging plan.

'How does that look to you?'

'Ideal.'

It was a small memo pad of the sort that classier hotels place by the phone or on writing desks: one hundred leaves, a stiff cardboard back, and printed across the top of each page in blue-black ink, upper case, was the name 'INGRAM FRYZER'.

'You'd have been better off ordering at least a dozen,' the girl in PrintPak said to Adam. 'We'd have given you a discount. Seems very expensive for such a little pad.'

'It's a present,' Adam said, handing over a twenty-pound note. 'I may be back for more.'

He was leaving the shop when his mobile rang.

'Hello?'

'Primo Belem?'

'Yes.'

'It's Aaron Lalandusse here. I got your intriguing message.'

'Can we meet?'

'Do you really have all that material?'

'Yes, I do.'

Lalandusse suggested a pub in Covent Garden, not far from his magazine's offices in Holborn and Adam said he'd be there. It was beginning to come together. He called Rita and asked her if they could meet at the *Bellerophon*.

'My dad will be there.'

'I know. I need to have a word with him.'

CHAPTER 50

'Do you want a bite to eat? A drink?' Alfredo Rilke looked in his hotel room's mini-bar. 'I can offer you chips – or "crisps", as you call them – some chocolate, a nougat biscuit.'

'Is there any white wine in there?' Ingram asked, suddenly feeling the need for some alcohol. Rilke had taken a floor of the Zenith Travel Inn near Heathrow airport and had summoned Ingram there, necessitating an inconvenient journey out in the rush hour at the end of the day. What was wrong, Ingram thought, with Claridge's or the Dorchester, for heaven's sake?

Rilke unscrewed the top from the wine bottle and poured out a glass for him. Ingram could tell as he accepted it that it wasn't nearly cold enough. What was the point of being the fourteenth richest man in the world, or whatever he was, and choosing to live in this style?

'Cheers,' he said, raising his glass, 'very good to see you, Alfredo.'

'I'm basing myself here for the next few days.'

'Excellent. You can come to our press conference.'

'I'll be there in spirit, Ingram.' He paused, and

re-set his face as if he had serious news to impart. 'I wanted you to know that I just heard, unofficially, secretly – an hour ago – that we'll get our FDA licence. Zembla-4 is going to be approved.'

Ingram inhaled, needing more oxygen. He felt his hand tremble and put his glass down.

'To say that's "good news" sounds mean-spirited. That means the MHRA won't be far behind.' His mind was going fast. 'But how do you know? It's unofficial, you say?'

'Yes. Let's say word has reached us. Our people have managed to learn enough about the reports, their content and recommendation. The advisory committee stage will be very positive, also. We heard it on the grapevine, as the song has it.' Rilke smiled. 'Don't look so worried, Ingram. We're not selling heroin. We're not smuggling weapons-grade uranium to rogue states that sponsor terrorism. Zembla-4 will save millions of lives over its licence period. It's a boon, a blessing to mankind.'

'Of course.' Ingram tried to make his features relax. 'Obviously I can't even hint at this at the press conference.'

'No, not even a tiny word. Just the business of the day. But I'll make sure you know our final buy-out price in plenty of time. It'll be very generous. Some analysts may even say more than generous. But not so generous as to prompt curious questions.'

'I see,' Ingram said, not seeing, wondering where this was leading.

'And then we get the FDA approval.' Rilke spread his hands as if to say: look how easy it all is.

'The ex-shareholders might feel a little irritated.'

'They'll be happy enough. We'll make a good offer. They'll have some Rilke stock to comfort them.'

'But when they hear about the Zembla-4 licence they'll suspect we knew.'

'But how could we know? The Food and Drug Administration guards its deliberations under utmost secrecy. Nothing is certain. The FDA refuses one out of four applications.'

'Yessss . . . Where will we manufacture Zembla-4?'

'Leave that to me. It won't be your company any more, Ingram. The days of these complicated, tricky decisions will be over. In fact you'll probably want to retire and enjoy your money.'

'I will?' Ingram queried – and then quickly made it a statement. 'I will. You're quite right.' He drank some more of his warm wine. 'Rilke Pharma bags Calenture-Deutz', the headline would run somewhere in the financial pages, Ingram thought. Not a headline, no big deal until the Zembla-4 news is announced. Then more plaudits for Alfredo Rilke's uncanny acumen – somehow cherry-picking a twenty-year licensed blockbuster drug for a few hundred million. A billion dollar revenue stream guaranteed for two decades. What would that do for Rilke Pharma stock? Not that Ingram cared, he would be enjoying his modest share of

Zembla-4 royalties. True, he thought, if I were an institutional holder of shares in Calenture-Deutz, happy to accept Rilke Pharma's generous offer, I might be somewhat aggrieved to know that I wasn't going to participate in that revenue stream or see its benefits. I might even start asking uncomfortable questions. Why sell a company when its new drug is up for approval? He looked back at Alfredo, who was at the window contemplating the traffic on the M4.

'My argument to the shareholders would be—'

'That you cannot guarantee a licence for Zembla-4. Not all applications succeed – only a few dozen drugs a year get a licence. Rilke Pharma's excellent offer is too good to pass up. Take your profit now rather than risk having an unlicensed drug on your shelf with all the costs of its development unreturned. Shrewd business sense.' Rilke wandered over and put his big hand on Ingram's shoulder. 'No one will query your decision, Ingram, believe me. You are just being a prudent CEO. Everyone will make a nice profit. Your more astute shareholders will have taken Rilke stock rather than cash – these people won't want to ask many searching questions. And, of course, no one knows about our little arrangement.' Rilke smiled. 'Which is one of the reasons I meet you in these charming hotels.'

'True. Yes . . .' Ingram encouraged his excitement to bubble up again and sipped his wine – no, it was too disgusting. He put it down. In fact he was feeling a little nauseous. He'd open something decent when he returned home, celebrate properly. Then an unpleasant thought arrived, rather spoiling the party.

'We never found that Kindred fellow,' he said. 'Pity about that.'

'It doesn't really matter any more,' Rilke said with a reassuring smile. 'Now we have the licence in the bag, Kindred's moment has gone.'

'That's very reassuring,' Ingram said. 'Actually, is there any brandy in that fridge? – I'm feeling a little off-colour.'

CHAPTER 51

The framed poster was for an exhibition of Paul Klee paintings – 'ANDACHT ZUM KLEINEN' was its title – held in Basle in 1982 and there was a reproduction of a Klee watercolour, a pointed-roofed house in a moonlit landscape of stylised pine trees with a fat white moon in the sky. At the bottom of the watercolour was Paul Klee's signature and the painting's title written in his scratchy copperplate handwriting: *'Etwas Licht in dieser Dunkelheit'*.

Rita looked at Primo, who was studying it carefully.

'Do you like it?' she asked.

'It's lovely, thank you,' he said and kissed her.

'A flat-warming present,' she said. 'This flat needs more warmth.' She handed him another package.

'You shouldn't do this,' he said, tearing the paper off to reveal a small hammer in a box and a picture hook.

'No excuses,' she said.

They chose a wall in the sitting room and he hammered in the picture hook and hung the poster.

'The place is transformed,' he said, stepping

back to admire the poster. 'What does "*Andacht zum Kleinen*" mean?'

'I looked it up. I think it means "Devotion to small things".'

Primo considered this for a second or two. 'Very apt,' he said. 'Let's have a drink to celebrate.'

They had stopped for a pizza on the way back from Battersea and had bought a bottle of wine to bring home. They sat with their glasses on the leather sofa, watching the ten o'clock news on television, Rita leaning up against him.

'We've got to change this sofa,' she said. 'It's like a gangster's sofa. What made you buy it?'

'It was going cheap and I was in a hurry,' he said. 'We'll change it, don't worry.'

Rita wondered if he was picking up the subtext to this discussion.

'How was Dad?' she asked. 'I thought it was best to leave the two of you alone.'

'I put a proposition to him – I need his help with something. He said he'd give it serious thought.'

'What proposition?'

'Something to do with the hospital. About a new drug. In fact I gave him a present. I've bought him a share in a company, a drug company.'

'You're trying to turn him into a capitalist, aren't you?'

'He seemed quite pleased.'

'As long as it's legal,' she said, turning to kiss his neck. 'Let's get naked, shall we?'

CHAPTER 52

It came up on the screen: INPHARMA-TION.COM, black and red, the PHARMA letters pulsing an orangey-crimson. Adam registered, logged in – his nom de plume was 'chelseabridge' – and he went to the thread for Zembla-4. He read a few of the posts, mostly pleas from asthma sufferers who had seen the advertorials and were wondering when and if the drug would be available. And then he made his own post, typing in the names of the dead children and the hospitals where they died, adding that they were all participating in Zembla-4 clinical trials when they had suddenly died and then left it at that. He was following Aaron Lalandusse's instructions precisely: make your first post, then add others every two or three days. Watch it build.

Aaron Lalandusse was an unshaven, bespectacled, thirty-something, with a tangled mop of curly hair. He looked as if he'd slept in his clothes but his voice was deep and sonorous, counterposing the image of geeky adolescence with maturity and gravitas. He had looked with close scrutiny at

Adam's list of names and his other documentation making little popping noises with spittle on his lips as he did so.

'Mmm . . . Yes . . .' he said, then, 'bloody hell.'

Adam had mentioned nothing about Philip Wang's death, explaining that he had come across this list during his routine work at St Bot's and, worried about what it implied, had decided to have it checked out further.

'This is highly combustible stuff,' Lalandusse said. 'I mean, if you're wrong, then the litigation will be monstrous, unprecedented.'

Adam pointed to the cryptic annotations beside each name. 'This is the handwriting of Dr Philip Wang, I believe, the late head of R and D at Calenture-Deutz. I don't really know what they are.'

'I would say they're dosages, times,' Lalandusse ventured. 'But I'd need to do a bit of checking.' He held up the list. 'This is a photocopy – I'd have to see the original. I can't write anything without seeing that.'

'I can get it for you,' Adam said.

They had met, as agreed, in a small, dark, wood-panelled pub in Covent Garden. The blazing evening sun obliquely struck the pub's engraved, frosted windows and made the rear snug bar where they were sitting seem so crepuscular that they might have been in a basement. A good place to hatch a conspiracy, Adam thought, as Lalandusse went to the bar to buy them two more bottles of beer.

Lalandusse had then told him about the potency and reach of the bloggers on Inpharmation.com and had outlined the road ahead, as he saw it. First, set hares running on the internet and see what came back – perhaps someone who had worked on the de Vere wings in the other hospitals had some information. Or disgruntled or ex-Calenture-Deutz employees might want to contribute. At some stage the volume of the Chinese whispers of the internet rumour-mill would be such that Calenture-Deutz would have to issue a press release.

'You know the sort of thing,' Lalandusse said. 'Complete outrage, irresponsible, disgraceful, reluctant to dignify malignant smears with a response, etcetera.'

'What then?'

'Well, then I can write my story in the *Bulletin* – precisely because it's become a story.' He thought for a moment. 'Perhaps we can break the habit of a lifetime and print a facsimile of your list.' He smiled with genuine enthusiasm, the boy in him overcoming the cynical journalist. 'Then the shit really would hit the fan.'

Adam smiled as he logged out and exited the site. He was in a large internet café on the Edgware Road. Lalandusse had told him only to use large cafés with dozens of terminals and to keep changing café, and only to pay cash. 'They'll try and find you,' he had said. 'You've no idea what's at stake with a new drug like this. How much money.' He laughed. 'They'll want to kill you.' He stifled his laughter. 'I'm only joking, don't worry.'

Adam parked his scooter on the pavement, locking it to the railings, and then climbed over the fence into the triangle, pushing his way through the low branches and the bushes towards his clearing. It was late, almost eleven o'clock, and the rows of bulbs on the superstructure of Chelsea Bridge glowed brightly in the navy-blue night – four brilliant peaks, like the lights on a circus's big top. He unearthed his cash-box and folded Philip Wang's original list carefully before slipping it into his jacket pocket. He saw he had about £180 left from his original stash and decided to take it – the days of the triangle were over, he realised, now that he had re-entered society as Primo Belem. He stood up and looked around, thinking back to the weeks when this small clearing and its overarching trees and bushes had been all he could describe as his home. He wondered if he would ever come back – perhaps he would: on some nostalgic pilgrimage in the future.

He climbed back over the fence, smiling at this notion, and unlocked his helmet from its box on the rear of the scooter.

'Well, well, well, if it isn't my old churchgoing chum, John 1603.'

Adam felt his heart jolt with pure shock and turned slowly to see Vincent Turpin step unsteadily from the shadows. He walked towards him, smiling.

'You have no idea how many nights I've spent down here at Chelsea Bridge, hoping to catch a sight of you. No idea . . . Night after fucking night.' He was close now and Adam could smell the alcohol on his breath. 'Almost didn't recognise you, mate, what with the hair all shaved down, like, different beard and that. Yeah, did a double take. That's John, I said to myself. Sure as shit: John 1603. Remember that night we came down here, first time? You sort of ducked and dived, didn't want to let me know where you kipped down? . . . Well, you didn't see me, but I saw you – hopping over the fence. Stuck in my mind, luckily.'

'Nice to see you, Vince,' Adam said. 'But I'm in a bit of a hurry.'

'Spare a couple of minutes for a chat with old Vincey, yeah? Look at you: little scooter – voom, voom – all spruce and modern young bloke, suited up. Must be doing well, John.' Turpin linked arms with him and turned him round, heading back towards the bridge, where there was a wooden bench with a view of the Lister Hospital on the other side of the traffic lights at the wide cross-roads. Adam sat down, feeling the saliva leave his mouth.

'What can I do for you, Vince?' he said.

'Somebody's looking for you, mate. A right nasty customer. Big bloke with a deep cleft in his chin. Ugly bugger. He came to the church, asking about you.'

'Don't know him,' Adam said, his heart weighing

448

heavy suddenly, thinking: he'd traced me to the church – maybe that's how he got on to Mhouse.

'He says you're a good friend,' Turpin continued. 'Says you've come into a bit of money. Says he'll pay me two grand if I can find you.'

Adam thought: all I need to do is run away. I'm safe.

'But I don't want to do that – if you don't want me to,' Turpin said.

'I'd appreciate that, Vince.'

'Thing is, there's no point in fobbing off old Vince Turpin with a load of bollocks and thinking you can just disappear.' Turpin smiled again. 'Because when I saw you arrive on your smart new little scooter I took the trouble to write down the licence plate number. Committed it to memory.' He put his hand on Adam's arm. 'If I give that number to Ugly Bugger – who seems a capable bloke, ex-copper, I'd say – I reckon he could track you down in a jiffy.' Turpin now gripped Adam's arm and pulled him close to his big seamed and folded face. 'If Ugly Bugger will pay me two grand, something tells me you might pay me four to keep my mouth shut.'

'I haven't got four grand.'

'I don't want it all at once, John 1603. No, no. I'd blow it, spendthrift arsehole that I am. I want it bit by bit, once or twice a week, like a sort of retainer. A hundred here, two hundred there, keep old Vince ticking over, keep the Turpin head above water.' He paused. 'Keep the Turpin lips zipped.'

'All right,' Adam said. 'We can work something out, I'm sure.' All he could do at this juncture, Adam realised, was buy time. He could pay Turpin off over the next days and weeks while the Zembla-4 plan progressed. All he needed was time. He reached into his pocket for his wad of notes.

'I can give you £150, now,' he said, and began to count out the notes.

'Why don't I just take the lot?' Turpin said, as his big hands swooped and grabbed the money. 'Let's meet here, again, same time, next Wednesday night.' He gave Adam his full smile, showing both rows of teeth. 'No funny business, John. You can sell that scooter tomorrow – set it on fire and throw it in the river – but something tells me Ugly Bugger will still know how to find you.'

'OK,' Adam said, 'I'll be here, don't worry.'

'Make it 200 quid, next time. Nice seeing you again, John.' He stood up, gave a brief wave and wandered off over the bridge towards the Battersea shore.

Adam drove back to Stepney in thoughtful mood. Turpin was right, all that his pursuer – Ugly Bugger – required was the number plate of his scooter. There was, now, a paper and electronic trail that pointed the way directly from the scooter to Primo Belem and his Oystergate Buildings apartment, even if he dumped the scooter, resold it, even if he moved to a new address. There were tracks out there in the world, now, tracks that led

450

to him for the first time. He'd have to change identity again, stop being Primo Belem – but how would he do that? Go underground once more? . . . Stay calm, Adam told himself, soon all this will be irrelevant: all he had to do was keep Turpin quiet and contented for a short period of time. He mustn't be distracted from his key mission; he should just continue as if this unfortunate encounter had never occurred.

CHAPTER 53

Ivo, Lord Redcastle wondered if there had been some kind of sign or omen that he had missed. He was also wondering if he was beginning to lose his grip. That guy who had rung him up about the T-shirts, for example – he *hadn't even asked his name.* What kind of entrepreneur was he? Pathetic. And, worse still, he had invited this unknown, nameless man for a drink at his house to discuss the T-shirt crisis – to which, it went without saying, he hadn't even bothered to turn up. Of course he had drunk a bloody mary and a half – no, practically a full bottle of wine at lunch. Maybe that was why he hadn't been thinking straight. Anyway, the guy not showing up that night had been a real downer (and he had behaved appallingly to Smika, he admitted, and taken far too much cocaine in compensation, later that night – got totally pranged – trying to make everything seem better, and failing). He made no excuses for himself, though he was cross that he had bragged about it to Ingram at the restaurant, as if the T-shirt problem had been finally solved. Fool. Idiot fool.

And then, on succeeding days, had come the solicitors' letters, three of them, horrible, stern missives listing his serial failings as human being and businessman and detailing his mounting debts to various creditors. More worrying – in a kind of disturbing existential way – had been the jpeg that Dimitrios had sent him. It showed a pyre of ten thousand of his sex-instructor T-shirts ablaze on a beach on Mykonos. He had always regarded Dimitrios as a pretty decent guy, almost a mate, even though he didn't know him that well . . . But after this – Jesus, it was totally out of order. Beyond the bounds, etcetera.

What, however, to do about this latest communication? . . . It was only ten o'clock in the morning but Ivo felt he needed a drink so he opened a bottle of cold Chablis from the supply he kept in his fridge at the home office and called Sam at RedEntInc at Earls Court.

'Any news on tracing that call?' he asked. He was hoping to find a number for the nameless man who had telephoned him about the T-shirts. He had not only *not* asked what his name was but he'd also neglected to find out how he could be contacted.

'We think we've got it,' Sam said.

'You did tell the police that it was obscene? Really obscene.'

'Absolutely – that's why they were so helpful. They say it came from a payphone in Sloane Square.'

'Fuck. Thanks, Sam.'

Ivo took a large gulp of his Chablis – a great morning drink, he thought, light and very palatable – and picked up the piece of paper that, according to the evidence of his front-door CCTV camera, had been pushed through his letter-box at 7.47 that morning by a helmeted motorbike courier.

All the envelope had written on it was his name 'IVO' in capital letters, and inside was a sheet from Ingram's personal memo pad – his name printed across the top – saying, written in biro, also in capital letters: 'SELL YOUR C-D SHARES NOW. I WILL DENY EVERYTHING. I.'

The 'I' was Ingram's recognisable initial-signature – the two horizontal bars of the 'I' widely separated from the vertical stroke. Unmistakable.

Let's face it, Ivo said to himself, I'm fucking broke – or as broke as people like me ever become. The whole T-shirt fiasco/debacle had cost and would cost him tens of thousands. He had a small collapsing pyramid of unpaid bills on his desk. The rent of Smika's gallery and the *vernissage* party had still to be settled. Not to mention Poppy and Toby's school fees . . .

So, he thought, this instruction comes, hand-delivered . . . Maybe Ingram had sensed the crisis brewing when they had met that day at the restaurant and he was offering him this semi-anonymous lifeline with built-in deniability: 'SELL YOUR C-D SHARES NOW . . .' Of course Ingram had to ensure he was distant from such a transaction:

he couldn't openly advocate this – it had to be done within the family, as it were. Fair enough, he could keep a secret as well as the next man. He would just run a quick check.

He called Ingram on his mobile.

'Ingram, baby, it's Ivo. Have you got a second?'

'I'm about to go into a meeting.'

'I was thinking of selling my Calenture shares. Cashflow problems.'

'Don't sell, Ivo. Don't be a bloody fool. Do *not* sell.'

'Fair enough. Thanks, mate.'

He called his stockbroker, Jock Tait, senior partner at Swabold, Tait and Cohen. After the introductory pleasantries he asked him directly.

'Jock – hypothetical question – could you unload my Calenture-Deutz shares today? Like pronto?'

'All of them?'

'Hypothetically.'

Tait hummed and hawed and asked to be given ten minutes. Ivo drank another glass of Chablis and listened to some calming music before Tait called back. He said he could sell them: indeed, he had a single buyer who would take the lot.

'How much would I make?' Ivo asked.

'Well – ballpark figure at 420 pence a share, say . . . About 1.8 million. Less commission, of course.'

'You say you've got a buyer.'

'Yes.'

'Then sell. Sell, sell, sell.'

There was a silence at the end of the line.
'Jock?'

'How would Ingram feel about this?' Jock said, cautiously. 'It might send the wrong kind of signal to the market. Not that it's any of my business.'

'Precisely. But you can relax – Ingram's cool. All the same, you know, keep it under your hat. *Omertà.*'

'Good as done,' Jock said.

Ivo hung up, finished his glass of Chablis and refilled it. It was a strange feeling – to move from an anxiety-ridden, near bankrupt to a millionaire in under half an hour. Funny old world. He was essentially a good guy, was Ingram – *au fond* – even though Ivo knew that neither of them really liked each other much at all. He wondered if he could detect Meredith's hand in this covert rescue mission – sweet Merry, always looking out for little brother. It was Meredith who had persuaded Ingram, much against his will, to put him on the Calenture-Deutz board, to guarantee some income in a pretty much income-free existence (apart from the trust fund). And now this. Ivo would be in a position to pay off everybody – even that cunt on Mykonos – and still have a million clear (less bloody tax, of course). He wondered: maybe this was the time to go non-domiciled, reinstate the Irish residency . . .

He poured himself another glass. Perhaps he and Smika should go out to lunch and celebrate – discreetly. Actually, he wouldn't tell her about the money – just say some film deal looked like coming off – in fact he'd better make sure it didn't go anywhere near the joint account, come to think of it, stick it in the Isle of Man bank for a while, yes. He picked up the phone and dialled Ingram's home number – praying for voicemail – if anyone answered he'd just hang up. Voicemail – thank Christ.

'You've reached Ingram and Meredith Fryzer's number. Please leave a message.'

'Ingram, it's Ivo. I just want to say thank you. Thank you. Bless you.'

Ivo hung up. Ingram would know what he was referring to – so no need for him to make any histrionic 'denials'. All was suddenly well in the Redcastle household. He wandered out of his study and called up the stairs to Smika's studio.

'Darling? Fancy a spot of lunch?'

CHAPTER 54

There was a good turn-out, Ingram could see, as Luigi drove them past the entrance to the Queen Charlotte Conference Centre in Covent Garden – some dozens of people still queuing to pick up copies of the agenda and press release and to have their names verified as bona fide shareholders. Can all these people own bits of my company? Ingram demanded, as he looked at the shuffling queue. He realised he was in his usual troubled state of wonder: it always happened at the AGM, as well, when he had the chance to contemplate these earnest amateur speculators – these mums and dads, these eccentrics with their thermos flasks and packs of sandwiches. All these hundreds, thousands of individuals around the world who possessed a little bit of Calenture-Deutz paper and who turned up, along with the smart young men and women from pension funds, the investment banks and the financial institutions, to listen to what the chairman and the board had to say about the proper functioning of the company they had invested in. It seemed extraordinary and, as at the AGM each year, he found himself in two minds, trapped: was this a healthy sign of the democratic, accountable base of Western capitalism, or was it an indication that the system was hopelessly soft and too lenient? Due diligence, fair practice, corporate responsibility – or raw, lean, energetic commerce being forcibly called to account for its actions and agenda on an annual basis, in an unreal situation where it could find itself at the mercy of rivals, special interest groups, selfish investors and the occasional random lunatic.

Talking of which, Ingram thought, there was a peach, a prime specimen. They were driving past an elderly pony-tailed man in a wheelchair holding up a placard that said: 'ZEMBLA-4 KILLS CHILDREN' – and underneath that the address of a website that Ingram couldn't read. He chuckled, heavy irony colouring his semi-laugh. He was used to these posters – he'd seen worse. There had been a 'FRYZER = MENGELE' banner a couple of years ago. He smiled again – this drug was specifically designed to *save* children's lives, for fuck's sake. Here was the problem when you opened your doors to the public, even an interested public – such gatherings were announced weeks in advance, discretion was an impossibility, word was circulated everywhere – you didn't even need to be a shareholder to cause trouble. Big Pharma was a legitimate target these days – like the banks, the arms dealers and the oil companies – any anarchic, eco-madman-warrior could take it on himself to make a symbolic protest, even against a perfectly harmless medium-sized Pharma company like Calenture-Deutz. At one AGM Ingram had had green paint sprayed over his £2,000 suit by a demonstrator wearing a skull-mask; at another, people in loin-cloths and with suppurating wounds painted on their bodies had lain on the pavement outside the venue feigning toxic death. All their public meetings were routinely picketed and targeted – moronic ape-chanting carrying into the hall as the financial report was read out, banners draped over the building, silent lines of young people wearing gas masks – and so it was something of a relief to see they only had one solitary dickhead to deal with this year. Security would see to him but the sooner the whole thing was over, the better.

As he stepped out of the car Ingram experienced one of his new disorientating swoons. He staggered, Luigi grabbed his elbow, and after a couple of deep breaths Ingram felt fine again. Blood spots, ferocious itches, fainting fits, the word confusions – plus, he had to say, intermittent nausea and very short-term headaches that were so short term they were over by the time he had reached for the analgesic. It could only be stress – stress caused by this whole delicate, secret accommodation with Rilke and Rilke Pharma, the aggravation imposed by Keegan and de Freitas, not to mention extraneous factors like the brutal murder of his chief researcher: all these symptoms must stem from these pressures – he was only human after all.

Lachlan McTurk had said he had run out of tests – everything had shown up completely clear – all there was left now was the body-wide ultrasound and the MRI brain scan and so he had been duly booked in. There was no alternative, Lachlan said, he could find nothing. Perhaps once this whole Zembla-4 licensing was over and as soon as the company was safely sold to Rilke Pharma his health would return to its old state – robust, uncomplicated, normal.

He went in through a back entrance and was guided along corridors to a form of green room where the board of Calenture-Deutz was gathering before it went on stage. Pippa Deere busied around him and had him fitted out with a lapel microphone. She assured him that all the international video-links had been checked and were fully functioning. Yes, yes, fine. Ingram couldn't really concentrate – he still felt a little light-headed and he ordered a coffee to quell his resurgent nausea. He smiled and nodded at his colleagues – the doctors and the Oxbridge professors, the ex-cabinet minister and the banking supremo – and there too were his nemeses, Keegan and de Freitas, looking over at him knowingly—

There was a gentle squeeze on his elbow and he turned to find his very own 'Lord on the Board', his brother-in-law, Ivo, smart in a tight dark suit, his thick hair gelled into glossy quiescence.

461

'Ivo . . .' Ingram said, drawing the name out, playing for time, then paused legitimately to accept the coffee brought to him by Pippa Deere. He took a quick sip, searching for a topic of conversation. 'Did you see that lunatic outside?'

Ivo chose not to answer his question, posing instead a question of his own.

'Did you get my message?'

'I did. But I didn't understand it.'

'Exactly.'

'Exactly what?'

'I knew you'd say that. Exactly.' Ivo pulled down the lower lid of his right eye. '*Exactly.*'

'Why would you leave a message I wouldn't understand? Why were you thanking me?'

Ivo leaned close. 'For what you did.'

'I did nothing.'

'*Quod erat demonstrandum.* Q.E.D.'

'What has been demonstrated?' Ingram was growing irritated at this ambiguity.

Ivo sighed. 'I had to say thank you, for god's sake. It's only reasonable, decent.'

'For what?'

'For what you did.'

'I did nothing.'

'You did not do nothing.'

Ingram began to feel he was in a Harold Pinter play, involved in a sinister duologue that could conceivably go on for ever.

'I. Did. Nothing.' He repeated the words with heavy emphasis.

'I know.'

'You admit I did nothing.'

'Yes, so to speak. But I thank you all the same.'

'For what?'

'For doing "nothing".' Ivo used his fingers to make histrionic air-quotes. 'I know that you know. And you know that I know you know.' Ivo tapped the side of his nose. 'I can read,' he said, conspiratorially.

'I don't know what the fuck you're talking about.'

'Exactly. Point taken. No worries. Good man, Ingram, I love you.'

Pippa Deere interrupted to guide them on to the stage and their appointed seats.

Ingram forced himself to stay awake as Professor Marcus Vintage, who was chairing the press conference, spoke about the year's progress the company had made, and the tragedy of Philip Wang's sudden and shocking death (silence in the hall), making no mention of Zembla-4, in his Yorkshire-accented monotone before handing over to Edward Anthony, the company secretary, who would present a brief financial report. The hall was nearly full, Ingram saw, full of part-owners of Calenture-Deutz, all apparently listening intently. He glanced down at the agenda: welcome from the chairman, welcome from the company secretary, statement from Ingram Fryzer, CEO. 'Statement' – that was when he would detonate his little fiscal bomb. Little did they know, he thought, looking out over the audience, that everyone in this room was going to leave richer than when they'd come in. Theoretically. He allowed himself a small smile.

It seemed several hours later that he was called to the microphone, though a glance at his watch told him only thirty-five minutes had passed. Ingram waited for the mild applause to die down and unfolded his notes.

'My lords, ladies and gentlemen. I want to make a brief special announcement that greatly affects the future of the company. As you all know, Rilke Pharmaceutical holds a 20 per cent stake in Calenture-Deutz. I want to let you know today that I have agreed to sell my personal shareholding in the company to Rilke Pharmaceutical. This will give them a controlling interest.' The room was completely silent. 'However,' Ingram continued, 'Rilke Pharma are proposing a complete buy-out of Calenture-Deutz as a share offer with cash alternative. Rilke is offering 600 pence a share, some 20 per cent higher than our current capitalisation. I, and the entire board of Calenture-Deutz, strongly recommend that you accept this generous offer. We envisage the takeover—'

'Point of order!' came a loud shout from the rear of the room. 'Point of order, Mr Chairman!'

Ingram felt an itch spear through the sole of his left foot. He stamped down on it hard behind the lectern.

Marcus Vintage looked at him questioningly – should he yield the floor to this interlocutor? Mutterings sped round the room, the sound of hushed shock, speculation and calculation as people wondered how much money they were going to make. Ingram looked round to nod assent at Vintage and saw his hugely magnified image on the video screen nod assent . . . He looked back at the auditorium, shading his eyes against the spotlights, trying to see who had interrupted him. Stewards were approaching an elderly, pony-tailed man in a wheelchair but someone had already handed him a roving microphone.

'I would like to ask the board,' his amplified voice sounded nasal and aggressive – the voice of hate, Ingram thought – 'if they could inform us of the exact number of children who died during the clinical trials of Zembla-4.'

Outrage, shouts, a collective drawing-in of breath erupted before the stewards bore down on the man, seized his microphone and swept him bodily out of the hall, wheelchair lifted off the ground, the man bellowing 'We want answers! We want to know the truth!' Ingram saw that one of the men operating the video cameras for the international feeds had swivelled round and projected wheelchair-man's uncompromising expulsion on the large screen.

The crowd were now applauding. What, Ingram wondered? His own fortitude, the swift removal of the voice of anarchy, the prospect of riches?

Professor Vintage was banging his gavel on the desk and crying 'Order! Order!' in a faint voice. Ingram felt the blood leaving his head and the room darkened. He grabbed the lectern with both hands and managed to stay upright. The room calmed, people who had stood up to see the disruption now sat down. Ingram drew in deep breaths as he consulted his notes, now worried that he might vomit at any moment.

'As I was saying before I was so rudely interrupted . . .' Laughter. 'The buy-out of Calenture-Deutz by Rilke Pharmaceutical should take place over the coming weeks once the various takeover requirements have been met. Calenture-Deutz will continue as a brand name but we will function within the unparalleled security and financial might of the third biggest pharmaceutical company in the world. As your chairman and chief executive I cannot urge you more strongly to accept this most generous offer.'

Loud applause, fervent applause, resounded through the room. Ingram looked across at the board to see them all clapping him – and there were Keegan and de Freitas clapping also, but formally, without the fervour of the room. What were their bonuses to be? Ingram wondered. Keegan was looking at him – and gave him a nod of acknowledgement as their eyes met – but not smiling. If anything, Ingram thought, he looked a little worried. De Freitas stopped clapping and whispered something in Keegan's ear. Ingram turned to the room, gave a small bow and managed to walk off the stage.

He tried to vomit as quietly as possible, a difficult thing to do – but very aware there were other people using the toilet beyond the stall he was occupying – repeatedly flushing the WC, hoping that the flow of water would cover the sound of his retching. Good god, he thought, must be some kind of food poisoning: he was empty, spent. He dabbed his mouth with a tissue, checked that his shirt and tie were free of bile-spatter, and flushed the loo for the seventh time. Funny how copious vomiting could make you feel both hellish and better, he thought, unlocking the door to the stall. You became a simple organism in a state of spasm, voiding your stomach your only aim and purpose, a creature of instinct, all intellectual function shut down. But it somehow rejuvenated as well as exhausted, it was a brief visit to the primitive being you once were – time travel to your lost animal self. He was alone in the toilet, everyone else gone off to lunch, and he washed his hands slowly and carefully, telling himself to stay calm – perhaps he'd better go back to Lachlan one last time.

He stepped out of the toilet into the corridor to find Ivo waiting there.

'I'm fine, Ivo. Good of you to wait. Don't worry, I'll be—'

'I don't give a toss about you, mate. You miserable

467

cunt. Do you hate me that much, really? How could you do this to me? To my family?'

Ingram sighed. 'You've been talking in riddles all day. What is it now?'

'600 pence a share.'

'Yes, an excellent offer.'

'I sold at 480.'

'Sold what?'

'All my Calenture-Deutz shares. Three days ago.'

'Well, then you're a fool.'

'You told me to sell.'

Ingram looked at him. 'Are you mad? Of course I didn't: I told you the opposite.'

'Exactly.'

'Stop saying "exactly" all the time.'

Ivo stepped threateningly closer and for a split second Ingram thought he was going to hit him, but Ivo said, in a trembling voice, 'I'll get you for this. I'll ruin you.'

He strode away towards the exit, shouting imprecations without looking back, 'Complete bastard! We're family, you wanker, family!' Ingram felt more itches springing up: one on his left buttock, one on his chin. He scratched them both simultaneously.

'Mr Fryzer?'

It was Pippa Deere – she looked a little worried, her nose and cheeks gleaming.

'What is it, Pippa? I'm not feeling so good myself – I'm going to skip facsimile.'

'Sorry?' Pippa Deere's face registered bafflement.

'Lunch. I'm going to skip lunch.'

'There are some journalists here, they want to speak to you.'

'Journalists? What do they need me for? They've got your press release, everything's there.'

'Yes, they have. They still want to speak to you.'

'Tell them I'll see them next week.'

'It's about that "point of order" that was raised.'

'For god's sake.' Ingram looked at the ceiling in supplication. 'Some crazy idiot crackpot shouts out some ranting nonsense and I'm meant to talk to journalists about it? We get these demonstrators all the time. Nobody wanted to talk to me when I was spray-gunned with green paint. Who let him in, anyway? What's the point of hiring security?'

Pippa Deere seemed about to cry. 'It turns out the man who was ejected from the hall is a shareholder. When he was thrown out he injured himself, fell out of his wheelchair and cut his head. He gave an interview to some of the journalists . . .' She sniffed. 'I've only heard the tape once but he said something about fourteen little children dying during the Zembla-4 trials. I'm terribly sorry, Mr Fryzer, I didn't know what to do.'

Ingram felt weariness descend on him, a great heavy cloak of weariness.

'It's all utter, abject, malicious nonsense. All right, take me to the gentlemen of the press.'

CHAPTER 55

'I can't thank you enough, Primo,' Jeff Nashe said, his voice almost hoarse with sincerity. 'It was absolutely amazing. I haven't felt that . . . *alive* since my accident.'

'You were tremendous,' Adam said. 'Couldn't have gone better.'

He was wheeling Jeff in his wheelchair down Kingsway, heading for a bus stop where they could catch a bus to Battersea. Jeff's cut (on his forehead) had been dressed by one of the security men who had thrown him out of the conference centre. It was more of a gash than a cut – and was now hidden by some sticking plaster – but the trickle of blood that had run down his face was perfect pictorial testimony to the violence of his expulsion – thoughtless strong-arm tactics used by fascistic security thugs to silence and eject an old, semi-crippled, wheelchair-bound man from a meeting that he had every right to attend and at which he was merely exercising his duties as a bona fide shareholder of a public company. This was more or less what Jeff had told the journalists who had interviewed him – he was articulate, angry and

470

expressive. Two of the journalists had taken photographs of his bloodied face and Adam had every hope the image would make tomorrow's papers.

It had been Aaron Lalandusse who had alerted his fellow reporters to the place and time of Calenture-Deutz's press conference – and to its potential disruption. Jeff had provided individual colour to what might otherwise have been a bland and self-congratulatory corporate exercise – and would be ably backed up by the evidence posted on Inpharmation.com. Calenture-Deutz would deny everything, of course – no doubt the press release was already circulating about the proposed Rilke Pharma buy-out – but now there was rumour and counter-rumour out there, enough accusation and denial to stimulate curiosity and further investigation. Aaron had everything he needed to write his piece for the *Global Finance Bulletin* – the key object of the exercise, after all.

Adam – as a Calenture-Deutz shareholder himself – had been in the room across the hall from Jeff. He had travelled with him from Battersea, in a taxi with the wheelchair and the placard, but while they waited for his moment, Adam had concentrated on what he could make out of Lord Redcastle's demeanour. There was no way of telling if his little ruse had worked – not that it made much difference to the main action of the day. It had been prompted by something Aaron Lalandusse had said when they had met. We need a *simultaneous* plan B, Lalandusse had

471

recommended, not a subsequent one: when you took on a powerful enemy it was always as well to attack on more than one flank: 'You know – go for the jugular with both hands but knee him in the balls as well.' And from what Adam could glean from his study of Calenture-Deutz's board members, Ivo, Lord Redcastle seemed the most obvious target to try and destabilise – though he'd also been tempted by the ex-cabinet minister – and so Ivo had been chosen.

Adam kept his eyes on Redcastle as the AGM progressed – he seemed serious and pensive and had applauded dutifully, always following the lead of others, never initiating a response. There was nothing to indicate in his reactions and be-haviour that he was now a richer but shareless board member, Adam thought – immediately rebuking himself: what did a man who had sold his shares in a company look like? Maybe Redcastle hadn't sold his shares but he hadn't looked at all happy when Fryzer made his announcement about the takeover. The main thing was that Jeff's point-of-order outburst had created enough fuss and brouhaha to justify Aaron Lalandusse asking pointed questions about the Zembla-4 clinical trials. Phase one had gone well, very well.

They had reached the bus stop. Jeff Nashe stepped out of his wheelchair and folded it up.

'I hate buggering about with these things on buses and trains,' he said by way of explanation.

'You don't need to worry, Primo,' he said. 'I can get home on my own.'

'Rita's asked me for supper,' Adam said.

Rita had made a lasagne with a big bowl of salad to go with it and cheese and grapes to follow. The initial concern that she had shown over her father's injury had been almost immediately dispelled by his obvious euphoria. Adam met her brother, Ernesto, for the first time, when he arrived ten minutes after he and Jeff had boarded the *Bellerophon*.

'What have you done to him?' Rita asked Adam. 'I've never seen him so happy.'

'Re-birthing, I think it's called,' Adam said. 'The old sixties radical is living again. He was great, by the way. He might even be in the papers tomorrow.'

They were talking in the *Bellerophon*'s galley – she was checking on the lasagne – and he reached for her and they kissed.

'What's this really about, Primo?' she said. 'Why are you asking my dad to attack a drug company?'

'Not attack – just raise an awkward question . . . It was something I discovered – at the hospital,' he said, trying not to lie too much. 'Something's wrong. And I thought: why should they get away with it? . . . But don't worry, Jeff's done his bit, his moment of glory come and gone. Now it's in the public domain.'

'Why didn't you ask the question?'

Good question, Adam thought. 'Because of my

job,' he said, improvising, 'I don't want to lose it. Conflict of interests. Calenture-Deutz have pumped a lot of money into St Bot's.'

'Yeah? . . .' She looked sceptically at him. 'I never quite saw you as a dedicated do-gooder.'

'We should all be dedicated do-gooders, shouldn't we?' he said, a little defensively. 'In fact, isn't that your job description?'

'Touché,' she said. She shooed Adam out of the galley.

In the sitting room he spoke to Ernesto about his forthcoming trip to Dubai.

'Forty per cent of the world's tower cranes are in Dubai at the moment,' Ernesto said. 'It's a tower-crane Klondike. I'd be a fool to miss out – I can quadruple my salary.'

Jeff came down the steep stairs from the deck bringing with him the exotic whiff of weed. He had a can of Speyhawk lager in his hand.

'Primo,' he said, swaying slightly, though the boat was perfectly still. 'Do you know why I called this ship the *Bellerophon*?'

'No idea.'

'Because Bellerophon slew the monster Chimera. A fire-breathing monster, half lion, half goat – if my classical mythology serves me well.' He took a swig from his can.

'Good name.'

'And today we slew the modern Chimera.'

'Slew might be a bit strong. Inflicted wounds with a bit of luck. Thanks to you.'

Jeff brandished a clenched fist above his head. '*Vinceremos!*' he shouted at the top of his voice.

'Hello?' Rita appeared with the steaming tray of lasagne in her hands. 'Dinner is served, you guys.'

Adam ate the lasagne and salad and drank too much red wine – to such an extent that he experienced a form of benign sensory deprivation. As Jeff and Ernesto argued about the moral consequences of, and the moral opprobrium attendant on, accepting work in a dynastic dictatorship such as Dubai – and Rita tried vaguely to keep the peace – their voices seemed to dim and muffle and Adam contented himself with watching Rita pouring wine and serving second helpings as if she were in some kind of aural bubble that only he was privileged to access. He looked entranced at her strong features and the way she peremptorily hooked falling locks of hair behind her ears, took in her lissom grace and ease as she hefted plates and bowls about the table – silencing her father with a palm across his mouth as he became too abusive – and he felt that familiar bowel-melting sensation in his innards, that abrogation of intellect in favour of emotion.

But his mildly inebriated, self-indulgent love-fest was spoilt by a small, insistent, keening voice at the back of his mind, like the buzzing of a fly or the thin siren-whine of a mosquito. Everything might have gone well today but there was still another problem: what was he going to do about Vincent Turpin?

CHAPTER 56

The leaves on the plants seemed so green and shiny that they looked as if they'd been cut from very fine tin or PVC, Jonjo thought, and then re-touched with glossy enamel paint. He gazed around the Risk Averse Group's lobby – there seemed to be even more plants in pots than the last time he'd been here. They must have someone come in and dust and wash the leaves, they were so healthy and lush they looked artificial, he thought, which rather defeated the point of having them growing in the place, absorbing the lobby's CO_2 and exuding oxygen, or whatever it was that plants did – photo-something . . .

Jonjo's mind was wandering in this way because he was bored, tired of waiting. He looked at his watch – close to forty minutes now. This wasn't on, out of order – they'd asked *him* to come in for this meeting with Major Tim Delaporte himself, for god's sweet sake. He stood up and approached the blonde girl at the reception desk.

'Major Delaporte will be five minutes,' she said

476

before he could utter a word. 'He's on a conference call – he apologises.'

'Oh, right – no worries.'

'Can I get you anything? Water? Soda? Cappuccino?'

'Cup of tea, please,' Jonjo said. 'Milk and two sugars, thanks.'

In fact it turned out that Major Tim was closer to twenty minutes finishing his conference call. The tea had been consumed as had the chocolate biscuit provided with it. Jonjo was about to say he couldn't wait any longer when he was summoned by a secretary and led down a long curved corridor to Major Tim's office.

He was still on the phone and he waved Jonjo to a seat. Jonjo examined his ten fingernails in close detail as Major Tim finished his call – it sounded as though he was talking to his wife about who was coming round for supper. Bloody hell, Jonjo thought.

'Jonjo,' Major Tim reached across the desk to shake hands. 'Sorry to keep you – crazy morning. How're things?'

Jonjo said things were fine and he was glad of this opportunity to talk directly with Major Tim as he'd changed his mind about Iraq and Afghanistan, and indeed all other Arab countries, come to that. He was ready to go, more than happy to—

The Major held up his hand and Jonjo stopped talking.

'People like you made the Risk Averse Group

what it is,' Major Tim said, solemnly, with feeling. 'We couldn't have built up to the size we are today, couldn't have such a presence worldwide, such a reputation, without men of your calibre and quality.'

'You're the best officer I've ever served under, sir. No two ways about it.' They always liked hearing that, the officers did.

'Which makes it all the harder for me to have to tell you that we're letting you go.'

'Sorry?'

'You're off operations, Jonjo. We're overwhelmed with young soldiers in their twenties – god knows who's out there fighting for us – so here at RAG we're reconfiguring our personnel. You know the army way, Jonjo: first in, first out, I'm afraid.'

He stood up. Jonjo noticed the darkness of his suit, a navy-blue so intense it might have been black, the cinched tightness of the waist of the jacket, the white shirt setting off the apricot blush of his silk tie.

'I wanted to let you know personally, man to man, not in some ghastly formal letter. I wanted to thank you as a fellow soldier. You've done us proud, Jonjo, and I'm sure you'll agree it's been mutually beneficial.'

Jonjo felt an unfamiliar lump in his throat. 'You don't want to lose old soldiers, sir.'

'We won't lose you – you'll be on our reserve list.' He laughed dryly. 'Just in case the Yanks decide to invade any more countries. No – it's a young man's business now. We need soldiers with

478

IT qualifications, telecommunications, languages, management skills.' He laughed again. 'The old days have gone – we can't just rock up and kill the bastards.'

Somehow Jonjo was steered towards the door. Major Tim shook his hand again and patted him on the back.

'There are a lot of security organisations out there, Jonjo. Not as exciting as Risk Averse, but you can make a decent living. We can give you any recommendation you like, glowing reference, etcetera.'

Jonjo thought it was worth one more try. He lowered his voice.

'I'm on to Kindred, sir . . . I've almost got him.'

Major Tim smiled vaguely. 'I don't know what you're talking about, old chap.'

'Kindred – I've got a new lead. A licence plate. It's only a matter of time before I catch him.'

'You've lost me, Jonjo. Communications gone down.' He stepped back into his office, a hand raised. 'We'll stay in touch. Good luck.'

Jonjo walked slowly along the curving corridor towards the leafy glade of the lobby, thinking hard. Something smelt, something ponged horribly, something else was going on here, he thought – such as Jonjo Case taking it right up the arse. He had said the name 'Kindred' twice. If Major Tim hadn't recognised the name wouldn't he have repeated it? 'Kindred? Kindred who?' That's what people did when they were confronted by an unfamiliar name. That was the natural expression of ignorance – repeat the name. 'Never heard of this Kindred person, Jonjo.' No, there was none of that: blank stare, blank denial. Jonjo thought on, a flutter of anxiety in his chest – no, he knew who I was talking about so what was the real agenda? Why had he been called in for this meeting? He didn't buy it – no fucking sale, Major Tim. He'd been there well over an hour now, what with the journey in, and all—

Outside the building he called Darren. He could feel a form of excitement building in him, the anxiety gone. He was experiencing the same adrenalin-creep as when you waited to go into combat.

'Darren – it's Jonjo.'

'Jonjo, mate. How're you—'

'What's going on? What the fuck's happening?'

'Happening? Nothing . . . I don't know—'

'For Terry's sake, then. Tell me. I saved Terry's life half a dozen times. Tel would never let me down. Never.'

There was a silence.

'You've got two hours, I reckon,' Darren said. 'They'll look like cops, most likely.'

'Two hours to what?'

'Two hours to cut and run. Fuck off out of it. They got you, mate.'

Jonjo clicked his phone shut.

★   ★   ★

Jonjo sat and watched his house for thirty minutes, just to confirm that it wasn't occupied, before he strolled to the front door, unlocked it and went inside.

The Dog was pleased to see him and then was clearly puzzled to be ignored as Jonjo moved carefully through every room. They had been good but not that good. Chairs were in almost their original positions, a door that had been open was closed. What were they looking for?

Then down in the garage he saw that his weapons were gone, all of them – the Tomcat, the 1911, his .870 Express Security – and the ammo. He searched for a chisel and with it worked free the semi-cemented brick in the garage rear wall. In the cavity behind it he kept, wrapped in thick plastic, a Glock 9mm, £10,000 in cash and an unused mobile phone and charger. It was all he needed. Cut and run, Darren had said. So he would.

CHAPTER 57

Ingram felt a little overwhelmed. A nurse had come into his room and said he had a visitor. She was swiftly followed by two young men who did a quick search and politely escorted her out. Then Alfredo Rilke entered with a bunch of flowers – full-bloomed, near-wilting roses, Ingram saw, a sure sign of last thoughts – and had drawn up a chair to his bed as the two men stationed themselves at the door.

Then he had removed from his pocket something the size of a slim old-fashioned transistor radio and had switched it on. Ingram cocked an ear: silence.

'Ultrasonic,' Rilke said. 'Ambient interference – no one can hear us.'

'Alfredo,' Ingram said, reproachfully, 'this is one of the most eminent and expensive private hospitals in London, not to say the world. This room is not bugged – I swear on my life.' He suddenly wished he hadn't said that, given his current state of health.

Rilke ignored him.

'So, how are you doing, Ingram?'

'I feel perfectly well – apart from the odd strange symptom now and then – but apparently I've got a growth in my brain.' He paused. 'My doctor suggested I had a brain scan and that's what they found.'

Rilke winced in sympathy. He said something under his breath in Spanish that Ingram didn't quite catch. It sounded like '*Madre de Dios*'. It was very rare to hear Alfredo speak Spanish.

'Ingram, Ingram, Ingram . . .'

'Alfredo . . .'

'What are we going to do?'

'I don't really know.'

'It pains me – what I am about to say to you.'

'Well, I'm about to have brain surgery, Alfredo. My priorities are very clear cut. My resilience is supercharged. Please don't worry.'

Rilke lowered his eyes and picked at the sheet edge around Ingram's chest, then he looked up and made full eye contact.

'I am not buying your company.'

Despite his supercharged resilience this surprised Ingram, jolted him somewhat. He thought about his impending brain surgery – they were going to 'debulk' his brain they said – and he regained some perspective and composure.

'These crazy allegations about the dead children – is that what it's all about?'

'No, no, no.' Rilke brushed invisible flies aside with both hands. 'This we can deal with. You are already suing three newspapers and two magazines.

There is a court injunction preventing future press speculation—'

'*Me?* I'm suing?'

'Calenture-Deutz is suing. Burton has had the lawyers in and they've gone to work very effectively. It's a scandal.' Rilke uttered the word in a very unscandalised way, as if he'd said 'It's a snowdrop' or 'It's a sausage' or something equally unremarkable, Ingram thought.

'Malicious, nasty lies,' Ingram said. 'It's the real downside of our business.'

'Lies we can deal with, easy. We would have "ridden this out", no problem.' Rilke pronounced the phrase as if he'd only just learnt it. His expression changed – Ingram could only interpret it as sad. 'Yes, we have these accusations – every week – about our products. We deal with them, we make them go away. But this time, I'm sorry to say, there is a complication.'

'A complication?'

'Your brother-in-law, Lord Redcastle.'

'Ivo . . .'

'He sold 400,000 shares two days before your announcement of our buy-out of Calenture-Deutz.'

'I know.'

Rilke moved his jamming device closer.

'I'm sorry to hear that,' he said.

'Ivo's a fool, a complete idiot.'

'An idiot who looks like he knew something was going to happen. That there was something rotten in the apple barrel.' Rilke explained how it appeared

484

from his angle, his point of view: Ivo sells all his shares. Then comes the announcement of the buy-out. Then the allegations about the children's deaths. 'Did you see the fall in Calenture-Deutz's share price?'

'I've been in the hands of doctors for two days. Tests, tests and more tests. I'm going to have brain surgery.'

'Your company's lost 82 per cent of its value.'

'That's absurd.'

Rilke shrugged. 'The market doesn't like what it sees. A board member dumping shares. It seems to everyone he knew something bad was going to happen. That there was some kind of cover-up going on in the Zembla-4 trials.'

'But there's no cover-up, is there?' Ingram thought immediately about Philip Wang. It was like condensation slowly beginning to clear from a fogged-up windscreen. What had Philip Wang discovered?

'Of course there's no cover-up,' Rilke said with iron assurance. 'But the company is going to be turned over, now, picked apart because of your brother-in-law's actions. Rilke Pharma cannot be associated under these circumstances. I'm sure you understand.'

'Ivo is a man with no money. He's lost a fortune on stupid, hare-brained schemes. He was broke: he needed cash.'

'I hope you can make a good case to the investigation.'

485

'What investigation?'

'The Financial Services Authority. The Serious Fraud Office – who knows?' He reacted to Ingram's genuine incredulity. 'Someone really should have told you, Ingram: Calenture-Deutz shares have been suspended, the company is under investigation by the FSA.'

Ingram tried to feel rage against Ivo but, to his vague consternation, he could muster none. He felt an ironic laugh building in his chest. He coughed it away.

Rilke spread his hands. 'You see our position: Rilke Pharma has to withdraw its offer. Burton will stay on as acting CEO – see what we can salvage.'

'Salvage?'

'We spent a lot of money on Zembla-4, Ingram. We have to find a way of recouping our investment. We can buy PRO-Vyril, the hay-fever inhaler, some of your other lines perhaps. Not all will be lost.' He reached over and squeezed Ingram's hand. 'It's over, Ingram. We nearly did it, nearly. And it would have been magnificent.' He called for his two men and stood up, switching off and pocketing his jamming device.

'But what about Zembla-4? The licences? The FDA? Surely—'

'The FDA rescinded its approval this morning. The MHRA has put everything on hold in the face of this scandal. There will be no Zembla-4, Ingram. We will not cure asthma.'

Rilke leant forward and kissed Ingram's cheek.

'I like you, Ingram. I was looking forward to our triumph. And now I'm sorry for your ill health. I wish you *buena suerte*.'

He walked out of the room and one of his henchmen closed the door behind him.

CHAPTER 58

Aaron Lalandusse frowned, then shrugged resignedly. 'There's nothing I can do. They won't run any of my pieces about Zembla-4 and Calenture-Deutz. I can't even mention their names. There are armies of lawyers out there, just waiting to pounce.'

'But that's outrageous,' Adam said.

'Of course it is,' Lalandusse said. 'But everything, so far, is pretty circumstantial, you have to admit. We have no smoking gun. What we need is a grieving family. An inter-office memo. Sure, it's all on the Web . . . But so are ten thousand other conspiracy theories. I think you're bang on to something sordid. And the legal might arrayed against us would seem to indicate that you were, but – from the journalism side, we're stymied.'

Adam sat, thinking.

'I'd relax if I were you,' Lalandusse said. 'Calenture-Deutz has had its shares suspended. Rilke Pharma has abandoned the buy-out, it seems. No drug authority in the world is going to dare to license Zembla-4, what with all these rumours about the trials and the dead children swirling around.' He smiled. 'If I were you I'd be feeling pretty chuffed.'

'Fourteen children died during the clinical testing of Zembla-4,' Adam said. 'Those are the simple facts. And they covered it up in order to get a licence that would allow them to make billions and billions of dollars selling a potentially fatal drug.' He would have liked to have added that they covered it up to such an extent that they had had their head of research and development murdered when he'd discovered what was going on; that they had tried to kill me, Adam Kindred, because I was some kind of witness with a key piece of evidence; and that, in trying to kill me, they killed a young woman called Mhouse and orphaned her son. He felt his powerlessness and he felt his smallness. What could he do? So all he said was, 'Somebody should be called to account. People should be prosecuted. Fryzer should be in jail, charged with manslaughter.'

'A noble cause, Primo,' Lalandusse said. 'Are you going to take on Calenture-Deutz's phalanx of lawyers? My editor has thrown in the towel. As has the rest of the British press, it seems.' He drained his bottle of beer. 'Don't get me wrong: there is a story to tell, but it may take a while to come out . . . Do you mind if we step outside? I need a ciggy.'

Adam and Lalandusse stood outside the pub under an awning, watching a persistent drizzle fall, while Lalandusse laboriously lit up. He puffed

away like a schoolgirl, producing vast dispropor-
tionate clouds of smoke, as if he'd only just learnt
what to do with a cigarette.

'What do you think will happen?' Adam asked.

'I suspect they'll break up Calenture – a fire sale
– sell off its profitable lines. They've got a new CEO
– they sacked the old one. He's "ill" so they say.'

'Fryzer?' Adam waited for Aaron to stop
coughing.

'Yeah . . . Sorry . . . "Sick leave" – the handiest
euphemism around when you've destroyed your
company.'

'What happened to Redcastle?'

'Kicked off the board, pronto. Fled the country
before the Fraud Squad got to him. He's in Spain,
so I hear. He'll be ducking and diving for the rest
of his life.'

Adam allowed himself to feel a momentary
relaxation. Maybe this wholesale collapse meant
he was finally safe – those people, whoever they
were, would stop looking for him now, stop trying
to kill him. Why bother with an Adam Kindred
when there was no Zembla-4 to protect any
longer? Surely the hunt would be called off . . .
And he did feel good about that, for all the unan-
swered questions buzzing around in his mind and
for all the guilt he felt about Mhouse . . . And
what had happened to Ly-on? . . . Had he been
taken into care? Fostered? . . . Thinking about
them was the strangest experience: to recall his
life with Mhouse and Ly-on in The Shaft – it was

like another person's biography. Still, Ly-on must be out there somewhere, and now things seemed to be calming down he should try and find out what had happened to him.

Lalandusse was lighting a second cigarette – it took him three matches and another coughing fit before he had it going to his satisfaction. Practice makes perfect, Adam thought.

'I'd better go,' Adam said. 'I've got an appointment.' He shook Lalandusse's hand. 'Thank you, Aaron,' he said, 'you've been a fantastic help.'

'No, thank *you*,' Lalandusse said. 'It looks very like you've stopped a killer drug in its tracks – doesn't happen every day. I'll get in touch when I write it all up – there may be a book in it – once the dust's settled.'

'Yeah, let's see if we can nail that evil bastard Ingram Fryzer.'

'You bet.'

Adam said goodbye and walked off towards the Tube station.

He sat on the bench by Chelsea Bridge waiting for Turpin – who was late. It was well after 11.00 now and the traffic was quiet on the Embankment. He had stood on the bridge for a while when he had arrived, looking back at the triangle, remembering. The tide was turning and was flowing strongly back down to the estuary and the sea. While he was waiting there had been a heavy shower that had driven him under the trees by the triangle to take shelter – a few people hurried by, heads down under umbrellas, but the streets were surprisingly empty. Adam took a woollen beanie cap out of his pocket and pulled it over his wet hair, down to his eyebrows. The night was cool, he shivered.

He had called Rita and told her he was working late and that he hoped to be home around midnight. She had her own keys, now, to the flat in Oystergate Buildings and she asked him if he'd like something to eat when he came in. He said, no, don't bother, don't wait up – I'll just slip into bed. The thought of slipping into bed with Rita excited him, of reaching out under the sheets for her warm body – he stood and paced up and down – how he wanted to be back there with her now, not waiting to meet his blackmailer, Vincent Turpin, this figure from his past, still haunting him, making demands. This was his third payment to Turpin, another £200, and he was running out of funds, borrowing money from Rita to make ends meet. He decided it would be his last – now he had spoken to Lalandusse and discovered what was happening at Calenture-Deutz: they had more than enough corporate chaos in their lives to be worrying about me, he thought. The dogs must have been called off.

He saw Turpin lurching down Chelsea Bridge Road, weaving across the pedestrian lights opposite the Lister Hospital, holding up one hand to stop non-existent traffic. He slowed down as he saw Adam, tried to straighten himself. Adam saw he was wearing a shiny new leather jacket, too long in the sleeve. So that's where his money was going.

'Got a smoke, John?' Turpin said, breathing beer fumes over him.

'I don't smoke,' Adam said, handing over the money and watching as Turpin laboriously counted it.

'You're short. I said £300.'

'You said two. Like the last time.'

'It always goes up a bit, John. Bad boy. Vince is not well pleased.'

'You said two. It's not my fault.'

'Tell you what, sunshine. You must have a credit card now you've got so successful. Let's go to a cash-point – see how much we can get – I'm in need of funds, as they say.'

'No, this is it. It's finished.'

Turpin sighed histrionically. 'You're making it very easy for me to earn two grand, John. I'll just call Ugly Bugger. Give him your scooter number. Where is it, by the way, you sold it?' Turpin prattled on, drunkenly verbose, and Adam was thinking: of course, of course, *of course* – he's *already* told him. He's got his two grand already. Why would Turpin do the honourable thing? Not in Turpin's life, not his way of dealing with the world. He tuned back in to hear Turpin saying, '. . . and I can get the money from you or I can get it from him. I got his phone number. Call him up, give him the licence plate. Bingo. Two thousand pounds to Mr Turpin, thank you very much. Makes no odds to me.'

Adam thought fast: he wanted to get away from here, away from the triangle. Was it worth the risk of alienating Turpin for another £100? He should keep him sweet: it would give him more time, more time to figure out how to erase the Primo Belem trail once and for all – one final bit of security. But maybe he was safe – this man hunting him, whoever he was, wouldn't work for nothing. And if Calenture-Deutz had gone to the wall—

'Make your mind up. Your call, Johnnie.'

'All right,' Adam said, turning towards Chelsea. 'There's a cash machine at Sloane Square.'

'I'm not that fucking stupid,' Turpin said, belligerently. 'No, I know another one. You might have friends waiting for old Vince at Sloane Square. No, we'll go to Battersea, mate.'

They headed off across the bridge, Turpin trying to hold on to Adam's arm to steady himself. His drunken instability seemed to have accelerated. Adam shook him off.

'Don't touch me,' he said.

Turpin stopped, angry. He put one hand on the balustrade.

'Don't you talk to me like that. What am I? Filth? . . . Anyway, you're the one going to fall over, you stupid cunt. Your shoelace is undone.' Turpin found this fact very funny all of a sudden and doubled up in a wheezy laugh.

Adam looked down to see that his right shoelaces

494

were trailing on the wet pavement. Turpin, still laughing to himself, leant back against the purple and white, thick cast-iron balustrade of the bridge, resting on his elbows – like a drinker resting, at his ease, Adam thought, leaning back against a bar. A late-night bus rumbled by, the light from its upper deck flashing across Turpin's seamed and folded face.

'I heard a funny joke today,' Turpin said. 'Didn't half laugh. It's good to laugh, clears out the system. Doctors will tell you that. A tonic.'

Adam stooped to tie his shoelace.

'There's this woman social worker, see?' Turpin began. 'And she's talking to a little girl, pretty little chicken. And she says: do you know when your mummy has her period? – You heard this one before?'

'No,' Adam said, beginning to re-tie his other shoelace for good measure.

'It's bloody good. Hilarious. So the little girl says to the social worker' – now Turpin put on a piping falsetto – 'Yes, miss, I know when my mummy has her period. Social worker: how can you tell? . . . And the little girl says: because daddy's cock tastes funny.' Turpin shook with laughter again.

It all became clear to Adam at once, in a flash of insight, what he could do, here and now, and how easy it would be. At the very least it would be some recompense, some rough justice, for all the grief Turpin had visited on his various wives and his little children. Adam quickly reached out, while Turpin was still rocking drunkenly with mirth at his joke, and slipped two fingers under the cuff of Turpin's right trouser leg. He gripped it, holding it firmly, and rose suddenly to his feet from his crouching position. Turpin went up and over the balustrade so fast and fluently he had time only to utter a short bark of surprise, his hands grabbing vainly at thin air. And then he was gone, falling into the dark beyond the bridge's lights. Adam heard the splash of his body hitting the water. He thought for a second about running across to see if there was any sign of him downstream, but Chelsea Bridge was awkward to traverse – he would have to vault two sizeable structural barriers on either side of the roadway – and anyway, it was dark and the tide was strong and surging and would carry Turpin away so quickly, he knew. Adam didn't pause any longer, he turned and walked on towards Battersea. The whole moment had been so fast – a mere second – no cars had passed by, no one else was on the bridge. At one moment there had been two men; the next moment there was only one. So easy. Turpin was gone, Adam thought, as he walked away, and he didn't feel anything, to his vague surprise, he didn't feel changed in any way and he didn't feel guilty. It was a simple act, a decision that had occurred to him spontaneously – bringing about an end to Turpin as if a roof tile had fallen on his head or as if he had been hit by a speeding car. A fatal accident. Adam strode calmly, steadily, on to Battersea and bussed home to Rita.

496

CHAPTER 59

Life's journey was very strange, Ingram decided, and it had recently taken him to places he never thought he would have visited on his personal itinerary from cradle to grave. He sat upright, now, in his hospital bed, leaning back against a fat pile of pillows, with his shaven, massively scarred head wrapped in a neat, tight turban of bandages. He had a drip in his arm and his left eye was covered with a black pirate's patch – something he'd requested himself, to see if it would subdue the firework display that glittered and sparkled against the shifting grey mica dust that was all his left retina was currently supplying as vision. With light not coming in, the darkness seemed to quell the pyrotechnics. Only the occasional supernova or atom bomb blast made him flinch – otherwise he felt pretty well, if 3 out of 10 could be regarded as a norm: nausea, parched throat, out-of-body trances not being included in the audit. He could speak, he could read (out of one eye), he could think, he could eat – though he was never hungry – he could defecate (effortfully, meagrely), he could drink. He craved sweet, cold drinks – he asked all visitors to bring chilled colas – Pepsi, Coke, supermarket 'own' brands – he did not discriminate.

It was three days since his operation – the urgent 'debulking' of his brain – and he had been informed that his tumour had been removed along with the other tissue. His chemotherapy was underway and he could receive visitors. His wife, Meredith, had left five minutes before – trying to hide her tears but failing.

Currently, Lachlan McTurk sat heavily on his bed, helping himself to a toothglass of the malt whisky he had brought as a present.

'You'll like this, Ingram,' McTurk said. 'Speyside. Aberlour. I know you don't enjoy West Coast.'

'Thank you, Lachlan. I look forward to it.'

McTurk topped himself up again.

'Who was your surgeon?' he asked.

'Mr Gulzar Shah,' Ingram said. He had popped in an hour previously, a tall, gaunt, softly spoken man with dark eye sockets, as if he had applied eye-shadow to them.

'Oh, very good man. Top man. Did he give you a final diagnosis?'

'Glioblastoma multiforme,' Ingram pronounced the words carefully. 'I think that's what he said.'

'Ah . . . yes . . . Hmmm. Oh, dear . . . Yes . . .'

'You're wonderfully reassuring, Lachlan. Mr Shah said he wanted to wait for more biopsy results before he confirmed. But that was his provisional judgement.'

'It's definitely something you don't want to get, old son, is all I'll say. Very nasty.'

'Well, I seem to have got it, by all accounts. I don't have much choice.'

'Yes, I suppose so.'

'You're my doctor, Lachlan – what's your prognosis?'

Lachlan sipped his whisky, thinking, sucking his teeth.

'Well . . . If you follow the usual pattern you'll probably be dead in three months. Don't give up all hope, though. Ten per cent of glioblastoma multiforme sufferers experience remission – some have lived five years. Who can say? You might be the exception. You might prove medical science wrong: live a long, fulfilled life. It is a rare and virulent cancer, though.' Lachlan reached forward and patted his hand. 'Exceptionally. Still, I'll put my money on you, Ingram. At least five years.'

'Many thanks.'

There was a knock on the door.

'I'll haste awa', laddie,' Lachlan said in his best Rabbie Burns mode. He pushed the whisky bottle towards Ingram. 'Do have a wee dram of this. No point in holding back, eh? Chin up.'

As he left he passed Ingram's accountant, Chandrakant Das, coming in. Chandrakant was in an evident state of shock – he couldn't speak for a while, his face pinched, his eyes moist, he gripped Ingram's hand with both his hands, looking down and breathing deeply for a minute, composing himself.

'I feel surprisingly well, Chandra,' Ingram said, trying to put him at his ease. 'I know everything is collapsing around me but I feel in sufficiently good health to want to enquire about the state of my finances. That's why I asked you here. I do apologise.'

Chandra was finally able to speak. 'It's not good, Ingram. Not good, not good, not good, not good.'

Chandra explained. Calenture-Deutz shares were currently trading at 37 pence and heading south. Rilke Pharma had made a buy-out offer to the other shareholders of 50 pence a share but were reconsidering as the company rapidly devalued. Ingram had been voted off the board as chairman and CEO and it was only his 'health crisis' that was keeping the Serious Fraud Office at bay.

'But I didn't make a penny from this fiasco,' Ingram said. 'I've lost a fortune. So why are they after me?'

'Because your brother-in-law has absconded with £1.8 million,' Chandra said, anguished. 'They can't touch him in Spain so they're after you. You obviously advised him to sell, they say. Clear case of insider dealing.'

'On the contrary. I explicitly advised him *not* to sell.'

'Can you prove it?'

Ingram fell silent.

'I don't want you to worry, Ingram. Burton Keegan is holding everything together, keeping the police at bay. It would look very bad to arrest and prosecute a man so close to – so seriously ill.'

'Good old Burton.'

Chandra took his hand again and said with real feeling, 'I'm so pleased to see you, Ingram. And I'm so sorry this has happened.'

Ingram frowned, gently releasing his hand from Chandra's grip. 'That's the thing: I really don't understand *how* it happened. That's what bothers me: everything seemed on course, all was fine and dandy.'

Chandra shrugged, spread his hands. 'Who are we to speak? To seek neat answers? Who can predict what life will bring us?'

'Very true.'

Ingram asked Chandra to pour him half an inch of Lachlan's whisky. He sipped it – throat burning. He smelt burnt barley, peat, clear Scottish rivers. It emboldened him.

'I want to know where I stand, Chandra. Bottom line. Don't spare me – now that everything's gone pear-shaped.'

'I did some quick analysis before I came,' Chandra said, retrospective disbelief distorting his features for a moment. 'It's not good . . . Last month you were worth more than £200 million. Now . . .' He took out his phone and punched numbers into it. Ingram wondered for a moment

501

if he was calling someone but he remembered you could do everything on a mobile phone now, everything.

Chandra held the phone away from him as if he were dubious of the reading he was receiving. 'Now I would say your assets were worth £10 million – give or take £100,000 here or there. Baseball park figure.' Chandra smiled. 'Of course, I'm not including your properties.'

'So there is some light in this darkness.'

'A gleam of light, Ingram. You can still live reasonably well. You are not a poor man. But you must be prudent.'

He handed Ingram a few documents for signature. Ingram might have well been signing his remaining assets away, for all he knew, but he trusted Chandra. And you couldn't live in a world without trusting people, as he had so recently and callously discovered. Chandra would make sure he was all right, that Meredith and his family were all right with what remained. There might have to be some down-sizing, some belt-tightening, but, as Chandra said, he was not a poor man. Or so he hoped, he thought, suddenly less sanguine. Who could predict what life would bring us? – as Chandra had just reminded him.

Chandra gathered up his documents, shook Ingram's hand and reassured him all would be well. As he left, a nurse poked her head around the door.

'Are you up for any more visitors, Mr Fryzer? Mr Shah said not to tire you out.'

'It depends who it is,' Ingram said, thinking that if it's the Serious Fraud Office, I'm comatose.

'It's your son.'

'Oh, well, that's fine.' He called out: 'Guy, come on in.'

Fortunatus stepped into the room.

' 'Fraid it's me, Dad.'

He had a bunch of flowers in his dirty hand, dark purple flowers with waxy leaves that were already giving off a powerful scent, filling the room. Forty handed them over.

'What're these?' Ingram asked, immeasurably touched.

'Freesias. My favourites. I just cut them for you. We do a garden not far from here.'

Forty looked as though he'd just come out of the front line – the usual filthy combat jacket over baggy, greasy jeans, his head now shaved egg-smooth. Ingram looked at him in wonder.

'How're you doing, Dad?'

'I've decided to adopt your hairstyle. Trying to look like you.'

Fortunatus laughed nervously.

'They shaved all my hair off and then hoiked out half my brain.'

'No need to go that far,' Forty said.

They both laughed at that. Ingram laughed harder and felt his body heave in response.

'I love you, Forty,' he said. 'That's why I want to look like you.'

'Dad,' Forty said, awkward. 'Please don't cry.'

CHAPTER 60

I t was strange seeing your picture in the newspaper, Jonjo thought, particularly if you'd never had your picture in any newspaper before. It was a photograph taken some fifteen years earlier, he calculated, when he'd been in the British Army, and was captioned: 'John-Joseph Case, wanted by police to assist in their enquiries into the murder of Dr Philip Wang.' He crumpled the newspaper into a ball and hurled it at the rear window of his camper-van. It bounced off the angled Perspex on to the carpeted floor where The Dog immediately pounced on it, picked it up and brought it back, dropping it at his feet and stood there waiting, tail wagging, for this new game to continue.

Jonjo picked The Dog up and heaved him into his arms, turning him on his back like a baby. The Dog enjoyed being held like this and he licked Jonjo's face with his big wet tongue. Jonjo hugged The Dog to him, confused by the emotions he was experiencing and said out loud, 'Sorry, mate, but there's no other way,' and dropped him carefully on the floor again. It was two hours to high tide, no point in hanging around.

Disturbed by this personal publicity, Jonjo went into the camper-van's tiny toilet and looked at himself in the mirror above the sink. The beard was coming on pretty well – the black still intense, though he might need to re-dye it in a couple of days if it kept growing at this rate and in a funny sort of way he thought that he suited being dark: he looked better than he usually did with his normal gingery-brown crew cut and it was an added bonus that his most recognisable feature, the cleft in his chin, was now obscured by the facial hair. Perhaps he should have grown a beard ages ago, he wondered, but at least he now looked nothing like the picture in the paper, he was glad to say. Following Kindred's lead, he thought to himself, uncomfortably, taking a leaf out of Adam Kindred's book of disappearance and evasion. Everything in his life had been running fairly smoothly – no complaints, thanks – until Kindred had arrived. He had survived the Falklands War, Northern Ireland, Gulf War I, Bosnia, Gulf War II, Iraq and Afghanistan – and only when the Kindred element intruded had everything gone arse-over-tit. He told himself to calm down.

He put his Glock in his pocket and picked up the spade.

'Come on, boy,' he said. 'Walkies.'

He stepped out of the camper-van and inhaled. It was a fine afternoon – sunshine and thin high clouds invading the sky from the south-east – an English summer's day with a cool breeze coming off the estuary. He had found himself a berth in a new caravan/campsite – not far from the seafront – on Canvey Island, Essex, a curious, sunken sea-walled enclave on the Thames between Basildon and Southend-on-Sea, a strange backwater of abandoned oil refineries with grassed-over concrete roads and rusting street lights, and huge functioning oil refineries and storage depots, gleamingly lit at night, venting steam and orange flares behind their diamond-mesh perimeter fencing, serving the vast tankers that docked at great steel jetties that poked out into the river estuary. Dotted along the Canvey sea wall were occasional neat art deco cafés that recalled the island's past as a Londoners' convenient holiday resort but that now, as far as he could tell from the few days he had been living here, kept their own bizarrely sporadic hours of opening and closing: sometimes you were lucky, sometimes you weren't.

During his Canvey Island sojourn Jonjo had kept himself to himself, going for walks with The Dog, circumnavigating the island by way of the sea wall path twice, clockwise and anti-clockwise, deliberately not becoming over-acquainted with his camper-van and caravanning neighbours on either side, ensuring that any conversations were brief but friendly enough, all the same.

The problem was The Dog. Basset hounds, that was the problem – he couldn't go ten paces without some kiddie stopping to pet The Dog; some mother saying, aw, what a lovely doggie; some bloke wanting to pontificate about breeds and breeding. He thought he might as well be carrying a placard: 'WANTED MAN ON THE RUN WITH INTERESTING LOVEABLE DOG'. The Dog was exactly what you didn't need when the fucking police were searching the country for you. He swore at himself for his sentiment: he should have left The Dog with Candy. Popped a note through the door asking her to look after him, saying he 'had to go abroad' or something for a few months. Candy would have been thrilled – it would have been so easy.

He and The Dog left the campsite, with no encounters, and headed east, walking through the town towards Smallgains Creek, where the marina and the yacht club were to be found. He walked up and over the sea wall, past the yacht club building and behind the boat yard, looking for the path that led through the tidal salt marsh – the saltings, as they were called – to Canvey Point, the flat easternmost promontory of the island.

Thinking back, he understood now what the plan would have been. They would have come for him, as Darren had warned. Having removed his weaponry earlier, they would have simply taken him away and quietly slotted him, then hidden his body, never to be found or seen again – end of problem, Plan A. However, because he wasn't there when they came, because he'd done a runner (thanks, Darren) they had resorted to Plan B.

The newspaper article had told him everything: in his house, when the police searched it, acting on an 'anonymous tip-off', they had found a photograph of Dr Philip Wang and blueprints of Anne Boleyn House, Chelsea. A gold watch that had belonged to Dr Wang had also been retrieved. DNA samples in the house had been matched with fibres found in Dr Wang's flat.

You're not stupid, Jonjo had told himself as he plodded along the path away from the boat yard, and that was why he knew he was well and truly reamed, royally shafted. Even if, supposing he was caught and arrested, he told them the truth, everything he knew, he would still take the murder rap. There was no connection that could be made between his freelance jobs and the Risk Averse Group – and whoever it was who had employed Risk Averse to employ him. Everything he said would be interpreted as wild, desperate accusations. Perhaps there might be a bit of embarrassment for Risk Averse (he could see Major Tim making a rueful face, expressing his total shock and surprise) but a disgraced ex-soldier, recently dismissed – who could say what paranoia might build? What fantastical plots might form in a traumatised brain?

No – there was nothing for it, he had to run and hide, that was all. Like Kindred – Jonjo acknowledged the irony again but did not savour it. Luckily he had been well trained; luckily he had concocted plans for unforeseen eventualities and worst-case scenarios. He had made one tele-phone call on his unused mobile phone to his friend Giel Hoekstra, who lived near Rotterdam. He and Giel had met during the Bosnian tour, found themselves in a few scrapes together, rubbed along and, in the way you do, in the way all the special forces guys did, fully recognising the risky and dangerous nature of the post-army lives they would be living, they had made plans for mutual help and emergency aid should it be required: parachutes provided, potential exit doors left ajar, safe houses identified, friendly ports avail-able in stormy seas. He could have telephoned Norton in St Paul, Minnesota, Aled in Aberystwyth, Wales, Campbell in Glasgow, Scotland, or Jean-Claude in Nantes, France or half a dozen others – but he had decided Giel was the handiest man of the moment and had called that marker in.

All he had said to Giel was that he had to leave England, now, immediately, clandestinely. By boat. Giel had decided what to do after a moment's reflec-tion: find a small provincial seaside town with a functioning harbour. Canvey Island, Jonjo had said instantly, recalling his childhood holidays – that's where you'll find me: Canvey Island, the Thames estuary, Essex. They had chosen a date and time and Giel had outlined a notional plan. From Canvey Island to another small seaside town with a harbour and a busy marina, boats coming and going all the time – Havenhoofd, it was called, near Rotterdam. Then from Rotterdam to Amsterdam to a flat Giel's sister owned. 'Be a tourist for a few weeks,' Giel said. 'I have many friends. There's a lot of work for someone like you, Jonjo. You can be as busy as you want, we get you new passport, become a Dutchman.' Thank god he kept the stash of money aside, Jonjo thought. He had dumped the taxi and had bought a fourth-hand camper-van for £2,000 cash and had driven out of London heading east through Essex for the coast and freedom.

He had parked up in Canvey and waited for his appointed rendezvous with Giel Hoekstra. He felt both pleased at his resourcefulness and mounting anger that he had been obliged to rely on it. What was going to happen to his house, his stuff? Don't even think about it, he told himself, you're free, the rest is history and junk. Major Tim Delaporte, move to the top of the shit-list. No, not quite the top – the number one spot was permanently reserved for Adam Kindred.

Jonjo stopped: he had come a few hundred yards from the yacht club and the boatyard, now, it seemed quiet enough. He led The Dog off the coastal path, let him off the lead, and picked his way through the coarse brown grass of the saltings and stepped down on to a small beach. He turned through 360 degrees and saw no one. The Dog was bounding about on the sand, sniffing at sea-wrack and chasing sand crabs, his tail a blur of excitement. Jonjo looked across the river estuary and saw the tall chimney of the Grain power station on the Hoo Peninsula opposite. That was

Kent over there, he thought idly, a mile or so away. He walked back to the grassy humps at the edge of the beach and, with his spade edge, measured a rectangle in the thin, shell-choked shingle and began to dig down quickly and easily into the moist, sandy loam beneath, excavating a neat dog-sized hole, two feet deep, with an inch of water in the bottom. He whistled for The Dog and soon heard him panting up from the beach.

'Go on,' Jonjo said, 'get in.'

The Dog sniffed around the edge of the hole, clearly not sure about this game. Jonjo put his boot on his rump and pushed. The Dog plumped down.

'Sit,' Jonjo said. 'Sit, boy.'

He sat, obediently.

Jonjo took out his Glock. He held it close to his leg and checked the area again, in case any ramblers were heading for the point across the flat, dark brown humps of the saltings before the tide rose, but there was no one. Opposite, on the far side of the mouth of Benfleet Creek, were Southend's crowded streets and the long arm of its pier. He felt oddly alone, a man and his dog on the extreme, bleak, salty tip of a small island in the Thames estuary and, simultaneously, oppressively suburban – all Essex was out there, just across the water, half a mile away.

He looked down at The Dog and began to experience very odd sensations, all of a sudden, as if his head were fizzing. He pointed the gun at The Dog.

511

'Sorry, mate,' he said. 'I love you, you know that.'

His voice had gone weird and croaky and Jonjo realised he was crying. *Fuck!* He was falling apart – he hadn't cried since he was twelve years old. He was past it, well and truly washed up, over the hill, pathetic, disgusting. No wonder Risk Averse had kicked him out. He swore at himself – get a grip, you pathetic *girl*, call yourself a soldier, some kind of fucking warrior, you are. He levelled the Glock at The Dog's head. The Dog looked up at him, still panting slightly from his exertions, blinking, unperturbed.

Squeeze the trigger. Slowly.

At high tide, as they had arranged, Giel Hoekstra was waiting for him on the quayside at Brinkman's Wharf on Smallgains Creek where visiting boats were allowed to moor. Giel was standing on the quayside, pacing around, smoking, a squat, burly man with his longish hair in a small pony-tail. He'd put on weight, had Giel, since they'd last seen each other, Jonjo thought, quite a gut on him now. They embraced briefly and slapped each other's shoulders. Giel showed him the powerful cabin cruiser moored by the quayside that he'd crossed the Channel on: white, raked, clean lines, two big blocky outboard motors on the stern.

'We be in Havenhoofd in three hours,' he said. 'Nice little marina. No questions. I am friend for the harbourmaster.' He grinned. 'Let's say – new friend.'

'I can pay for all this,' Jonjo said, handing him a wad of notes. 'Look, they're all euros.'

'No need, Jonjo,' Giel feigned being offended. 'Hey. I do this for you – you do it for Giel Hoekstra, one day. No need, please.'

'It's your money, Giel.'

There was something different about his tone of voice. Giel took the money.

Jonjo stood in the cabin with the wheel in his hand – Giel had gone down to the head to take a leak – and enjoyed the sensation of steering this powerful boat, with its creamy boiling wake, away from England towards his future. The remorseless vibration of the twin engines drumming through the deck reinforced this idea of steady purpose, of smooth untroubled progress, of the inevitability of their arrival at their destination.

He took a deep breath, exhaled. He had hoiked The Dog out of the hole, fitted the lead to his collar and walked back towards the yacht club and the boat yard. Then he had removed the collar (with his name and address imprinted on the dangling steel coin) and had improvised a noose, of sorts, and tied The Dog to the railings by the boat yard. He gave The Dog a pat, said a hoarse goodbye and strode away. He looked back, of course, and saw The Dog sitting on his haunches, licking at something on his side, completely unperturbed. Jonjo had tossed the collar into Smallgains Creek and had walked on. A bark, a yowl – was

513

that too much to hope for? Somebody would take charge of that dog in ten minutes, that was the thing about basset hounds – they were irresistible.

Still, he felt reassured, obscurely pleased at his weakness, not condemning himself, concentrating on the feeling of the engines thrumming through the decking, the vibration travelling up his legs, almost sexually arousing, in a funny sort of way. Quiet, steady purpose. Yes, that would be his motto, now he was free, now he was shot of everyone and everything. And his quiet steady purpose would be directed, he decided, towards one end: he would find Adam Kindred. He had the scooter's licence plate number – he had paid that piece of filth £1,000 for the scooter's licence plate number – and that was all he needed. That had been Kindred's downfall: there was a trail now – electronic and paper, from the scooter to its owner – where there had never been a trail before. When it all went quiet, when the toxic dust had settled, when everyone had forgotten about John-Joseph Case, he would come back from Amsterdam to England, secretly, silently, find Adam Kindred and kill him.

CHAPTER 61

Allhallows-on-Sea. A good name for a place, a place on the Kent shore of the Thames estuary. Adam stood and looked north across the mile or so of water to Canvey Island opposite, on the Essex shore. It was as good a spot as any, he thought, to claim that here the river ended and the sea began. He turned to the east and looked at the high clouds – cirrostratus – invading the sky from the south, lit by a strong, afternoon late-summer sun. Could be bad weather, threat of thunderstorms . . . You felt yourself on the edge of England here, he thought, surrounded by sea, continental Europe just over the horizon. The air was bright and hazy and there was just a hint of coolness in the estuarine breeze. Autumn coming, finally, this year of years beginning to draw to its close.

Adam, Rita and Ly-on had left Allhallows-on-Sea with its vast caravan-amusement park and had walked along the coastal track towards Egypt Bay. The great flat expanses of the Kent marshes, with their winding fleets, their dykes and drainage ditches, were on their left, the wide river glinted, with a nacreous sheen, on their right, and their shadows were cast strongly on the path behind them as the sun occasionally broke through the ragged, high film of clouds. They sauntered along, carrying their plastic bags that contained their picnic, Ly-on occasionally scampering down to the small strips of sand and shingle to pick something up or shy a stone into the water. Ly-on was taller and slimmer, Adam thought, since he had last seen him, his pot belly gone. He was still not sure if he was any happier, however.

When Adam had decided to go looking for Ly-on, his conscience prodding him, he had been reluctant to return to The Shaft – too many risks, too many people who might recognise him – so he had revisited the Church of John Christ, thinking that, of all places, this was one that had known Mhouse, might have some record of her and what had happened to her son. He put his badge on, for old times' sake, and presented himself at Bishop Yemi's office. Bishop Yemi wasn't in, he was told, the Bishop was running late at a meeting with the Mayor at City Hall. Adam said he'd come back another day. But as he was leaving he saw that the door was being opened for the evening service by Mrs Darling, 'John 17' herself, who was also setting up the welcome desk, a few blank 'John' badges fanned out in front of her in case some potential converts wandered in.

Adam introduced himself: John 1603.

'I remember you,' she said suspiciously. 'You've smartened up, John.'

'Do you remember Mhouse?' he asked.

'Course I do. Poor dear Mhousie. Bless her. Horrible thing that happened. Horrible.'

'Do you know what became of her son, Ly-on?'

'Ly-on's very well, being well looked after.'

This news had cheered him, unbelievably. He felt a sense of relief wash through him that was so intense he thought he might need to sit down.

'Where is he? Do you know?'

'He's at the Church of John's orphanage in Eltham.'

'Can I visit him?'

'You'll have to talk to the director – but seeing you're a fellow "John", I think that might be OK.'

'Who's the director?'

'Hang on – I'll get a letter with his name on.' She went and found some headed notepaper and pointed the name out: Kazimierz Bednarczyk, 'Director of Special Projects'. Adam noted the empurpled, embossed solidity of the letter head – 'THE CHURCH OF JOHN' and its prominent sunburst logo, its registered charity number. Some C-list celebrities were on its roster of 'honourable patrons', a devout backbencher, a chat-show host, a born-again member of a boy band. The Church of John was not sitting on its hands, that was for sure. An avenue of bright tomorrows stretched ahead for Bishop Yemi.

Later that day Adam telephoned the number on

the notepaper and was told by a friendly young woman that they did indeed have a young boy at the Eltham orphanage called Ly-on. Ly-on 'Smith' – nobody knew his last name, including the boy himself, so he'd been called 'Smith' pending any future adoption. Adam said he was a family friend and would like to take him out for the day, if that were possible. Oh yes, we encourage visits and trips out, he was told. There would need to be a brief meeting with Mr Bednarczyk first and of course there was a fee of £100.

'A fee? . . .'

'Yes, that's the fee for a day's outing.'

Adam had given his name and made an appointment for the following Saturday.

So Adam and Rita hired a car and Rita drove them to Eltham on the following Saturday, mid-morning. Adam had told Rita that he just wanted to see the boy again, see how he was getting on, make sure he was happy and being looked after properly. Rita said she was perfectly prepared to be their chauffeur, thought it was an excellent idea and looked forward to meeting Ly-on. They stopped on the way at a supermarket and bought food and drink – sandwiches, pies, scotch eggs, water, colas, juices – and a travelling rug and paper cups and plates, some plastic knives and forks. On a whim, passing a toy shop two doors down, Rita had suggested they buy some beach games – a Frisbee, a diabolo, some flat paddles with a ball to hit.

The Church of John's orphanage at Eltham – Adam noticed that the claim 'John Christ' was more and more frequently absent in the light of the church's new prosperity – was a detached Victorian brick villa in a large garden with a car park where the front lawn had once been. Rita said she would wait in the car and Adam went into the building for his appointment with Mr Bednarczyk.

Inside, it was like stepping into an old school, Adam thought. A smell of cooking, of rubberised floor coverings, dusty radiators and chipped paint-work. A struggling prep school that had seen better days and whose pupil numbers were remorselessly dwindling, was the image that came to mind. Through a rear window Adam could see half a dozen little boys in jeans and matching emerald-green fleece jackets kicking a football about on a piebald rectangle of grass fringed by a tall cypress hedge. He could hear a piano being played badly in an upstairs room: chords struck heavily, wrong notes amongst them. A young, hot-faced woman in a nylon overall clattered down the stairs with a mop and a bucket.

'I'm looking for Mr Bednarczyk,' Adam said.

'Down the corridor, first left.'

Adam followed her directions to find a door with a plastic nameplate: 'K. Bednarczyk'. He knocked and a voice invited him to enter.

Kazimierz Bednarczyk was sitting at a desk covered in papers and files and behind him could be glimpsed a partial view of the orphanage's front car park through the dangling, dusty, oatmeal louvres of a vertical blind. Adam could see their hired car and Rita walking around, taking the air, exercising, windmilling her arms. Badnarczyk's peroxide-blond hair and neat blond beard failed to disguise the man Adam knew as Gavin Thrale. They looked at each other for a few seconds. Thrale remained utterly impassive.

'Mr Belem,' he said offering his hand. 'Do take a seat.'

They shook hands and Adam sat down.

'What are your plans for the day?'

'I thought we might go down to the coast, find a beach, have a picnic.'

'Sounds delightful. Ly-on would need to be back by six o'clock.'

'Not a problem – I understand.'

'Just fill this in and sign – there.' Thrale pushed a release form across the desk towards him. 'I think we can waive the fee – seeing as it's you.'

'Thank you,' Adam said.

As Adam filled in the form Thrale picked up the phone, punched out a number and asked, 'Is Ly-on ready? Good. We'll meet him in the hall.'

They sat there looking at each other.

'How are you?' Adam said.

'I'm surprisingly well, considering. And you?'

'I'm fine.'

'The church has been very good to me,' Thrale said, cautiously. 'I believe you had the same opportunity offered.'

'Yes. But it just wasn't the right time.'

'Bishop Yemi is a most accommodating man.'

'One might say a remarkable man.'

'You've heard he's standing for parliament. Rotherhithe East. As a Conservative.'

'He *is* a remarkable man,' Adam said.

'My friends call me Kazio,' Thrale said.

'I'm Primo.'

'What about meeting up one day, Primo? Have a drink. Talk things over.'

'I'm not so sure that would be a good idea, Kazio.'

'Yes . . . You're probably right. Funny old life, eh?' Thrale said, standing up.

They walked down the corridor to the hall where Ly-on was waiting, wearing the same jeans and emerald-green fleece uniform of the other boys.

'John!' he shouted when he saw Adam, and ran towards him. Adam fell to his knees and they hugged.

'I know you come for Ly-on,' he said, smiling broadly. 'Green, green peas, man.'

Adam stood up, a little overwhelmed, as Ly-on went to fetch his bag.

'You knew his mother, I believe.'

'Yes. She used to serve the food sometimes, at the church. You probably remember her,' Adam said.

'It's all a bit of a blur, those times, I have to confess,' Thrale said, as Ly-on came back. 'Enjoy your day, Mr Belem.'

'Thank you, Mr Bednarczyk.'

521

And so Adam, Rita and Ly-on had driven east towards Rochester and Chatham until Adam saw a sign for the Hoo Peninsula and he said, 'Let's go to Hoo. Sounds interesting.'

'Hoo,' Ly-on repeated. 'Hoo, hoo, hoo.'

They followed the signs until they saw one that said 'Allhallows-on-Sea' and 'Beach', driving through the village until they came to a dead end by the caravan site. They skirted the holiday park with its rows of static caravans and its covered swimming pool and leisure centre, and parked the car where the metalled road turned into a track. Then they discovered that the various games they had bought – the Frisbee, the fat-paddled tennis bats and ball, the diabolo (or Chinese yo-yo) were missing. Rita remembered putting the bags down in the shop but thought that Adam had picked them up and stowed them in the boot. Perhaps they were still in the shop, Adam ventured – they could call back on the way home, it didn't matter – they could improvise. So, carrying the plastic bags that contained their picnic, they walked along the coastal path heading for Egypt Bay.

They found a spot on the edge of the bay, spread their rug and ate their sandwiches and pies and drank their fizzy drinks. Adam felt he was in a kind of time warp – the flat marshlands behind him, the refulgent estuary in front, and beyond the hazy mass of the Essex shore, Canvey Island, the Maplin Sands, Foulness. Ly-on took his jeans off and changed into his swimming trunks behind a towel held out by Adam. He went paddling in the shallows, shouting out, 'Remember you promised to teach me to swim, John!'

Adam looked up and down the river's coastline. There was an empty tanker temporarily moored offshore, riding high in the water, and it reminded Adam that this was where, after the Napoleonic Wars, all the prison hulks were berthed, old, rotting, mastless three-deckers full of convicts destined for Australia . . . Australia – where his father and sister and nephews were living. Don't think about it. So Adam wondered what it must have been like for the convicts in the hulks, looking out at this, their last sight of England, the flat Kent shore and the dark Cooling Marshes, their minds full of desperate thoughts of escape—

'He seems all right,' Rita said, gesturing at Ly-on. 'Doesn't talk about his mum.'

'Yeah,' Adam said. 'I hope so.'

Rita put on her sunglasses and lay back to enjoy the weak but warming sunshine. Adam felt in a turmoil of emotions as he sat watching Ly-on, his arms hugging his knees, and, triggered by the thoughts of escaping convicts and prison hulks, found himself wondering if Turpin's body had made it this far downstream.

He had thought very little about Turpin since their last encounter, and suffered no guilty conscience. Sometimes he wondered if there was something wrong with him that would explain this unfeelingness he experienced about what he had done, as if his new life and everything that had happened to him over the last few months had changed him in some crucial way, hardened him. Perhaps it had – perhaps he *was* a different person, to some significant extent, from the man he had been. But there was nothing to grieve about as far as Turpin was concerned – he couldn't imagine Turpin's wives and children missing him, speculating amongst themselves as to why Vince had disappeared from their lives all of a sudden. Anyway – all he had done was tip him into the river, after all. He just hoped, somehow, that Turpin's was one of those bodies that the river took with it, along with the rest of its rubbish, and that Turpin's corpse had made it through the dangling southern loop of the Isle of Dogs, with its reverse currents and collecting pools, and that the ebb tide that night had carried him past Greenwich and Woolwich and Thamesmead and Gravesend, spewing him out eventually into the fathomless cold waters of the North Sea. He would bob up at some stage, bloated and decomposed, be washed up on a shingle bank somewhere, on Foulness Island or the Medway estuary, or perhaps even more further afield, on the beaches of Northern France, Belgium or Holland – but nobody would make much of a fuss about the drowning of Vincent Turpin.

He turned and lay down beside Rita and gently kissed her on the lips.

'You're very quiet,' he said.

'I've been thinking,' she said, and sat up. 'Do you remember that murder I told you about? That one I found in Chelsea?'

Adam said he did – they had talked about it a couple of times, Adam not saying much, just listening. It just proved to him what he had always suspected: that the myriad connections between two discrete lives – close, distant, overlapping, tangential – lie there almost entirely unknown, unobserved, a great unseen network of the nearly, the almost, the might-have-been. From time to time, in everybody's life, the network is glimpsed for a moment or two and the occasion acknowledged with a gasp of happy astonishment or a shiver of supernatural discomfort. The complex interrelatedness of human existence could reassure or disturb in equal measure. When Adam had realised that Philip Wang had played a part both in Rita's life and his own it had stunned him at first but, as time had gone by, it began to seem almost commonplace. Who knew what other invisible couplings, affinities, links and bonds between them lay out there? Who could ever precisely locate our respective positions on the great mesh that unites us?

'What about it?' Adam said.

'Have you seen this?' She took a newspaper clipping out of her handbag and showed it to him.

It was a picture of a man, a soldier in combat gear, and the caption said his name was John-Joseph Case and he was wanted by the police to aid their enquiries into the murder, in Chelsea, of Dr Philip Wang.

Adam looked at the photograph, trying to keep his face still. This was an image of a younger man than the one he had encountered – the one he'd seen unconscious on the cobbles of the mews behind the Grafton Lodge Hotel – but the aggressive stare, the weak chin and the cleft in the chin were unmistakably those of the man who had been hunting him all these weeks and months. Ugly Bugger, Turpin had called him.

'What about it?' Adam said again, carefully.

'This was the man I arrested,' Rita said. 'The one with two automatic pistols. The one who was let go.'

'Right . . .' Adam said, feeling the nape of his neck tighten.

'And now they want him for murder. That particular murder. Don't you think it's an amazing coincidence?'

'You should tell them,' Adam said. 'They had him, thanks to you, and then they let him go. Outrageous. Sounds like a conspiracy to me.'

'You're very gung-ho,' Rita said. 'Maybe I should let sleeping dogs lie. I told you what happened when I tried to push it.'

'So what?' Adam said quickly, then qualified his certainty. 'Listen, it's up to you. But it seems to me people shouldn't get away with disgraceful mistakes like that. If he's guilty he should be prosecuted.'

'Mistakes? I thought you said it was a conspiracy.'

She thought for a second, frowning. 'Maybe it explains what he was doing in Chelsea. Maybe this Wang was involved in some secret top-security thing . . .'

'Maybe.'

Ly-on came up from the beach at that moment with his fist clenched around something. He half opened his palm to reveal a small semi-transparent crab.

'It's a sea-spider,' he said. 'I catched it.'

Adam and Rita congratulated him and suggested he put it back in the water. He agreed and wandered back down to the shore.

Adam was thinking fast – if this John-Joseph Case man is the one they're looking for then perhaps I might be free again. Perhaps I really am free – already, now – he thought. I could be Adam Kindred again . . . He looked up at the slowly gathering clouds.

'Primo?' Rita said. 'Are you all right?'

'I was just thinking, dreaming, imagining something . . .'

Rita put the photo away in her bag, stood up, stretched, and sighed, 'I just don't understand,' she said, plaintively.

'Who can predict life's course?' Adam said. Then suddenly he looked over his shoulder at the marshes.

Rita laughed at him. 'Easy, boy.'

'I don't know. I thought someone was watching us.'

'Oh, yeah. Some monster's going to rear up out of the ooze and seize you – turn your life upside down.'

'It has happened before, you know.' He reached for her hands and made her sit beside him again. She lay back.

'What?' she said. 'Your life turned upside down?'

'Hey, John!' Ly-on shouted from the beach. 'I found another.'

'Why does he call you John?' Rita asked, kissing his neck.

'It's just a nickname we had.'

'Oh, yeah?'

'Yeah.'

Now he kissed her on the lips, his tongue touched her teeth, his hand on her breast. She moved her thigh against his.

'Do you think we might live out here?' he said quietly, his lips on her throat. 'What do you think?'

'Here? . . . It would be a nightmare commute, wouldn't it?'

'I suppose so. But there's something about this place . . .'

'Do you want to live in a caravan?'

'No. No, no. In a house. I was thinking: we could buy a little house in Allhallows. A cottage. Pool our incomes, get a mortgage and live out here, on the estuary.'

'Pool our incomes, get a mortgage, buy a house . . .' Rita drew herself back a few inches so she could look him in the eye. 'Is that a proposal?'

'I suppose it is,' Adam said. 'What do you say?'

She kissed him. 'Anything is possible,' she said. 'Who can predict life's course?'

'Good point.'

They lay silent, side by side, on their backs, silent for a while on the turf of the Kent shore of the Thames estuary, the wide flat marshes behind them. He reached for her hand and their fingers interlocked.

'I love you, Rita,' he said quietly, feeling his enormous weakness in the face of his enormous need for her.

'And I love you,' Rita said, evenly.

He felt an inward sigh of relief and release within him. It had been said so calmly, so straightforwardly, as if what they felt for each other were part of nature, as obvious as the marshes at their back, the wide river at their feet and the clouds in the sky above their heads.

'And I know for sure your name is Adam.'

Now it was Adam's turn to draw back and look at her.

'What did you say?'

'What?'

'What did you just say?'

She thought, puzzled at the need to repeat herself.

'I said: "I know for sure I had those games, I had them".'

'Right, yes, those games—'

'The Frisbee, that tennis paddle game, the diabolo,

I can't believe I left them in the shop. Someone must have stolen them.'

'No, no, no. We were in a bit of a rush,' Adam said, reassuringly, playing for time, allowing himself to calm down. 'All the stuff we'd bought. Food, drink, flasks, paper cups, travelling rug. We had masses of bags. We must have left them . . .'

'We'll check on the way home.'

'Yes.'

Adam sat slowly upright, realising. She was bound to find out, he thought, not letting go of her hand. The network was revealing itself. And she was a clever young woman, a police officer, too smart and shrewd not to find out one day, one day soon, and now that they were living together there would be, inevitably, too many unsuspecting clues revealed in their casual conversation, too many candid talks, too much circumstantial evidence of another, previous life for a clever young woman not to notice, not to draw conclusions, not to deduce. Perhaps he should just tell her one day, confess . . .

He felt light and weightless all of a sudden, as if he might float away if he let go of her hand. He would welcome that day, he thought, it would bring an ending, a conclusion of a rather miraculous kind . . . He experienced a few seconds of breathless, blinding exhilaration: perhaps, with Rita's help, he might reclaim his old life, become Adam Kindred again, whatever dangers lurked out there in the world, become Adam Kindred and make clouds yield up their rain. He had a strong sense that everything would be all right now, even though he admitted to himself, simultaneously, that he knew full well that it was impossible for everything to be all right in this complicated, difficult, mortal life we lead. But at least he had Rita, and that was all that really mattered: he had Rita, now. There was always that, Adam supposed, that and the sunshine and the blue sea beyond.